Goblin Market

Goblin Market

MARYANNE COLEMAN

www.blkdogpublishing.com

Other titles by Maryanne Coleman:

Pandemonium

No Faff, No Fuss, Just Food

For Taliesin, the Singer ....

With love.

BEFORE

The embers were burning down and the only sound was the drip of water from the roof. It was so quiet, that it seemed almost possible that you could hear the stalagmites growing on the floor. On the little pile of skins in the darkest corner, the Child stirred and began to whimper. The Mother detached herself from the little group near the fire and tiptoed over to where he lay. 'Ssshhh.' Her current man didn't like this Child, offspring of two Springs ago, half-orphan of another, vanquished. She laid a finger to her lips, for quiet, but the Child still whimpered. She lay down next to it and began, in what words she had, to sketch a story, a story of the light-foot ones, who flew around the rolling downs outside the cave. Of the chosen, winged ones who did not work, or die. The golden ones who did no harm; but still were best kept happy with some milk now and then, or perhaps a piece of her charred, unleavened bread. The Child slept but the Mother kept up the tale, mostly to herself. She told the Child to watch for the black ones, the ones who flew too near the mouth of the cave and sometimes inside it. Who, with their sharp, sharp teeth and grabbing hands could make off with a Child in a winking, while its watching Mother was distracted. By a golden one, perhaps. Perhaps the black and the gold were one.

The embers were burning down and the only sound was the creak of the drying timbers in the roof. It was so quiet, that it seemed almost possible that you could hear the rushes in the thatch whispering to each other as they had on the river bank. On the little pile of straw in the darkest corner, the Child stirred and began to whimper. The Mother detached herself from the little group near the fire and tiptoed over to where she lay. 'Hush, little one.' The men were tired from the day in the fields, the women were still busy, weaving their fabric to cover themselves in the coming cold. The Child could be amused by a story. A tale of little Brownies who came and helped when no-one was watching. The lovely Faeries, the Tuatha da danaan, who lived in the wood and must not be approached, for fear they would steal the most beautiful Child in the house. The Unseelie, the black-hearted crew who tore and rent men or women limb from limb – or Children, the Mother said, with a meaningful look – who were out too late or looking where they shouldn't look. Be a good Child, said the Mother, and none of these will harm you. Because even the beautiful woodland faeries were not to be trusted; you must always keep them happy with fair bread and milk and the best lengths of the most beautiful cloth. Do not ever, warned the Mother, speak to strange women in the road, do not take money from a green-skinned man, do not go anywhere with anyone, even if they look like your own Mother; they will be Shape-shifters for sure. The Child looked at the Mother with huge eyes and sleep was long in coming.

The embers were burning down and the only sound was the soft susurration of a needle pulled through linen. It was so quiet that it seemed almost possible that you could hear each stitch settle down into the fine seam on the hem of the nightgown. On the little trundle bed in the corner by the fire, the Child stirred and began to whimper. The Mother put aside her sewing and went over to the crib. She leant in. 'Hush, my little one, my bantling,' she crooned. 'I will tell you a story of faerie and wood and weald. A tale of the Childe Rolande, of Tam Lin, of True Thomas. I will tell you such a tale of …' The Child turned in its sheets and lisped at the Mother. 'Tell me a tale of Black Annis, the fachan and the bogle. Tell me a tale of the nuckalevee and bean-sidhe.' The Mother stood up from the crib. 'Ssshhh,' she begged. 'They will hear you and come for you when the candle is out. They will drag you down to their lairs beneath the mountains and keep you there as their servants. I put cream out every night to keep the faeries at bay. No cream ever milked will keep the Unseelie hordes from us if you call them. Hush, now, child and go to sleep.' In the other chimney corner, a dark shape stirred. A Hound raised its head and could almost be said to smile. It edged closer to the crib. The candle guttered down. The Child slept a fitful, dream-filled sleep.

The candle guttered and the Child whimpered in its sleep. The nanny walked crisply across to where it lay. 'Hush, now,' she said, without bending down. 'Tell me a story,' whispered the Child. 'Story, I'll give you story,' said the nanny and walked smartly to the door, blowing out the candle as she went. In the darkness, something snickered.

The dimmer switch hummed very faintly and, in its tubular steel bunk bed with built in entertainment centre, the Child whimpered. The alarm picked it up and the Mother came up the stairs and into the room. 'Mum!' screamed the Child. 'I had a bad dream.' The Mother walked over to him, stroking the damp hair back from his hot forehead. 'Darling,' she said, kissing his cheek. 'Was it a bad dream about monsters, about bad things in the closet?' 'No.' 'Then was it a bad dream about flying things, faeries and dragons?' 'No.' 'Then what was your dream about?' 'I dreamed I didn't have my television. I dreamed I lost my Gameboy. I dreamed my X Box didn't work. I couldn't find my mobile phone. My iPod wouldn't download tunes. It was horrible.' 'No monsters then?' 'Mum! There's no such thing as monsters, faeries and dragons.' The Child lay back down. 'I'm all right now I know I still have all my stuff.' The Mother walked to the door and turned. 'No faeries at all?' 'No, none.' With a sigh, the Mother walked to the top of the stairs and, with a heavy heart, floated down them, landing clumsily at the bottom. She sighed. 'I think you may be right,' she said. 'I think you may be right.'

I

A spectacular sunset, the sort you always get when you haven't got a camera, had just given way to a grey dusk with a cold rain falling. Not that the Weather had mentioned this; that sparkly woman on the telly had shimmered right through to the end.

The doors whispered closed behind the women as they left work. Their heels clattered and splashed in the puddles as they made their way past the abandoned ice-cream kiosk and the stacked rows of trolleys. Almost every one groped in her bag for a cigarette – This Is A Smoke Free Zone – and called their goodnights through a haze of exhaled smoke, drawing in the weed as though their lives depended on it. They straggled off to beat-up cars parked round the back of the supermarket, next to the bins overflowing with slimy cabbage and bent French sticks, the world the public never sees. A few went to wait for buses. One started to walk.

'Hey, Tania,' Madge called from her car. 'Come on, you're thin enough already.' What other use did walking have, except to walk off the lunch time burger and chips? 'I'll give you a lift.'

'No, really, I shall be fine.' It wasn't meant to sound stuck up. It just did.

The woman wound up the window and drove on, muttering 'suit yourself' as she did so. It was a bit of a bugger, that. She thought that at last they might get to find out where she lived. And better, who with. Tania had a secret, that much was clear. Almost all the shelf-fillers thought she was foreign; she spoke so precisely and didn't really seem to get the whole price and weight thing. If you told her beans cost £20, she would have shown no surprise, just put the label on. The checkout girls thought she was just thick. Well brought up, maybe, with her posh voice. But definitely thick. What about that time they'd tried to train her for the till? The scanner light really scared her and she'd got her sleeve caught up in the conveyor and she was back to shelf-filling in very short order.

There were various theories of course and a book going on it. Madge reckoned she was a university drop out from some la-de-bloody-da school, but then Madge's granddad had known Arthur Scargill and was caught in some sort of class-war time warp. Anita's money was on the fact that she was Jeffrey Archer's love child, or was it Cecil Parkinson's? Anita was very hazy on her politicians, past, present or manqué. Trace and Viv couldn't make up their minds, but that was Trace and Viv for you. They gravitated from an asylum seeker to a famous actress in disguise, working in Tesco's to get the feel for a part in a new film, maybe Planet of the Grapes or something. Nobody had laughed when Trace came out with it either.

Of course, if Madge had waited, got Brian to drive slowly, she might have learned something about Tania. There again, it might have confused her still further.

Tania was making light work of her journey home. She was, indeed, thin enough, even in the company overalls and they didn't fit anybody. She was so light on her feet she seemed to almost skim the ground, whipping the evening puddles into tiny ridges and she never seemed out of breath or tired. Alison's theory was that she was 'on something'. She had to be, with all that energy, whizzing along the aisles, coping with spillages and coffee shortages and lost children in her stride. And strong! When the Home and Wear manager had tried it on in the store room, she'd nearly broken his arm. The Home and Wear manager was Trevor, oily as an anchovy and about as intelligent. He strutted around the store, talking loudly on his mobile, eyeing the talent at the check-outs, lingering by the lingerie, undulating past the undies. Trace and Viv had been astonished when they'd coaxed the story out of Tania. They knew a grope with Trevor could bring quick promotion. He wasn't too bad looking, if you didn't mind his breath. Even so, Trevor had sailed through the air with the greatest of ease before crash-landing in the cardies, his ego more bruised in fact than his portfolio.

It was Bron who filled her thoughts as she walked home. She was turning into a bit of a nag, she thought, especially with him. A smile flitted across her lovely face as she thought that perhaps she had always been a nag and especially with him. A long, long time ago, as it seemed to her as she glided past the library, a man had come up to her and Bron when they were on a picnic. She could barely remember where it was now – Arden? Was that it? The man was very keen. He was scratching away with his quill while she and Bron talked. In the end, he said he was delighted with what he'd got and he'd be in touch. He never was.

If only Bron would do a bit of work, now and again, she was thinking as she slid past Laura Ashley. The rain had stopped now and the town night was fresh and, for a while, clean. She missed Arden and the cobwebs in the morning. Work had never been Bron's strong suit, she had to admit, but when there had been someone else to sweep the dust behind the door, it had been just about acceptable. Now, when she got home, he hadn't done a stroke.

Ellesmere Crescent curved, in the way that crescents do the world over. Number Thirteen stood next to Number Eleven. In fact, had any silly prankster in the night decided to swap the numbers, you'd never know, because Number Thirteen and Number Eleven were identical, not just to each other, but to every other house in the Crescent. That was town planning for you. She floated down the path that sloped to the door, past the less-than-neat borders and the little bank with its wild thyme.

There was a dim light in the hall beyond the bubbled glass, twinkling like the frost that would lace the garden before morning. After the first time she'd suggested to Bron he do something around the house, and he'd managed to suck up everything not nailed down, hoovering was out of the question. It had taken her hours and hours of work to replace the things he had broken. But she hadn't bothered to replace the vacuum cleaner. What was the point? Anything with a plug and a switch was a mystery to him. Except television. He had taken to that like a duck to water... although she was pretty sure ducks didn't watch television.

Home now, she pushed open the door. There was no point in locking it. Everyone they knew well could beat any lock, evade every motion sensor and security camera ever made.

'Honey, I'm home!' Wasn't that what they said? She'd heard it several times on the television, knitting while Bron snored beside her.

Grunt. Actually, several grunts, in several different voices.

She'd closed the front door quietly, but now she slammed the sitting room door back on its hinges, in time to see something out of the corner of her eye vanish through the wall.

Bron lay sprawled on the sofa, looking rather like Pierce Brosnan with tumbling curls.

'Have you been here all day?' she asked him coldly. 'Just playing cards with your nasty friends? I wish you'd never discovered the damn things.'

'Sweetie,' Bron's voice slunk like velvet over the carpet and up her spine. 'Sweetie, darling, I just had a few of the boys round. I get... lonely.' His voice could be had up for sexual harassment.

She shook herself free of it. 'Don't waste your glamour on me, you... pig.' There was a mild squeal of protest, from deep within the plaster. She glared at it and there was silence. 'I work all day and get home to what?' She looked around the living room. It had not changed since this morning. 'Nothing done. Have you done the washing? Well, have you? Have you?'

He smiled, and undulated to his feet. She was doing what she'd told herself on the way home she wouldn't do; she was nagging. And he was very, very gorgeous. She supposed it was just as well he hardly went out. He would collect a crowd, women would walk into lamp posts. His musky smell filled the room and there was just a brief hint of goat feet, low music and flickering firefly light. She stamped her foot.

'Sweetie, darling, you know I love you when you're angry.' He started towards her and his approach seemed to take years, from across an arc of space and time.

She snaked out an arm and slapped him, a slap that would have broken a mortal's arm, as Trevor of Home and Wear knew only too well. He hardly flinched, but slumped back on the sofa anyway, sulking.

'You never want to play, these days,' he muttered, his voice now mutinous, but wheedling. Every sinew in her body fought to resist, but she sat beside him and stroked his curls back from his beautiful face.

'I get tired,' she said, kissing his ear. 'It's hard work, this human business. I'm having to remember how to talk. You know, with my mouth. And how to listen with my ears, instead of just reading their minds. I have to eat their horrible food muck at lunch time. What a waste of time that is. What is a burger, anyway? And chicken tikka? What's all that about?'

He shook himself. 'I was watching a programme on the television the other day that was called "From recovered meat to burger".' He looked down, reflectively.

'And? What is a burger, then?'

'You don't want to know. It involves hooves.'

There were quizzical grunts from beyond the wallpaper and an outraged bulging of the wainscoting.

'Not cloven,' Bron turned in the vague direction of the movement and it subsided.

'Ah.'

Bron sat up straight, as big and muscular as she was frail. He put his arms around her and she curled up in the nest they made and together, they dreamed of happier times. Times when a drop of dew started the day, nectar fresh from the flower. Or any bread and milk that some hapless human had left out. The time of faerie when mortals believed. Really believed, as in were scared shitless of annoying the wee folk. Every move the poor creatures made was designed to avert the wrath of the fairies. There was as much bread and milk as you could eat. Cream, sometimes. The most beautiful human babies were theirs to take, leaving their own in their place. Fairy babies were, by and large, homely, to be generous about it. The less generously inclined would say they were bloody ugly. Mortal men and women could be lured to their kingdom – too much inbreeding was bad, even for the tuatha de danaan. And some of the men had been... Tania smiled in her sleep. Bron poked her in the ribs.

'I've told you about that. It's that Tam Lin again, isn't it?'

She started awake, scarlet with embarrassment. 'No, no, you know I never got anywhere with him. And his girlfriend was called Janet. Janet, I ask you! One of the girls on the deli counter is called Janet. Well, I say girls! When she goes out for lunch.

'Did you know that you have become very boring?' he suddenly said, in a conversational tone.

She was stopped in her tracks. Her lip trembled. 'You've never called me boring before.'

'That's because you never were. You were Titania once, trailing stars through the arc of night. You were bossy. Jealous. Overbearing. The list could go on. I'm always being accused of not being over-bright, and I grant you that that is a fair comment. But no-one's ever been bored while I'm around. I am Oberon, your lord. But I'm bored now. You're boring.'

She tried to face up to him, but was suddenly exhausted and burst into tears. Tears that ran the length of her perfect nose. No red nose for Titania, the Queen. 'It's... it's just, I get so tired.'

'You said that.' He deliberately didn't even hold her hand. A fairy king isn't made of stone; one little hint of weakness and he would be putty in her hands.

'Why did they stop believing in us? It was so wonderful in the old days. It wasn't too bad, even a hundred – is that right, a hundred?' he nodded, 'years ago. There were a few... not many, but a few. That nice Mr Barrie and that poetess Christina something... But now, no one. Where are the children? Why don't they...'

Before she could finish, he pointed at the television. It was on all the time, because he couldn't work out how to switch it off. A small child on the screen was sitting in front of another screen, making little animals run about. They couldn't work out how.

'That's why. Where is the magic in their lives? They control it all. They make things move without touching them. They can talk to people from any distance, on little things they hold up to their ears... oh, what are they called?'

'Mo-biles.'

'Yes. Those. Anyway, there is nothing they can't do. So where is the space for us?'

'Us? *Us?* We are Titania and Oberon! People quake at the sound of our names. Our Faerie Rades brought terror to the countryside. Children would be quietened with stories of what we might do.' She had risen from the sofa, and hovered there in all her angry glory, hair flying and sparks shimmering over her dress, which was no longer the rather unpleasant puce and beige of her supermarket uniform, but a gossamer creation, filled with teeming pictures which came and went before you could see them fully, in a kaleidoscope of colour.

She saw, through the back of her head as she used to, a puzzled boy beyond the window. He'd dropped his mountain bike at the radiance that filled the lounge at Number Thirteen, scattering his paper round over the lawn. Perhaps he'd better lay off the computer games. They were making his eyes go funny.

She felt his stare, behind her back, and subsided. 'See,' she said sadly, still looking at Oberon. 'He saw that, and still he doesn't believe in us.' She heard the clatter and whir of his bike chain as he pedalled down the Crescent. She grabbed Oberon's wrists and pulled his face down to her. 'What can we do? I'm going mad, and if I get much madder, we'll be stuck here, in this misty house, with these nasty mortals, for ever and ever and ever and...'

He kissed her gently and said, so softly she could hardly hear it, his deep voice a hum in the depths of her brain, 'Not for ever, my sweetness. Not for ever.'

'Not?' She brightened up. 'Do you have an idea?'

He shook his magnificent head and turned away. 'No, my love. I just mean that, if we become like them, we won't be here for ever. I mean that we will grow old and die.'

Her heart felt colder than ice and the fear of death which all mortals live with swept over her like cold water down her back. 'Die?' she whispered.

'Yes, although I fancy the growing old is worse.'

She became pale, grey and almost transparent, as she lost her will to survive. He grabbed for her, but his hands went through her as she faded slowly. Then suddenly, she was back. 'Bollocks!' she shouted.

'Bollocks? What in earth and sky are they? Or should it be, is that?'

'I don't know,' she said. 'But I hear them called upon a lot at work. He or they, I don't know, is some sort of god, I think. Whenever Madge stubs her toe, she cries to him. Anyway, whatever, I am not going to die. Or grow old, either.' She twirled in her own spiralling light, stronger now and less translucent. 'It's time to fight back. Get your little friends back out of the wallpaper.'

The wainscoting thumped and the scampering began under the plaster, with little sniggers and playful snorts. 'It's time for a council of war.'

2

They had been so excited. Council of war, just like the old days. But after the initial euphoria, they all sat round the table, just looking at each other. The edges of the room seemed blurred, with the scent of moss and autumn leaves in the air, moonlit shadows in the corners where no shadows could be. The table, covered in a gingham cloth, seemed out of place in the kitchen diner, which was now positively bosky in its decor.

Titania had a bit of difficulty, to start with, with Oberon's Goblin Card School. At one time, of course, she had been surrounded by his Court all the time and that was what she needed – time, to get used to them again. Humans looked a weird lot to fairies, by and large. Their faces were too lumpy, too pink. Their teeth were too big, too square and blunt. Their eyes were just... holes. What was it they said? The lights were on, but no one was at home. To fairies, the humans' lights weren't even on. But now, she was quite used to the great lumpen things and the Card School looked – she felt ashamed of herself for thinking it, but they were just so, not to put too fine a point on it, so frankly *hideous*.

It wasn't as if they were even the same. The main problem was that, although they owed their main ancestry to pigs, Oberon had tinkered quite a bit and the brighter ones had added a few embellishments of their own. But although the noses were all different, they remained resolutely snouty. Only one had felt strongly enough to do something about his ears, and all he had done was to plait the sprouting hairs; not a fashion which was going to catch on in a hurry, Titania was pretty sure.

But, as she was about to make a suitably cutting remark, she looked round the table again, and bit back her spite. Apart from pigness, the little faces looking anxiously up at her from round the table, receding chins practically on the cloth between their grubby little hooves, had another thing in common – shining hope in their little red-rimmed eyes. Their muted grunts of excitement made her heart melt. These were her people – to be generous with the term – and she was their Queen, after all, and they were pinning all their hopes on her.

Even Oberon was looking at her in open admiration. He didn't see how she could fail. If he – Lord of Faerie – was scared of her, then he didn't see why the world shouldn't be. So what if they had so diminished that they lived in Thirteen, Ellesmere Crescent instead of East of the Sun and West of the Moon? So what if their Court – present company always excepted, he hastily added, in case any of the School were listening to his thoughts – were scattered far and wide and, in some cases, gone completely native? Titania was back, and in fine form. They weren't bickering between themselves over a page boy now. She was fighting for her life.

She pulled herself together and managed a smile. She put up a shield in her head, should Oberon come calling. She was feeling less certain now she saw what she had to work with, but no less determined.

'First,' she said, 'we need a plan. What they call at the supermarket a Marketing Strategy.' She beamed round at the assembled goblins. Blank stares met her, but they made encouraging little noises in their snouts, and tried their best at smiles. The effect was quite unsettling. She sighed.

'All right. Let's keep it simple.' Oberon let out a silent whistle of relief. If it wasn't for the boys, he'd have felt very stupid. Say what you like about them, it was easy to feel clever when they were around.

'What did we used to do in the Old Days?'

Oberon looked puzzled. 'We didn't do anything. We never fought with anyone. We just... *did* stuff. Who was going to argue with us?'

She looked around furtively and dropped her voice. 'The Unseelie Court. They were always trying to unseat us.'

He laughed so loudly it shook the furniture and made the neighbours in Number Fifteen shake their heads and tut. 'No need to whisper, is there? If we're having trouble, I hardly think they're doing any better. People at least *liked* us. That black hearted lot, everyone was scared of them. Who has a good word to say for fachans, hags and bogles? I shouldn't think there's a one of them left!'

Titania shook her head. Oberon and the gang were glad to see sparks run through her tendril hair.

'No, I would bet,' the goblins looked up hopefully, but she quelled them with a look, 'I would bet my throne, such as it is, (hat they are flourishing somewhere. Evil has its own reward,' she quoted, though she didn't know who, 'and so their rewards are probably great. I can't feel any nearby, but I know they are in this world somewhere. If I know them, whatever it is they're doing won't be nice.'

A dank chill settled briefly on the room, and the smallest goblin, as it were the runt of the litter, shivered and gave a little whimper, shuffling closer to Oberon as it did so. He gave it a matey poke in the ribs with his elbow to cheer it up and it briefly disappeared under the table with a small thud.

Titania waited until the poor little thing had scrambled back up onto its chair, anxiously smoothing down its bristly hair and adjusting what it was pleased to call clothing. Then she continued, in the relentlessly patient voice which in better times Oberon had dreaded.

'We can't afford to overlook anything. I just know the Unseelie are still around. All we can hope for is that this time, they're on *our* side.'

The table fell silent. That was a big piece of information for them to take in. Since before the dawn of time, it seemed, the two Courts had been at odds. When the goblins assembled were just twinkles in their Lord's eye, the Unseelie Court had been driven back to North of what men called the Border, into Scotland, and there they had stayed, finding the mountains, bogs and unseen valleys more to their taste than the sunlit lands to the South. Dark land for dark deeds, and the war between them had ceased. But memories are long when you're immortal, and fairy babies, either in their cradles under the hill or in the farmhouse kitchen as changelings, had been taught to dread the dark host of the Unseelie Court.

'Come on, dear,' said Oberon, chancing his arm. 'Let's not meet trouble halfway. It's mortals we've got to persuade, not that black crowd. How are we going to do that? I watch a bit of television, as you perhaps know.'

Titania and the goblins all raised their eyes, with varying degrees of success.

'...and I have to say, I don't think I've seen one single fairy, except the Tooth Fairy, but she would be furious if she were here to see how they think of her, poor old soul.'

'Oh?' Titania didn't watch much television.

'Show her as a chap, ad-ver-tising,' Oberon tasted the unfamiliar word as he spoke it, 'something for keeping your teeth clean.'

Titania couldn't resist a small nag. 'Ah, if they stuck to dew, not donuts, they wouldn't need...'

'Yes, yes, my point being that they don't think of us. Not ever. And that's why we're in this state. And if we keep on going round in circles like this, we'll never get anywhere. In the Old Days, I'd just get Puck to circle the world a few times, drop a word where it was needed and before you knew it, the Fairy Rade was on its way. I won't embarrass you now by mentioning you know who and Janet, or that idiot with the donkey head, but usually, it worked rather well, although perhaps I shouldn't say so.'

They all smiled in remembrance and allowed themselves a little rueful shake of the head. The goblins were soon distracted by Titania's sparkling hair again. She was getting more beautiful by the minute. They sighed, chins on trotters.

Oberon glared at them and they shuffled back to attention.

Titania asked him, 'Do you know where he is now?'

'Puck? Haven't a clue. Boys?'

One of them, whose small sartorial conceit was a row of

striking green freckles across his nose, grunted, 'I fink he's a milkman.' They all looked at him, waiting for more information, like, how did he know that? But the unaccustomed and sudden attention startled him, and he blushed bright scarlet, making his freckles stand out alarmingly.

Titania came to his rescue. 'Clever lad,' she said, only slightly patronisingly. 'Any idea where, or do we have to follow every milkman in the country till we find him?' Her voice rose at the end of the question into an exasperated shriek.

The goblin looked mulish, a good trick for a pig with green freckles. Oberon tried to calm things down. 'Come on, Freckles, old lad. Have a little think. Who told you? You don't see many folk; it can't be that hard to remember.'

The little creature furrowed its brow and tapped its trotter against its front teeth, in what was an unexpectedly disarming gesture. Suddenly, its eyes brightened and it squeaked, 'I know, I know!'

'Who?' they all chorused.

'What?' It was puzzled.

'Who?' This time there was rather an edge to it.

'Who what?' it whimpered. 'Don't you'se mean "where?"'

'What?' They were all puzzled now, but Titania saw the answer to the problem first.

'It means, it hasn't remembered who told it, but it does remember where Puck delivers his milk. Is that right?' She turned to Freckles with a smile and it blushed again and nodded violently, but said nothing.

They all waited for a moment until Oberon snapped. 'Where?'

The goblin gulped and said, 'Woodford Green.'

Titania, bearing in mind its speech impediment asked, 'Is that Woodthord Green, or Woodford Green?'

'Woodford.'

'Yes, but is that...?'

'Titania!' snapped Oberon. 'My boys aren't daft, are you lads?' Delighted squeaks and grunts answered him. 'I know where it is. It's in Essex.'

'Vat's in Thuthex, ain't it?' one of the others asked eagerly.

'No, Thydney, Essex is in Essex,' Oberon was patience it-self.

'How ever do you know that?' Titania was impressed, in spite of herself.

'Kilroy,' came the simple reply. 'Most of the people on his show seem to come from there. Mostly someone called Tracey.'

'I know this is getting off the subject,' Titania said, 'But it can't be the same woman all the time, can it?'

Oberon shrugged his rippling shoulders. 'They all look the same to me, my love. It's you who can tell mortals apart.' He looked at her from under his lashes. 'The men, anyway.'

The goblins squeaked with pleasure. Their Lord and Lady were getting at each other again. Just like the Old Days.

'All right, then,' Titania rapped lightly on the table to bring the meeting to something resembling order. 'We know where he is. Freckles, do you know what name he goes by these days?'

'Robin Goodfellow.' The goblin drew itself up a little, de-fiantly. 'And I mean *F*ellow.' The goblins on either side drew back from the shower of spit that accompanied the word.

Titania had the grace to look a little shamefaced. 'Next thing, then, do we get to him first, or make plans first and then find him?' She mentally slapped herself, for giving the massed brain cell of the Card School a choice. She went on, without waiting for an answer, 'I think we ought to find him first. He always had a quick brain...'

'Too quick for his own good,' Oberon put in, and the gob-lins sniggered. They weren't any too bright, but they were bright enough to hate anyone or thing more intelligent than they were – and to persecute the few forms of life less so.

'If he is dealing with mortals, he'll be useful to us' she went on as if he hadn't spoken. Puck's loyalty had always been in question and they both liked to think of him as their own servant. In point of fact, Puck was no-one's servant but his own. Fortunately for him, they had never found that out.

'If he hasn't gone native,' Oberon growled.

'No, no,' Titania was less sure than she sounded. 'Not Puck.'

'If he hasn't, then why didn't he stay in touch?' Oberon demanded. 'Why did he go off by himself?'

'He might not be by himself,' she shot back. 'Until a few minutes ago, we didn't even know where he was. How can we be sure he's on his own?'

There was a hasty whispering among the goblins and the tiniest one, still a little dishevelled by his fall, piped up, 'I think he's with Cobweb.'

'*Cobweb?*' Titania was appalled. It was a well-known fact that everyone only loved *her*. Worshipped the ground *she* floated over. '*Cobweb??*'

'Steady on, dearest,' Oberon tried his best. 'Probably just a rumour.' He glared at the littlest goblin, but it was so full of its own importance, it couldn't take a hint.

'That's what I heard,' he asserted proudly.

'Did you?' Titania's voice was a steely hiss. 'Did you really?' She looked around her motley crew. 'Right. You. You. You.' She pointed at Freckles and Tiny and to an astonished Oberon; no one pointed at the King of Faerie. 'Get out to wherever he is, delivering his milk, probably curdled, I wouldn't be surprised. Find him. Bring him here.'

'And Cobweb?' Freckles asked, in a tiny voice, designed to sound as if someone else had said it.

Her silvery laugh fooled no one. 'Oh, yes, bring Cobweb. *Definitely* bring Cobweb.' She smiled around the company. 'Well?' she asked, smiling like an icicle. 'What are you waiting for? Off you go. The rest of the boys and I will do a little light planning while you're gone. Won't we, boys?'

The remaining goblins gulped and nodded. It was going to be a dark and stormy night.

3

They found themselves suddenly standing outside, in the dreary garden of Number Thirteen. Oberon slumped down on the bank, overgrown with thyme and, sadly for him, several clumps of nettles.

'Ow!' he sucked the side of his hand petulantly.

'You want a dock leaf, Sire. That's what you want,' asserted Tiny. Like many brightish creatures, he wasn't always bright enough to see that; sometimes, acting dumb is safer. By way of a lesson in this aspect of life on earth, he got a hefty clout round the ear from Oberon.

'I know I want a dock leaf,' the King snarled. 'What I don't want are the stings. In the old days...' the goblins' eyes glazed over, '...in the old days,' he repeated, in a heavier, rather threatening tone, which made them stand up as straight as their pig ancestry would allow, 'I could sit *where* I liked, *on whom* I liked, and I never got stung, bitten or otherwise attacked by anything. Now, every bloody plant I go near seems to want to poison me in some way.'

'Not just nettles?' asked Freckles, confused.

Oberon looked out from under beetling brows and in a low rumble which made Tiny's ears sing, said just one word.

'Broccoli!'

'Yeurghh.'

'I rest my case. Now, to work. You, Smartarse. Freckles. Where is this Woodford Green, then?'

Freckles looked startled. He'd only come along because Titania had told him to. He didn't know there was going to be *geography*.

'Dunno,' he muttered, mulishly.

'What's the magic word?' Oberon hissed in his ear.

'Dunno, *Sire*.' He ladled on what his little goblin brain took to be heavy irony. But Oberon, without a subtle bone in his body, took it at face value and Tiny breathed again. Despite his diminished powers, he knew that Oberon could snuff them out as easily as winking. More easily, in fact. All he had to do was stop wanting them around, and that would be it. There would be just a goblin shaped gap in the Universe. A thought began to form in Tiny's brain. He mulled it over and decided to save it for later. For when he could persuade Oberon that he had thought of it himself. Tiny was indeed more than the sum of his parts and, unlike so many of his kind, he could learn from experience, a scary talent he knew he must hide from his master.

Oberon wrinkled his brow. This was hard. He raised his hand to knock and go back inside for a bit more information. The knocker turned, rather disconcertingly, into Titania's face, and he got a nasty nip from her beautiful, even teeth. He leapt back, his heart in his mouth. Even Faerie Kings can get the shit scared out of them when things like that happen suddenly.

'H... hello, dear. I was just...'

'I know. It's in Essex.'

A tiny echo from inside could be heard. It sounded like 'Thuthex,' and ended with a small squeal, as of a pig kicked in the ribs by a delicate faerie toe.

'But, how do we get there, my love?'

'Don't creep round me, Oberon. Do what fairies do, or do what humans do. I don't really care. Just find Puck and get him back here.'

The face melted back into the slightly peeling paint and the three stood there, looking puzzled. Before any of them could speak, her voice was heard from behind the knocker.

'Fly.'

Their lips moved, but before they could ask, her answer

came.

'Or get a lift. I believe they call it "hitching". Just get on with it.'

This time she was really gone. Oberon looked down at Tiny and Freckles, with their little trusting faces turned up to him. He was not a sentimental being, but he was suddenly overcome with an emotion which frightened him for two reasons. Firstly, it was a bit scary to feel such overwhelming love and affection for two things as unprepossessing as they. Secondly – and this was by far the worse – he had a sneaking suspicion that love and affection was a bit... human. He was on the turn. He snapped himself out of it and gave them both a manly clap on the shoulder. He beamed benevolently and then asked, 'Does either of you know what she means?'

'Well,' Freckles said, 'I fink she means we have to fly or do vat fing vey do, where vey stand vere wiv bits of paper wiv writin' on. Cars and lorries and fings stop and vey get in.' He lowered his voice and sounded rather awestruck. 'I don't know what happens to vem after vat.'

'That sounds a bit hard,' said Oberon, who had never really taken to either cars or writing. 'We'll fly, shall we?'

The two goblins shuffled their feet and looked embarrassed.

'We can't,' Tiny said.

'Can't? Can't fly?' Oberon chuckled. 'But we can *fly*!'

'Well, we can't,' replied Tiny.

Freckles added, 'You said, when you fought of us, vat vere wouldn't be no call.'

Oberon looked startled. That sounded a very Titania thing to have said. Things were worse than he had imagined. He tried to put a brave face on things.

'Come on, lads, don't be downhearted. I expect you could if you wanted to.'

They shook their heads and in a minute voice, Tiny said, 'Can't. Tried. Can't.'

'Oh, look, lads, I'm sorry,' Oberon said. 'I could... carry you.' He suppressed a shudder. He hadn't built in hygiene either, when thinking up the goblins and he was rather fastidious.

Their faces lit up and they held up their arms to him in such a trusting way he was quite overcome. He tucked one under each arm and breathed through his mouth as much as he could, in an attempt to minimise the smell. He closed his eyes and soared over the rooftops, his mind fixed on the mythical land of Woodford Green. He pictured it as an expanse of verdant woodland, quietly waiting in the silver moonlight. Here and there, small houses lay in clearings, surrounded by grazed sward, cropped close by the deer and ponies which wandered at will beneath its shining, whispering leaves.

Every now and then, the silence was broken by an owl's hoot, a baby murmuring itself back to sleep, the quiet words of lovers wrapped in a cloak in a secluded glade. The world of Ellesmere Crescent was very far away and he smiled gently to himself. If he could just locate those lovers, he could set himself gently down behind them and watch as...

'Sire?'

He opened his eyes. He was still on the path outside the house.

'Sire? When are we going to start flying?' Tiny asked, his piggy eyes downcast and furtive.

'Ah, yes. Just having a bit of a think, you know. It's a while since I did any flying.'

'No call?' ventured Freckles, who was beginning to feel rather stupid and not a little exposed, out in the open street, tucked under this idiot's arm, like a badly wrapped parcel.

Oberon considered dropping the horrible freckly thing on its head, but dismissed the idea as being unbecoming a monarch and also pointless, as all goblins' heads were as hard as iron. 'No, as a matter of fact,' he said, haughtily. 'Not in recent... times.' Faeries have a very slight grasp of time. 'Then' and 'now' are all the terms they really need. 'Future' was something they were having to address, so he tried again.

'A few inches, that time, Sire,' urged Tiny, trying to be helpful. And, it was true, they had risen a little from the concrete paving slabs unevenly placed near the front door.

Oberon sighed.

This time, the whole of Titania appeared, blazing mad

and standing, arms akimbo, in the doorway.

'Still here?' she said, a mirthless smile playing over her lips. 'And here's me, with the kettle on and everything. Waiting for Puck and Cobweb.'

The trio flinched. How, they wondered, could such a gossamer light word as 'Cobweb' be imbued with such venom and scorn. The goblins couldn't remember her – to be frank, all the faeries, fluttering about aimlessly from flower to flower, all looked alike to them. When you spend your days rootling around after truffles and similar fungi, sparkly things with wings don't really cross your path very often. Although, they added quickly and loudly in the invaded privacy of their heads, they all knew and, of course, simply adored Titania. She looked at them slightly less sternly.

But Oberon remembered Cobweb more fondly. A fluffy creature, much given to mending spiders' legs and putting a final buff on beetles' wings. She tended to be the one to watch the human babies, stolen from their cradles, putting on the likeness of their mothers, so as to startle them less in their new beds made of gossamer and leaves. She could be very friendly. A rather silly smile spread over his handsome face.

Smack! Titania soon wiped it off for him and he stood there, rubbing his cheek, like a schoolboy.

'Don't sulk! Just get off and find them. If you can't fly any more, you lazy toad,' and something in her tone suggested that the word was chosen for a reason, 'then use your legs. You can't hitch a lift with these two visible, their faces could stop a clock. Both of you, do that disappearing thing you do and hide somewhere.'

There was a pop and a giggly grunt, as of two goblins off the hook. They disappeared.

'No, fools,' Titania sighed. 'I mean hide somewhere on him. There's room enough, after all.'

Oberon's clothes rustled and he adjusted the hang of his jacket a touch.

'Comfy?' Titania asked.

'Not really,' he answered.

'Never mind. Off you go. The main road is over there. I have to walk down it every day on my way from work. You know, that thing I do while you lie here forgetting how to fly. So off you go. Stand there, look gorgeous and you'll soon be whisked off to where you want to go by some lovely, lonely woman with a fast car.'

He perked up.

'And remember,' she poked him in the goblin with a firm forefinger, 'you're not alone, is he boys?'

Delighted grunts and squeaks answered her.

Oberon thought it was perhaps time to mend a few bridges, before the wisps of smoke became a total conflagration and their plan collapsed in ruins. He reached out a tentative hand and stroked her arm, so tenderly she nearly burst into tears. Even without his full fairy glamour he was still good – oh, so frighteningly good. She knew he would be a vital part of their comeback, especially if any women stood in their way. She shook herself; it was so easy to fall under his spell. Animal magnetism was wafting through the air. You could smell it. It wove its magic in growing, invisible clouds, into the air around the house and along the street. Mr Jones at Number Fifteen awoke to the surprise of his life – Mrs Jones, clad only in curlers, undulating across the thin carpet of the back bedroom, whence he had been banished twenty years before. She almost tripped over the scurrying form of their old cat, sadly neuter, but still with his memories, as he dashed for the cat flap on an errand of his own. Alas for Mr Jones, Titania removed Oberon's hand from her arm, though not unkindly and, with a light kiss and a shove, sent him on his way to find Puck. The glamour faded and Mrs Jones awoke in confusion. Mr Jones sighed and turned over, but who could say whether the sigh was one of disappointment or relief.

Out on the pavement now, Oberon bent reluctant steps towards the main road. He felt in his pocket, to check if there was any money, which even he knew he would need, if he was to get very far. Nothing. He glanced round, furtively, and plucked a handful of dry leaves from under the hedge and managed to turn them into a couple of fivers. He gave a little smile and a hop and a skip, which he was happy to feel kept him in the air just a touch longer than might be expected. He began to feel better. He was going off to do something. His powers were still there, though less than in the glory days. Titania would be pleased with him and soon they wouldn't be on their own. The two would become four, as soon as he found Puck and Cobweb. Four would soon become... more. Arithmetic wasn't Oberon's strong point, either.

The goblins quietly hid in his coat lining, hardly daring to stir. The master was happy. Things were on the move. Soon there would be truffles, bread and milk, maids to pinch, old women to frighten, babies to change. They slept, snuffling quietly and dreaming goblin dreams, as Oberon stood on the side of the road, looking gorgeous and waiting for Miss Right to drive by.

4

Back in the kitchen, less mossy now, more flowery, as befitted Titania's bower without the overwhelming masculinity of Oberon, the remaining War Council waited for Titania's next big idea. They smiled brightly at her as she slumped at the table, with her lovely head cushioned on her arms. Her hair lay on the gingham tablecloth in long tendrils, through which a ghost of a faerie garland wove and a few last sparks twinkled and died. She stayed there for a long time and the lads became a bit embarrassed, wondering what to do next. A small sob escaped from under the curling hair.

Thydney said, 'She'th crying.'

'No, I'm not!'

'Yeth.' Thydney's neighbours backed away. They had seen what happened in the Old Days to anything that crossed the Queen, and getting exploded goblin out of your hair took ages.

'Yeth, Mithtreth,' he sprayed. 'I can hear you. We all can.' He looked round, nodding encouragingly at the others, who tried to pretend they weren't there. 'Pleathe don't cry. We... we love you. We hate to thee you thad. And,' he gave a gulp to swallow his own sob, 'it'th *thcaring* us.'

Titania's shoulders squared and her head came up. She tossed her hair carelessly back from her forehead, where it immediately arranged itself to best effect. She gave one small, ladylike sniff and smiled at them. Dear things. Not handsome, possibly, but certainly loyal. And that was what they needed. Oh, yes. Not like that – her lip trembled again and she fought for control – not like that ungrateful beast, Puck. She grasped the edge of the table, took a deep breath and said, 'Thank you, Thydney. Boys. I'm sorry about that, but I do get rather tired these days. All the excitement has rather taken it out of me. But I'm all right now.'

The little creatures showed their pleasure in a variety of rather stomach churning noises and she held up a languid hand to quieten them down.

'Right, now, while Oberon, Freckles and Tiny find Puck and Cobweb,' she managed to keep her voice even, 'we must plan our next move.'

'I thought we were going to wait for Puck,' piped up a goblin, a little larger than the rest, who liked to wear what he fondly believed were human clothes.

Titania fought down her instincts as she answered him. He didn't seem as devoted as the rest and he had a gleam in his eye which in any other creature might be called arrogant. *Watch him* said her subconscious, but aloud she said, 'Yes, of course we are. But what if he *has* gone native? What if he and Cobweb are mortal now and don't remember us?'

The goblins were aghast. Puck had always been Jack the Lad, everyone's friend, good at games, good with the ladies, a bit slapdash perhaps, but a *good bloke*. He wouldn't have forgotten them. Would he? They turned anxious eyes on their lady.

'Let's not meet trouble half way. I'm sure it will all be fine. Just fine.' Suddenly she raised her head. 'What time is it?'

'Time?' Thydney asked. 'We can't tell the time. Time is for mortals,' he added smugly.

She turned an exasperated glare on him. 'Yes, Thydney. Time is for mortals and for me. I have to work, you know.'

'But surely, Mistress,' ventured the third goblin, who slicked down his bristles with a parting in the middle and tried to model himself on Bertie Wooster, to rather ghastly effect, 'surely you won't be going to work any more? Not with the plan, and everything?'

'This is just when we will need me to work,' she snapped.

'Plans don't just pay for themselves, you know. Are any of you prepared to get a job instead of me?'

With a grunt and a rustle, they all disappeared.

'Come back, you idiots,' she sighed. 'I don't expect there's an employer in the land desperate enough to take you lot on. I mean, look at you. For a start, you're only three feet high. And green, in some cases.'

Bertie was rather hurt and muttered, 'We do our best.'

She patted him on the head, and surreptitiously wiped her hand down her dress before continuing. 'Yes, lads, I know you do, but you take my point, I'm sure. If I have followed things I hear at work correctly, we will have to advertise ourselves. And that costs a lot of money.'

Bertie brightened up considerably. 'I say, will we be on the telly?'

Titania hated to burst his bubble. 'I think we'll start smaller than that,' she said gently. 'When we've got a few mortals believing in us again, we can start thinking a bit bigger. I don't watch as much television as you chaps. In fact, how can I watch more than all day?' She sounded a little waspish and they looked suitably crestfallen. 'Even so, I realise that it is a very important thing for us to get involved in.'

'Mithtreth?'

'Yes, Thydney?'

The little creature cleared its throat and blushed. Its voice was a husky whisper and it twirled its trotters together in its embarrassment. 'You're very beautiful, Mithtreth.'

'Of course I am, Thydney. And your point is?' Titania was beaming from ear to ear.

Thydney was confused. He had thought that that was his point. He looked around frantically at the others.

Squeaky squared his porcine shoulders and said, 'I think what Thyd's getting at, is that you are as lovely as any mortal woman what we see on the telly.' He turned to the squirming Thydney. 'Is that right, Thyd?'

He nodded.

'Oh, I see.' Titania could hardly speak for the huge smile she wore. 'You are saying, you dear little thing,' she moved in closer and then reeled back as she caught the edge of Thydney's breath, 'that if I went on the television, they would know at once I am the Queen.'

'N... no, not exactly,' Thydney was forced to say. 'What I mean ith, that you could eathily get a job modelling clotheth, or thomething.'

'Can you cook?' asked Bertie and immediately regretted it. She looked at him so coldly that for several seconds you could see his breath as it swirled from his upturned nostrils in frightened pants.

'No,' he continued hurriedly. 'No, of course you can't. I only said, Mistress, because the mortals love to watch each other cook and that would be a good way to get lots of people to watch you.'

Titania looked doubtful. 'I can do dew,' she offered, tentatively. 'And nectar, if somebody collects the flowers for me.'

The goblins looked at each other and shrugged their shoulders.

'Not cooking, then,' said Squeaky.

Bertie suddenly gave a little bounce in his chair. 'What about interior decorating?'

'What?' Titania was completely nonplussed.

'Look around,' joined in Thydney. 'You've done wonderth with thith place. When the Lord went out, it just changed on itth own, jutht becauthe you were in it. That'th magic you can still do, Mithtreth. Loadth of programmeth on that, ath well.'

'Forget it!' she said sternly, looking round the table. 'If I go on the television, it will be in glory and not as some ninny painter or cook. So no, all right?'

They looked mutinous.

'And don't mention it to Oberon when he gets back. If he says anything about it, I'll know who told him, because he could never think of it himself.'

The goblins knew better, but said nothing. Was it not they who sat hour after hour watching TV with Oberon, hearing him comparing the women he saw with Titania, almost always in her favour? Titania meanwhile stored the idea away for future use. She would need some of her glamour back first, though. Unless, of course, she unleashed Oberon...

Unleashed was a good word, where Oberon was concerned. He had stood at the side of the road for only a few minutes before a long, sleek car drew up at the kerb and a manicured finger beckoned him inside. Because it was late at night, accidents had been kept to a minimum, as bus and lorry drivers were largely immune to Oberon's undoubted assets. There had been one rather nasty shunt, followed by a vigorous hand-bagging, but just as it began to get really amusing, the car arrived and swept Oberon away.

He really hated cars. He hated speed he wasn't in control of, he hated the feeling that he was going somewhere at someone else's behest. But if he had to be in a car, this was the car to be in. Its pale leather seats caressed him like liquid moonlight. The dashboard was softly lit with lights which reminded him of the gathered fireflies around his bower in the forest so long ago. The engine was a distant purr, with hidden power in its throat, ready to be released at a moment's notice. He stroked the leather and looked sideways at the driver, trying to avoid the view out of the windscreen; rapidly approaching tail lights had never been his favourite vista.

She was smiling like the cat that had got the cream. And there was something vaguely feline about the eyes and the small Roman nose. She held the wheel lightly and he wished she wouldn't – he liked to see a nice firm grip where mechanised speed was concerned.

'Hi, there,' she husked at him. 'How far do you want to go?' He noticed a slight, rather attractive accent, but he couldn't place it. All mortal voices sounded alike to him, by and large

'How far can you take me?' he asked, innocently. 'I really want to go to Woodford Green. And I need to be there around dawn, if that's all right?'

'I wasn't talking about where,' she laughed. 'I asked "how far?"'

Oberon was astonished. This woman was treating him like some sort of object. That wasn't how it was supposed to be. It was always he who made the running and, in this particular instance, he just needed to get to Woodford Green. Anyway, he didn't fancy her. Much.

She laughed again, back in her throat. She slid her green eyes round to look at him again. She tossed her amber hair over her shoulder.

'You are a very superior form of hitchhiker,' she said. 'Usually they are a bit smelly and dirty. Usually they are just a *tad* more grateful!'

'I'm sorry,' Oberon recollected himself and switched on the charm. 'It's not that I'm at all ungrateful, really I'm not, but I must get to Woodford Green. My wife was most insistent.'

The pale gold lids flicked down over the cat eyes and she licked her lips with a pointed little tongue. 'What if your wife never finds out we took a little... detour?'

Oberon gave a little gasp, as goblin elbows poked him in the ribs. 'Oh, I think she'd know,' he managed to say.

'I don't think she would, you know,' she said, her voice sharper.

Oberon gave a little chuckle and subsided into his seat. He was enjoying this, to his amazement. The lightly perfumed interior, the soft, soft leather, the dominant woman and, unexpectedly, the speed. He began to feel himself drifting off to sleep. Just as his lids dropped over his peat brown eyes, a blue light filled his vision.

'Damn!' spat the woman and he felt the car slow sharply as she pulled over. She wound down the window. 'Good morning, officer.'

'Good morning, madam. In a hurry, are we?'

Oberon kept his face turned away. He didn't really want to get involved. He felt rather than heard her get out of the car and through his increasing tiredness came a muffled conversation, which gradually became a monologue in the woman's voice, grown dreamy and smoky, as though heard over a huge distance. Then she was back in the car, smiling languorously at him. Had he had the strength in his neck to crane up to the rear view mirror, he would have seen the policeman standing there, staring after the car as it raced off, still well over the limit. Had he passed by three hours later, he would have seen him standing there still. In fact, he didn't move, until another squad car sent to find him and his partner stopped near them. They didn't seem to hear or see as they were gently led away to somewhere quiet and padded.

From a far, far distance, Oberon felt the car slow again. He felt hot, hot breath on his cheek and eager, taloned fingers pulling at his clothing. He raised a tired arm, as weak as string, to try and push her away, but his flesh was too weak, and his spirit none too willing. Deep in an abyss of his brain, he hoped she wouldn't scratch him. He still remembered what had happened the last time he had come home with scratches... he tried to remember what he was doing here, where he was going. 'How far do you want to go?' He could remember her saying that. Did he want to go this far? Who cared? He snuggled down in the seat, making himself more comfortable, more accessible to her searching fingers. He groaned and slightly arched his back as her nails dug into his belly.

Ow! They really were digging in! His eyes flew open and his first view was of her face, close to his and seriously angry.

'Are you taking the piss, laddie?' she hissed, not so genteel now. He remembered where he had heard the accent. He remembered the last time he had seen those eyes. He remembered the last time he had come home with scratches.

'What, by all that's hideous, are ye doing with a goblin in yer trousers?'

He was fully awake now, more fully than he had been for some decades.

'Leanan-Sidhe!' he breathed.

'The same!' she snapped, 'Although I prefer Leanne these days, if you don't mind.' She clicked on the courtesy light. 'Oberon!' She slammed her palms down on the wheel in frustration. 'How many hitch hikers are there to choose from on any night on that road?'

He opened his mouth to answer, but she spoke first.

'Dozens, that's how many, dozens. Although,' she looked down for a second and continued, more quietly, 'perhaps not as many as there once were.'

He gaped. 'You're not still doing the... the blood thing, are you, Le... Leanne?'

She tossed her hair. 'No. Well, yes. But not so much.'

There was a strained silence, then they both spoke at once.

'How did you learn to drive?'

'Still with Titania then?'

'No,' he said, 'please. You first.'

'Well, yes, all right then. I assume "your wife" is still Titania.'

'Oh, yes. Ha. Ha.' He strained a laugh. 'Still with Titania. Oh, yes.'

The goblins struggled in his jacket, trying to get round the back. They had seen what Leanan-Sidhe could do when she was peckish. Oberon was safe, but to a member of the Unseelie Court goblins were just the equivalent of a nice bowl of olives.

'To answer your question,' she continued, 'I don't see what's so hard about driving. We can all do that.'

The goblins sniggered. Oberon heard in his hindbrain little voices saying things like 'flying' and 'no call'.

Oberon gave what he hoped was a careless laugh and, shrugging his shoulders, managed not to answer.

'Oh,' she nodded slowly. 'So it's true, then. Your lot can't drive. Or work machinery.' She drew nearer. 'How are you on computers, my Lord? Pretty damn nifty on the World Wide Web, I would imagine, heh, Oberon, heh?' Her unpleasant laugh filled the car and Oberon was stuck for an answer.

'Still,' she purred, drawing closer, 'You're pretty handsome, Oberon. No paunch,' she slapped his tight stomach. 'Nice thighs. Nice...'

'Do you mind!' Oberon sat up sharply. 'I still have the scars from last time. You pretended to be someone else then, as well, as I remember.'

'Yes,' the woman snickered. 'Titania's look is an easy one to achieve.' With a flick of her hair and a horrible melting moment, Titania sat there. But Titania with nasty, cat green eyes and eye teeth which were slightly too long for beauty.

Then in a flash, she had gone and the Leanan-Sidhe sat there instead.

Oberon shuddered.

'Did the little woman believe you?' she laughed nastily.

'Of course,' Oberon said, haughtily. 'Eventually,' he added.

'Main question, though,' she said, 'is why you and your little mates here were standing beside the A34 in the middle of the night. Okay, so you can't drive. But, surely, you can fly?'

Oberon looked down at his lap and hurriedly rearranged his scattered clothing.

She snickered again. 'You can't, can you? You can't bloody fly. Just wait till the lads hear this.'

'Lads?'

'You didn't think it was just me, did you? Dearie me, no.

We're pretty thinly spread but... let's just say, we're around. *All around.* So, where were you going?'

Oberon knew he mustn't say. Although obviously less numerous than they once had been, the Unseelie hordes were stronger than his own and he smelled danger. He turned on his glamour. Whatever she might say, she really did find him attractive. She treated him like some village idiot, it was true, but oh, how she wanted to get inside his clothes. His musky smell filled the car. The goblins covered their eyes and folded in their ears to try and drown out some of the inevitable. But they could still tell what was going on and Tiny at least wouldn't sleep for a week. Unseelie or no, Leanne was not immune to Oberon's powers even when she was trying. And tonight, she wasn't trying. Yes, there were others from her Court in the mortal world, but an ugly, geeky lot they were. Girls just want to have fun, or so she was told. Just as she slipped under the cloak of his glamour, a tiny bit of her cold, analytical brain resurfaced to tell her she had been had. But by then she didn't really care. The last thing she remembered hearing was a soft voice in her ear saying, 'And no scratching this time, if you don't mind.'

5

Oberon and the goblins waved to the tail lights of Leanne's car as they dwindled into the pearly dawn light.

'Will she be all right? Driving with her memory gone, like that,' asked Freckles.

The other two gaped at him.

'Freckles, mate, she's a vampire. She drinks blood. She eats people. She doesn't *really* look like that you know. Only when she's... hunting. Really, she hasn't any...'

But Oberon stopped him. 'Yes. Thank you, Tiny. There is such a thing as too much information. She'll remember a few bits soon. But not where she dropped us or who we are. Let's just think of her as we last saw her.' He hitched at his trousers, reminiscently. 'And hope it is the last we see of her.'

He looked around him. So this was Woodford Green, hey? They were in a tree-lined road, with large, detached houses decently secluded from each other by large, manicured gardens. The dawn air was quiet, with just a few waking birds trying their voices in distant stands of trees, not quite what Oberon had imagined when he was trying to fly, but pleasant, all the same. In fact, and a pang of jealousy stabbed him, rather better than Ellesmere Crescent. Puck had always had ideas above his station.

'Well,' Oberon stretched his arms and yawned luxuriously. What he could really have done with right now was a nice few days kip on a mossy bank, as was his post-coital habit in the Old Days. Instead of which, they were searching for a milkman. 'Well, let's get going. Er... do either of you know quite what we're looking for. Milk just appears, as far as I'm concerned. I don't think I've ever seen what brings it.'

Tiny and Freckles tried to look like goblins of the world who were never up and about early enough to see a milkman.

But the truth of the matter was that Squeaky had been going out for runs lately, generally working his previously puny goblin body, and Tiny had gone out with him sometimes, for a jog. They were blissfully unaware that they accounted for the rise in unexpected jogger heart attacks in and around Ellesmere Crescent. The statistics were all over the place, thanks to them.

'We're looking for a humming cart sort of thing,' said Tiny.

'Really?" Oberon said, trying to look as if he knew what it was talking about. 'What does it hum?'

'Just "hmmmm hmmmm",' said Tiny.

'All right, you can stop now.' Oberon was striding off down the road, ears cocked, listening for humming.

Tiny scurried after him. 'That's not me. That's the noise I mean.'

'Well, that's good. I hadn't hoped to find him so quickly. Well, well, let's catch him up.'

'But, Sire,' gasped Freckles, already slightly out of puff from Oberon's punishing pace, 'I don't think he's going to be the only one.'

'Nonsense,' blustered Oberon. 'He can put a girdle around the world in forty minutes. I'm sure delivering a few bottles of milk in a little place like this wouldn't take him long.' He charged round the corner and there, sure enough, was a small van, humming quietly to itself, pulled up on the pavement. They went round to the front. There was no one in the driving seat. Oberon looked round and tried a little experimental fly. Two feet! He grinned at the goblins foolishly and they clapped their trotters in encouragement.

From his slightly higher vantage point, he saw a flash of a white coat among the bushes by the house.

'Let's surprise him,' he whispered. 'Let's creep up on him and shout "boo". He used to love that game.'

'But, Sire...' Tiny was pointing to the front of the cart.

'No, no, I know it's not very kingly, but he'll love it.'

Giggling to himself behind his hand and bent over in an ostentatious crouch, Oberon set off up the drive, skimming over the grass and leaving hardly a trace of his passing. Panting and wheezing, the two goblins hurried along behind and arrived round the corner of the house just in time to take in the salient features of the scene before them.

In the doorway stood a woman, wearing a see through nightdress of such startling brevity that, wrong species though they were, made the goblins get quite hot and bothered. Clamped to her face in what mortals called a kiss, was a milkman, cap tilted onto the back of his head and the spare hand, the one not holding the crate, up the aforesaid brief garment. Creeping up behind them, giggling like a schoolboy, was their Lord, Oberon, Dread King of all the Faerie Hordes. As they watched in horrified stupefaction, he leapt in the air and shouted 'Boo!'

The two humans sprang apart as if electrified and the woman let out such a scream, just before she fainted, that Freckles' ears rang for days. The milkman stood transfixed and then ran down the drive as if Leanne and the Horde were after him, milk bottles flying in all directions. Oberon had caught a rogue blueberry yoghurt right in the middle of the chest, but even without this, would have been looking fairly foolish.

'That wasn't him,' he said, flatly. 'Not Puck.'

Tiny and Freckles could hear footsteps coming down the stairs inside the house, accompanied by some pretty disgruntled muttering. They tugged at Oberon's arm. It was surely important not to be seen. Although generally human in shape, Oberon was quite striking, especially since, in his shock, he had omitted to quite land and was hovering a fairly disconcerting six inches from the ground. They towed him, unresisting, down the drive and reached the road in plenty of time to see the cart weave away into the distance. They tugged Oberon down so that he was sitting on a low wall at the edge of the pavement.

'Not him. Not Puck.'

'I tried to tell you, Sire,' said Tiny, risking a clip round the ear. 'They have their names on the front of their humming cart.'

'Oh, ho, Mr Clever,' said Oberon. 'When did you learn to read?'

'Well, I can't read,' sulked Tiny. 'Not for want of trying, though. But I can count, as long as the numbers aren't too big. And I reckoned that "Robin Goodfellow", which is what Puck is known as around here, is probably... ooh, lots of letters. *That* milkman just then, only had a few letters on the front of his cart.'

Oberon looked at the goblin with new eyes. There were hidden depths to Tiny. Better watch out. Clever and goblin were two words Oberon had never intended to go together. He contented him with a terse 'well done, mate' and a friendly cuff round the side of the head which knocked the poor little thing several yards along the pavement.

Suddenly Freckles pricked up his ears. Were they humming because of that mortal's scream, or could he hear another cart? He gazed into the milky distance and over the brow of the hill came just such a thing, weaving from side to side in a rather haphazard fashion.

'It's that one I just jumped out at,' said Oberon, disgusted. 'Humans don't drive that badly except when they've had a shock or something.'

Freckles narrowed his eyes. 'Humans don't drive that badly,' he said. 'But fairies do.'

And as if to prove his point, the humming cart crossed the road crabwise and fetched up gently in a hedge. There was a soft fairy curse, a grinding of levers and it bounced backwards and went on its disjointed way.

Oberon shielded his eyes from the growing dawn glow and murmured, 'My lad, I believe you're right.' Throwing caution to the winds, he leapt, flew, ran down the road, crying, 'Puck! Puck! It's me!'

Mr Ernest Thwaite, bent over his prostrate wife in his doorway, made a mental note to write to the council as soon as he had had his breakfast. The neighbourhood was going to the dogs. First, lunatics assaulting his wife on her very own doorstep, and then language that no decent householder should have to listen to being yelled out in the road. There were, after all, ladies present, unconsciousness being no bar to being shocked by obscenities.

This time, Oberon had it right. It *was* Puck and Tiny derived a small measure of satisfaction from the huge number of letters adorning the front of the cart. The hobgoblin hadn't changed much. Even in his milkman's overall, he was lithe and lissom, with a face clear and unlined but, to Oberon, undistinguished. That he had a different effect on the ladies of the milk round, the King was unaware.

When he had recovered from the shock, Puck asked, 'How did you find me, Lord?' There was something in the tone which Oberon chose to ignore. An undercurrent of regret at being found, which was surely a misunderstanding. Puck had been around mortals much more than had Oberon and perhaps had picked up their speech patterns. Yes, that would be it.

Tiny gave a discreet cough and stepped forward. Oberon flicked him behind him again with his toe. 'Been looking all over for you, old friend,' he said. 'Titania and I, we missed you so much. I've been thorough brush and thorough briar...'

'Isn't that my line, my Lord?' ventured Puck.

'Whatever. Anyway, we've found you now, so you can come back with us...'

'No, Lord.'

'Pardon?'

'No. I live here now. I'm not the best milkman in the world,' he looked pensive. 'The milk doesn't seem to keep too well... Anyway, not the best, but I enjoy what I do. Cobweb – do you remember Cobweb?'

A faint light of fond remembrance twinkled in Oberon's eye.

'I can see you do. Well, we share a house just around the corner from here, just on the edge of a little park, not too near the dual carriageway... although quite near the railway line.' He brightened up. 'But sometimes, when the trains aren't running, because of track maintenance, and what mortals called "strikes" for some reason, it is quite quiet. Quite like home.' He gave a little wistful smile.

Oberon was puzzled. Puck had always been quite capricious and not always very careful over details, but he'd never actually refused point blank to do something before.

'Titania's with me, of course,' he wheedled.

Puck smiled absently. 'That's nice. That's really lovely.'

Oberon's heart constricted with fear. He had heard in Puck's voice a trace of Tracey from Essex. He was turning, faster than his milk. He grabbed Puck's shoulders and shook him. 'Look at me, you sprite. Look at me. I am Oberon, your Lord. Titania, your Queen commanded me... er, I mean... commands you to attend her. Oh, and she says, bring Cobweb, if you like.'

'I'd love to, Sire,' Puck said, already moving away. 'But I've got this milk, and Cobweb's got her babies.'

'Babies?' the hunting party chorused. 'You've got *babies*?'

Oberon added, under his breath, 'Titania will go demented.'

Puck hurriedly corrected the impression he had made. 'No, no, not our babies. Other peoples' babies. Cobweb visits babies in their houses, to make sure their mothers are looking after them properly. She's called a Health Visitor.' He looked a little doleful. 'There were a few problems at first, what with her bringing the odd one home now and again. And she had to learn not to talk about changelings too much. Some mortal babies can be very ugly, although not a patch on a faerie baby, of course.' He gave a reminiscent sigh. 'But she's quite good at it now, and she can't just get up and go. She'd miss them.'

'There are babies where we live,' Oberon put in hurriedly. 'I've heard them.'

'Where is it that you live, Sire?' asked Puck. 'Some leafy wood somewhere, is it? Some riverside idyll, where nightingales serenade you all night long and butterflies form a canopy where're our Lady goes?'

'Er... no, not so's you'd notice. We live...' he bent down to Tiny and whispered out of the corner of his mouth, 'where is it we live?'

'Guildford,' mouthed Tiny.

'Where?'

'Guildford,' a little louder this time.

'Yes, that's right,' said Oberon, none the wiser. 'There.'

'Oh. Nice.'

'Ellesmere Crescent,' announced Oberon proudly. Titania had made him learn that, after he had got lost for the umpteenth time. 'Number Eleven.'

'Firteen,' hissed Freckles.

'Firteen... er, Thirteen. Yes. Thirteen.'

'Unlucky for some,' said Puck.

'Pardon?'

'That's what they say, the mortals. At Bingo.'

Oberon was both aghast and puzzled. 'Bingo?' It sounded very, very mortal to him.

'It's a game. We play it on a Wednesday. They shout out numbers and you... well, I don't think it would be quite your cup of tea. Speaking of which, I must get on with my milk round.'

Oberon could see that it was time to get down to issues. 'Are you seriously standing there, telling me you would rather deliver milk to these mortals than come back with me, be with me and Titania, make Faerie great again?'

'Yes.' Puck's answer was quick and unequivocal. 'Yes. I would. I know you are disappointed, Lord, but... Cobweb and I are happy, in a way. We used to be miserable, about how we had come down, you know. We wondered where you were, how you had come to forget us. And, well, in time we started to forget as well and forgetting is easier than remembering. It doesn't hurt so much.'

Oberon sank down, very slowly, crumpling in on himself. It was like watching a glacier slide off an ice shelf, like watching a star implode, like some huge, slow, geological event from far away.

Puck stood over him, shifting awkwardly from one foot to another. He looked imploringly at the goblins, but they looked away, trying to whistle silently, but their lips weren't really made for it.

'Look, Sire... Please don't do this.'

Oberon just stayed quite, quite still. His shape grew less defined, misty and flowing.

Tiny grabbed the hem of Puck's white coat. 'Look, he's fading. Please, please say you'll come back with us,' he cried. 'Let's just say it's for a holiday. A bit of a change, let's say. Please, Puck, please. He hasn't got the strength to come back once he goes.' Tiny was pleading for his life, Puck knew. If Oberon went, then there wouldn't be any goblins any more either. And perhaps no more fairies, not at all. Puck wasn't sure he was human enough to survive without Oberon's faint influence in the Universe. He knew when he was beaten.

'All right,' he sighed. 'All right. We'll come with you. But just to stay for a bit. Not for too long.' He leaned down and shook Oberon's shoulder. 'Sire? Is that all right?'

Oberon nodded his head very slightly. It was only Tiny, from his lower vantage point, who saw one crafty, glittering eye creased round with merriment, twinkling out from under his tumbling curls.

Oberon uncurled himself to his full height. 'Okay,' he said, cracking his knuckles. 'Let's get Cobweb and be off.' He threw an arm around Puck's drooping shoulders and set off down the road. 'How's your flying these days, old man?'

The goblins chuckled and did a little dance. It was going to be *great*. Just like the Old Days.

'Ah,' Oberon was saying, as the strange little party disappeared over the brow of the hill, 'Cobweb is going to be *so* excited...'

6

obweb wasn't so much excited as gobsmacked. She was still in bed when they arrived at the house, rather nicer than Ellesmere Crescent, even Oberon was forced to concede. Oberon burst through the bedroom door and before she could react had swept her up in his arms and planted a huge smacker right on her lips. The sweeping up only lasted a second or two however. The lissom fairy who had specialised in spiders' broken legs and in disentangling moths caught in webs, had become rather fonder of mortal food than had Oberon and Titania.

'Cobweb, dear one,' Oberon crooned, massaging his left bicep, which had taken most of the strain, 'You're looking wonderful. You've... blossomed.' He beamed around the room, proud of his choice of word. The goblins were still too slack-jawed to reply and Puck was in the throes of seeing Cobweb through someone else's eyes. He saw a still attractive but rather large woman, with tousled hair and confused expression, sprawled where Oberon had dropped her on the bed Puck could rarely bring himself to share. He had always been more of a facilitator, rather than a participant, when it came to the arts of love, as he still rather coyly thought of it.

The silence was stifling, but not for long.

'Robin!' screeched Cobweb. 'What are these... people...?' her voice died away as Tiny and Freckles swam into focus. They wiggled their trotters at her in what they hoped was a friendly wave.

Puck shrugged his shoulders at Oberon, who had turned to him in puzzlement. 'She's almost gone, Sire. She never had much of a grip, if you remember, even in the Old Days. She was always wandering off in her head. If I had a quid for every time I had to fetch her back when she was minding the changelings...'

'Yes?' beamed Oberon encouragingly. 'If you had a quid...?'

'It's just a saying, my Lord,' sighed Puck. 'Anyway, you can see how she is. She hardly remembers anything. I told you. Forgetting is the easy way out. She took it.'

Oberon squared his shoulders and, sitting on the edge of the bed, patted Cobweb's hand in a paternalistic way. Her pudgy fingers pulled away from him and she lowered her eyes. He made another attempt to hold her hand, but this time she snatched it away and tucked it under her other arm, like a sulky child.

Oberon was puzzled. Women just didn't *do* that to him. He stood up abruptly and snapped at Puck, 'Let's leave the stupid female here. Titania didn't really want her anyway, that much was obvious before we left. It was you she wanted – Cobweb was just baggage.'

Puck hung his head. 'I can't just leave her, Sire. She'd never manage on her own.'

'Manage? Of course she'll manage. She's got a job, hasn't she? Titania has a job and has often said she doesn't need me.' He laughed in what he hoped was a devil-may-care way. 'She's just joking, naturally, but I think the point is soundly made. So,' he grabbed Puck by the shoulder and made to leave the room, 'Off we go.'

Puck pulled himself free. 'No, Sire,' he said. 'I won't leave her.'

Freckles, who had a soft heart beating in his rather peculiar body said quietly, 'Do you love her, then?'

Puck looked up and Oberon and his henchmen were shocked to see his eyes full of tears. 'No, I don't. But I should, and somehow, when it comes to decisions like this, that is almost the same.' He stood there, feet planted apart on the beige shag pile of Cobweb's bedroom, arms straight and fists clenched, ready for a fight or flight. In the old days, the anger in him would have had him soaring round the room, Cobweb flying at his heels, Peter Pan and Tinkerbell, as J.M.Barrie had seen them all those years ago as he struggled with writer's block in his orchard.

But now, they were just a defeated milkman, his face and body still eighteen, but with eyes a thousand years old and full of sadness, and a fat, stupid woman, who didn't know why her life was not as good as the lives she saw on the TV. A woman whose bedroom was full of strange things she knew in the back of her clouded brain she should recognise, beings who had started that itch on the tip of the tongue that only returning memory can scratch.

Oberon sighed and rubbed his face with his hands. Tiny wasn't sure, but he sometimes thought he saw a few sparks crawling through his master's hair. Now was one of those times and he heard a low piping in the background. Puck's head snapped up and he sniffed the air.

'Sire?' he asked.

Oberon shrugged self-deprecatingly. 'Sorry. I just find myself doing that since yesterday. I must say, despite this setback, I do feel rather well.' He shook his hair back and two small petals fell out onto Cobweb's bed.

The others looked at them as they withered and died immediately, but they had *been* there, and that was the main thing. Oberon shoved his hand into his pocket and brought out the crumpled money, looking a little brown round the edges, but more bank note than leaf. He coughed gently to draw their attention and basked in their respect.

Puck looked from Oberon to Cobweb and back again. He smiled, a ghost of his old wolfish smile and clapped the two goblins on the back. They crowed with pleasure and stamped their hoofed feet.

'Give me a minute with her. She'll need to pack. Mortals take clothes and things with them when they travel, and she will need a while. Go downstairs and help yourself to anything you fancy. I could murder a bacon sandwich... sorry, Sire. It's just a saying. I'll have what you're having.'

'Freckles,' Oberon ordered. 'Get outside and gather some dew, in a silver cup, if you can find one. I'm really quite hungry.'

Puck sighed as he closed the bedroom door. 'Come along, dear,' the others heard him say, as they made their way down the stairs, Oberon giggling with pleasure as he floated down with his fingertips on the banisters and feet six inches from the treads. 'We're going on a bit of a holiday.'

Finally, Cobweb was ready. She stood in the hall, with two bulging suitcases at her feet, trying not to look at the goblins who sat on them, legs swinging excitedly and their eager faces lifted to her. She hadn't acknowledged their presence since Freckles had winked at her in a matey way. She had worked it out to her own satisfaction that if she didn't see them, they weren't there. Puck had managed to persuade Oberon to use the savings he had hidden in the coffee jar, rather than the faerie money, which was becoming more leaf-like with every hour. They were going to catch a train, and Puck reckoned that the journey was going to be traumatic enough, without getting arrested for passing dodgy notes in exchange for tickets. For a start, Oberon's money had a depiction of his own head where the Queen's should be.

They joined Cobweb in the hall and Oberon held open his coat for the goblins to hide in. With a pop, they disappeared. Cobweb vaguely felt that this should make her feel rather better, but it didn't. She kept glancing at Oberon from beneath her lashes, as if she couldn't quite believe he was really there.

Effortlessly lifting a bulging suitcase each, Puck and Oberon led Cobweb out through the front door. Puck let it slam behind him and then, after a moment's pause, posted the key back through the door.

'There,' he said. 'Now we can't come back.'

Oberon flicked two fingers at the door, and it swung silently open. He smiled, a tiny flicker at one corner of his mouth and said nothing. Puck closed the door again. It wasn't often his master got sentimental, but he knew that this was his way of saying that it wasn't a one way street after all.

The station was just round the corner, and as soon as

Oberon saw the large building, with people scurrying to and fro, and platform indicators whizzing round, he was glad that Puck was at his side. He stood with Cobweb in the middle of the concourse while Puck got their tickets, and he smiled benevolently on all the women who for some reason found it necessary to cross and re-cross the station, mostly with silly grins on their faces. He gave Cobweb a friendlier than ever squeeze now and again, which startled her and made her more like a rather portly rabbit caught in headlights.

Puck came back just as a curious crowd was beginning to coalesce from the commuters thronging the station and he hurried them off to the train. Puck was finding all this faintly amusing. He hadn't let his sense of humour out for many decades. He leaned towards slapstick; people walking into walls, falling over rugs. His favourite time in recent centuries had been the Victorian era, when humour was hardly subtle and the Queen herself could be reduced to paroxysms if a footman fell over. Ah, happy days. But he had found himself out of step since radio was invented. Word plays amused him, but the best pun out had nothing on a lovely squishy pie in the face, as far as Puck was concerned.

You didn't have to have a very subtle mind to see that they made an unlikely group. Cobweb looked very like every other slightly overweight, slightly harassed, slightly discontented woman on the train – and they were legion. Puck, though technically older than she, looked like a teenager still; slim hipped, dark haired with eyes which changed colour with light and mood, now dark, now twinkling like sunlight on a mountain stream under overhanging ferns. He smelt like the most expensive cologne ever made – sharp with crushed grass, mellow with the smell of moth wings and candlelight. He turned heads, he knew, and had sometimes had a difficult job fighting off the bored housewives. Alf Coe, his round partner, had had a wonderful time, picking up Puck's leftovers.

Oberon was... Oberon. No one could describe him when he was out of sight. He was as tall as you wanted him to be, dark, handsome. What more was there to be said? His beauty was as old as time and as new as the next second but one. His features shifted like smoke and no two people saw the same face when they looked at him. But he was certainly heart-stoppingly handsome, as some mortals who had looked too long could testify, were they able. In view of this, Puck was heartily glad that the goblins were out of sight. But not out of his mind, obviously, as a cheeky, green-freckled face briefly materialised out of Oberon's top pocket, and winked at Puck before disappearing in a twinkling.

'Stop that!' he said in his head, and was rewarded with a chuckling grunt.

They settled themselves in their compartment and Cobweb stared steadfastly out of the window. At the London end of their short journey, Puck decided against the Tube and instead hailed a cab. Oberon had been ill at ease enough on the train above ground; underground had never really been his forte. It reminded him too much of the really bad old days, when Pan had ruled and things had really been pretty rough. The Old Religion in its naked form was nasty and brutish. Men – and women – had had a softening influence eventually and their heyday was long and sweet. Sometimes, Puck thought, this twilight was just nature's way of winding everything down. But Oberon, more especially Titania, had called him, and he wasn't so far gone that he could do anything but answer.

The cab turned out to be less than ideal. The cabbie had many and varied political views, mostly aimed at foreigners and what he would like to do to them. Oberon quite rightly perceived himself to be about as foreign as you could get, and the cabbie was only saved from toad-dom by the simple fact that Oberon had forgotten how to turn people into amphibians.

Ensconced on the Guildford train out of Waterloo, Puck put Cobweb in the window seat, where she stared at the passing countryside again. She had persuaded herself they were going to Bournemouth, and was looking out in a desultory way for her first glimpse of the sea. Puck felt that it would be time enough to disillusion her when they got to Ellesmere Crescent. The goblins were getting restive and so he put Oberon in the other window seat, opposite Cobweb, where their wanderings around his jacket would be less noticeable. He leant back in his seat, dropped his head back and closed his eyes. Just to rest them – he wasn't going to sleep. Well, only for a minute.

He was woken by a scream. His eyes flew open and spun round momentarily before they focused on the space previously occupied by Cobweb. He leapt to his feet and raced down the train in the direction of the sound. It was coming from a locked lavatory several carriages down and he knew it was Cobweb. The register of the scream was becoming higher with each expelled breath and soon only bats would be able to hear her. He knew he had to get in there before she screamed herself into oblivion. He also knew that, even after years of disuse, he still had the power to slip like a waft of smoke through the key hole. The problem was that he was surrounded by people, more every minute as they were drawn by the screaming, now nearly off the human register. There was nothing for it. He backed away a little, mingling with the crowd and then, when no one was looking, dematerialised and made a dash for the hole in the door. He had to be quicker than a twinkle in a gnat's eye; he didn't have the power yet to stay that small for long and materialising halfway through would clearly be very serious. Safely in the loo, his worst fears were realised. Cobweb had gone in as a mostly mortal woman needing a pee and had, in front of the mirror, become a very scared mostly faerie creature with a weight problem and the worst hair day of her life. She screamed even louder when he appeared in the reflection behind her. She turned suddenly, a difficult trick in a train lavatory when you are not alone and weigh almost fourteen stone.

'Puck!' Her voice sounded like a steam whistle. 'Is that me? What's going on?'

'Hush,' he soothed, placing a finger across her lips. 'Hush, pretty Cobweb. What brought this on, eh?'

She pointed with a trembling finger at the glass.

'You've been... away.' He glanced over his shoulder as things suddenly fell into place. 'What happened to scare you into this?'

'Someone... a man... Oberon! Oberon is on this train! Did

you know? He was sitting opposite me. He...' she opened her eyes wide and was lost for words.

'Of course he did,' Puck sighed. 'He can't help himself. We'd better get back and make sure he hasn't done any more damage. Are you all right? We'll explain on the way.'

She opened the door and the gathered commuters stepped aside to let them both pass. Some of them were at their office desks later in the day before their brains let them wonder how it was that one had gone in, but two had come out. But that was Connex for you – nothing was ever quite what it seemed.

T

aking their way back down the train, Puck felt, was the longest journey of his very long life. He could hardly bear to wait to see what havoc Oberon was wreaking. On the other hand, ignorance was bliss and he narrowed his eyes as he approached their seats. But Oberon was stretched out asleep in his corner, snoring gently with a sound of distant bees. Slipping into the seat next to him, Puck felt more at home than he had for many years. It was as peaceful as a woodland glade in their little corner of the train, but he didn't dare sleep again. Besides, they were nearly at Guildford.

Cobweb was pushing petulantly at her suitcases, more than filling the seat next to her.

'What are these great heavy things?' she whinged to Puck. 'I haven't got any room.'

'It's your luggage,' snapped Puck, suddenly terribly fed up with her. She was whiney as ninety percent mortal, she was whiney as ninety percent faerie. This seemed to be a heads you win, tails I lose situation.

'I am a *faerie*,' she boomed. 'I don't do luggage!'

Puck lunged over the table, too small for usefulness, too big for comfort, and grabbed her by the sensible scarf wrapped round her chins.

'Listen, Cobweb,' he hissed. 'Don't push me, all right. You've been a great big lump of whinge for years, you haven't had a faerie thought in decades. You've done nothing but eat bloody donuts and chips since I don't know when. I've got you out of trouble more times than I care to remember. I've been stuck as a milkman for so long that I remember doing rounds with a horse pulling my cart, and I was stuck there because I was looking after you. So don't push your luck. We're going to Titania and you know how she feels about you, so watch your mouth and try to keep up. Otherwise...' he paused, searching for the right words, 'otherwise, we'll let you go.'

'Let me go?' she whispered through dry lips.

'Yes,' he said, in a tight voice. 'Let you go. You'll dwindle, you'll die. You'll blow away like a dandelion clock and every fragment will know every minute of your disintegration. So,' he let her drop back into her seat, with some relief, 'shut up about things when you are in the hearing of mortals. Our time isn't here yet. Leave things to Titania.' He sat back down.

Cobweb crossed her arms and sulked out of the window, muttering, 'Oh yes, leave it to Titania. *Titania* knows what to do. Oh, yes. *Titania* will soon sort it out. Where's *she* been all these years, then, eh? Oh yes...' Puck sighed, and set about waking Oberon.

'Sire. Sire. We're here.'

Oberon woke up slowly, one eye and, Puck suspected, one brain cell, at a time.

'Where?'

'Guildford, Sire. Where you live.'

He rubbed his eyes and did a quick goblin check. He glanced across at Cobweb. 'She's different,' he hissed in a stage whisper to Puck.

'She's back,' he said. 'In a way. Dumb still. Whiney.'

'And fat,' Oberon observed, without malice.

'Indeed, Sire. She is still fat.'

Cobweb roused herself. 'Fat? I think... comfy.'

Oberon was blunt as ever. He stood up and clapped her on the shoulder. 'No, fat,' he said. 'Never mind, soon get rid of that, old thing. Soon have you flitting from flower to flower again, eh?'

Puck covered his eyes with a weary hand. What was the point of shutting up Cobweb when the King stood there and bawled stuff about flitting along a crowded train. But in all his dealings with mortals, there was one thing with which Puck had never quite come to grips. And that was that if they heard something that didn't make immediate sense, they didn't try to work it out. They just assumed that the person saying it was potty, daft, mental or one of the other many words they had for anyone off the norm. The men who heard it smirked. Handsome he may be, but daft as a brush, they chuckled to themselves. The women just thought how the love of a good woman would straighten him out in no time.

Without Cobweb's luggage, which she happily abandoned, leaving the train was easier than getting on. Oberon had no clue at all how to get to Ellesmere Crescent.

'Ask the goblins,' suggested Puck.

'They've never been outside the house until last night,' Oberon replied.

A snicker came from his top pocket and a green freckled snout appeared.

'I've been to work with the mistress,' Freckles volunteered. 'It was great.'

'Was that the day when her piles of cornflake boxes kept falling over?' Oberon knew his goblin all right.

Snicker.

'Can you find the way back, then?' Puck asked.

'Yes, I fink so. From the supermarket, vo. Not from here.'

'Supermarkets are usually quite easy to find,' said Puck. 'We'll tell you when to start directing us.' He looked around. He was looking for a large building, new, probably red brick, intended to blend with the local architecture, but actually sticking out like a sore thumb. Ah, there it was. They walked over to its car park and poked the goblin through Oberon's jacket.

'Oy!'

'We're ready to start.'

'Can I poke my head out?'

'Are you joking? Mortals will see you. What did you do when you went to work with Titania?'

'Well, in the shop, I just hid. But on the walk back, I popped my face out of her bag. The mortal children have funny faces on their bags, so I just looked like one of them. Not,' the goblin added, 'that my face is funny. I had to dress it up a bit.'

'Naturally,' Oberon agreed. He'd always been quite fond of goblin faces because, handsome as he was, he was happiest with no competition.

'All right,' Puck said. 'Try that. It might just work.'

'No one's carrying a bag,' observed the goblin.

'Just stick a bit of body out then. If Oberon sticks his hand through your braces, it'll do,' Cobweb suggested.

Puck and Oberon looked at her in amazement. Freckles twisted his head round and even Tiny risked popping one eye out to look at her in admiration.

'How do you know they wear braces?' Puck asked. No need to let her know he was impressed.

'Tchah! After all the goblin braces I've mended...'

'Oh, yes,' Freckles agreed. 'She's a handy one with a needle, I'll give her that.'

After a bit of wriggling and adjusting, Freckles eventually got himself comfortable and they set off. Oberon made an arresting sight. A tall, dark man, as lovely as day, wearing clothes which seemed to flow around him in a way no tailor on earth could match, carrying a bag with a face that could turn milk and which appeared to be talking to him. He even seemed to be asking it things from time to time. Small children passing by wanted one for Christmas and would drive their parents mad for months. The one who got a bite was not quite so keen, but the nightmares kept its paediatrician occupied for years.

Quite soon, they turned into Ellesmere Crescent. Oberon was as pleased as if he had built it himself. He had no eye for mortal architecture and didn't see how tired and scruffy the whole road was. He had also found his way on his own – he discounted Freckles' contribution as soon as they were safely there – and stood there smiling and extending an arm. The smile became a little uncertain after a while and his arm drooped from the shoulder.

'Number Firteen,' whispered Freckles, out of the corner of his mouth.

'I knew that,' huffed Oberon, but made no move.

Puck led the way. He wasn't much at reading, but in his many years of milk delivery had learned numbers and the letters a,d,i,l,k,m,n,o,t and y – all that was needed for the notes he received. The housewives who had anguished over invitations to untold delights once their husbands were at work were not to know that he hadn't the first clue what they had offered. Many had settled for Alf instead.

At the door, Oberon stood uncertainly outside.

'Well?' Puck said. 'Aren't we going in?'

'Er... have we been long?' Oberon asked.

'I don't know. When did you leave?'

'I think... last night.'

'Well, no, then. You haven't been long. In fact, you were very quick. In fact, how *did* you get to me so fast? Can you still fly after all?'

Oberon coughed and didn't answer. He squared his shoulders and pushed the door open. He called, 'Titania? We're back! Look who's here!'

No reply. The house was clearly empty. The hall had the singing silence of a noise just ended, but that would be the goblins, having a bit of a roustabout while the Mistress was away.

Freckles jumped down, and bounced straight back up again.

'Er, Sire? Could you let go of my braces?'

'Hmm? Oh, sorry old chap.' Oberon let go abruptly and Freckles was off like a bullet and went straight into the wall head first. He popped back out again with the others, who clamoured around Oberon and Puck, all shouting together.

'One at a time. One at a time,' said Oberon, holding up his hands. Goblins aren't good at taking turns, but eventually they settled down and Thydney took a deep breath and began.

'Mithtreth hath gone to work,' he said.

'To work?' Oberon asked. 'At a time like this?'

'Yeth. She thaid she could athk about advertithing. She

thaid thomething about a notith board. Pothtcardth.'

Oberon was getting quite wet. He decided to let someone else have a go. 'Bertie. Your turn.'

Bertie gave a discreet little cough behind his trotter, smoothed down his bristles and began.

'Well, Lord, while you were gone – you've been very quick, by the way. How did you do it so fast? Can you fly again, Lord?'

Oberon looked at the ceiling. 'Time for our story later,' he said, kicking Tiny, who was sitting behind him, giggling quietly and tidying up his clothing, disarranged from travelling in Oberon's underwear.

'Yes,' Bertie continued, 'The Mistress said she had to go to work, because advertising needed money and also because the people at the supermarket knew stuff about how to sell things, and what we need is to sell ourselves.'

At this, Cobweb, who was nosing round the sitting room, wiping her finger along polished surfaces and being generally delighted by the layer of dust, said indignantly, 'Excuse me! There'll be none of that! I haven't done that since...' she subsided under the shocked stares of the assembled company. 'Well, I never have, as such, of course, but...'

'Do be quiet, Cobweb,' said Puck. 'You'll only embarrass yourself more than you have already.'

'And anyway,' said Squeaky, looking her up and down, 'You're not my cup of tea anyway, obviously, but how much d'you think you'd make?'

Cobweb reached to clip him round the ear and things could have got nasty. Oberon held up his hands for peace. He knew his Titania and if she came back to find they'd fallen out, he would be the one to get the blame. He had a sneaking feeling that when the details all came out, he was in deep trouble anyway. He didn't want it to get any worse.

Bertie took up the tale again. 'She said that we need to make people know we are still here.'

'Fair enough,' said Freckles. 'But in that case, why did I have to hide on the way back from the station? Those braces really chafed.'

'No, no,' Tiny piped up. 'Not just appear at people. Look

at that woman this morning when you jumped out at her, Lord. She might never recover.'

'You jumped out at someone?' asked Puck, incredulously.

Oberon mumbled, 'Er... mistaken identity. You know how it is.'

They were all silent for a moment, all busy with their own thoughts.

Bertie shook his head and carried on. 'So, she said she would work for a while longer, and then we could make some more plans. I... er, I don't think she was expecting you back so soon, Sire.'

Oberon preened. 'We *did* do rather well, didn't we?' he beamed round the room. It was obvious to everyone that no matter who had the ideas, who did the work, this great brainless... King, they hastily amended their thoughts, was going to get the credit. As he had through millennia.

'I thaid she ought to be a model, Thire,' ventured Thydney.

'Or a television cook,' said Squeaky, for whom his stomach always came first.

'Or a dethigner.'

'What about a singer?' asked Tiny.

'Have you ever *heard* her sing?' spat Cobweb. 'Mustardseed always did the singing, hidden behind a bush. She only mimed.'

'Please, Cobweb,' begged Puck. 'Let's not be catty.'

Oberon gave a little rueful smile. Catty. Slanted cat's eyes. Sharp little claws. Pointed eye teeth. A rough little tongue, lapping, lapping...

'Sire!' shouted Freckles urgently. 'I fink we should be a bit careful, don't you?'

Oberon jumped. 'What?' he roared, too loudly, as all beings, mortal or faerie do, when caught out in a rather illicit daydream.

'We should be a bit *careful*,'' said Freckles, looking pointedly round at all the interested faces. The world of Faerie had always been alive with gossip, with Oberon its main subject and old habits die hard.

'Mithtreth will be home thoon,' observed Thydney. He

rubbed his trotters together excitedly. 'Let'th make her a nithe cup of nectar and plump up the cuthions. She'll be *tho* pleathed to see Puck and Cobweb. I can hardly wait to thee her fathe!' The little thing wiped his snout, dripping with spit and dried his hand absent mindedly on the side of Cobweb's dress. 'It'th going to be *tho* exthiting! His little eyes twinkled with delight and anticipation.

Puck sat down as if the weight of Faerie was on his shoulders. Oh, yes. It was going to be exciting, all right.

8

As Titania wriggled into her overall in the changing room she was thinking hard. She wasn't popular with the other girls, she knew. She found talking to them very difficult, not just because she found their idioms hard to emulate, but because she was afraid she would let things slip.

Their husbands, after all, were far from being King of Faerie – mostly they were referred to as 'my old man' or 'that bastard'. On Monday mornings it was often 'that drunken bastard'. Not many of them seemed to be happy, except for Shania, who had only been married a few weeks and who got a lot of nudges and winks. Her baby was due in about three months, the others said and she seemed very happy. Titania had a bad feeling about it, though. She had met Shania's husband. The vibrations given off by the baby didn't really match. To a fairy that would mean nothing. What with changelings, love potions, disguises and confusions, no one was quite sure who anyone was anyway, from one dawn to the next. But Titania knew it mattered to mortals. In particular, she felt, it probably mattered to mortal men who wore their wife's name tattooed on one hand and 'Scumbag' on the other.

So, she was aware that her life was rather different from theirs. She didn't need to buy food, although she sometimes did, for the look of the thing, and Oberon was partial to peanut M&Ms. She would herself sometimes indulge in a small vodka and tonic and could see how drunken bastards could become quite hooked on it. She didn't go clubbing – it sounded rather violent and not really her type of thing at all. She couldn't knit very well, only scarves but she'd always enjoyed watching the spiders, and the sight of a new spiderling trying to learn could keep her amused for hours. Television she avoided. She knew herself well enough to be aware that she could easily become as hooked as Oberon on the square window on the mortal world. To be honest, it upset her to see so much sadness that she could do nothing about.

And so, she kept herself to herself. But now, she needed ideas. Mortals knew so much about how to get in touch with each other. They were always communicating; on their mobiles, by writing, reading, television and e-mails, whatever they were. They could travel; in cars, trains, aeroplanes. She had always found it got the job done just by thinking hard. The right faerie for the job would always turn up quick as winking. And Puck – she sighed to herself – he was always there, a shimmer on the edge of vision, always ready to do her bidding. Not always very well, but he did his best, and that was the main thing.

She set about filling the shelves which had been ravaged by the all-night shoppers. She was on bakery today. She hated that, because although the work was light, the smell of so many loaves and cakes quite turned her stomach. But still, she consoled herself, it wasn't as bad as the butchery department. She preferred food in tins and packets. It didn't smell and didn't leak.

The other problem with bakery was that there never seemed to be a time when the shelves stayed full. Tired-looking women, with mewling toddlers and dribbly babies would grab the loaves as soon as she put them down. So it was her coffee break before she got a chance to have a look at the notice board. She was looking for ideas. How did you organize a meeting? She could read a little, but checking the board was going to be a long job. She had to spell unfamiliar words out letter by letter and work out what it said. F.O.R.D. E.S.CO.R.T. That was okay. Ford Escort. She had a Faerie Escort whenever the Rade went forth. But that couldn't be what it meant. This Escort was in I.M.M.A.C.U.L.A.T.E. C.O.N.D.I.T.I.O.N. She sighed. This wasn't going to work. It would take her weeks, and the cards were changing all the time.

She turned away from the board and bumped into Trevor from Home and Wear. She backed away hurriedly, but he moved faster.

'Tania. I'm sorry,' he hurriedly said. 'I didn't mean to touch you. I wasn't looking. Honestly, I just bumped you by accident, there. I...'

She patted his arm and he flinched. 'Don't worry about it. An accident. I'm sorry.'

He looked suspiciously at her. He'd only just been able to stop wearing the neck brace. She was very lovely, though. Was it worth another try? 'Urn, do you need any help?'

She looked at him thoughtfully. He was easily overcome if he got too frisky. Keep upwind of him and it was not too bad. He obviously could read and possibly also knew about e-mail and meetings. She decided. 'As a matter of fact,' she slipped an arm through his, causing reminiscent pain to judder through his ribcage, 'I do. I want to form a... group.'

'Are you the singer?'

She laughed. 'Me? Goodness no. Why do you ask that?'

'Well, you said "group". I assumed you meant a musical group.'

'No, I mean a group of... people. With interests the same.'

'Oh, I see. Like a reading group, or,' his ribs twinged again, 'karate, something like that.'

'Yes,' she smiled at him and his heart turned over. 'Yes, something like that. But not that.'

'Ah, self awareness, perhaps?'

That sounded more like it. 'Yes. That would be the kind of thing. How do I start a self-awareness group?'

'Well, I don't think a card will do it. You need a poster.' He led her along to the other side of the Customer Service Kiosk. 'Here you are. Something like this.'

She looked up at the brightly coloured pieces of paper fluttering in the breeze from the automatic door, opening and closing endlessly. They meant nothing to her. Some had pictures, others just words, but it was all too much. She quickly considered her options and whichever way she looked at it the answer was clear. She was going to have to admit to him she couldn't read.

She cast down her eyes and looked up at him demurely. Yes, that was it. He was hooked. 'I can't read,' she whispered.

He felt this gave him an edge. If only he knew. He patted her hand. 'There, there. That's nothing to be ashamed of, dear. Let me help you. This one here, it advertises a bring and buy sale. Hmm, let me see. Alternative therapies? Yes?'

She looked doubtful.

'No. Right. Hmm...' he ran his finger over the posters. 'Nothing there, really, like the thing you want to start. I'll tell you what!' he raised a finger as though just thinking of a brilliant idea. As far as he was concerned, it was a brilliant idea; he wasn't to know that she was in fact more than one step ahead. 'Why don't you come round to my place, after work, and I'll design you a poster on my computer? Then we can put it up here and see what happens.' He smiled condescendingly at her. 'Who knows, some of the girls might join and soon you'll have lots of friends.'

'I doubt it,' she muttered under her breath. Aloud, she said, 'What a good idea. But I'll have to discuss it with my L... my friend, first. I want to get the details right.'

'Fair enough, fair enough,' enthused Trevor of Home and Wear. Was this his lucky day, or what? 'Tomorrow night, then. Shall we say, straight after work?'

'Shall we say, later?' Titania smiled. She needed time to gather reinforcements and it was no good expecting Oberon to find his own way anywhere. She didn't even know if he was home, yet.

'Er... okay, then. I live at Keswick Road. Do you know where that is?'

'Yes.' No need for him to know that she lived in the next road along. This was going to take very careful handling. 'See you tomorrow. What number?'

'Forty seven.'

Damn. She always got those two mixed up. She hoped there wasn't a number seventy four, or things might get a little difficult. 'It's a date, then.' She had heard the women say that quite often. How was she to know the things the phrase was doing to Trevor's physiology – his hormones would be out of whack for weeks. He went away, whistling to himself. She skimmed away back to bakery, only just remembering to let her feet touch the ground.

Right; the next thing was to work out the wording. And there, she came to a complete standstill. Whatever was she going to put? 'Calling all Faerie? Feeling Put Upon and Low? Don't Worry, Your King and Queen are living in Ellesmere Crescent with a load of Goblins hidden in the walls. Pop round and have a drop of nectar and a moan and end up more miserable than you were before?' Damn. 'Calling All Faerie. Our Moment Has Arrived. We Have Nothing To Lose But Our....' What? What had they to lose? Nothing. What had they to gain? Everything. But how do you design a poster for a meeting, when hardly any of the creatures you are trying to contact can read, none of them needed to buy food and they were spread so thinly that she might, apart from Oberon, be the only one for miles?

She puzzled over it all afternoon, restocking the bread automatically. As she was leaving, into the gathering twilight and the usual sounds of lighting up and banter, she was still no wiser. She had to endure a conspiratorial wink from Trevor and a whole lot more hostility from the girls from Toys and Gifts. They despised her when she had given him a hiding. They despised her more now for sucking up to the odious creep.

'Mortals!' she said to herself as she skimmed off up the High Street. 'I'll never understand them. Three thousand years and rising, and I still haven't sorted the stupid things out.'

She tried to cheer herself up as she got nearer home by thinking of who might be waiting for her. Her heart fluttered in her chest. Best case – Puck, on his own, handsome, boyish, full of fun, flying round her sitting room with the joy of living. No Cobweb. Worst case – Puck, in a knitted thing in a greyish colour, with short cropped hair and a moustache. Cobweb beside him, beautiful and intelligent. Undiminished. She laughed quietly to herself. How likely was that? Beautiful she had certainly been. Intelligent – no. This was a faerie whose favourite hobby was plaiting ribbons into babies' hair, polishing beetles. How much of a threat could she be, especially after all this time?

Poor Cobweb sat miserably at one end of the settee, eating the last of Oberon's M&Ms and watching a quiz show with a female quiz mistress so vicious she reduced Cobweb to tears most nights. She was starting to sniffle, even now. Puck and the goblins were robbing Oberon blind at poker. Oberon's little stack of transformed leaves was getting very small indeed and he was hunched over his cards, anger simmering just below the surface. The mossy overtones of the room held just a hint of sulphur.

They heard the door latch click. They all had different thoughts spinning through their heads as they heard Titania call, 'Honey, I'm home.'

9

Oberon leapt to his feet, scattering cards and leaves willy-nilly.

'Oh, sorry,' he grimaced. 'Null and void, sure-ly?' and he dashed into the hall. He wanted to reach Titania first. The competition had begun. Puck sat, twisted round slightly in his chair, watching the door with eager eyes. The goblins got very small and sidled into the skirting board, with none of their usual squealing and kicking. Cobweb didn't seem to notice anything. She knew she was the weakest link.

In the hall, Titania was hanging up her coat. She looked Oberon up and down, as he stood there, bouncing from one foot to another in his excitement.

'You're back!' she exclaimed. 'Any luck?' She tried to look past him into the sitting room but he dodged about to impede her view.

He pulled the corners of his mouth down in an elaborate show of remorse. 'No,' he said mournfully, 'no luck.'

She shoved him aside. 'Get out of the way, Oberon!' she snapped, though not unkindly. 'You never could lie to me.' She disappeared through the door.

Oberon took a few seconds out to marvel at his good fortune. As long as she thought he was a useless liar, he was safe. He was waiting for the cries of delight from inside the room, but heard nothing. Cobweb surely couldn't be causing that much of a problem. Ever since her moment of revelation on the train, she had sunk into what he could only assume was a black depression. This was unlike her faerie self, always so bright and merry. But it was also unlike her almost mortal self – overweight, plodding but at least content. He was worried. Perhaps they should have left well enough alone.

He followed Titania into the room and looked across at Puck. He was expecting him to be wrapped in his wife and was prepared to do his angry monarch bit. But no. Titania was sitting next to Cobweb, patting her hand, stroking her hair, and the two were in earnest, whispered conversation. Puck lifted his eyebrows at Oberon and shrugged his shoulders. He pointed at the door and made a strange gesture at Oberon which the king didn't understand.

They went out into the hall.

'What's going on?' whispered Oberon.

'The Queen appears to be looking after Cobweb,' Puck said, awe in every syllable.

'No,' Oberon said, laughing uncertainly. 'Titania doesn't do that. She never has had any time for faeries, except to be pampered by them. She never could keep her Rade for long; they got on her nerves, but nothing like as much as she got on theirs. If I had... what's that thing you say?'

'If I had a quid, Sire?'

'That's the one. If I had a quid for every faerie that's come crying to me...'

'Yes, Sire. I have often noticed.'

Oberon stood there, a faraway look on his face. He shook himself. 'Happy days, eh?'

'By and large, Sire, yes,' agreed Puck.

'But the question is, what is going on in there?'

'Is it because, Sire, the Queen has been lonely?'

'Lonely?' roared Oberon. 'Lonely? With me, and the goblins around all the time? Lovely creatures, every one. Loads of company.'

'Yes, Sire, but very *male* company. In fact, you are probably the most male being I've ever met.'

Oberon acknowledged the compliment with a regal inclination of his head. 'She's got women at work. She hasn't made any friends there and that's her fault. I've told her to bring some home, to meet me, but she never has.'

'That wouldn't have been entirely wise, Sire, would it? You know how you find it hard to... keep control.'

Oberon sulked for a moment. Then he raised his head with a smile. 'You're probably right. As always. So, what was that funny sign you gave me just now? Is it some arcane secret of the Milk Craft which you have learned?'

Puck was puzzled for a moment, then remembered what he had done. He did it again, raising one curved hand to his mouth, elbow raised.

'No, Sire. It is the sign mortals use to indicate that they would like to go for a drink.'

'Sorry. Are you thirsty? There is some dew in...'

No,' Puck broke in hastily. 'No. I meant... a drink. In a pub. Alcohol.'

'Ah, wine! Very nice, in its place. Elderflower, perhaps or...'

'Dew, yes I know. I was thinking more in terms of an export lager. Or vodka. Gin. Brandy. All four.'

Oberon struck a martyred pose. 'Titania doesn't agree with strong drink, except when she has had a hard day, sometimes, she'll have one or two...' His voice trailed away and he looked ruminatively at the closed door.

Puck grinned. It always amused him when his master showed his naive side. 'I'll get your coat.'

'I'm not cold,' said Oberon, automatically.

'Perhaps not, Sire. But mortals are at this time of the year. You should try to blend more.'

'Blend, yes,' Oberon said, as he shrugged into the overcoat Puck had found hanging under the stairs. 'Yes.'

'Where's your nearest pub?' Puck asked.

'I don't know,' Oberon said, testily. He was feeling a bit of a fool.

'Do the goblins know?'

Oberon felt that he was losing his grip on his tiny court of... what was it now... seven. 'Yes,' he said. 'They most likely do. But we're not taking them. They wriggle about so, and we can't let people see them, even if they have had a drink or two. It would cause a riot.'

'True, Sire. They aren't very beautiful, it has to be said. Let's go, then. It can't be far away. It never is, in my experience.' He stuck his head round the door and said, very rapidly and with all the signs of long experience, 'we'rejustpoppingoutforadrinkdearwon'tbelongdon'twaitup.'

Oberon was impressed. There was no murmur of dissent from inside and they were on their way out of the door in record time.

'How did you do that?'

'It's something I learned from mortal men. Just wait till they're doing something else, preferably talking, and just say what you want to say really fast and really quietly. They hear you but don't take any notice. But later on, when they start to shout, you just say, but make sure your tone is very meek, "I did tell you, dear" and often they don't hit you.'

Oberon walked on silently for a while, digesting this. He was so glad that Titania had woken them up in time, before he got too mortal. It sounded as if it was worse than he thought. He'd always assumed that the things he watched on the television were fiction. But the truth was stranger still.

As Puck had guessed, the nearest pub was just around the corner. As soon as they walked in the door, Oberon knew for sure that the goblins had been making their way there, without his knowledge. It was difficult to pick out any particular component of goblin odour, but, he realised, this was definitely there, sometimes almost overwhelmingly so. He made a mental note to punish them about it.

Puck walked over to the bar and, leaning on one elbow, gestured to the barman with a ten pound note folded lengthways and held up between his fore and middle fingers. The barman approached, polishing a glass. He looked dubiously at Puck and opened his mouth to speak. He seemed to struggle for a moment, and then gave up. He closed his mouth in a determined way and then tried again. This time he said, 'What can I get you, sir?'

Puck smiled benevolently and said, 'Two pints of Stella

and one for yourself.'

'Thank you very much, sir.' The barman was grateful, but confused. What he really wanted to say was 'can I see your ID, mate?' but those words refused to come. 'I'll have a lager top.' He poured the drinks and turned to use the till. With his back turned, he tried the words again. Yes, no problem there. Can I see your ID, mate? He turned back, poised to repeat the phrase.

'C...c... that will be five pounds ninety, sir,' he heard himself say. 'C... c... ten pounds, thank you, sir.' He gave Puck his change without trying to say anything more.

'What happened there?' Oberon asked, when they had found a seat at a rather sticky table in the corner.

'Oh,' said Puck, sinking his lip gratefully into the froth, 'He didn't think I was old enough to drink.'

Oberon snorted into his pint and blew froth over the back of the woman at the next table. He reached over to brush it off, but Puck stopped him with a warning look. 'You? Not old enough? You must be...' the number was a bit big for Oberon '...easily old enough,' he finished.

'Yes. True enough. But I only *look* teenaged. I just don't seem to show the years.' He sighed. 'It's meant a lot of moving about. People get funny about you when you should look sixty and you look sixteen.'

Oberon nodded. 'As King and Queen of course,' he said, causing the damp woman at the next table to give him a funny look and edge her chair a bit further away, 'we've been here for a shorter time than you. But I do know what you mean. If Titania doesn't get us sorted soon, we'll have to move on.'

Puck punched him playfully on the arm and the woman got a bit damper. 'Two things, if you don't mind me mentioning them,' he said. 'First is, can you speak a bit more quietly? People are looking.'

Oberon raised his head from his pint and sure enough, eyes were definitely turning their way.

'Secondly,' he dropped his voice even lower, 'Of course, she'll sort everything out. Doesn't she always?'

'Eventually,' muttered Oberon. 'I say, Puck...'

'Can we make that Robin?' Puck said anxiously. 'When we're out?'

'Oh... yes, okay. I say, Robin, do I have to drink this? It tastes like pee.'

Puck, already at the bottom of his glass and feeling a bit better already, slid the unwanted pint over the table until it was in front of him. 'I must say, I've always taken exception to that phrase.'

'Why?'

'Well, how do you know what pee tastes like?'

'Well, I don't, obviously. But I would imagine it would be similar.'

Puck chugged the pint and wiped his mouth with the back of his hand. 'There must be something you like the taste of.'

Oberon thought for a moment, nearly said 'dew' and then thought better of it. 'You seem to be a bit of an expert. You choose.'

Puck walked over to the bar. This time the barman didn't even try to ask to see his ID. Oberon saw him point at the upturned bottles high up at the barman's back. He came back, weaving carefully round the tables, carrying two small glasses. Oberon was relieved that at least he wasn't going to be presented with gallons of whatever it was.

Puck put the glasses down on the table. One was clear and one was orange.

'Which one's mine?'

'Whichever,' Puck said, shrugging off his leather jacket onto the back of his chair.

Oberon sniffed them both gingerly. Difficult to choose. One smelt of fruit, peaches and oranges. The other had no smell at all as such, though as he inhaled it, the inside of his nose wrinkled of its own accord.

'What's the clear one made of?' he asked. 'I doesn't smell like water.'

Puck shrugged. 'Potatoes, or something.'

'Yeurghh," grimaced Oberon. 'I'll have the fruity one,' he said, and took a sip. It was really surprisingly delicious. It tasted of sweet peach juice, dripped into his mouth by a beautiful slave girl in one of his mountain strongholds, more years ago than anyone could count. He could almost taste the musk of her skin, washed down with the sticky juice running from the red heart of the fruit. Somewhere at the back of the taste was another flavour – fruit still, but sharper and clean. It made his throat feel warm and open, relaxed and ready for more. 'Hmm,' he licked his lips. 'That is really, *really* nice.'

Puck smirked. Oberon wondered if his ears were usually that pointed. 'Another?' he asked the king.

'Why not?'

'Ah,' Puck smiled at him. 'Why not indeed. Same again?'

'Are there other fruit ones?'

'Oh, yes,' Puck laughed. 'More fruit ones than you can possibly imagine.'

'One of those, then. But not blackcurrant. I never could stand those.'

'I remember, Sire,' said Puck and wandered a little less steadily back to the bar. He came back with two more glasses. A deep red one, this time, and another clear one.

'Bottoms up, Sire,' he muttered, and knocked back his drink in one. He screwed up his eyes and shook his head violently as the alcohol went down.

Oberon sniffed and sipped. Cherries, warm from the sun, with a hint of the stone, almondy and rich. Even nicer than the last. He put the glass down, but for some reason, the table was much nearer than he thought it was and he slammed it down hard. The damp woman looked round with a disapproving look and clicked her tongue. He decided to ask for another drink.

'Nuvver,' he said.

Puck suddenly remembered that his Lord had never really been exposed to the demon drink before. He had no head for it. 'Perhaps not, Lord,' he whispered.

But Oberon slammed down his glass again and, rather louder demanded, 'Nuvver!'

Puck was none too sober himself, but he was sober enough to know that he had let something loose than should never have been allowed out. Titania was going to kill him. Or at least, do something rather long term and painful. It had involved bees last time, and it still stung him in hot weather.

Nonetheless, to give himself thinking time, he went back to the bar and got another drink. He carefully placed it in front of the king.

'Plum!' announced Oberon, proudly. He poked the woman with the wet back in the ribs. He waved his empty glass at her and told her, ''s plums.'

She wrinkled her nose at him, picked up her bag and left.

'Sh's gone,' Oberon confided in Puck, 'p'raps sh' dun't like plums. Waddya think?'

'You're probably right, Sire,' said Puck, placatingly. 'What if we go home now?'

'I know!' cried Oberon, delightedly raising one finger in the air. 'I know! We'll take some a'dis plum stuff for Tit-Tit-Titania and Thing. They'll love it, won'ey? Waddya think? Ay? Ay? Shall we?'

Puck tried to quieten him, flapping his hands at him and shushing him madly. But Oberon was on a roll. He got to his feet, and, swaying about, started to sing. He was on the second verse of an obscene catch from five hundred years before when for no apparent reason, he started to make for the door in a surprisingly purposeful way. He looked down at his feet, as amazed as anyone. The barman ran round, in great relief, to open the door to let him out. He hadn't been looking forward to throwing him out – he was a big bugger and his mate looked a bit dodgy as well, but they seemed to be leaving of their own accord, and a good job too.

Puck grabbed his coat and ran after him, righting tables as best he could after Oberon's passing, nodding, apologising, sobering up fast. The cold night air finished the job and he stood there stupefied as Oberon swayed around, several inches from the ground.

'Thank goodness he decided to leave,' he muttered to himself.

'Dethided to leave, fiddlethickth,' said a voice from up Oberon's left trouserleg. There was a soft pop and Thydney stood on the pavement, dusting himself down. 'We couldn't thtand the crying in the houthe, tho we dethided to have a drink.'

Another pop deposited Freckles alongside him, followed

by the other goblins in quick succession.

'Whatever made you give him drink?' demanded Bertie.

'Yes,' volunteered Squeaky. 'Why did you think we always sneak out when we fancy a quick one?'

'Because,' Tiny continued, poking Puck rather hard in the knee, 'because, cleverdick, he can't hold his drink. He's made a fool of himself more times than enough over the last three thousand years or so.'

Puck said, in his defence, 'I don't think I've ever seen him really drunk. Well, not this drunk, at least. Can somebody sit him down? He's making me giddy weaving about like that.' Indeed, Oberon was wobbling about like a helium balloon tethered lightly to the ground and about to make off as soon as the ribbon should be cut.

Squeaky and Freckles tugged on the hem of Oberon's overcoat and he subsided in an untidy heap.

'I think,' said Puck, 'that we should continue our recriminations back at the house. You lot are a little bit noticeable, don't you think?'

The goblins scampered off, Freckles calling over his shoulder as they turned the corner, 'You fink we 're noticeable! Look at His Nibs.'

Puck spun round and caught Oberon by his ankle just as he floated away, giggling softly. With difficulty, he turned him the right way up and, half carrying, half towing him, turned into Ellesmere Crescent to face the music.

10

As Puck towed Oberon up the garden path, he was wondering what reception would be awaiting them. He had grown used to Cobweb's ranting when he got home a bit the worse for wear. He still remembered, with a faint ringing in his ears, Titania's fury when he had over-stepped the mark, or made one of his little mistakes. But, to the best of his knowledge, he had never had them both at once. He patted Oberon's pockets, looking for his key. He had found that it was best to at least let yourself in. Nothing annoyed them more, he found, than ringing the bell. It also gave them time to work out their strategy while they were on their way to opening the door. It even gave them time – he shuddered – to pick up something like a rolling pin. He had never mastered the art of opening all locks. Sometimes it worked, mostly it didn't. He just couldn't click his fingers very well. It just made a dull noise, like a kiss through a blanket. And he couldn't click the fingers on his left hand at all.

Oberon didn't seem to *have* a key. Thinking about it, he didn't go out much and probably wasn't in the habit. Puck lay him down on the bank of... he sniffed. Could it be wild thyme? He smiled and looked down fondly at his recumbent lord. What an old softie!

Holding him down by standing on the hem of his coat, he raised Oberon's hand in the air and tried to click his fingers for him. No good.

'Sire? Sire?' he shook him gently by the shoulder and spoke softly right in his ear.

Oberon shook his head and flapped one hand at him. 'Shoo. G'way. Sleeping.'

'Yes, Lord, but we can't get in the house. Can you click your fingers, Lord?'

'Yes. I can,' he replied, with unusual assertiveness. He rolled over gently and began to snore.

'No, no, I mean, can you do it *now*? Please?'

Oberon extended a languid arm, clicked his fingers and the door swung open.

Puck chuckled and pulled him to his feet, as light as thistledown and about as useful. He swung him round and turned to go in. Not looking quite where he was going, he walked straight into Titania, standing there with her arms folded and in one hand – not a rolling pin, surely!

'Ahah!' crowed Puck, helplessly. 'Mistress! Fancy you...'

'I am disappointed in you, Puck,' his mistress said, coldly. 'Not only do you appear to have broken poor Cobweb's heart with your cruelty and thoughtlessness, but you also seem to have got the King of Faerie absolutely rat arsed.'

'Rat arsed, Mistress? This is a curious phrase for you to use.' He played for time frantically.

'Er... yes. It took a little persuading, but the goblins told me in the end. I admit, I wasn't sure what they meant until you finally got the door open. Look at him! Did you give no thought to that time in Athens? It was a total embarrassment.'

'I wasn't there, Mistress. I was in disgrace, if you recall and when I heard, I put it down to exaggeration.'

'Unfortunately, it wasn't an exaggeration, Puck. In fact, it was worse than the stories. Most people had gone by the time the baklava started flying around.'

'Ah.'

Yes, ah.'

'Mistress...'

'Yes?'

'Why are you holding that rolling pin? And may I put my Lord down? He's starting to weigh something again and he's quite heavy.'

She pulled Oberon off Puck's back and gave him a push towards the sitting room door. He spun off down the hall, only to land in a heap just in the doorway. 'He hasn't quite got that mastered again, yet, has he?' she said, almost fondly. 'As for the rolling pin, I haven't got the first idea. It just seems to be a mortal thing to do and so I did it in case anyone was watching your performance outside. I just thought it would make things look a bit more normal.'

Puck thought to himself, *normal?* Aloud, he said, 'You're right, Mistress. Things have begun to slide a bit.' He thought for a moment and then brightened. 'But that's good, isn't it? If people see us gliding along, or flying, or clicking our fingers to open doors, won't that make them believe in us again? We wouldn't have to do anything, then. Our powers will come back on their own.' He grinned happily – the cheeky sprite who always had the good ideas.

She smiled at him fondly, and patted him on the shoulder. She wanted to hug him to her, kiss him, cry, say how lonely she had been – but she was the Queen and wouldn't get anywhere by being soppy. 'Dear Puck,' she patronised. 'If only that were true. But, sadly, mortals have got over being surprised. They see magic everywhere. Films these days are full of the impossible. When I first saw a film, I couldn't believe it. Mortal actors, their heads being cut off! Then, pictures of them, smiling and waving, perfectly well and healthy. And alive! How could it be possible? Then Oberon explained. The whole thing was an illusion. Well, those I understood. Faerie glamour, all the changelings, faerie gold, hundred year sleeps, all that was stock in trade for us and all illusion.'

They smiled at each other, each with their own thoughts.

'But, Mistress,' said Puck, 'Mortals know it is only film magic. If they saw it in the street, in the shops, with their own eyes. If they could reach out and *touch* someone floating inches from the ground...'

'They would just assume it was what they call mass hypnosis. I've heard of these things from the women at the supermarket. Stage shows where the hypnotist makes everyone believe they are a chicken, or something similar.'

'Do they lay eggs?' Puck asked with his cheeky grin.

'Don't push it, Puck,' she snapped. 'You're not forgiven yet,' she tossed her lovely head in the direction of Oberon, curled up snoring peacefully in the doorway.

'No, Mistress!' he said hurriedly. 'I mean, if they don't lay eggs, it isn't *real* magic! We could make them lay eggs. We could make them grow feathers. We could make them *be* chickens, not just *think* they are.'

She looked at him for a long minute. Then she *did* kiss him. A faerie brush of her lips on his forehead. 'Oh, Puck,' she breathed. 'You can't know how glad I am that you're back.'

They stood there, faces only inches apart, looking into each other's eyes in the dark and dingy hall. A sparkle of faerieland hung in the air and a faint smell of flowers and tiny sounds of rustling leaves transformed the dull suburban corridor. Puck reached up and stroked a tendril of hair from the Queen's face. A small moth, with golden dusted wings, flew out and landed on his forefinger. They looked at it and a single tear rolled down the rose petal surface of Titania's cheek. He reached up to kiss her, as mortal instinct vied with faerie.

A resounding belch from the recumbent heap behind her broke the spell and the moth imploded with a faintest pop and a shower of golden scales.

'Oh, very nice,' came a petulant voice from beyond the door.

'Oh, bat's droppings,' muttered Puck. 'I'd forgotten her!'

'Yes,' said Titania. 'A bit of a habit with you, or so I hear.'

'So, you've been swapping girl talk while we were away?' Puck said, nastily. Cobweb had been bringing out the worst in him lately. In well over a hundred years, a faerie could let itself go in a big way and Cobweb and big were now synonymous. Puck had worked something out, in his long solitary hours delivering milk. When a faerie started to slide, they just got to be more of what they once had been. So gentle Mustardseed, and he had very fond memories of her, had just become sweeter and sweeter. Her slide into being a mortal had been swift but painless and Puck had stood by helplessly as she became a gentle old lady, smelling of powder and Horlicks, nodding away her final days in a rocking chair in Hove.

He could still move pretty fast then and visited as often as he could. The staff were enchanted by her good-looking grandson, even as they wondered whether he should encourage her in her rather disturbing memories of flying and stealing bread and milk. But it made her happy, and they were very fond of dear old Mabel. They even called her by her nickname sometimes, when they tucked her up in bed. She was such a sweetie – just a bit senile. But no trouble and so easy to look after. She hardly seemed to weigh a thing. And then she died, and Puck was inconsolable for decades. But Cobweb, for all her caring ways, had always been a whinger. At the time of Mustardseed's death, Cobweb was already rather tiresome, but Puck was never one who liked the sound of being alone, so he stuck by her. They had come to an uneasy arrangement whereby he didn't bother her if she didn't bother him. And if neither of them was happy – well, that's what mortality was all about. It was good practice.

And now, she was here. Whingeing and lounging about, her two best talents. The Mistress wasn't going to take too much of this, he was sure. Except... he wasn't all that sure. She seemed to be taking the great thing's side. Something of mortal woman must have rubbed off when she was in that supermarket, after all.

'Cobweb does tend to exaggerate, Mistress,' Puck threw over his shoulder as he elf-handled Oberon into the sitting room.

'I do not,' squeaked Cobweb. 'I do not so exaggerate. You've always ignored me, ever since you...'

'Yes?' said Puck, nastily. 'Go on. Ever since I... what? Ever since I found you making a rather dodgy living in Soho?

'I was a milliner,' she said, sniffing haughtily.

'Yes, if you say so. Then you were a nursemaid. Then a parlour maid. Then...'

'Yes, all right, all right,' she said crossly. 'You weren't so special yourself.'

'Oh, come on now, you two,' Titania intervened. 'No squabbling, I beg. Oberon and I brought squabbling to a fine art aeons ago and you can't even come close. Let's sort this out now, once and for all.' She turned to Cobweb and said,

'You've been crying to me all evening about how Puck doesn't understand you. Why should he? You don't understand yourself. You've got fat, lazier and stupider than you ever were before. As for the... behaviour, shall we call it, before Puck found you, well,' she stole a glance at Oberon, curled up now on the hearthrug and smiling to himself as he slept, 'you always had that tendency, as I recall.'

Cobweb snorted, not a pretty sound, and Titania continued, 'Please don't snort at me, Cobweb. Your reclamation begins right now, with what mortals call a diet and what I call a good telling off. You *will* be nice to Puck; you *will* be polite to me and Oberon, your lord; you *will* be helpful round the house and, lastly, you definitely will be nice to the goblins.' Faint noises and cries of 'hear hear' came from behind the sideboard. 'They may not be pretty, but they have been a help to us when the rest of you had all cleared off to look after your own interests. I won't hear a word said against them, especially by a fat old fairy like you.'

The goblins, heartened by what they overheard, appeared, one after another, and stood proudly to attention in front of the settee, smiling broadly. Cobweb recoiled slightly and Freckles seized the advantage.

'Look, Mistress, she's doing vat fing again. Vat flinching fing.'

Titania sighed. 'You're as bad as she is, Freckles. Don't wind her up. She's under a lot of strain, as are we all, plus she's not any too bright, don't forget. When your Lord wakes up, tell him we have gone to bed and he can sleep down here. I have been making plans while he's been out drinking,' she made the word sound positively obscene, 'and I will explain in the morning. Also tell him that I have wasted quite a bit of glamour today to make sure he has a nice headache in the morning. He can't avoid it, so tell him not to bother with an aspirin – it won't have any effect.'

With that, she swept out of the room, with Puck at her heels. After several false starts, Cobweb managed to clamber up off the settee and follow them out. As she passed, each goblin stuck their tongue out – tongues in the case of Thydney – and blew a fat raspberry. Squeaky added a gesture which he had seen mortals use, but which had less impact somehow, when given by a trotter. It made him feel better, though, and that was the main thing.

Cobweb stumped up the stairs and into the spare room. Puck wasn't there, but she had hardly expected him to be. She looked at herself in the mirror inside the wardrobe door. Looked at bits of herself, because she couldn't get a view of all of her body at once. She sat down on the edge of the narrow little bed and wept softly. Perhaps Mustardseed had had the right idea after all. At least mortality had one thing going for it. At least you could die.

II

Oberon didn't open his eyes. Something told him that it wouldn't really be a very good idea. The faint pink light that made its way through his eyelids was bad enough; daylight was going to be far too much. Someone was banging a kettle full of stones on an old tin tray, somewhere just behind his left ear. He wished they would stop it, because it was really hurting his head.

Slowly the sound resolved into someone stirring a spoon around in a cup of liquid. A desire for a drink gripped him, followed by instant nausea; surely, he would never be able to drink anything again. The thought of opening his mouth and taking anything in seemed a total impossibility; whereas, the opposite seemed increasingly likely.

The noise stopped and he decided the best thing to do was to just lie still and wait for everything just to go away. He began to feel a tiny bit better. Everything was quiet. The room beyond his closed lids was no longer spinning round, just swaying gently from side to side. Just like a clock, he thought to himself, a pendulum, swinging gently, hypnotically, from side to side. Tick. Tock. Tick. Tock. He began to drift into a healing sleep.

Then all the bells on all the chimes on all the clocks in all the world all rang together. Striking thirteen, they filled his aching head. He covered his ears with his hands and curled up tighter, but the noise didn't stop. The only peace would come if he could get out of there, back to somewhere quiet. Back to the woods, he thought through the clamour, it was always quiet there. He turned over and struggled onto his hands and knees. Miraculously, and all at once, the bells stopped ringing. He carefully raised his head and looked gingerly from side to side.

To his left, the goblins were gathered in a porcine huddle. Their little eyes looked at him from under their varied height of brow, from non-existent to several bristles high. Their expressions were always hard to read, for obvious reasons, but the general impression was one of glee.

To his right, the view was much less rosy. Titania sat in the middle of the settee, arms folded, expression stern. Behind her stood Puck, also with his arms across his chest, but his posture had more of the proprietorial than the censorious about it. Of Cobweb, there was mercifully no sign. Oberon was not sure he could stand the crying and moaning this morning. He had a feeling he would be doing plenty of that on his own account.

One of the goblins spoke, apparently from the bottom of a deep well, while inhaling helium.

'We haven't had a chanthe to exthplain about the headache yet, Mithtreth,' he said, happily.

'Don't worry, Thydney,' Titania said kindly. 'I think the king has got the gist, don't you?'

Goblin giggles pierced his skull.

Puck leaned forward. 'How are we this morning, Lord?' he asked, a smile beneath the surface breaking through before the question was properly asked.

Oberon closed one eye to get the elf in focus. 'You look okay,' he whispered thickly. 'I'm not too well, though, for some reason.' He looked at his queen. 'I assume you are at the bottom of this.'

She smiled and said, archly, 'I take some of the credit, but I think that most of it, you did yourself.'

He risked a nod, then quickly wished he hadn't. 'Can you call it off now, beloved one?' he tried to wheedle, but it didn't seem to be coming out quite right. He screwed up one eye again and twisted his neck to look at her. 'I can't think straight.'

'Nothing new there, then,' Titania said crisply. 'However, you do look odd. You haven't been green for years, although I grant it quite suits you, in an odd sort of way. Perhaps I'll let it clear up shortly. We have work to do, after all.' She turned her head and smiled up at Puck, who returned a cheeky grin. 'Shall I get rid of my Lord's poorly head, Puck, do you think, or shall I let it stay a while?'

Puck looked at Oberon with his head on one side. He looked at the goblins, wriggling with excitement over in the corner. Squeaky had just accidentally pushed Tiny back through the plaster and only a leg was sticking out, rather disconcertingly. He said to Titania, 'Perhaps we should let him get better, Mistress. The goblins are getting a bit over-excited and I think as soon as we start planning, giving everyone a job to do, the better. We should harness their energy before one of them explodes.'

'You're right,' shuddered Titania. She remembered last time; that had been bad enough, and then there had been faeries galore to clean up the mess. She waved a languid hand at Oberon and the hangover left him in a bone-crushing wave, from his toes to the top of his head.

'Ow,' he complained. 'That was almost worse than having the thing.' He sat up, pushing his fingers through his curls and massaging his scalp.

'Well,' said Titania dismissively. 'You shouldn't do it, then, should you? You know you have no head for drink.'

'I have!' How could the Lord of Faerie not have a head for drink? Why, many nights he... reality bit. Many nights he had passed out on some mossy bank, totally off his face on elderflower wine. He gathered himself together and lurched onto an armchair, where he sat, looking hurt and noble. Puck came round from behind the settee and sat, cross legged, in front of his Lord, like he always had in the Old Days. Oberon beamed round at his motley court. Tiny had dusted himself off and was now standing with the others in an excited gaggle. Titania sat, composed and beautiful, on the settee. Puck was at his feet. He smiled and sighed happily. Things were on the up and up.

'Where's Cobweb?' he asked.

'Still in bed, Lord. She still doesn't like early mornings. She hasn't quite shaken off the last sixty-odd years,' Puck told him.

'Even so,' Oberon said, majestically. 'She should be here.' He clicked his fingers in the direction of the goblins. 'Squeaky. Go and fetch her.'

After the goblin had left the room, Titania turned to Oberon and asked, 'Why Squeaky? Of them all, that's the one that would give me the biggest shock if he woke me up suddenly.'

'Why?' asked Oberon, puzzled. To him, one goblin was much like another.

Puck answered for her. 'Because, Lord, Squeaky is trying so very hard to be mortal. It's the biggest, the nearest to pink, the least...' he shot an apologetic glance at the others, '...like a pig, of them all. It's trying just a bit too hard. And the effect is a bit, well, a bit *spooky*.'

Oberon was more confused than ever. 'Spooky is good, isn't it? Don't we do spooky? The whole glamour thing? I don't understand.'

Titania threw him a fond look. 'Sometimes you are just so sweet,' she said, absently. 'Spooky is excellent, yes. All our powers will soon be bent towards making mortals believe in us and to do that, we will have to move things, make things disappear, frighten late walkers, turn horses in their stables... or whatever it takes these days. But *we* aren't supposed to think anything is spooky. We *are* it, we're not supposed to be scared by it.'

As if to reinforce her comments, a shrill shriek, cut abruptly off, sounded from upstairs.

'See? She was scared out of her wits, waking up to that.'

Oberon looked crestfallen, and was about to launch into an abject apology to keep the little woman happy, when Squeaky suddenly barrelled into the room, tripped over Puck's legs and fetched up with a screech of trotters at Oberon's knee.

'Sire, Sire,' he stuttered.

'What?' snapped Oberon. 'Scared her, I suppose.'

'No, no.' Squeaky twizzled his head round, rather too many times for comfort. He tried to talk to everyone at once, whilst meeting no-one's eye. 'She scared me. Oh, please, Mistress, someone, go up there and see for yourself.' He rushed over to the other goblins and wriggled to the back of the small crowd. He huddled down and the others patted him absentmindedly with gentle trotters.

All three faeries felt a cold hand grip their heart. Titania floated to her feet and disappeared, leaving a light wind wafting the curtains. Puck was right behind her, moving faster than a spark. Oberon leapt to his feet and skimmed two feet before catching his toe on the edge of the settee and coming down with a bang. He got up, gave his clothes a tug and ran, on foot, through the hall and up the stairs.

Puck was standing in the doorway of the little box room. Titania was inside, sitting on the bed, bent over the still form stretched beneath the thin duvet. Oberon couldn't see Cobweb, but she seemed to be somehow... less. The covers were hardly shaped at all and, surely, she must make quite a mound. He edged past Puck and round the other side of the bed. Lord of all Faerie or no, he gasped and sat down heavily on a wicker chair which Puck had thoughtfully materialised behind him.

Cobweb lay still as death, her face ethereal on the pillow. She was like a ghost of the faerie he remembered, but a faerie grown old and withered. Her face was beautiful, high cheekbones underlining her large eyes, closed now and fringed with lashes as long as a calf's. Her hair spread in loose tangles around her head, the colour of thick cream, shot with cowslip stamen yellow. Her lips were like the tiny petals on the edge of a dog rose, pink and velvet. But her beautiful face was covered with fine lines, her hair was thin and dry, her lips sunken over teeth which he knew would be black or missing. She was that impossible thing, an old faerie.

He leaned forward and took her hand, light as thistledown, a silken bag full of pin-like bones, which lay lifelessly on the quilt. It twitched in his. 'She's alive,' he breathed.

As he spoke, she opened her eyes, their tawny depths milky with cataract. Her lips twitched in what may have been a smile, but the movement was small and fleeting and he couldn't be sure.

Titania swallowed her tears and said, 'Cobweb. What happened? Can you tell us?'

Cobweb swallowed, and forced a harsh whisper through her dry throat. 'I wished I could die,' she said.

'You can't die,' Puck said from the doorway. 'We need you, Cobweb. Please don't go.'

She turned her eyes to him and shook her head. 'I've been so unhappy,' she croaked. 'You don't love me. You,' she turned her face towards Titania, 'hate me. You,' she turned to Oberon, 'have forgotten me. I wished I could die. And now,' she smiled, a small triumphant smile, 'and now, I am. So, please, leave me alone. It doesn't hurt or anything,' she said, slightly louder. 'I don't know why I was frightened of it all these years. And at least I've got my looks back.' She gave a dry little laugh, which made her cough.

Titania patted her hand. 'I don't hate you,' she said, her smile false and bright. 'We had a lovely chat last night, didn't we? All girls together.'

Cobweb turned her death's head to Titania. 'You didn't mind a fat, stupid old woman. You would have minded a faerie. I don't think there's room for the two of us, especially,' again the ghastly little coughing laugh, 'in a poky little place like this. As I recall, the world was a bit small for us both.' She closed her eyes, weak with the effort of speaking.

Oberon clutched her hand and she gave a little cry of pain. 'Oh, sorry. Cobweb, I hadn't forgotten you. Really, I hadn't. You know how much I...'

She opened her eyes and looked at him for a long minute. 'How much you what?'

He didn't answer, but hung his head.

She smiled and reached across with an effort and held his hand in both of hers. 'You want to say you love me, but you don't. With the Queen around, who could love me? Especially as you had come to think of me, in my nearly mortal skin. So, don't feel bad. I understand.' Her eyes wandered across to the doorway, where Puck still stood, stricken with emotions he hardly knew he could feel. Regret. Remorse. And, Cobweb would be surprised to learn, a sudden rush of love.

He spoke to his Lord and Lady. 'May I be alone with her for a minute, please?' he asked.

They rose as one and bent down to kiss Cobweb's wrinkled cheek, each kiss as soft as a wing beat. They left the room and quietly went down the stairs, to shush the goblins and sit in hope that Puck would be able to create life in her where they could not.

Puck crossed the room and stood looking down at her. She raised her eyes to him and, in answer to his unspoken question, gently shook her head. He gently lay his lithe and sinewy body alongside hers on the bed and, wordlessly, he held her softly, until the fluttering beat of her heart slowed and stopped. It was the loving thing to do.

The little group waiting silently downstairs all lifted their heads as he walked slowly into the room. He shook his head, the tiniest movement, but one which said everything there was to say.

Tiny burst into noisy tears. It broke the ice which had held them all in its grip and they all wept, thinking their own thoughts, fearing their own fears, letting go of their regrets and guilt.

Upstairs, Cobweb's body dissolved into a handful of shimmering dust. Puck had opened the window as he left the room, and a sharp dawn breeze crept in over the sill and stirred all that was left of Cobweb and carried it away, into the air where it belonged.

12

Titania was the first to recover. She blew her nose gently on a scrap of tissue and wiped her eyes. The goblins had crowded round her for comfort and she looked down at them fondly. Oberon and Puck were across the room, the elf at his master's knee, and, for once, Oberon seemed to be thinking of someone other than himself. He had his arm round Puck's shoulder and their heads were together, bent in shared grief.

'We have wasted too much time,' Titania said, but her tone made it clear that she did not mean on mourning Cobweb. 'If we hadn't waited around for things to get better on their own, Cobweb would be still...' she dropped her voice, and stifled a small sob, 'she'd be still with us.' She drew a deep breath, placed her hands on her knees and stood up abruptly, scattering goblins as she did so. Tiny, who had actually managed to clamber onto her lap, bowled over several of the others in his flight and by the time they had sorted out whose leg was whose, she had put on her coat and was going out of the door.

'Where are you going?' asked Puck.

'To work, of course,' Titania replied.

'But surely,' Oberon said, 'Not today.'

'Especially today,' she said. 'I have plans for tonight to move us on, and if I'm not at work today, they might not work out.' With no further explanation, she was gone.

'Oh, by the way,' her voice rang through the air, although she herself was skimming across the puddles at the corner of Ellesmere Crescent, 'I shall want some ideas from you lot when I get back. An Action Plan, at the very least.'

Oberon mouthed, 'Action Plan?'

'What'th an action plan?' asked Thydney.

They all looked at each other in bewilderment.

'Oh, get the cards out,' said Oberon, pulling up the table. 'It'll help us think.'

Crossing the High Street, Titania shook her head ruefully. Cards, indeed. If you wanted a thing doing, you must do it yourself. A golden dust settled gently on her hair, and she went on her way, to work and the inevitable leering of Trevor of Home and Wear.

It really was a stunningly bad day. Titania felt on the verge of tears most of the time, sorrow and loss being compounded by the sneers and snide remarks of the girls jealous of her dubious honour of being temporarily Trevor's favourite. The day dragged by, hot and stuffy in the storeroom, over-air-conditioned in the shop, dark and rainy outside, the occasional bursts of sunshine only serving to highlight the massed banks of dark cloud away to the west.

As she made her way home, walking not skimming, shoulders hunched with dread at what awaited her later at Trevor's – he had reminded her with a grin and an ill-advised pat – she tried to marshal her thoughts, but they spun round, out of control, and the main direction of the spin was downwards.

The door of Number Thirteen swung open at her approach and she heard a lot of shushing and suppressed giggling from the sitting room. She pushed the door open with difficulty and walked into a positive bower of flowers, the settee transformed into a swing hanging from a gnarled branch of an oak tree which was inexplicably sprouting from the skirting board in the corner. Puck, Oberon and the goblins were grouped anxiously near the fireplace, wringing their hands.

'Do you like it, Mithtreth?' said Thydney, too loud in the hushed, over filled room.

She was speechless and tears were hanging on her lower lashes. She pressed her lips together and nodded.

They smiled at each other, nodding and bobbing about with relief. She liked it. They had done the right thing after all. That afternoon, with nothing done and Oberon in serious deficit to Squeaky, who played a mean game of poker, Puck had decided that, in the absence of a plan of any kind, the best thing to do would be to disarm his Mistress with a nice gesture.

'Cheer her up,' he had said. 'Then, when she's feeling better, *she'll* come up with a plan!'

He and Oberon had put their heads and their meagre powers together and had come up with the flowers. It had been the goblins, concentrating so hard their little brows had met even more decisively over their snouts, that had produced the tree – a triumph of over-the-top goblinery, a tree so gnarled it was a wonder it could stand at all. The leaves trembled faintly as if in a light breeze, from no direction mortals would know. Petals fell gently around it all the while, but the grass was never covered with them. Bees hummed quietly among its endless blossom, but they were perfectly behaved bees – heard but never seen and they certainly would never sting. No spotted snakes with double tongue could be found among its roots, however hard they looked. It was a perfect faerie tree.

Exhausted with all the conjuring, they had rested among the blossoms for a while, until they felt rather than heard, her approach. Oberon had swung the door open with the last of his power, while Puck sat frowning, trying to click his fingers.

They helped her up onto the swing, which moved gently of its own accord. She swept a hand from chin to ankle and transformed her drab uniform into a shimmering gown of silver and pale blue. The others sat in the grass and looked, love shining from their eyes. She put her head back and swung gently, dreaming, dreaming...

The goblins started to get a bit restive. Bertie nudged

Freckles in the ribs.

'Ask the Mistress if she has a plan, old boy,' he whispered in Freckles' ear.

'Do you fink I'm mad?' asked Freckles in alarm. 'She's having a bit of a rest. Anyway, one of vem,' he pointed a disgruntled trotter at Puck and Oberon, 'should do ve askin'.'

Puck could hear a faint mutter of conversation beneath the susurration of the leaves and the murmur of the bees. He decided it wasn't any of his business. He let himself swim away on the current of warmth and gentle noise.

A sharp trotter poked him in the side.

'Oy, Puck,' a whisper accompanied by breath which could strip paint brought him more completely out of his reverie.

'What?'

'Are we gonna ask 'er? About the plan?'

He stirred himself reluctantly and poked Oberon idly in the side.

'Sire?'

'Wassup?'

'Are you going to ask her? About the plan?'

Oberon sat halfway up and looked for someone to poke in his turn. Damn! He was the last in line. The buck was stopping right there. He cleared his throat. 'Hrrrmm. Dear one?'

Titania didn't open her eyes, but said, 'Yes?' in a suspicious and, Oberon thought, potentially threatening tone.

'We were wondering,' he carried on, looking frantically at the others, but they were all looking at the ceiling, or carefully examining a speck on a trotter, 'we were wondering if you have come up with our next move?'

She sat upright abruptly and the swing stopped dead. 'Next move? I wasn't aware that we had made a first move yet?'

'Yes, dearest,' said Oberon, placatingly. 'We found Puck.'

'That wasn't a move,' Titania said sharply. 'That was more like preparation. However,' she jumped lightly down from the swing, 'you're right. Let's go into the kitchen and sit round the table and all tell each other our ideas.'

Puck and Oberon looked at each other frantically. The goblins tried to creep away, back into the wall.

'Stop right there!' she snarled. 'You lot, into the kitchen when I tell you.' Her head snapped up. 'It's been a bad day today, for all of us but especially me. When I have a bad day, everyone has a bad day. Understand?'

They nodded and filed obediently into the kitchen. They pulled out chairs and sat round the table; those who were chairless stood, resting their little chinless faces on their trotters.

'Right,' she smiled mirthlessly round. 'Who goes first?'

Only silence met her.

'No one? All right then, I'll have to choose someone. Now, who shall it be?' She tapped her perfect fingernail on her perfect teeth and looked around at the company, all of whom refused to meet her eye.

'Well, let's start at the top, shall we? My Lord?'

Oberon appeared to have gone deaf.

'Oberon? Lord of Faerie? Dread Lord of the Kingdom Under the Hill?'

He pretended to hear her for the first time and made a very bad job of being surprised. 'What, dearest? Sorry, what was that?' He smiled wanly, but knew he was rumbled.

She slammed both hands down, palms flat on the table. The room trembled and ornaments fell off shelves in Number Fifteen. 'Just tell me you haven't got any idea what to do next,' she roared, 'and then perhaps I can ask someone who has!'

'I haven't... sorry, what am I supposed to say?'

'You haven't... well, go on then. Repeat it after me.'

'I haven't.'

'Got any.'

'Got any.'

'Idea.'

'Idea.'

The goblins and Puck were embarrassed and scared in approximately equal amounts. They knew that if she treated Oberon like this, it was only to practice for something worse when she came to them.

'What to do.'

'What to do.'

'Next.'

'Next.'

'Well done. That wasn't so hard, now, was it?' She smiled around them again. 'Well, who *has* got some idea?'

Tiny coughed and swallowed hard. In a small hoarse voice, he said, 'I have.'

'You?' everyone said together.

The little creature crossed its arms over its barrel chest and half turned away, snout in the air.

Puck, the nearest, gave it a conciliatory pat. Tiny shrugged him off.

'Come on now, mate,' crooned Oberon. 'We didn't mean it. Come on, now, what's your idea? Eh? Tell us. Go on, you know you want to.'

The goblin just clamped its mouth shut more firmly and shook its head.

Titania snapped first. Jumping up from her seat, she grabbed hold of the back of its coat and shook it and shook it until everyone could hear its teeth rattling. She dropped it and its teeth rattled on. 'Just tell us your idea, you idiotic creature,' she yelled.

Eyes relatively wide with shock, the little creature composed itself a little before taking up a declamatory stance and beginning.

'Well, we all know how our Lord Oberon thought us up.'

'Yes, of course,' said Titania testily. 'Although I have always thought he might have done a better job of it.'

Tiny looked a little hurt, but continued, 'Well, why doesn't he think of some more. Then, we could spread out a bit, and look for some more faeries. That way, they could then spread out and look for some more, and so on, and so on until we had found all of them.' It stood there, looking pleased with itself and the others slowly realised that that was it. The idea. They were quiet for a moment.

'Rubbish!' said Oberon. As the person who would have to do the thinking up, he was none too keen on this idea. It would take him *days*. And give him a headache, if he was any judge.

Titania though was thoughtful. 'You might be on to something there, Tiny. We'll need a basic infra... something or other, I can't remember what it is mortals say, but once we've got it, more goblins would be very useful. But,' she added hurriedly, 'not until we have done a bit more groundwork.' The smell was something awful some mornings and she wasn't sure she was meant for a world where goblins outnumbered faeries by quite such a margin.

'Structure,' said Squeaky.

'What?'

'Structure. That's the infra thing you were talking about.'

'Yes, that's it,' said Titania thoughtfully, looking a little askance at Squeaky. He was far too interested in mortal life – he would have to be watched or he might blow their plan. 'Anyway,' she continued, 'Now that Tiny has got the ball rolling, I must be off. I have a meeting with a mortal this evening, who might have some big ideas we can use. So I'll leave you to carry on thinking – and that will be without using the cards, if you don't mind – while I get on with it.' She got up and made to leave the room.

Puck and Oberon were suddenly barring her way.

'A mortal?' they chorused.

'Yes,' she said, shortly. 'There are a lot of them out there, in case you hadn't noticed.'

'Which one?' asked Oberon suspiciously.

She dropped her voice to a mutter. 'TrevorfromHomeandWear,' she said.

Oberon almost exploded. The goblins ran for cover. 'You mean the one you threw through the display because he tried t...'

'Yes, yes,' she interrupted him impatiently. 'That one. But I'm sure he's learned his lesson,' she added, trying to push past them.

'I'm sure he hasn't,' Puck said, memories of Alf Coe in his head. 'That sort never do. You can't go there on your own.'

'I can't go with any of you lot, though, can I?' she retorted. 'Oberon will break his legs as soon as look at him. Puck, you will be a little more subtle, I'm sure, but mortals today are a bit sophisticated for the whole donkey's head bit. So, please, out of my way. I'm late.'

Oberon followed her out into the hall, as she changed her dress into jumper and jeans and added a coat. 'Please,' he begged her. 'Just take a goblin or two, eh?'

'And they'll do what? Breathe on him?'

The goblins looked hurt, as they popped their heads out through the wall.

'We'll protect you, Mistress,' said Freckles, ingratiatingly. 'We'll come and get Puck and the Master if he tries anyfink.'

Titania wrinkled up her lovely nose in thought. 'All right then,' she said, holding open her coat. 'Just Tiny and you then, Freckles.' They jumped out of the wall and disappeared in one movement under her jumper, wriggling to get comfy. She reached under her clothes and hauled Freckles out again, holding him at arm's length. 'And none of that! Any more of that kind of behaviour and you'll be very sorry, you odious little creature. Far from being more goblins there will be one less. Do you understand?'

Freckles nodded, as best he could dangling in mid-air. She tucked him away again and he lay very, very still. She reached up and kissed Oberon, stroked Puck's cheek lingeringly and went out.

As the door slammed, Oberon looked searchingly at Puck. 'What was that all about?'

Puck decided to ignore him and, gathering the goblins in front of him said, a shade too loudly, 'Well now, chaps, better get some ideas thought up, eh? The Mistress is doing her bit, after all, so we ought to do the same.'

Oberon was left standing in the hall, wondering. He needed eyes in the back of his head to watch these two. He might be making more goblins sooner than they thought. He followed them into the kitchen and sat down.

13

It was only a few steps to Trevor's house, a surprisingly neat modern terrace, with dwarf conifers in window boxes and a brightly painted front door. The knocker was a brass dolphin and Titania rapped its tail smartly against the wood. Trevor opened the door so fast that Titania correctly guessed that he had been waiting behind it for her to arrive.

He looked more friendly, less predatory, than he did at work. He was wearing a sweatshirt in a pale, washed out blue, jeans and slippers. He looked more like Suburban Man than Shark. Titania felt the butterflies – or was it goblins – under her solar plexus subside. Could it be she had misjudged him?

'Hello,' he said, with smile. 'So glad you could make it. Come in,' and he stretched out an arm to show the way into a neat little room, elegantly furnished with two white leather two seater sofas, a low merchant's chest as coffee table and a pine cupboard, obviously housing the television and stereo, as soft music was emerging from two speakers, expertly placed to give unobtrusive surround-sound.

He held out his hands for her coat, and she shrugged it off her shoulders, taking in the detail of the room. On the faux-driftwood mantelpiece was a single piece of glass, enhanced with a touch of granite. On closer inspection, it turned out to be a modern piece, depicting a mermaid on a rock. She knew that some of them had come ashore, but – surely, not Trevor.

The kelpie women were known for their beauty, but the mermen she had met were an ugly bunch and, although not gorgeous by her own high standards, she could tell that Trevor was a perfectly good example of mortal man.

She felt his hot breath on her neck and spun round, nearly sending flying the two glasses in his hand.

'I poured you a drink, if that's okay,' he said, handing her one.

She looked at it dubiously. It was a glaucous yellow, fizzing slightly and smelt like the bottom of a vegetable rack — and she should know.

'What is it?' she asked, holding it up to the light.

'Cinzano and lemonade,' he said, proudly. 'A bit of a favourite with the ladies, I've always found.'

She took a cautious sip; it made her cough. 'Not a favourite with this lady,' she wheezed. 'Do you have any gin? Vodka? I like those clear drinks that don't taste of fruit or veg.'

He looked a little crestfallen. 'Er... no. I only have the Cinzano.'

She handed him the glass, keeping her arm straight and therefore Trevor at a bigger distance than he seemed happy with. 'Just a lemonade, then, if you don't mind,' she said firmly. 'I am here to work, after all.'

He reluctantly went back into the kitchen and she heard him slamming doors and muttering to himself. Freckles popped his head out under the edge of her jumper and winked at her.

''E's mad now,' he giggled. 'I bet 'e was gonna try and get you drunk, so 'e could 'ave 'is wicked way wiv yer.'

She slapped him back into hiding just as Trevor reappeared with a tall glass of lemonade. 'Sorry,' Trevor said. 'Did you say something?'

'Er... no, just what a lovely room this is.'

'Yes, I like it,' Trevor surveyed the room smugly. 'Usually quite a success with the ladies.' He smiled at her, but his eyes were calculating, looking her up and down. Perhaps he wasn't nicer in his own surroundings after all.

She sipped her drink. Ah, that was better. 'Right, let's get our thinking caps on then, shall we?' she said, sitting down on the sofa furthest from where he stood.

He crossed the room in a few strides and sat beside her. 'Yes, we'd better get on with it,' he said, leaning in nearer, and gave a little laugh. It sounded like a nail down a blackboard and the goblins shivered inside Titania's jumper. Trevor saw the movement and patted her hand.

'Not nervous, are you?' he leered. 'No need to be nervous with old Trev.' In fact, he was the nervous one. His neck had been twingeing all afternoon and he had looked out the neck brace, just as a precaution.

'Not at all,' said Titania frostily, and indeed, she wasn't. She had protection, of a sort, and anyway had subdued this mortal once before. 'Where is your computer?'

'Upstairs.' How could one word sound so sinister?

She re-crossed her legs, giving him a light kick in the process.

'In that case,' she said, 'let's have a bit of a think before we go on to that stage.' She tried to move away. His breath was becoming a bit upsetting. In his turn, he was thinking that she didn't smell so good this evening. Instead of her natural smell of new mown hay, a smell which he found himself craving when she wasn't there, there was a definite waft of farmyard. Not strong, but coming in waves, whenever she moved. He edged away a little.

He leaned forward and picked up a pad and pen from the table. He had put it there as a bit of window dressing, hoping he wouldn't need it. But, never mind. If she wanted to make a production of it, that was quite okay with him. A bit of a chase was a favourite with some ladies, he had found. He clicked the pen and turned to a clean page.

'Now,' he said, turning to her. 'What is this group of yours all about?'

'Well,' she realised that she had no idea what to say. *I want to find a load of lost faeries, who might well look just like you, or like the things hidden under my jumper* seemed hardly a good place to begin. 'I want to get in touch with a group of people I've lost touch with.'

'Ah, you mean, like, old school friends, that sort of thing?'

'That sort of thing, yes, but these friends are... very old friends. We go back a very, very long way.'

He looked at her in mock amazement, his face a mask of wry disbelief. 'How can you go back a very, very long way with anyone? You're only, what, twenty two, twenty three?'

She punched him what she hoped was playfully on the arm.

'Ow.'

'Sorry. I don't always know my own strength.'

His neck twinged again as he remembered. 'It's all right. Really. Go on.'

'I meant to say, that is very kind of you. I am in fact older than that.'

He looked more closely, as she held her breath, and could see no sign of age in her petal skin, clear eyes and lustrous hair, which seemed to be in slight motion, even when she was sitting still and there was no wind. He had decided it must be an optical illusion of some kind and, of course, he was almost right.

'Well, whatever,' he shrugged. 'Do they all come from around here?'

'No. They come from all over.'

'How many are there?'

How many indeed? Who had ever counted the faerie hordes? 'Many.' He didn't like the faraway look in her eyes. The hairs on the back of his neck, distributed more or less evenly among the spots, began to prickle.

'Do you know their names?'

'Not all. And anyway, they have many names, depending on who you ask.'

He sighed, and put down his pen. 'This is going nowhere fast, is it? Are we talking about old lags?'

'I beg your pardon?'

'Old lags? Prisoners? Are these people you have met in prison, or...' it wasn't his imagination, her hair was moving. And her eyes... they seemed to draw him in, '...some kind of institution?'

Her voice dripped ice. 'I have never been imprisoned. No, these are just friends I have lost touch with, as I said.'

His smile reached only one twitching corner of his mouth and he made a little sound in his throat that may have been a small, nervous laugh. Perhaps she was a spy. The girls all said she was foreign. Oh, God, perhaps she was going to put a hit out on him, when she had used him. Perhaps she would kill him herself. Oh, God! He got up abruptly and then, after a quick turn round the room sat back down again, on the other sofa, much to her relief. She didn't know what she had done, but he had moved away, and that was the main thing.

'Do they speak... English?' he asked.

'By and large.'

'That's a start.' He made a note.

'But they don't read too well.'

He crossed out his note and put down his pen with an exasperated sigh. He rubbed his hands over his face and looked up at her. 'May I recap?'

'Please do.'

'Your friends, who you want to find are from all over, from way back, you don't know their names, they can't read... are you taking the piss? If you just wanted a date, you only need have said.'

She got up and stood there, faint sparks flying from her hair. 'You said you could help me,' she snarled, through gritted teeth. 'Otherwise, you hound-breathed fool, nothing would have induced me to come here.'

He stood up as well and faced her. God, she was lovely when she was angry. The goblins stirred.

'Oh, oh.' Freckles whispered. 'Time to fetch the Master?'

'No,' Tiny mouthed. 'I somehow think the Mistress can fend for herself. It's this mortal who needs help.'

Trevor stepped forward and, taking his cue from screen heroes from Rhett Butler to Mr Darcy in his wet shirt, grabbed Titania and clutched her to him, bending her slightly back and sideways, in preparation for the kiss which would make her tonsils melt. Everything went well at first, but suddenly, for some reason he couldn't fathom, he suddenly found himself on his back behind the sofa.

He hauled himself up, and there she was, sitting demurely as if nothing had happened. With dignity in tatters, he came round and sat down again, but nice and far away. He adjusted his sweatshirt, which had ridden up over his rather pallid, tv-dinner fed paunch and smiled ingratiatingly.

'Sorry about that. Must have tripped. Where were we?'

'I think you had just said you couldn't help me,' she said, mildly.

'Oh, yes, well, it is a bit of a problem. I'm sure you see. What you need is radio or television. That gets round the not reading thing, doesn't it? The Internet is another possibility, in that you could use pictures, or something, but that is a bit beyond my expertise.'

She smiled at him and, although he had a faint memory itching around in the back of his head, warning him to stay back, he moved forward again.

'This guy don't learn very fast, do he?' asked Freckles in a whisper.

Trevor was on his knees now, beside the Queen where she sat in the corner of one sofa, pressed back on the cushions. She was soft-hearted, as Queens of faerie go, and she didn't want to hurt him too much. After all, his heart was in the right place, she could tell that. Beneath the Lothario exterior was a husband with 2.4 children trying desperately to get out.

She put a hand on his arm. 'Please, Trevor,' she said quietly. 'Can't we just be friends?'

Trevor knew what that meant. That meant 'Oh Trevor, take me, take me now!' Women often asked if they could be friends, but he always knew the subtext, and once he had been right.

He lunged forward and managed to fasten his lips over her mouth. She bit down hard and he fell backwards. God, her teeth were sharp. She stood up quickly, so quickly, it seemed to him, that she hovered in mid-air. The goblins hung on tight, making themselves as small as they could. They felt the sweatshirt dissolve around them as its place was taken by a gauzy dress of every colour and none.

Trevor lay where he had fallen, down between the sofa and the chest. She skimmed over the rug to hover just above him, clothes and hair streaming in a wind he could see but not feel. She bent over him, her face close to his and hissed,

'Don't do that, Trevor!'

He clawed back, trying to dig himself into the carpet. 'Who are you?' he whispered. 'What are you?'

Her face softened, and with a sigh, she said, 'Once, I was your dearest dream. But now, I suppose, I am your worst nightmare.'

He was huddled now in a corner, hands over his face. 'Just go away,' he muttered. 'Go away and leave me alone.'

She put out a hand and stroked his head. 'Forget me, Trevor,' she said. She had learned enough about mortals to know that their brains were very fragile. Cobweb had been a lesson which she wouldn't forget in a hurry. 'Forget tonight and what you've seen. Just remember that Tania wasn't too forthcoming and then you'll cope all right.'

She waved her hands down her body and was dressed in jeans and jumper again. The goblins breathed a sigh of relief and jumped down to the ground. One of them crept over to Trevor and with a gentle trotter lifted one eyelid.

'Out for the count,' it said.

'He'll be all right,' said Titania. 'He won't remember a thing in the morning.'

Tiny, looking back at Trevor's huddled body, trembling uncontrollably every few seconds, as he whimpered in his dream, wasn't too sure. But the Mistress had always had a temper. He trotted off to catch up with the others.

She was standing in the hall, putting on her coat and he looked up into her face. She said nothing for a moment, then, 'Perhaps we'll not mention this to the Master and Puck, eh, lads? They might not understand.'

The goblins nodded and, risking being seen, they each took one of her hands and they strolled through the chilly moonlight, back to Ellesmere Crescent, each busy with their own thoughts. In Freckles' case, this kept him busy just until they reached the corner. Titania's would keep her awake all night.

14

Titania pushed open the front door of Number Thirteen, turning as she went in to remind the goblins not to tell Oberon or Puck about what happened. She told herself it would be because they would be angry at Trevor. Deep down, though, she knew that she had over reacted and that their anger should really be directed at her. If she couldn't keep herself in check, their re-emergence would be scuppered before it had begun. Despite their fall in the world, she knew that there were sleeping powers that would wake and imprison them forever if they went around unbalancing things. And behaving as she just had would, if not checked, certainly unbalance things.

But the goblins had already gone. They knew where they wanted to be when the Mistress was in this mood, and that was with Oberon, who would protect them if he felt like it. That wasn't terribly reassuring, but it was definitely better than a poke in the eye with a sharp trotter.

She went into the kitchen, where an eerie silence suggested to her that they had just managed to sweep the cards away as she went in. A drift of leaves on the floor, their suits fading into the brown as they dried up before her eyes, confirmed her suspicion.

Oberon looked up. 'How did you get on?' he asked, brightly.

'Yes,' said Puck, as though scripted. 'How did you get on?'

She pursed her lips and took a deep breath through her nose, to calm herself down.

'Not too helpful, I'm afraid,' she said, sweeping a goblin from its chair and sitting down. The goblin tried to creep away. She grabbed it by the back of its coat and turned it to face her. 'Wait a minute. I don't know you, do I?'

The little creature shook its head, twisting its eyes round frantically to get some help from Oberon. Oberon looked studiously the other way.

Titania held it closer. 'It looks a bit like a chicken,' she said, eventually. And indeed, it did have a rather beaky nose, and its eyes, on the sides of its head, were very beady and never still. Its hair was streaked with twenty different shades of brown and flopped over its low forehead in a rather fetching quiff. This was its only attractive feature, however. It smelt of wet chalk and mouldy corn. 'Can it talk?' she asked.

The goblin gave a squawk of annoyance.

'As you can possibly tell,' sighed Puck, 'it can't. The snag is, it thinks it can. It's been driving us mad since it turned up.'

'Turned up?'

'Yes, all right,' said Oberon, giving in. 'Thought up, rather than turned up. I just thought it might be nice to have something not quite so piggy.' Outraged grunts filled the air. He flapped a dismissive hand at the older set of goblins, poking their heads from the plaster, except in Squeaky's case. He extended a trotter in an unmistakeable gesture. 'They know what I mean,' he said, sulkily. 'They're just jealous of its hair.'

'They certainly can't be jealous of its brain,' muttered Puck. 'It doesn't appear to have one.'

Titania was nonetheless impressed. 'At least you've been getting on with things,' she said, in a rather patronising tone. 'I hit a snag, which we should have foreseen.'

'What?'

'Well, we can't read, can we?' She looked at Puck. 'I know you can manage a bit, and I've picked up a few words. S.A.L.E.,' she added proudly. 'That's "sale". I'm all right with the odd thing like that. But a whole *lump* of writing, we've not really had the practice.'

'So?' said Oberon, still rather hurt that she wasn't more

impressed by his new goblin.

'So,' she said, 'my plan had been to have posters, things through likely doors, that kind of thing, like they do at the supermarket. Advertising, you should know all about that, it's on the television all the time.'

'Yes,' said Oberon, 'I know about that. But they have someone reading it to you, as well. So I don't need to read. '

'That's my next point,' she said. 'If we could get on the radio, we might be able to reach some more faerie. But even if we do, what do we say? "Hello, are you a faerie? If so, come round to Thirteen, Ellesmere Crescent, Guildford, where your King and Queen live in a tiny little house with some goblins who look like pigs...'

Squawk!

'...and chickens, and an elf." I don't think that will do it, do you? And anyway, advertising on the radio costs a lot. I've heard the manager at the supermarket complaining. It increases his over-heads, whatever they might be.'

They all sat silently, deep in thought. Occasionally, Oberon or the chicken would raise their head, mouth open, as if to speak, but would subside immediately, on realising that the idea wouldn't work. Or that's why everyone assumed the chicken said nothing, but who could tell with chickens?

After a while, Puck stirred in his seat and then stood up. He paced around the table, until they all felt rather giddy.

'Please sit down, Puck, dear,' begged Titania. 'You're upsetting the chi... new recruit.'

'I think I've had an idea, but I've got to get it straight before I tell you, otherwise I will get all tangled up,' said Puck. After another few circuits of the table, he sat down and leaned forward on his elbows. The goblins all emerged completely and settled down to listen. Puck's ideas had always been worth listening to in the Old Days, even if they did turn out to be mad and completely unworkable.

'Right, now, we've all watched the telly, right?'

They all nodded, except Titania, who couldn't help adding, 'Well, only the news, really and the wildlife programmes.'

Puck ignored her and continued. 'We've all seen those mortals who stand in front of buildings, usually, but some-

times fighting, or whatever, and tell us what is going on behind them.'

'Yes,' said Tiny. The idea was beginning to dawn in his
larger than average goblin brain.

'When it is fighting, there isn't usually a crowd, but for
every other thing, there is. Just people who were passing, saw
the camera and decided to watch. Sometimes they wave,
have you noticed, and sometimes they shout things.'

'Yes!' Tiny punched the air. He was there. He'd got it.

Puck smiled at him as he hopped up and down from one
trotter to another in his excitement. 'Keep it in, Tiny,' he
said. 'Let me finish.' The others smiled encouragingly, except
the chicken-goblin, who was scratching in a desultory way at
the pattern on the carpet. 'What we need to do,' he continued, 'is to get ourselves out and about, and get on those news
things they have. We haven't changed much. In fact, my ears
are definitely getting more pointy than they were when I was
a milkman.' Oberon was glad to hear him say that – he'd
thought his eyes were going funny. 'I don't see that any of our
Folk out there could fail to recognise us. And as for the goblins – well.'

'Yeth?' asked Thydney. 'Well what?'

'Well, you chaps couldn't be taken for mortal, now, could
you?' said Oberon, in a bracing sort of tone.

'Why not?' asked Squeaky, menacingly.

Oberon stared at him, lost for words. Titania rescued him.
'Because you are unique, every one of you,' she said, with a
queenly condescension. 'Precious and different. Who wants to
look like an old mortal anyway? There are loads of them and
they all look the same.'

Squeaky was mollified, but not completely convinced. He
backed away, muttering and looking out from under his piggy
ginger lashes.

'That is a very, *very* good idea, Puck,' Titania continued.
'But...'

'But how do they find us, once they've spotted us?' asked
Bertie, for once ahead of the pack.

'Yes, how?' Titania patted him, wiped her hand automatically and turned to face the elf.

'I... I hadn't got that far,' Puck conceded.

Oberon's brow had been furrowed, but it began to clear. 'What we need,' he said slowly, 'is something that isn't words. Something that tells our people something, but without writing.'

'A pitcher!' cried Freckles.

'What, like a big jug?' asked Bertie.

'What?'

'A pitcher. A big jug.'

'No! Not a *pitcher*! A *pitcher*. You know, a pitcher of us or sunnink.'

'Oh,' Bertie turned his snout up to an almost impossible angle. 'A picture!'

'That's what I said, wunnit?' Freckles spread his trotters and looked round the company.

'More or less,' Puck said, patting him on the shoulder. 'More or less. But he has got something there, you know. If we could think of a picture that would show what we were doing, then perhaps we could be found that way.'

'I've got an idea,' said Thydney. 'What if we waited, nearby, after the broadcatht had finished. Tho, Freckleth, for inthtanthe...'

Titania took over before they all drowned. 'Yes, one of the goblins makes sure he is on camera. Meanwhile, a few of us who look...' she glanced sideways at Squeaky, who was cracking his knuckles and looking mutinous, '...a bit more like mortals,' she continued in a quieter voice, 'could wait nearby for a few hours. If anyone else turns up that we think might be faerie, then, hey presto,' she clapped her hands and a rather startled looking pair of nightingales materialised in the middle of the table. 'Oh, sorry,' she said, and jumped up to open a window to let them out. She turned back to the table, and everyone was suddenly talking at once. They all had refinements to add to the plan, from the sensible; someone waiting quietly nearby, to the insane; that Oberon could think up a goblin with a flashing arrow on its head.

She let their ideas run, waiting for a consensus to develop. She was quietly grateful that no one had seemed to want more details of her evening, although she had a feeling that

Oberon would be asking questions later. Finally, the talking faltered to a stop and all faces turned to her.

'So, we are generally agreed, then, are we? We get a goblin on camera, and then someone – I suggest Puck, to start with – waits nearby to see if any one turns up. Is that it?'

Nods all round.

'Fine. The next problem is to find out where these camera things are going to happen.'

Everyone looked at Oberon. He was, after all, the one known to be addicted to the television. 'I don't know,' he said. 'I don't watch those news things. All those mortals fretting over stuff they can't change.'

'I watch a bit,' said Puck. 'A lot of them come from a place called West Minster. It looks like a park, with a big building in it. There's something from there most days. It's in London.'

'Is that far?' asked Bertie, nervously. He hadn't travelled much. Tiny and Freckles, fresh from their trip to Woodford Green, tutted condescendingly.

'No,' said Tiny. 'Not far.'

'We've been there,' nodded Freckles.

'Okay, no travel stories,' begged Oberon. 'We've all been around.'

'Yeah,' menaced Squeaky. 'But not lately, eh?'

Oberon narrowed his eyes at the goblin, and put him at the top of his deconstruction list. The chicken suddenly squawked in its sleep and made them all jump.

Titania looked at it thoughtfully and hauled it to its feet. 'You know,' she said, 'I think it would be a good one to practice with. Doesn't say much, looks like a very ugly kid to mortals, but unmistakably goblin to faerie, and it frees the others up to patrol around for a while. What do you say?'

The chicken didn't know whether to be pleased or insulted. It said 'Squawk!' anyway.

'Good idea,' said Puck. 'I'll take them all up to London tomorrow and scout around for a camera. When we find one, we'll put... what's its name?'

'Bill,' chortled Freckles.

'Nice one. Bill, here, in the crowd. You two, Mistress,

Lord, can stay here and watch out for us. Oh, sorry, Mistress. I suppose you'll be at work.'

Titania looked thoughtful. No,' she said slowly. 'I think I've finished with work.'

'Or it has finished with her?' whispered Tiny to Freckles, who nodded. She clipped it round the ear.

'Right then,' Puck rubbed his hands together and to everyone's astonishment, including his own, turned a back flip that encompassed the whole room. He landed and faced them with a grin that lit up the kitchen, 'Let's get a bit of rest; it's an early start tomorrow and Bill needs to look as much like a goblin as he can.'

'Which is *very much* like a goblin indeed,' said Bertie.

'Squawk,' Puck, his Lord and Lady heard Bill say as they shut the door behind them. They didn't hear the sound of breaking furniture as they went up the stairs.

Oberon softly shut the bedroom door.

'Now,' he said, growing larger and somehow more lush, 'What really happened tonight, My Lady? Hmm?'

Titania looked at him for a moment and then, waving an arm, was immediately dressed in a gauzy nothing that almost made Oberon forget his question. His attention span was short, even for a faerie, and as she stood there, firefly lights glimmering around her head and the scent of frosty stars filling the room, he found he didn't really care much what had happened at Trevor's. What was happening here was enough for even the Lord of Faerie to cope with. She crooked her finger and he was pulled forward till he could feel her breath on his cheek. She circled his waist, locking her fingers behind him and they were lifted up, lips touching in a gentle faerie kiss, coming to rest on the bed, now covered with fragrant herbs with, some part of Oberon's brain was glad to notice, not a single nettle to be found.

'I'll tell you in the morning,' Titania whispered into his curls. 'Nothing I was proud of, but nothing to bother you either.'

Content, Oberon let Titania spread her glamour until he could have sworn he saw stars winking overhead and that he could hear wind through the trees.

Puck, in his room across the landing, tried not to listen. Apart from the odd goblin oath from below, and a strange billowing of the plaster as the fight spread beyond the bounds of the kitchen, the house was still and quiet. So quiet that, when he closed his eyes, he imagined he could hear wind soughing through green leaves and starlight pricked through his closed lids. When Titania spread her cloak, more than she knew was encompassed by it. Puck wasn't jealous – he'd got over that in the millennia that had passed – but he was lonely. As far as he was concerned, the New Day which would replace the Old Days couldn't come quickly enough. He just hoped that they were all ready for it. Cobweb had known she wasn't; and he had a feeling that it wasn't going to be as easy as all that.

He screwed his eyes tight shut, ran through a couple of heavy metal favourites – he liked *Fear of the Dark* best – in his head to drown out the nightingales which seemed to be singing in his ear, and finally, fitfully, he slept.

15

Anything later than dawn was a lie-in for the occupants of Thirteen, Ellesmere Crescent. Oberon, it was true, liked his bed, and would wallow in it all day if he could. But even he liked the occasional sun-rise, if he could catch a nap later. To watch the sun rise, even if it was through rooftops and satellite dishes, was the only way to start the day. Puck had chosen his employment as milkman for that very reason – he had seen dawns of every type; grey, wet, dry, but today's was a peach. A pearly sky, shot through with the palest pink, a hint of thrush-egg blue at the corner of your eye, no matter which way you turned, this was a dawn which promised a lovely day. Looking back, and he could look back a long, long way, Puck couldn't remember ever having been disappointed by a day which began like this. He drew a deep breath, filling his lungs with the smell of damp earth, lightly crushed grass and a hint of woodsmoke from a distant, illegal bonfire.

He went back into the kitchen, rubbing his hands and up for a bacon sandwich, nice crispy meat with lashings of HP sauce. He opened the fridge. Two bottles of tonic and half a lemon. The bread bin held something which had once upon a time been a crust of brown bread and a spider, which looked at him balefully.

'Okay, okay, don't look at me like that,' Puck said to it, reproachfully. 'I was only looking for something to eat.'

'It's a lovely morning,' sang a voice from behind his back. 'The dew is as fresh as can be.'

'Sorry, Lady,' said Puck, turning. 'I got into the habit of eating mortal food. I don't suppose you've even got any milk, have you?'

She grinned. 'I'll see if the milkman's been. I get it for the goblins.' She went down the hall and he heard the front door open, followed by the clink of bottles. 'You're in luck. He isn't usually this early.'

'You don't get the service these days,' said Puck wistfully. 'When I first started in the milk business...'

She laughed and said, 'Not like you to reminisce, Puck. As I recall, you always had a tendency to live for the moment.'

His smile was rueful. 'It's what living with mortals does to you, haven't you found that? And of course, poor old Cobweb, she liked to talk about the old times. That was until she discovered donuts, and then she didn't do it so much.' His voice died away and he filled the moment by getting up, pouring himself a glass of milk and then putting the other bottles away.

'No need to do that,' Titania said, turning her head to watch him. 'They aren't bothered whether it's fresh or not.' She paused, watching him as he stood with his back to her, leaning on the sink, looking out of the window to watch a thrush open a snail on the path which led to the totally unused washing line. 'Puck?'

'Yes, Lady?'

'Nothing. Um, how did you sleep, last night?'

He turned to face her, still leaning on the sink. He had a milk moustache, which made him look about fourteen and suddenly very vulnerable. 'I... couldn't seem to drop off. But then I was all right.'

She stood up and wafted over to give him a light kiss on the tip of his perfect nose. 'Good. I... think of you sometimes. Worrying, you know, that perhaps you can't sleep, or something.'

He looked at her and then pushed her gently away. 'Don't worry about me. You're where you should be. Don't rock the boat – we may be sinking anyway.'

She reached out, arm at full stretch and wiped away the milk. 'I don't know how you bear that stuff,' she muttered, and wandered away to wake Oberon, always the last to rise. 'Get the goblins up,' she said, over her shoulder. 'We've got to give them their instructions again. It's no good expecting them to remember anything from last night.'

Puck pushed off from the sink and flew across the room, just to get in a bit of practice. As he looked down, he was glad he had, since this meant he had not trodden in the white splashes of drying chicken shit decorating the vinyl floor just by the skirting board. He tapped on the wall.

'Wakey, wakey, chaps. Time we were up and out.'

Shufflings from behind the skirting board were followed by a few cries and shouts of 'Watch where you're standing!' 'What was that I just trod in?' 'Bill's laid a bloody egg!' 'Squawk!'

Finally they were all assembled, more or less in a line, in the kitchen. They were all trying to tidy themselves up, in their own way. Bertie's bristles were positively alive with grease, Squeaky had buffed up his leather jerkin, cut to reveal his biceps, and Bill kept running an anxious hand, somehow too big and broad for his arm, through his luxuriant quiff.

Titania and Oberon made their entrance, dressed soberly for faerie, but undoubtedly regal. Their clothes were dark green, but shot with colours that moved and danced about, so subtly that no eye on earth or in the world of faerie could say where they came from, where they went. Titania's long coat covered a soft, velvety tunic which looked like the softest moss. Her trousers were cut close to the ankle and she wore low boots with a wide rim, edged with suede as soft as a sigh. Oberon had on a business suit and overcoat, but all in the softest leather. The goblins and Puck were dumbstruck. Puck recovered first.

'Sire, Mistress,' he said, licking his dry lips, 'you both look wonderful, but...'

'But?' Oberon said, giving a twirl for the benefit of the goblins who were, in their quiet way, dedicated followers of fashion.

'I thought the idea was that we were going to blend.'

Oberon shrugged his leather clad shoulders. 'Blend? Who wants to *blend*?'

'Well, Sire, we do. We don't want to attract a random crowd. They'll all be mortal, or mostly mortal, and we don't want to have to waste a lot of time getting rid of them which we could be using in getting in touch with our own kind.'

Titania nodded in agreement and closed her eyes, gave a ladylike shudder and toned down her clothes a notch. Oberon looked stubborn but, with a lot more effort, did the same.

'But, hold on a minute,' piped up Tiny. 'I thought that the Master and Mistress were going to wait here and watch for us on the television.'

'That's right!' said Puck. 'When did that plan change, Sire?'

Titania smiled and looked down for a moment. When she looked up, her eyes shone with excitement. 'We want to be there, Puck. We want to see what's going on. To be where...' she turned to Oberon, 'what is that saying?'

'Where the action is,' Oberon finished for her, doing an embarrassing little boogie on the spot and clicking his fingers. Doors opened and shut at random all over the building, including next door, fetching the cat a nasty one and propelling it into the lounge at a rate of knots. It hated those beings at Number Thirteen; they didn't smell right. But how does a cat tell anyone?

Puck sat down heavily. Oh, no! His Lord was going to... mingle. It was going to be a bad day after all, no matter what the weather.

The goblins were shuffling uneasily. They didn't know whether it would be worse to be there, watching and taking part on the spot, or back in Ellesmere Crescent, watching the television, watching it all go pear shaped. Each one was trying to get to the back of the group, hoping not to be chosen. Puck was one step ahead of them and stayed between them and the wall – he had had years in which to work out the fairly simple workings of a goblin's mind.

He spoke. 'In view of that, then, Sire, Madam, perhaps we all ought to come.'

The goblins sagged with relief. They really didn't want to

be parted at this vital point. Oberon looked sulky. He didn't want Puck to be there, no matter how many goblins he had to have up his vest. He wanted to go out on the town with Titania – to soak up the admiring glances and cut a swathe through any crowd. But Titania was speaking.

'Good idea. You know more about mortals than we do, Puck. And we'll need help carrying the goblins. Two is about my limit and I don't think Oberon can manage the rest on his own, can you dear?' she turned an innocent gaze on Oberon and he knew when he was beaten.

He grunted in reply.

The goblins all ran forward, each wanting to be one of the chosen two. She pointed to Tiny and, to everyone's surprise, Bill. They hopped up and disappeared under her coat. There were shufflings and delighted, muted squawks. She poked her midriff and it rustled. 'No eggs, by the way.'

'He lays eggs?' Oberon asked in amazement. 'That wasn't in the plan.'

'No,' Freckles said wearily. 'I shouldn't fink it was. And eggs ain't all 'e does, niver.'

'Sorry, lads. I'll try something else next time.'

'Dunnow what's wrong wiv pigs,' Freckles muttered, as he hopped up and disappeared under Puck's jacket.

The others distributed themselves around the King and his elf, and they walked down to the station, Oberon and Titania arm in arm, Puck fetching up the rear, there in body, but in his head already on Parliament Green, running through all the disasters that could happen. They were many and varied and all ended up with Oberon being arrested. He sighed. Never mind, perhaps it would all go all right after all. Pigs might fly, said the dark Puck in the back of his mind.

'Oy,' said Freckles. 'We would if we could, you know. No need to be like that.'

'Sorry,' said Puck, and followed his King and Queen into the station concourse.

'Can we use my money?' Oberon asked eagerly. 'It's got the right head on it this time. And the edges haven't curled much at all, really.'

'Why not?' said Puck. At worst he could be arrested now;

or was that at best? At least it wouldn't be too far to visit him in the cells.

But the clerk was busy; commuter time was just hotting up. And anyway, Titania was smiling at him. Oberon could have paid in lavatory paper (which in a way he had) and he wouldn't have said a thing.

Safely ensconced on the train, Puck sat soaking up the essence of the mortals who surrounded him on all sides. He had felt his rapport with them lessen in the few days in Ellesmere Crescent. It was easy to lose your grip on the mortal side of things when you were with Oberon too much. Their Universes may be parallel, but if you tried to keep a foot on each rail, you might do yourself a serious mischief.

At Waterloo, he led the way. They would walk to the Houses of Parliament. They had plenty of time, and he hadn't forgotten the taxi driver who had nearly changed species. He had to be mindful that their powers were more now that they were together, and Oberon was full of it, what with the door opening thing and what he kidded himself was flying. He was going to take a lot of watching.

The bridge stretched out into the sparkling day and they ambled along it at their own pace, with their own thoughts. Oberon leaned on the parapet and gazed down at the water. He'd never really had much to do with water in quantity – woods were more his thing. And this water looked sluggish and somehow thick, not bouncing and sparkling as he thought it should. He turned away and carried on to the other bank. Titania had been ambushed by a troop of Japanese tourists, bulldozed into stopping by clicking shutters and whirring cameras. Little men, hardly reaching her shoulder, stood proudly by her while their wives crossly took photographs of them. Then, they thrust the cameras at her and posed smiling, gesturing to her to take their picture. She copied what they had done, but without a clue what she was doing. Most of them would get back to Tokyo with two mementoes of the Faerie Queen; one of a dazzlingly beautiful woman and the other of her thumb.

Puck mooched on, head down, kicking at the paving stones moodily. The goblins were making his back ache. He had a premonition knocking at the back of his skull and his feet hurt. Pavements always did that to him. He wished that he could fly to where they were going. He had been having little practice flights in the past 24 hours and he was pretty sure that, if he tried, he would get to Parliament Green without dumping in the river. But... they weren't at that stage yet. But, oh, what fun it would be, to finally take flight, leave all this behind, find some quiet place to just... what? How were they going to keep them, down in the glade, after they'd seen Wolverhampton?

They all eventually got to the opposite bank, and Titania and Oberon stood there, rubbernecking like the most hardened tourists. They hadn't been to London, at least, not for nearly four hundred years. Their last visit had been to the Rose, in heavy disguise, to see a play some bloke had written. It was supposed to be about them, but, apart from the names there wasn't anything they recognised. Titania was played by a man, for a start. She had been rather embarrassed about the donkey storyline, though, and her blushes had brought about some pretty heavy questioning from Oberon for a while.

Back in the here and now, they were getting bored with waiting, and Puck bought them both an ice cream, to keep them occupied. It didn't seem to count as food, so they both had a lick, just to keep him quiet.

'This is lovely,' Titania said, indistinctly, 'but it's very cold. Can I wait while it warms up a little?'

'No, Mistress,' said Puck, earning himself a very funny look from a passing shopper, 'It will melt then. By the way,' he added, as the shopper stumbled off the kerb in her attempts to cross the road while staring at the trio, 'Can we decide what to call each other while we are in a crowd? Perhaps Tania?'

'No,' Oberon boomed, reacting swiftly. 'Our Tania and Bron days are over, Puck. If you must, don't call us anything. But call me Bron and I will personally see to it that you hop everywhere for a while.'

'Hop?'

'I will turn you into a toad,' hissed Oberon, eyes ablaze.

'Take no notice, Puck,' Titania sighed. 'I've seen him practicing and the only way he'll make you hop everywhere is if he stamps on your toe.'

Puck hardly dared ask. 'What has he been practicing on, er...' he dropped his voice to a whisper, 'Mistress?'

'The postman. The milkman. Mr Jones, from next door. Mrs Jones.'

'I must interrupt here,' said Oberon, drawing himself up, 'I think I had a bit of a success, there.'

'Mrs Jones *always* looks like that,' said Titania impatiently. 'You made no difference at all.'

Oberon looked crestfallen and said, under his breath, 'Well, just don't, that's all.'

To change the subject, Puck nudged him. 'We're here, Sire. Let's split up and look around for a camera crew. Whoever finds one, send out for the others, and we'll meet back here.'

'What signal shall we send?' Oberon asked, excitedly. This was just like the television. Only realer.

'Anything,' said Puck. 'If we get a message, we'll know what it's for, won't we?'

Titania nodded.

Oberon said, 'No, no, I've seen this in films. There has to be a password.'

'Such as?' Puck said, testily, ready to set off.

'Oh, I don't know. Something that only we would know.'

'How about "camera crew"?' said Titania, although she knew irony was wasted on Oberon.

'Hmm, too obvious, perhaps?' he replied. 'What about...?' Oberon's imagination was small and slow.

Tiny stuck his head out of Titania's coat and said, nastily, 'Is this all really necessary? I'm stuck in here — beging your pardon, Mistress — stuck in here with a goblin that is still three parts *hen*. Can you imagine what it's like? Bloody feathers everywhere! Just say "found it" or something. Who else will be calling inside your head?'

'He's got a point,' said Titania, who was beginning to itch, now she knew about the feathers. 'Let's just split up and search. Call our names or something, anything, when you find one. See you,' and she skimmed off, remembering to touch the path, for the look of the thing, but so excited that she sometimes did several steps in the air. Oberon and Puck looked after her fondly, sighed and walked away in different directions.

It had begun at last.

16

Oberon wandered off across the grass. It was better than walking on the pavement, and there weren't so many people. In fact, there didn't seem to be anyone else walking on the grass at all – he couldn't quite understand why, it was so much more comfortable on the feet. He looked around him, squinting a little into the autumn sun, warming the mellow stone of the huge building away towards the river. Puck had told him it was where mortal laws were made – it seemed an awful lot of trouble to go to, when, if his television watching had taught him anything, most people spent most of their time breaking them. There didn't seem to be anything happening, so he just ambled about, enjoying the sun. The goblins were quiet; they had gone to sleep somewhere around his waist and he could hear their gentle snores from time to time. In fact, he felt a little sleepy himself, so he found a park bench and settled down, with his coat wrapped around him, for a bit of a snooze.

Puck walked off towards the mountain of golden stone. He looked up its sheer sides and his feet itched with longing. He wanted to soar around those fairy-tale turrets, trailing mist and sparks. He missed Cobweb, suddenly; if only this harebrained scheme could possibly succeed!

Titania was as happy as the day was long. It had stopped raining, she was out on the town, by herself, not dragging to or from work, just *out*. She revelled in the admiring – and occasionally slightly puzzled – glances of the passers-by as she danced along. It wasn't raining, she was the Queen and soon everyone would know it. It was good to be alive. She swept her eyes from horizon to horizon, and saw a little group of people gathered near the end of the huge building away to her left. For a moment, her heart stopped – it wasn't Oberon, was it, doing something noticeable? But no, as she looked to her right, she could see him, stretched out on a bench, obviously asleep. She lightened her lips and sighed – nothing new there, then, but at least he was being no trouble.

She moved off in the direction of the little crowd. She saw from a distance the thing that looked like a small shaggy dog on a stick which the man in front of the camera always seemed to have with him. She wondered whether it was a pet, or whether it was a working animal. She was quite excited to be so near, to see them in their real skin, not just through the glass of the television set. She knew the man who was talking. Most mortals looked the same to her, but his face was familiar, as they went. He was talking to the man with the camera, and pointing to the sun, which was unseasonably bright. The whole crowd shuffled round a bit, so that his face was half in the shade, and she shuffled with them. He was talking again, seeming to introduce himself to the man with the camera. Didn't he know who he was? It occurred to her that perhaps mortals didn't always recognise each other, either. How interesting.

She gave her goblins a little gentle poke and was rewarded by a load squawk.

The presenter swore and threw down his script in disgust. The sound man leapt in the air, clutching his ears.

'What in God's name was that?' he yelled. 'It sounded like a bloody chicken!'

'Go again,' the presenter said, picking up his script and giving it a quick shuffle. He looked at the crowd. 'Quiet please, everyone,' he said. 'I have to get this segment taped, and the quieter you are, the quicker I can do it.' He nodded to sound and camera. 'Okay?' They nodded back.

Titania called frantically for Puck and Oberon. She turned to see the elf skimming as fast as he dared across the grass. Of Oberon, there was no sign, but at least Puck had heard.

She ran to meet him. 'They've nearly done,' she gabbled. 'Puck, quick, do something.'

'Well,' he said, 'You've got the two goblins we need. Get them in there, in the crowd. I'll stand back and look in that little television thing they've got set up, and see if you can see them all right. Ready?' he said to her coat.

'As we'll ever be,' came Tiny's voice, somewhat muffled.

'Okay then. Go!' said Puck, and with a slither and a wriggle, Tiny and Bill hit the ground running and disappeared into the crowd.

This take was going rather well. The presenter was summing up, gesturing with his arm towards the building behind him.

Titania shook Puck's arm. 'If he finishes,' she hissed, 'we've lost our chance. Make a noise or something. Make him start again.'

Puck stood on tiptoe and crowed like a cockerel. It was his party piece and was always guaranteed to bring things to a standstill.

This time, the sound man ripped off his earphones and reeled away, clutching his head and cursing loudly. The cameraman looked on in mild interest. These sound guys – so sensitive.

'It's a bloody chicken,' the sound man said. 'It is, it is a bloody chicken. It's that countryside lot, isn't it? They've gone and released bloody chickens.' He stamped about, massaging his ears.

The presenter stepped forward. 'Come on, now, Jeff,' he said, putting an avuncular arm around the man's shoulders. 'There aren't any chickens. Look around. I see no chickens. Do you?' he peered into Jeffs face.

Jeff looked up, now his ears had stopped ringing and his balance had come back on line. 'No,' he admitted. 'Although, hold up, a minute,' and he peered into the crowd. He dropped his voice and said, 'When we've done this, I think I'm going to put in for a bit of leave.'

'Okay, old son, if you want to. But why?'

'I... thought for a minute there that there was a big chicken. In the crowd.'

The presenter looked thoughtful, then patted the man's arm. 'Okay, then, Jeff. I'll see the producer about a little bit of a break for you. How about if I can get you a holiday programme for a few weeks? Bit of a rest, eh?' He gave him a penetrating look and then walked back to his mark. As the cameraman caught his eye, he made a little gesture, a finger screwing for a second at one temple.

Trembling, and looking around furtively, the sound man resumed his position, and the presenter adjusted the hang of his jacket, cleared his throat and began again.

Puck had a peep in the monitor, and, sure enough, just over the reporter's shoulder, Bill was beautifully outlined against the mellow stone. He appeared to be a little unsteady on his feet, but Puck put that down to excitement.

He nudged Titania gently and asked, 'Should he be that tall?'

She looked over at the scene and said out of the corner of her mouth, 'No. I told him to stand on Tiny's shoulders, so we could see him better.'

'Good call,' Puck said, admiringly. 'I would never have thought of that.'

She had the grace to look ashamed. 'Actually,' she confessed, 'Neither did I. It was Tiny's idea.'

This time, the recording went without a hitch. 'It's a wrap,' said the soundman with relief and the presenter wandered off for a fag and to sign a few autographs. Even political editors have fans.

An elderly lady went up to him rather diffidently and asked, 'When does this go out? Only, I have a sister in Ruislip who will be looking out for me. I think I was visible over your shoulder you see, and she will be so excited.'

He beamed down at her, his fake tan orange in the unexpected sun. 'It will be a part of tonight's six o'clock bulletin,' he said. 'It will definitely go out, because it will be tied with a larger item linked to this afternoon's Parliamentary Questions. About six fifteen, or so, I imagine.'

'Oh, thank you so much,' she twittered. She reached up to

his shoulder and picked something off the fabric. 'I think I'd better remove this, don't you?' she giggled. She handed him a tawny feather, which had been resting there since the filming finished. A chicken feather. The sound man, coiling up his leads and nestling his microphones in their padded boxes, took one look and fainted dead away.

The presenter looked down at him dispassionately. 'Er, Tony,' he called to the cameraman. 'Sort Jeff, will you. He's finally flipped.' He smiled once more at the old lady, who stood there horror-struck by her hero's callous attitude, and he wandered away, pulling at his tie. 'I think we'll have a new team, next time, Melissa, don't you?' he remarked to his PA as they drove away in the studio car. 'These sound guys, they get flakier every damn time.'

Melissa nodded and made a note on her pad. The political editor looked over her shoulder. She had doodled chickens in the margins. He tapped a musing finger on his pursed lips and made a mental note to watch the news tonight – and hope he saw no poultry.

Puck meanwhile was reporting back to Titania. 'It will be on tonight just after six,' he said. 'So we've got quite a while to wait. But Bill was in full view the whole time. And he gave the sound man the willies, but no one else, so we shouldn't start too much of a panic. It seems that most mortals only want to see what they want to see. It seems their eyes aren't really designed to detect a six foot half-chicken-half-goblin when they see one.' He looked around. 'Where are they now?'

Titania patted her midriff. 'I got them tucked away again. I felt *so* sorry for that poor man. He was really quite upset.' She looked round and saw him, propped up against the wheel of the outside broadcast van. 'I must go and have a word.' She wandered over to the sound man before Puck could stop her.

She squatted down beside him. 'Hello,' she breathed.

He looked up. He had been trying to look down, when he could. He didn't want to see any more tall chickens, if he could help it. He couldn't believe the woman whose face filled his view. She was more beautiful than... no comparisons were possible. He'd always had a bit of a thing for Catherine Zeta Jones, but this woman put her totally in the shade. Her face was perfect and seemed to almost glow from within. Her skin was like the down on the palest peach, her eyes seemed to have depths in them no one could plumb. They were deepest violet, or were they brown, or possibly blue? Her lips, palest pink and soft as a petal, parted and she asked him, 'Are you feeling better, now?'

He could only nod, blushing furiously, and looking down. He felt as embarrassed as a schoolboy. It was while he was looking down that he saw the chicken, peering out from under her coat, looking sideways at him, in the way that chickens do.

He scrabbled to his feet and ran, screaming, across the grass, Tony, the cameraman in hot pursuit.

'Well,' said Titania, going back to stand by Puck. 'That wasn't very polite, was it? I only asked him if he was feeling better.'

It was an unusual response, Puck had to agree. It was only Tiny, smacking Bill smartly round the head in the privacy of Titania's coat lining, who really understood.

A yawn in her ear made Titania turn round. Oberon stood there, rubbing his eyes and looking puzzled.

'What time is it?' he asked. 'Do we have to stay here any longer? Why is that man screaming? Is anyone doing any television thingies? Can we go home?'

'Half past two,' said Puck, taking each question in turn, 'Yes, until at least this evening. We don't know. They've done it. No.'

'Pardon?' Oberon hadn't been listening to anything he had said; the questions had left his mouth without intervention of his brain.

'Never mind,' Titania said. 'It's all done. All we have to do is wait and see who turns up.'

'Do you mean I missed it?' Oberon was disappointed.

'There wasn't much to miss,' Puck said. 'Tiny and Bill worked well, not too much damage was done, really.' He and Titania exchanged a look. 'Plenty of coverage, so all we have to do is wait here. But not until after six, because the recording won't be on the television until then.'

'What shall we do?' Titania hugged Oberon's arm and grabbed Puck's as well. She held them both tight. 'I'm so excited. What do you say if we put the goblins somewhere safe for a bit and go off by ourselves. I must admit,' she gave a little wriggle that Puck and Oberon both found quite disturbing, not to mention the two City types walking across the green, 'I must admit, I feel like an afternoon off.'

'The zoo?' Oberon suggested.

'No, Sire, I don't think so,' Puck scolded. 'You know the effect you have on animals. Especially the big ones, lions, bears, those sort of creatures.

Oberon looked chastened. 'They don't like me,' he sulked.

'It's your fault,' Titania told him. 'You tease them.'

'Well,' Oberon looked stubborn. 'I'm King of the Forest. Even now,' he added.

'Whatever,' said Puck. 'No zoo. What about a nice walk?'

'Boring,' muttered Oberon.

'Shopping?'

Oberon brightened up. 'Yes,' he said. 'Shopping. I can make some money. Lots of leaves around here.'

'Make that *window* shopping,' Titania said firmly, 'and I'll come. Your money doesn't always look quite... right.'

Puck gathered them up before they could change their minds. 'Window shopping it is,' he said. 'Where do you lot want to be dropped off?' he asked his goblins.

Bertie stuck his head out of Puck's chest, briefly, to say 'Hyde Park'.

'Any particular reason?'

'Grass. Trees. Lots of places to hide.'

'Courting couples,' leered Squeaky, from Oberon's trouser pocket.

'Not at this time of the year, surely,' said Titania.

'You never know your luck,' Squeaky said, in a voice that made Titania shudder.

'Hyde Park it is, then,' Puck said. 'How are we travelling, Your Majesties? Shall it be Air, Under Ground or by taxi?'

'If you can control yourself, Oberon,' Titania said coolly, 'I rather fancy a taxi.'

'A taxi it shall be, my Lady,' Puck said. They walked to the edge of the Green and he held up an arm. 'Harrods,' he said to the driver, 'via Hyde Park. And please, no politics.'

IT

The taxi driver didn't show his surprise. He'd seen most things, in his years behind the wheel in the London streets. But it was a little odd, all the same, to do a detour so that three grown people could get out on the edge of Hyde Park, stand there for about ten seconds and then turn and get back into the cab. But not before the woman – a right cracker – had shouted, 'And don't forget – come when we call you. No messing about.'

He dropped them outside Harrods. What a good job it was that he had no inkling what his handsome tip would have turned into by morning.

Titania, considered at Number Thirteen to be an expert on retail, thanks to her supermarket experience, stood outside the store and gaped. Its windows were so full of things she had never dreamed of, they were so brightly lit, so elegant, she was struck dumb. The doors were swinging constantly with mortals streaming in and out, carrying baskets and green bags with gold lettering. She had only heard of this place – no wonder mortals had stopped believing in her kind. Here was fairyland and everyone could enter. It was sweetly smelling, sparkling, magical. She went inside as if drawn on a silken thread.

Oberon whispered to Puck, 'What's the matter with her? I've never seen her like this.'

'She's shopping,' Puck replied. 'She's not slipped far down

the slope to mortality, but she'd slipped far enough to like shopping.'

The two followed her into the scented interior of the store. She was standing mesmerised at the glittering display of glass and china. She was happy as long as there was a glass to drink out of when she was at home. But now, she wanted, really wanted six matching Stuart crystal brandy balloons as if her life depended on it. She clicked one with a fingernail, and it rang out with one glorious, clear note. She turned to Oberon, with her eyes shining.

'Oh, listen to that,' she breathed. 'Isn't it lovely? Isn't it all so lovely?'

'I think,' Puck said urgently into Oberon's ear, 'that we'd better get her out of here. Quickly.'

'Oh, I don't know,' said Oberon, looking around. 'I can see why she likes it.'

'Sire, please, we must. I thought she could take it, that she would enjoy it...'

'Well, she's certainly doing that,' Oberon said wryly, as Titania took off through an archway. They could hear her cooing over, of all things, handbags. They followed her. 'Oh, come on, now,' Oberon said. 'Even I know it's not nice to make bags out of crocodiles.'

'Stylish,' muttered Titania, smoothing its scales.

'Get her out of here,' said Puck through clenched teeth. 'This is doing damage. These few minutes have done more to make her mortal than all the years that went before.'

'Why did you bring us here, then?' Oberon said, shaking him by the shoulder.'

'I thought she would enjoy it. She'd been so much stronger the last day or so.'

'Well, she isn't stronger, is she? This shop is stronger. Let's get her out.'

They took her, one each side, and propelled her out of the shop, through the double door. She stood on the pavement, still looking bewildered.

'What happened in there?' she asked eventually.

'It appears,' Puck said, 'that you can't handle shops.'

'Can't handle shops?' Her voice rose to a squeak. 'I work,

worked, I mean, in a shop.'

'No,' Oberon said, 'I think I understand this. You worked somewhere that sold things people need. Food. Soap. That sort of thing. Mortals have to have those. But who in their right mind,' he was still quite horrified, 'wants a handbag made out of a crocodile's skin?'

'Yeurggh,' shuddered Titania. 'How horrible.'

'You wanted one back there,' Puck told her. 'That's how dangerous it was for you.'

She walked away up the road. She suddenly turned. 'I wanted a bag made out of a crocodile?'

'Yup.'

'No wonder nobody believes in us,' she said. 'They can't concentrate on an idea when they can wallow about in… stuff!' she threw her arms wide. There was just so much *stuff*. She looked around. Everyone in sight was carrying a bag. Most of them had two or three. Children's buggies were piled high with shopping. In several cases, the child was being pulled grizzling behind, having been usurped by carrier bags. She smiled at one little chap being dragged along towards more shopping. She wiggled her fingers at him and to their mutual delight, a bluebird flew upwards and away, trailing little stars.

The child stopped, and sat down suddenly. His mother yanked him to his feet.

'Birdie, Mama,' said the boy.

'Come on,' said his mother. 'No birds here.'

'Lady made a birdie. Harry want the birdie.'

'I'll buy you one later,' she said, swinging him in front of her. 'Just hush.'

The three faeries watched in dismay.

'He saw me do that,' said Titania heavily. 'A few more minutes, and he'd have believed in me. A few more like him…'

'You have to deal with the mothers,' said Oberon with a gleam in his eye. The child's mother had shown a very well turned buttock through her Calvin Kleins.

'Children,' retorted Titania. 'They're the way to go.'

'Television,' Puck reminded them both. 'Let's not run before we can walk. We need more recruits before we can start a campaign on any single front. There is a woman on the television; it is made to look as if she appears by magic in a child's room. She solves the problem he is having with his computer.'

Titania looked crestfallen.

'Then, she waves an arm and, in a twinkle of light and glitter, she disappears. So, you see, you can appear to children in all your glory, Lady, but they'll have forgotten you in a moment. They have the attention span of...' some train of thought made him turn to look at Oberon. He had wandered off down the street, in general pursuit of a pretty girl with long, swinging auburn hair. Puck trotted off and led him back.

'Well,' he continued, 'I rest my case. In the meantime, we'd better get back to where the broadcast took place. We only have about half an hour to get there.'

Oberon beat his chest with a clenched fist. It got him a few odd looks. Titania nudged him.

'What?'

'Blend!' she hissed.

He threw out his arms, and announced, 'I was just trying to indicate that I feel fit as a flea and can get there in as many seconds.'

Puck laid a restraining hand on his arm. 'Yes, Sire. You can. The Queen can. I can. But unfortunately, these mortals who surround us on every side, can't. And I think we've already had the conversation about blending.'

Oberon's lovely brow wrinkled in thought. 'Have we?' he said.

A passing woman seized her chance. The loveliest man she had ever seen was standing, right in her path, looking confused.

'Are you lost?' she said hopefully, looking up into his forest-green eyes, 'Can I help you?'

He looked down at her. A plain little thing, with anxious eyes in a pale, thin face. And – he'd never seen this in the flesh, as it were – a metal bar through one eyebrow. His lip curled. 'I hardly think so,' he said dismissively and turned away.

'No need to be rude,' she said. 'I only asked.'

Puck leaped to the rescue. 'Thank you so much,' he gushed. 'I'm sorry, he's foreign.'

She nodded understandingly at the second most gorgeous man she had ever seen in her life. 'I thought so,' she said and dropped her voice. 'Royalty, is he?'

Oberon spun round. 'How perceptive of you, my dear...' he began, but Puck and Titania bore him away. 'But she knew I was the King...' the woman heard him saying as the crowd swallowed him up.

'The King?' she said to herself. That explained it then. Obviously a loony. But what a waste, eh? What a waste.

They skimmed through the crowd like thistledown, on their way to pick up the goblins. They arrived at the edge of the Park and sent out a call, silent to everyone but their target.

'Tiny?' cooed Titania's inner voice. 'Bi-i-i-ll?'

'Lads?' boomed Oberon, silently. 'Lads? It's time to go!'

'Come on,' snapped Puck. 'We haven't got all day!' He'd had nothing to eat all day, just the glass of milk and an ice cream. He was finding food the hardest habit to break and he was a bit testy.

There was a rustling in a nearby bush and two goblin faces appeared, wreathed in smiles. It was Bertie and Thydney.

'We've had a spiffing afternoon,' Bertie breathed, hopping under Puck's coat and disappearing with a pop and a happy sigh.

'Yeth,' agreed Thydney. 'Thuper.'

'It's bin great, yeah,' agreed Freckles, appearing suddenly. 'Bit of fresh air, loads of space.' He stood at his master's feet, showing no sign of tucking himself away. Squeaky appeared and stood there too, feet planted in what looked like a defiant gesture to Puck. He waved his hand at Oberon's coat, held invitingly open.

'Get in, then,' he said. 'We've no time to waste.'

'Don't wanna,' said Freckles. Squeaky just clamped his mouth shut, crossed his arms and scowled out from under his brows.

Oberon made a grab for them, but they were too quick for him, jumping backwards into the bush and peeping out from the depths of the branches. The King leaped on the bush, ripping leaves and twigs away in handfuls.

Puck dragged him off. 'Blend?' he said, quizzically, raising one eyebrow.

'I'll give them blend!' snarled Oberon. 'I knew there'd be trouble. I just knew. Well, we'll just have to leave the little buggers behind then. They weigh me down, anyway. Ruin the cut of my overcoat, wriggling about all the time.' He turned his back in disgust.

Tiny and Bill had arrived on the scene in time to see Oberon attacking a bush. They looked at each other in alarm. They too had enjoyed their afternoon. Bill had spent most of it, it was true, scratching happily in some dirt at the base of a tree.

Tiny had climbed up into its branches and swung there, in a handy fork, enjoying the sun and the chatter of the children playing nearby. It had been idyllic and the nearest to the Old Days he had experienced in a long time. He'd had a little doze, a little dream; he felt ready for anything. And now, the Lord appeared to have gone bonkers. They edged carefully round him and tugged at Titania's hem.

Dragged away from watching Oberon venting his temper, she bent down. When she saw the two of them standing anxiously there, arms up, waiting to hide in her coat, she remembered what it was all for. To rescue her people from dissolution and death. To give them somewhere to live where they could be themselves, not some horrible mixture, neither fish nor, and she mentally apologised to Bill, fowl.

'Don't worry, dears,' she muttered. 'Just a bit of a problem with Freckles and Squeaky. They don't want to hide.' She opened her coat and they popped straight in and hid, quietly for once and with no squawking. Bill just got on with cleaning out his nails and flicking the bits at Tiny. Tiny didn't notice – he was busy with his own thoughts. He was quite fond of Freckles, but Squeaky he could take or leave. He crossed his trotters, hoping that the choice would come down on the side of 'leave'.

'Let's go,' said Oberon, making up his mind. 'They'll soon be sorry. Out in the cold. On their own. When we have found more of our Folk, won't they feel silly, eh?' he nodded and winked at the others, who made noises of assent. They turned to walk away, but slowly, glancing back to see if they had seen sense.

They were almost out of sight when Freckles suddenly shot out of the bush and, moving so quickly any watching mortals would have been hard pressed to make out the details, caught them up and hopped under Oberon's coat. He stuck his head out briefly and in a breathless, whispery voice said, ''E still won't come. There's... stuff going on in that park, vo. Let's go.' He disappeared abruptly.

Puck said, 'Stuff? What stuff?'

'I dunno,' Freckles' voice echoed in their heads. 'Fings. In the bushes, but mainly where there's mortals. When they walk along, you know, talking to their hands

'Ah!' said Oberon, looking intelligent, 'Mo-biles.'

'That's the fings, yes. Well, some of them, they've got... I couldn't see vem properly, but just *movement*, yer know, just wind where there's no wind, light where there's no light.'

'In short,' Titania said, looking thoughtful, 'What you look like to mortals, when you don't want to be seen.'

'Yes,' agreed Freckles, in a worried tone.

Oberon gave a shudder. 'I try not to get too near those mo-bile things,' he said. 'They make my head ache. It kind of... buzzes in my ears.'

There was a chorus of general agreement from the hidden goblins.

'So...' Puck was gathering his ideas together. 'So, there appear to be goblins, who we don't know, who *like* that feeling? Is that right? And what about Squeaky?' He poked Oberon in the general area of Freckles.

'Ow,' said Oberon and the goblin in duet.

''E seemed to like it,' said Freckles. 'Or, at least, not mind it.'

'He's always been far too close to mortals for my liking,' added Titania. 'I'm glad he's not here.'

Puck was thoughtful. 'I don't think we've heard the last of

him, all the same,' he said. He glanced at the sky. Time was getting on and they still had a fair way to go. 'We'd better step out, Your Majesties. We don't want to be late.'

18

In a penthouse flat, high above the sluggish river, Benedict lay back in his blonde leather chair and flicked through the hundreds of channels available on his state-of-the-art wide screen television, set behind automatically sliding doors at the end of his study-cum-den. He was looking for a news programme, more specifically, BBC News, which he still preferred. He liked change, often for change's sake, but some things, you just got used to. From the first days of the cat's whisker radio and that nice little Italian gentleman and his experiments, he had stayed loyal to BBC News. Being a snappy dresser himself, he rather decried the lapse from evening dress, but still, one couldn't have everything.

His languid arm outstretched, he pressed 'select' and Michael Buerk began to keep him up to the minute. He'd checked his share prices and off-loaded a few duds, he'd updated his personal calendar, he'd answered his messages, e-mails, voicemails, faxes. He'd checked his website, to make sure the designers had done the tweaking he had asked for. And all without leaving his chair. And now, the world was unrolling in his study. Life was grand.

He put down the remote and clasped his hands behind his head. At dead on seven, he knew, James would be in with his light supper. At dead on eight thirty, his rather beautiful companion would arrive and they would go for a cocktail somewhere stylish. He didn't like to be out long, so at eleven, he would drop her at her equally stylish apartment, and fifteen minutes later, would be ready for bed. Here, he would sleep dreamlessly until exactly six thirty, when he would be woken by James, to begin another perfectly ordered day.

With a martyred sigh, Michael Buerk was describing a tense day in Parliament. The Government was bringing in an unpopular bill. Since it didn't impinge on Benedict's life in the slightest, he turned the sound low and let the flickering images amuse him. The Leader of the Opposition was silently ranting and banging his desk. The camera panned back to show rows of MPs, all yelling, then the Speaker, shouting, he supposed, for order. Then the picture changed to the political editor, outside Parliament, earlier in the day to judge by the sun. As usual, a crowd had gathered and he thought the reporter was looking a little strained, although the story was by no means earth-shattering. Perhaps the crowd was bothering him. Benedict chuckled. He despised people who couldn't cope with their jobs.

But suddenly, he was on his feet. He rushed over to the television and practically pressed his nose against the screen. What was that... *thing* doing there? Over the political editor's shoulder, as plain as day, its bemused face staring vacuously at him? A goblin, that was what. A damned goblin, and not one of his.

Then it was gone. He sat back suddenly, yelling for James.

'Sire?' What was his master doing on the floor?

'James? Have you been watching the television?'

Oh, I see, James thought to himself. Checking up on me! Aloud, he said, 'Certainly not, Sire. I was preparing your supper.'

'Don't be paranoid, James,' snapped Benedict. 'I just wanted to know if you had seen the news.'

'I watched it earlier today, Sire. During my luncheon break.'

'Did they have the outside broadcast? From outside Parliament?'

'I believe not, Sire.'

'Where can I find a rerun of it?' Benedict muttered, pressing buttons at random. 'I need to see it again.'

'News 24, Sire, will have it on again shortly. You could watch for it on that.'

'Good thinking, James.'

'Sire.' James turned to go.

'No!' he grabbed his wrist. 'Stay here. I want you to watch it with me.'

The butler subsided onto the floor beside his master. He hadn't seen him this flustered in years. They led an orderly life, high above the City. A place for everything, and everything in its place. A time for everything, too, and the hairs on James's back and palms began to stand on end. He felt change in the air, and he wasn't sure it was going to be for the better.

Having found the right channel, Benedict relaxed a little, but didn't take his eyes off the screen.

'Er... what are we watching for, Sire?'

'I told you,' he snapped. 'An outside broadcast. From outside Parliament. Just shut up, now, and watch, will you?'

After a while, the scenes of Parliament which preceded the broadcast appeared on the screen. Benedict grabbed James' sleeve and leant forward.

'Watch,' he breathed. 'Watch behind the reporter's shoulder.'

'A little old lady?' ventured James.

'No, no, the *other* shoulder! Look! There!'

James let out a long, whistling breath. 'Well, I'll be!' he exclaimed. 'It's a goblin.'

Benedict let go of his arm and clambered back into his chair. He looked white and a little shaky. 'Well, at least I'm not losing it, James. You saw it too.'

'I certainly did, Sire. A little crude, I can't help thinking. Not like your own rather more sophisticated models.' He smoothed down his fur and smiled, showing all his teeth.

'What's going on?' Benedict muttered. 'Why would any goblin make himself visible, like that. I'll bet O.. .O...'

'Oberon,' concluded the butler, helpfully.

'I know,' snapped his master. 'Well, him, I'll bet he doesn't know about it.'

'I understood that he and his lady were no more, Sire.'

James was back in full butler mode now, regretting his little lapse earlier. But that goblin had been a shock.

'Really?' Benedict asked, snapping his head round. 'And who told you that?'

'Grapevine, Sire,' James muttered.

'Backstairs gossip,' Benedict dismissed it. 'I hate that. No, I'd heard they had diminished and were living in the Home Counties somewhere. I can just see Oberon and Titania as Lord and Lady of some decaying manor. Just suit him. Hunting, shooting, fishing.'

'My Lady Titania wouldn't allow any of that, Sire, would she?'

'No,' Benedict sighed. 'It's true she doesn't like hurting things. Not so much as a fly. Not so much as a wing off a fly....' His voice died away, lost in memories.

James coughed, a sound from prehistory.

'What?' Benedict looked up. 'Still here? Shouldn't you be getting our coats?'

'Coats, Sire? But surely, supper...? Lady Leanne...?'

'Yes, coats. Supper and Leanne can wait. She has her own amusements, she can fall back on those, as it were, tonight. And I'm never actually hungry, James. You know that. It's only ever for the look of the thing.'

'Yes, Sire.' He turned in the doorway. 'Ermm, where are we going, Sire?'

'Why, to Parliament Green, of course. To see if that goblin is still knocking about the place. We've let that goodie goodie lot slip from our minds, James. We must make a progress check.' He picked up his mobile and slipped it in his pocket. He clicked on his 'away from desk' icon on his email, switched on the answerphone and stood up, patting his pockets. 'Car keys?'

James let go a piercing whistle from between his pointed teeth. An answering bleep came from under an envelope on the desk. Benedict walked over to them and picked them up. Without turning he said, 'Oh, by the way, James. Can you put some clothes on, please? I still haven't forgotten that incident with the woman on the floor below.'

James looked stubborn. 'Well, what was she doing, getting

in the lift at that time of night? I wasn't expecting her.'

'She's allowed to get in the lift, James, whenever she wants. She was away for weeks, at that health farm. It cost me a fortune. I should have stopped your wages.'

'But you don't pay me wages, Sire.'

'True, true. Privileges, then. No more going out at night.'

'But, Sire...'

'Just be more careful, then. Meanwhile, get our coats. We won't be the only ones who saw that goblin. We'd better get moving. Call me when you've got the lift.'

'Sire,' said James out loud. In his head, he was muttering, pompous arse. I remember him when we lived in a cave. Sometimes, I wish we'd never left it.

'I heard that,' he heard his master's voice. 'Don't think I couldn't arrange it. With a nice boulder over the opening.'

James slammed the door and shrugged into some clothes; just for devilment, he chose the tartan anorak. It reminded his master of the Old Days and that always annoyed him. He hated clothes, they mussed up his fur and made him itch. And he had such a lovely pelt, everybody said so. Well, not said so, as such. But he was pretty sure that that was what they meant. If only they could talk! But he was almost certain that his current squeeze understood every word he said.

He went back into the study, carrying his master's coat. He was getting quite excited. More goblins! Perhaps he would meet a friend. He pulled the hood of his anorak well down over his face and pressed the button for the lift. You couldn't be too careful, living near to mortals. They got scared so easily, and all he'd wanted to do was make friends. Perhaps he shouldn't have jumped up like that, but old habits – and they were very old habits – died hard.

The lift arrived, mercifully empty, and he called his master. They went right down to the basement garage and got into their Bentley. It glided out onto the road, his master's hands firm on the wheel. James sighed happily. His master should get out more, stuck in his room, bent over his computer all the time. He lowered the window and sniffed the breeze. An adventure. Just like the Old Days.

19

Parliament Green was almost deserted when Titania, Oberon and Puck arrived, at about half past six. The commuters had gone, the dog walkers and lovers hadn't arrived. Everyone was, Puck hoped, at home watching the TV. He wasn't too happy with arithmetic, beyond 'two yoghurts and a semi-skimmed every other day except when that is a Wednesday', but he had done a rough working out in his head and had got the answer to either 2,000,000 or twenty faeries living in Greater London. If half of those were watching the news, and half of those the BBC, then they could expect... well, certainly *some* to arrive on Parliament Green during the course of the evening. He shoved his hands deep into his pockets and prepared for a long wait.

His original plan had been to split the three up and watch different sectors through the evening, finishing just before midnight, when the last train back to Guildford would leave from Waterloo. He was pretty sure that they would be able to get back under their own steam, but Titania was clearly tired and with Oberon's miniscule attention span, nothing was certain. If the worst came to the worst, they could sleep out, but it was getting cold these nights, and they were all out of practice. So he was planning on the train.

The plan he put into operation, however, was for Oberon and Titania to patrol together. His Lord had been showing definite signs of wandering over the course of the afternoon, and His Lady was getting crosser on a corresponding scale. So, they were walking the perimeter, he was watching near the building, where the broadcast had actually been filmed.

Glancing across, he could see their figures now, arm in arm, silhouetted against the glow of the streetlights. He walked over and looked out over the Embankment. A few slow boats were moving downstream, one of them brightly lit. Music and laughter wafted from it and he was reminded of the royal barges of the Old days. Unseen and unsuspected, he had often ridden them as they plied the waterway, sometimes cleaner, sometimes dirtier than now. He had picked sugar plums, sipped wine from a lady's glass, watched assignations that no mortal ever knew had happened.

His ears began to buzz. Looking to his left, he saw a woman, walking quickly, talking into a phone. His head ached and his eyes wouldn't focus so well, but he was sure he had seen her before As she came into view, and earshot, he could just catch through the buzzing, fragments of her conversation.

'Well, I'm on the Embankment now... Why not...? There's someone in the way, otherwise I could probably see you, I'm so close... Don't treat me like a fool, Ben... I've got to talk to you, anyway... No, it won't keep... Because I'd forgotten most of it. .. .Now I'm beginning to rem...'

She took the phone away from her ear and looked at its display in disbelief. She shook it and shouted into it, 'Ben? Ben? You total bastard!' She flipped it shut and in a sudden petulant gesture, drew back her arm and threw it into the river.

Puck was shocked. He had always had the impression that mortals treated those things like gold. Always had them with them, went mad if they were lost. And now, she had thrown it away. He had heard the splash. He looked back to where she had been a moment ago, to check her reaction, but she had gone.

'Hello,' a voice suddenly purred in his ear. He straightened up, and found himself inches from the woman from the river path. How could she have moved so fast? The buzzing in his ears was replaced by a drumming, of hot blood racing round.

She had red-gold hair, tumbling over one shoulder, and strange, cat-like eyes. When she smiled, her teeth looked slightly pointed, but not so much that it made her unattractive. She seemed faintly familiar.

'Waiting for someone?' she whispered, stroking his hair back from his face with slender fingers. He felt her sharp nails lightly graze his temple. Suddenly, she stopped. He grimaced with pain as she grabbed one of his ears tightly and wrenched his head back.

'Ow!' he cried. 'That hurts!'

'Puck!' she spat. 'What are you doing here?'

He jerked his head back to focus on her better, to take in the whole. Now he looked properly, she was unmistakeable. The sinuous body, every muscled curve showing through the clothes. The eyes, the teeth, the nails.

'Leannan-Sidhe,' he breathed.

'The same,' she said, throwing his head to one side viciously. 'But I prefer Leanne these days. More in-keeping.'

'With what?'

'The image. City girl about town. Professional single lady. You know the kind of thing.'

'Is that what they call vampires these days, then?'

'Theatrical agent, dear. That's what I do.'

'Come on,' said Puck, derisively. 'I don't believe you've gone completely native.'

'Well,' she licked her lips. 'A girl has to have her fun. But you're all right, dear one,' she said, chucking him under the chin, taking care to keep her claws sheathed. 'I've never enjoyed the taste. A bit... musty, I've always thought. Like chewing a moth. But you haven't told me what you're doing here,' she said, narrowing her eyes.

'Ah, you know,' said Puck, lightly, throwing up his arms. 'This. That. Just out for a stroll.'

'London based, are you?' she asked, lighting a cigarette and blowing smoke into his face.

'No, not really,' he said, coughing gently. 'Nearby. Makes a change, though.' He smiled vaguely in the direction of the river, Big Ben. 'Bit of sightseeing.'

'I see. A tourist.' She suddenly grabbed his wrist and bent

it back, so that he nearly overbalanced. His goblins jumped for safety. It would hurt if he landed on them, almost weightless though he was. 'And you have friends with you,' she smiled down at them. 'How sweet.' They tried to creep away. 'Stay right there!' she ordered, and they sidled back, to be as near to Puck as possible. The world was big and scary, suddenly. They didn't quite know where they were, and an Unseelie vampire was on the loose. They never thought they'd say it, but how they wished they were back behind the wallpaper in Number Thirteen, Ellesmere Crescent.

She drew on her cigarette and the tip glowed brightly. 'I'm going to have a guess,' she breathed out, with the smoke. 'I think you saw that goblin on the news. I think you're here to see what's going on. I don't think you'll have thought of that yourself. I think it must be Titania. Oberon's too stupid.' She released his arm and he rubbed it to get the blood flowing again. She looked around.

'Yes,' he nodded, frantically, looking down at the goblins, encouraging them to join in.

'Yeth,' said Thydney. 'That'th right.'

'Yuk,' she said, giving Thydney a kick. 'He's repulsive! He's wet my leg.'

'Thorry,' Thydney said, contrite. He huddled up to Bertie and they looked very frightened indeed. Puck rounded on her.

'Leave him alone,' he shouted. 'He's done nothing to you. Why don't you clear off and do whatever it is you do. You've obviously managed all right without us, so just go away.'

'Oh, no,' she said, menacingly. 'I admit, that was my first, my gut reaction. But Ben is interested, so that makes me interested. He doesn't usually come out, so it must be important.'

'Who's Ben?'

'Don't you... oh, of course. He wasn't called that when you knew him last. The Dark Lord of the Unseelie Court, Monarch of the Glen, as our more unruly goblins called him, is now known as Benedict Macadam.'

Puck reeled back. A mortal name. For the Dark Lord? 'Why?' he asked, dumbstruck.

'Because,' she said patiently, taking his arm and leading him off across the grass, the goblins trying hard to stay in their shadow, 'because when you are buying and selling, wheeling and dealing, mortals think it's odd if you haven't got a name. Lots of them *pretend* not to have names, of course, but they have got them. Their wives, girlfriends, business partners, call them something. When you're starting out, you have to introduce yourself as something.' She put on a voice she thought sounded like a banker. 'I am Claude Poshness. And you are?... oh, Dark Lord of the Unseelie Court, but I can call you Sire? Get out!' She gave his arm a squeeze. 'See the problem?'

Puck nodded. He could see Oberon and Titania, standing on the pavement, looking towards a dark, sleek car, parking a few hundred yards away. They were in earnest conversation and Titania was glancing anxiously back over her shoulder. When she saw Puck, she broke away from Oberon and came skimming over the grass towards him.

'She's still very beautiful,' muttered Leanne.

Titania pulled up short when she saw the Unseelie, with its arm through Puck's.

The vampire got in first. 'Yes, Queen,' she said, holding up her hand. 'It *is* Leanan-Sidhe. But I prefer Leanne. Yes, it's been ages. Yes, I've done well for myself. I thought you were gone, until the other night.'

'The other night?' Titania asked, touching down lightly on one delicate toe. She had allowed her hair to flow out around her head and she looked very royal.

'Yes,' said Leanne dismissively. 'Oh, the old man didn't tell you, I suppose. Hmph, typical.' She looked a little wistful. 'Mind you, I can't remember everything.' She brightened. 'But the bits I *do* remember, they were very good bits.' She looked the Queen directly in the face and folded her arms defiantly.

Freed from her grip, Puck sprang to Titania's side, leaving the goblins to cover the ground as best they may. 'Take no notice, Mistress. That doesn't matter. But this does. Listen – the Dark...' but before he could finish, they heard a car door slam expensively shut. They heard, unnaturally loud, the click of expensive shoes on the pavement.

'He's here,' breathed Leanne.

Puck and Titania spun round. Oberon stood where Titania had left him, staring at the figure approaching him from the car. The walk seemed to take forever as the two Lords, Dark and Light, came together on the edge of the green.

Everything seemed to stand still, as if there wasn't enough energy spare for the light, the air, leaves spiralling down from the plane trees to move in the vicinity of the faerie kings. What greatness would fill the city skies? What creatures of air and darkness would materialise to witness this great meeting? The City held its breath. The faerie watchers, down to the tiniest goblin, waited.

'Hello,' said Oberon, stiffly.

Benedict nodded and muttered, 'Hello, y'sel.'

'Long time, no see,' Oberon added.

'Right enough,' the Dark Lord agreed. His Scots accent had broadened in the presence of his lighter half. They stood, facing each other, in silence. The spell was broken and Titania and Puck, with Leanne, with the goblins scampering at her heels, bringing up the rear, hurried over to them. They took their places, at their respective Lord's elbow, factions facing each other on a city street.

The goblins jumped about excitedly. They outnumbered the Unseelies by, ooh, loads. So, what if he could drive a car? What if she could drive a car? Their Lord could *fly*. And the other lot didn't seem to have any goblins. Even Bill felt very superior. They looked over at the low machine pulled up onto the kerb. The passenger door opened and a dark shape slid out. It straightened up and slunk over to stand at Benedict's side.

He turned to it. 'Ah, James,' he said. 'Perfect timing. I was forgetting myself a little, there. Everyone, this is James. My butler.'

Titania gave the thing a piercing look. It was taller than an average goblin, but clearly a goblin, nonetheless. Despite his anorak hood pulled down low, it was clear from his deep set eyes under shaggy brows, and a nose tending to damp, that his master had found his inspiration among the hounds of his dank Highland castle. It was a Bogle, a nasty piece of work, much given to creating mindless damage in cottage kitchens, making chimneys smoke and turning horses in stables. It didn't strike her as the obvious choice for domestic help. She had spent one rather uneasy evening in the company of the Dark Lord, an evening over which they were both happy to draw a veil, and this creature was definitely there then, creeping around in the shadows and flicking globs of porridge at the unsuspecting.

'You used to be known as Jimmy, didn't you?' she asked it.

It ducked its head and muttered, 'Yeah.'

Leanne couldn't keep out of it. 'Well,' she said, archly, to Benedict. 'You didn't want me around, but you brought him with you. I wonder you dare let him out at night. You know how he carries on!'

'James knows how to behave in company,' Benedict said smoothly. 'We haven't had any trouble for weeks.' He turned an innocent smile on Oberon. 'What are yours based on? Pigs, is it?'

'And chickens,' Oberon added, ushering Bill forward. 'It was Bill you saw on the television news. At least, I expect that's why you're here.'

'I didn't know that you were behind it, my Lord O.. .O...'

'Oberon,' finished James, happily.

Benedict turned on him. 'I know, I know,' he said.

'Still having a bit of trouble with using his name, I see,' said Titania.

Benedict laughed with a hollow sound, 'A bit out of practice, my Lady,' he said. 'I didn't think we'd be meeting again.'

'We heard you were dead,' James said happily, smiling round at the company. 'Gone to dust.'

'Gone to dust?' Titania spat. 'The King and Queen of Faerie?' Her eyes sparked and James had the presence of mind to hide behind Leanne, paws on her shoulders.

She shook him off. 'Don't hide behind me, you coward,' she said. 'Fight your own battles, you great hairy thing.'

'More a case of *a* King, isn't it?' asked Benedict coolly.

Oberon grew taller, more dreadful. He fixed Benedict with a glare that would have fried any mortal or goblin in its path. '*A* King? I should say not. I was always considered The King of Faerie.'

'By whom?' Benedict asked, mildly. He spread his arms. 'Look around. See any signs of the Faerie Rade, cantering over the greensward?' He shaded his eyes theatrically and looked from horizon to horizon. 'Hmm, no, 'fraid not. Face it, Lord, you're finished.'

Oberon looked down on him in a condescending way. 'I don't notice you surrounded by your Horde,' he smirked. 'And after all, it is dark, their natural time to be out and about.'

'Just because you don't see them, doesn't mean they aren't here,' Benedict said. 'In fact, my Horde are all around. In almost every home, you'll find at least one of my Folk. In every shop, in every street, they're there.'

Puck stepped forward. 'Is that what Freckles was talking about, Lord?' he asked Oberon. 'Wind where there's no wind, light where there's no light.'

Before Oberon could answer, Benedict was nodding gleefully. 'That's my lads,' he said. 'Every phone, fax, PC, every piece of technology that they have gathered about them, each one has one of my lads. Mortals even have names for them, though they've never seen one. Gremlins, they're called. Posh mortals call them *deus ex machina*.'

Puck thought he'd call his bluff. 'Go on, then, let's see them.'

The Unseelie Court, all three of them, didn't reply. Puck knew that, had Oberon had a Rade that size, he wouldn't have been able to resist summoning them, with a click of his fingers and a wave of his arm. 'Go on,' he goaded. 'I bet you can't.'

Leanne answered. 'No, he can't.'

Benedict spun round on his heel, eyes blazing.

'Well,' she continued. 'You can't, can you?' She turned to the others. 'They're tied, more or less, to the thing they accompany. They can't move far from a source of power, battery or mains, without fading. Also, they don't have enough strength to be visible. Well done to Chuckles, or whatever...'

'Freckles,' the goblin said, stepping forward, 'if you don't mind, Lady.'

'Freckles, then, for spotting them at all.'

'It's a glitch,' said Benedict stubbornly. 'I'm working on it.'

'So, you know about computers, and things,' asked Titania, impressed despite herself.

'Oh, yes,' he replied. 'It's my business. I run computer companies; software, hardware, programming, websites, ISPs, you name it,' there was no chance that they could, so he continued, 'I'm there.'

'We've never really got to grips...' Oberon said, humbly. 'But,' he brightened, 'I can fly again. And I can open doors.'

'I can do those,' Benedict snorted.

'With planes and keys,' Puck said. 'Any mortal can do that.'

'Whatever. Anyway, you haven't explained how you came to let young Beakie here appear on the news. Wasn't it a bit of a risk, discovery-wise?'

'But we *want* to be discovered!' Titania cried. 'We thought that, if a few of our Folk saw us, they might come here to find us. We could spread the word. We're on our way back to the top. But, then,' her face fell and the faint glow which had surrounded her dimmed a little, 'only you turned up. We thought you were diminished, too. We weren't expecting you at all.'

Leanne looked through narrowed eyes at Oberon. Details were beginning to come back to her. She pointed at the King. 'He at least should have expected something,' she said. 'After the other night.'

'The. Other. Night.' Titania said, her words falling like stones.

'Er... didn't I tell you, beloved?' Oberon began. 'It... it wasn't anything, not really.'

'Not anything?' said Leanne, staring forward.

Oberon held up his hands to them both. 'Well, something, of course,' he said to the vampire, 'And, on the other hand,' he turned to his Queen, 'Nothing.'

They didn't reply and the silence was deafening.

'Puck?' he said. 'Puck? Help?'

But Puck wasn't listening. 'Yes, yes,' he flapped a dismissive hand. He'd heard this conversation so many times over the years. They'd be all right. But, meanwhile, over by a low-growing herbaceous border cut into the grass, he could see a small figure, trying to both hide and be seen all at once. 'What's that?' he said, pointing.

They all peered into the gloom, but could see no details. Whatever it was wasn't too tall, and appeared to be dressed in a long, brown coat which nearly swept the ground. The goblins sniffed the air, their sense of smell being more acute than their sight. Bill turned his head one way and another, trying to get the little person into focus. It was Puck who recognised him first.

'Hey!' he called, and waved. The figure shrank back a little. 'Hey, Mr Dobie. Over here.'

'It's not Mr Dobie, surely?' said Titania. 'Fancy him still being around.'

But, sure enough, the figure detached itself from the shade of a litter bin and slowly, shyly made its way across the grass.

20

Titania turned urgently to Benedict. 'Please,' she said, touching his sleeve lightly and looking up meltingly into his eyes. 'Can you just give us a bit of space? Mr Dobie is terribly shy. It must have been very hard for him to make the decision to come here tonight.'

Benedict looked at Mr Dobie with contempt. 'Call that a faerie?' he asked.

'Strictly speaking, he's a brownie,' said Titania. 'But really, terribly shy. Look, we'll stay in touch, shall we?'

'How?' asked Leanne, reasonably. 'I don't expect for a minute that you're on the phone.'

'Well, there is one,' Titania said dubiously, 'But we never use it. None of us can remember the number.'

'What's your address, then?'

'Thirteen, Ellesmere Crescent, Guildford,' Puck interrupted. 'See you there, perhaps. Now, will you please go? You're making Mr Dobie nervous.'

The small Unseelie Court retreated to Benedict's car. There was a slight scuffle as James objected to going in the back, but they were soon on their way. The last the others saw of them was James' tongue making a slimy mess of the back window. The last they heard was a faint cry of 'Down, James,' before the roar of the engine drowned the voice and then died away.

The brownie stood there shyly, head down and one toe

drawing an invisible pattern on the pavement. The goblins had gathered round and were tentatively patting him and saying, 'Hello, Mr Dobie,' and, in Freckles' case, 'Wotcher, mate.'

Titania walked over and looked down at him fondly. Mr Dobie was a gentle soul, and he'd always been knocking about, as it were, but his speciality – the care of old men, in particular – and hers – men, in general – had never really crossed. He looked up briefly but was then overcome with confusion. He'd never been this near to the Queen before. He didn't even know she knew his name.

Oberon clapped him on the back and said, 'Glad to have you join us, old chap.' Mr Dobie blushed some more.

'Saw you on the telly,' he said, in a surprisingly dark brown voice, which sounded rusty with lack of use. He pointed to Bill. 'Thought I'd come and see what was going on.'

Puck turned a somersault with pure delight, and didn't notice when he went round three times without touching the ground. A passenger in a taxi going by did notice, however.

'Driver,' he said. 'Not Planet Hollywood, after all. I think I'll just go home, please.'

The cabbie sighed. He had been interrupted in mid flow in a particularly vitriolic rant against the government, and he'd totally lost his thread, now. What a good job his fare was going all the way to Dulwich. He'd have plenty of time to get back into his monologue.

Titania craned her neck round, her eyes meeting those of the startled man. 'I think,' she said, 'that unless we want to blow our cover before we're ready, that we all ought to calm down and get ourselves back home.' She put a friendly hand on Mr Dobie's shoulder. 'You *are* coming back with us, aren't you?' she said.

Mr Dobie screwed his hands together with embarrassment and delight. 'Can I?' he asked, huskily, looking round at every face.

'Glad to have you,' boomed Oberon, annoyingly stuck in King mode.

'Love you to,' said Puck, smiling. To Titania, he said quietly, 'I don't have to share with him, do I?'

She nudged him excitedly. 'If you have to,' she said. 'Who knows, we might have *hundreds* more, yet. I think Freckles and Tiny should stay a while longer, just to make sure no one else comes.'

Tiny overheard. 'Why me?' he said. 'I'm the littlest and so you can't expect me to do anything, Mistress. What if something horrible from the other lot turns up. What if the Fachan turns up? Black Annis? Jenny...'

'You're frightening yourself unnecessarily, Tiny,' Puck reassured him. 'None of that lot will be out without Benedict's say so. Anyway, a twelve foot, one legged giant would be a bit noticeable, wouldn't you say?'

'He could be in disguise,' muttered Tiny.

'All right, a twelve foot, one legged giant disguised as a rabbit would be a bit noticeable, wouldn't you say? Anyway, I'll just get the Master, Mistress and Mr Dobie safely home, and then I'll come back for you.'

'There won't be any trains, not by that time,' protested Tiny. 'We'll have to wait all night and then hide in the morning. What if any of our Folk turn up? What'll we do with them?'

'If they do, we'll tell them what's happenin',' said Freckles, joining in. 'It'll be a good larf, Tine. Don't worry.' He looked at Puck. 'How will you get back, though?'

Puck clasped his hands and then thrust out his arms straight, cracking the knuckles. 'I don't know,' he said, 'It's a lovely night. I fancy a bit of a fly.' He jumped in the air and floated down like a dandelion seed, caught on a faerie's breath.

'Oh, Puck,' cried Titania. She grabbed him and hugged him. 'You're my favourite elf in the whole world – in both worlds!' She gave him a very un-Queenly kiss, interrupted finally by Oberon's cough.

'Glad you're pleased, Madam,' he said, coldly. 'Perhaps we ought to be getting on.'

'Don't cough at me, Oberon,' she said, tossing her head. 'I shall want details about The Other Night when we get back.'

Oberon smirked behind her. She turned to face him. 'And don't think you can lie to me. I always know.'

He smirked again.

'Smirk all you like. I always know – it's just that sometimes, I choose not to let it show.'

Oberon was crestfallen. Now he'd never know for certain.

Tiny and Freckles took shelter behind the litter bin where they had first seen Mr Dobie. The others swept off in the direction of the station, the remaining goblins hopping up, trying to catch hold of a fold of coat as it swirled past their ears. Eventually, they made a moderately conventional group, making its way, a touch fast possibly, along the road. They suddenly felt very, very lonely.

'I'm scared,' Tiny whispered.

Freckles took on the role of big strong goblin. 'You'll be all right,' he said, unconvincingly. 'What about old Squeaky, eh? All by himself, in that other park?'

Tiny nodded. Although he felt sorry for Squeaky, he wasn't sorry he wasn't right here, right now. Squeaky had an unpleasant habit of undermining the rest of them, making them feel nothing was worthwhile. Tiny couldn't help but think that all Squeaky wanted was to be like the mortals. Only better.

'What do we do,' he asked, 'if we see any of our Folk?'

'Well,' said Freckles. 'First off, we have to check that they really are one of us.'

'How?'

Freckles hadn't really thought this one out too well. 'Well... we recognised Mr Dobie all right, din' we?'

'Er... yes. Puck recognized Mr Dobie.'

'Dun't matter, dun't matter. I've got me eye in, now. I fink we're capable of spotting any ovver faerie wot turns up.' He adopted an alert pose, scanning the edges of the green.

More mortals were out now, strolling in pairs through the unexpectedly lovely evening, walking city dogs, pooper scoopers at the ready. They all were purposeful, with somewhere to go, even if that somewhere was nowhere. No one ambled. No one seemed to be looking out to see what they could see. No one, in short, was behaving like a lost faerie.

'Bit of a shock, that, wasn't it?' Tiny said, suddenly, making Freckles jump and clutch his chest.

'What was?' Freckles cried, over the thumping of his heart.

'That lot, that Unseelie lot, turning up like that.'

'Well, we knew about Leanan-Sidhe.'

'Yes, but the Lord! What about him, eh? That car and everything?'

'And old Jimmy, as well. Done up like a dog's dinner.'

'I like that,' said Tiny. 'Dog's dinner!'

'It's the way I tell 'em,' laughed Freckles, who had made the joke completely by accident. He went back to scanning the horizon. Tiny giggled and punched Freckles weakly on the arm. Freckles punched him back, stifling a laugh.

'I hate goblins who laugh at their own jokes,' choked Tiny, and pushed him over, good naturedly. Before long, they were tumbling over and over on the grass, punching and giggling uncontrollably.

'Oh, how like goblins!' a censorious voice said, nearby. 'Or should one say, how like pigs?'

They leapt apart and looked around frantically, looking for the source of the voice.

Against the litter bin leant an elegant figure, clothed in what looked like a one piece, tightly fitting skin, the colour of tree bark, which looked wet and shiny. Over it, it wore a cloak, green and textured like woven leaves and on its head it wore a hard-looking hat, in the shape of a half-nut.

'One has been watching for some time,' the voice continued, 'and one has come to the conclusion that if one didn't intervene, you two... it bridled and its voice trembled a little... 'things would give one's game away entirely.' It bent up an elegant arm and began to inspect the nails on one twiggy hand. It seemed to have finished, so Tiny spoke.

'What are you?'

'What? How common you are. Surely, *who* would be more polite?'

'Who, then?'

'Ah, introductions! One was beginning to despair.' It extended a languid arm, sinewy and strong under its bark coating. 'I,' it spread the fingers of its other hand over its narrow chest, '*I* am the spirit of that hazel tree, yonder. Past its best now, poor thing... pollution, you know. But, home, none-theless. And you are...?'

'Tiny,' Tiny said, reaching up and pressing his trotter against the birch spirit's twigs.

'Dear thing, indeed. But your name is...?'

'Tiny,' said Tiny.

'Ah, how sweet.' The spirit turned towards Freckles. 'Now, don't tell me, don't tell me. Let one guess. Er... Ugly!' The smooth brown face under the curious hat split in a grin, showing the colour of a newly peeled stick beneath the crack-ing bark.

'Freckles,' growled Freckles, putting his trotters firmly be-hind his back.

The creature bent in the middle, suddenly, like a tree in a gale. 'One apologises,' he said quietly. 'One doesn't get about much, and one is out of practice at social niceties.'

'S'orlright,' muttered Freckles.

'A mistake anyone could make,' added Tiny, brightly. 'But may I ask why you're out here like this? You can't have seen the television broadcast, surely?'

'Television,' said the spirit slowly, as if tasting the word for the first time. 'You are quite right, dear thing, one has indeed no access to the television. But, out here on one's own, one learns to watch, as it were. And there has been a lot of very strange behaviour on this green tonight.'

'Such as?' Freckles said, suspiciously.

'Such as,' said the tree spirit, drawing itself up, 'The King and Queen of Faerie, *and* the Dark Lord of the Unseelie and his ghastly Mistress, *and* a load of goblins and a bogle, not to mention dear old Mr Dobie, all gathered in one spot on the pavement, having a conversation.' It folded its hands smugly across its middle. 'Not something one sees every day, one is sure you chaps will agree.' It smiled again and looked en-couragingly from one to the other.

'You've got us there, .. .er, do you have a name as well?'

The tree spirit looked confused. 'Why, Hazel, of course,' it replied.

'Doesn't that make it rather confusing, you know, when you meet other Hazels?'

'No. Should it?'

Tiny and Freckles exchanged a look. 'No, no,' Tiny said, hurriedly. 'Not at all. Well, ...may I call you Hazel?'

Hazel inclined several degrees and smiled encouragingly.

'Hazel, you seem to have seen everything. Titania and Oberon, the King and Queen, are trying to gather our Folk together. We have become a bit spread out in the last few hundred years, and some of us have gone altogether.' He pressed his lips together to stifle a sob. Poor Cobweb. 'But the Lady is ready for action again, so we planted...'

'Ah, good plan,' said Hazel, nodding approvingly.

'Er... planted a goblin on a television broadcast and we're here, waiting to see if any of our Folk saw it and maybe turn up here.'

'And so far,' Hazel précised the situation, 'Only Mr Dobie has turned up.'

'And you,' said Tiny.

The spirit laughed, a rustling sound. 'Yes, and, of course, one!'

Freckles spoke. 'You talk nice, Hazel,' he said, impressed.

Hazel swept its hand over its head and patted the hat back into place. 'One does one's best,' it said, modestly. 'One's tree is after all the repository of knowledge. But of course, one is sure that you knew that.'

They didn't.

'One tries to set a good example, but really, some of these shrubs have spirits that are really not quite up to one's standard. Conversation is almost impossible.' It stepped forward and put an arm round each goblin. The weight was considerable and they buckled at the knees.

'Cor,' Freckles said, 'you're heavy for your size.'

'One carries the essence of one's tree around with one,' sighed Hazel. 'Sorry.'

'Don't worry,' Tiny said. 'I think you might turn out to be very useful.'

'How?' asked Freckles rudely. 'Stuck in this park, in'e?'

'By no means, my dear fellow,' rustled Hazel. 'One can move about.'

'Yeah, I mean, I know you're over here, when your tree is

over *there*. But I'm talking about getting to Guildford.'

'It sounds delightful,' Hazel said, closing its eyes and throwing back its head. 'Positively sylvan.' It sighed, like a soft breeze.

'Er... perhaps,' said Freckles, having no clue what the stuck up thing was going on about.

'Anyway,' the spirit clapped its hands and stood up straight. 'One can go anywhere, provided one is provided with a piece of one's tree. So,' it bent down and patted Tiny in the small of the back, to encourage him on his way, 'trot over there, dear chap, and break off a branch, Gently, though. No damage, one begs.'

Looking furtively from left to right, Tiny legged it across the open space, a blur in the blackness. He jumped up and broke off a twig, which he brought back to the tree spirit.

'Ow,' complained Hazel. 'One doesn't like to make a fuss, but that always stings. No matter. One can follow you anywhere now.'

'Oh, good,' muttered Freckles, already fed up with it. Had it swallowed a dictionary, or what? 'We've got to wait for Puck, now,' he explained. 'Then we can join the others.'

They crouched down behind the litter bin, keeping an eye out for any more faerie, but the next one they saw was Puck, spiralling down from the orange backlit sky.

'Hazel!' he said. 'Long time, no see.'

'Puck, old fellow!' cried the spirit. 'One hasn't seen you since one was a sapling.'

Puck slapped him at the back of his slender trunk, and said, 'Into the twig, Hazel,' he said. 'Guys, hop up. We're off. If we time it right, Master and Mistress will have finished their argument and made it up again.'

'Poor Mr Dobie,' said Tiny, as he snuggled down into Puck's coat lining. 'He'll wonder what he's let himself in for.'

Puck hopped twice, getting used to the extra weight, and then soared away over the trees, heading South West to Ellesmere Crescent.

'One is so excited,' said the twig.

'Oh, bog off,' muttered Freckles.

21

As Puck flew – high enough to not be visible, low enough to miss aircraft coming in to Heathrow and Gatwick – he mulled over the train journey. It hadn't been too bad, all things being considered; the atmosphere between the King and Queen was just a touch frosty, but she had been concentrating on making Mr Dobie feel at home, and so Oberon had folded his arms and pretended to sleep. The train, being the one used by home-going theatre-goers, had been full, with a particularly thick gaggle of women finding it necessary to stand just near their seats, looking dotingly at Oberon, or Puck if their view of Oberon was impeded. Titania got the occasional jealous glance, but she was with the funny little old guy, so obviously she was no competition.

Puck had shepherded them off the train at Guildford with a grateful sigh. Mr Dobie was looking around him dazedly. Before his dash up to London from the Sussex countryside to try and find more of his kind, he had never really been into a large town before. He usually hung around in villages, looking after the oldest inhabitant, or, more recently, in sheltered accommodation, keeping the old folks company. He had heard a rumour, from a Mr Dobie in a neighbouring village, that there was a place in London full of little old men who wore red clothes – such a cheerful colour, Mr Dobie thought – but he reckoned that if they were in London, they probably had plenty of company already.

He didn't know why he'd just dropped everything to dash up to the Big City. He felt a bit lonely. The Mr Dobie Socials which they used to have in the Old Days hadn't happened for decades now. He had only met another Mr Dobie by accident once or twice, on the road, or in the corridors of Dunroamin or Twilight Villa. He just needed... well, friends. He wasn't as young as he was.

And now, here he was, being ushered by the Queen herself into her very own home. Humble enough, he could see, but still... And the King himself, offering to take his coat, sitting him down. And all those goblins, such friendly little chaps, although a bit boisterous for his taste, perhaps. And Puck. Everybody's favourite. Puck, who had been so kind to him, who had spotted him first, as he hid shyly by the litter bin. Puck, who had been so excited to see him, he had turned a triple somersault.

But the excitement was beginning to take its toll and he was nodding off in the chair before he knew it. So Puck had taken him upstairs and had given him his very own bed, before flying off to get the others. Mr Dobie was happy. He snuggled down, pulled the covers up to his little wrinkly ears, and slept like a log.

As soon as Puck had gone and with Mr Dobie asleep upstairs, Titania and Oberon, with a withering glance at the goblins which sent them scurrying for cover, got down to the business of a bloody good row.

'So,' she began, as was her privilege. 'The Other Night, eh?'

'Ahah,' Oberon began, his breath caught in his throat. 'I told you about that, surely?'

'No.' A snowflake swirled out on her breath and softly landed on Oberon's cheek, where it melted with a miniscule sizzle.

'Oh, well, nothing to tell, that's why,' said Oberon heartily. He clapped his hands on his knees and pushed himself up from the sofa. 'I'm glad we've had this little chat. Clear the air, eh?'

'Sit!'

His knees gave way and he sat.

'Let me tell you what I think happened,' she said. 'On the way to fetch Puck and Cobweb, you met Leanan-Sidhe.'

'She prefers Leanne.'

'Leanan-Sidhe. She gave you a lift, I expect. Something like that. One thing led to another. And another. And then you decided not to tell me.'

'No, no,' said Oberon, desperately. 'Well, yes, but only so she would take me to Puck. We'd never have got there otherwise, would we, boys?' The wall stayed resolutely silent.

'Well, we wouldn't. I couldn't let her know why we needed to get to Woodford Thingie. I didn't have a clue how to get there myself. I thought... if I gave her something else to concentrate on, as it were, she'd forget the whole thing. I used a bit of glamour, a bit of...'

Titania held up her hand and turned her head away. 'I don't want gory details,' she shuddered. 'Just the excuses will suffice.'

'No, really,' he slid across the sofa and slithered onto the floor to land with his head in her lap. Her fingers began to play with his curls, almost automatically. He gave himself an internal thumbs up. This was a good sign. 'I only did it for the good of the Plan. Otherwise,' trump card coming up, 'Otherwise, we'd not have Puck with us, even now. And just look how useful he's been. We wouldn't have got anywhere without him, now, would we?' he twisted his head round, to look up into her face. 'Eh? Titania? Would we?'

She didn't answer for a moment, just carried on playing with his hair. Then she came to a decision. She gave one curl a tug, and then said, 'All right. Last chance, though. No more of it. You know what she's like.'

Oberon looked innocent. 'Oh dear me, yes,' he said, hiding his grin in her skirt. But at the back of his mind, there was now that teensy doubt. Was she taken in? Was *she* taking *him* in. He'd always wondered about that time she was North of the Border. Never mind. Save that one for next time. Time to change the subject. He sat up.

'I wonder how old Tiny and Freckles are getting on?'

Titania shrugged. 'Who knows?'

He turned her face to his. 'Don't get fed up. We've got Mr

Dobie.'

She gave him an indulgent smile. 'Not the brightest sandwich at the picnic, though, is he? Do you remember what the faerie nursemaids would call the babies if they did something silly?'

'Er... Dobie?'

'Correct. But,' and she heaved a sigh and dropped her voice, 'he is quite a sweetie, and he isn't any trouble.'

'And he *is* a faerie,' encouraged Oberon.

'Well, a brownie.'

'Don't split hairs. He's one of Ours, and that's the main thing. With that other lot out there, able to work all sorts of things, and with one of their goblins on every machine, we need all the help we can get, even if it is only from a brownie. At the very least, he can get out a bit and find some more. He's an inoffensive little creature. Very likeable.'

'You're right,' Titania said. 'Are we going to wait for the others?'

'Do you want to?' he said.

'I could do with a hug.'

'All right, then,' he said, moving in nearer.

'Just a hug. I haven't forgotten the vampire thing yet.'

He whispered in her ear.

'I keep telling you. There was nothing in it.'

He took her hand and they went up the stairs.

'And anyway,' she whispered to herself. 'It was a long, long time ago. In the Old Days.'

✦ ✦ ✦ ✦ ✦

Puck touched down on the path outside Number Thirteen and shook the goblins out of his coat. He put the twig down gratefully – it seemed to weigh a ton. Hazel stepped sideways and picked the piece of wood up.

'Thank you so much, Puck, old man,' he said. 'Probably the smoothest flight one has ever had.'

'Fly a lot, do they, trees?' asked Freckles, sarcastically.

'Figure of speech, figure of speech,' said Hazel crossly. To

Puck, he said, 'These goblins have no social graces, do they?'

Puck smiled down at them. He had quite a soft spot for them, really. They had stuck by the Master and Mistress through thick and thin. It couldn't only be because they liked beating Oberon at cards. 'They're good lads,' he said. He tried to click his fingers, but no luck.

'She's probably left it on the latch for you,' said Tiny. 'Try it.'

Sure enough, the door swung open and they tiptoed inside.

'You lads get off to bed,' said Puck, quietly. 'I'll be on the sofa, Mr Dobie has my bed. Poor old thing was shattered. Hazel, presumably you...?'

'One doesn't need anywhere special, dear boy,' intoned Hazel. 'Although my twig could probably benefit from a drop of nice fresh H20.'

'Get that, Freckles, will you?' said Puck, 'before you go off to sleep.'

'I would if I knew what it was the poncy great thing wanted,' complained Freckles.

'Water, dear boy. A soupcon of fresh water. Spring, if you have it. Tap if not.'

'Ice and a slice?' Freckles asked, straight faced.

'Too kind,' said Hazel. 'But no. Straight as it comes will be more than a sufficiency.'

Freckles hefted the incredibly heavy stick over his shoulder and a tap was heard running in the kitchen.

''S'on the windersill, all right?' he said, coming back into the room.

'South facing?' asked Hazel, arching an elegant lichen eyebrow.

'Of course,' said Freckles, with an ironic bow.

'Lovely,' said Hazel, leaning against the wall and closing his eyes. He opened them again, suddenly. 'One doesn't sleep, of course. But one finds it beneficial to close one's eyes.' He began to snore gently, a sound like a slow march on gravel.

Tiny and Freckles merged into the wall.

''Ere,' Puck heard Freckles say to Tiny, as he settled down.

'What?'

'What's brown and sticky?'

Bearing in mind Bill's habits, the answers were many. But Tiny obediently replied. 'I don't know, what is brown and sticky.'

Freckles snorted with laughter. 'A stick,' he said.

Puck fell asleep to muffled bangs and shouts of 'Get off,' 'Shut up,' 'Squawk,' and 'Ow!'

22

Despite the excitements of the night before, Puck was, as usual, first up. He was in the kitchen, drinking a glass of milk, when Titania swept in, pointing back through the doorway.

'Puck,' she said, almost trembling with excitement. 'There's a tree spirit leaning against the wall through there.'

He smiled at her, and wiped the milk moustache away with his sleeve. 'There is indeed, Mistress. He approached the guys last night; he saw all of us on the green, and wandered over to find out what was happening.'

She clapped her hands, and did a pirouette. Her nightie billowed out and Puck tried not to look. 'That makes two\ Oh, Puck, this is so exciting! What tree is it?'

'Hazel,' he said quickly, and turned to the sink to rinse his glass, so as not to have to watch her reaction.

'Hazel? Oh, no! What a bunch of knowalls. It'll drive us all mad.'

'No, Mistress. Hazel's not so bad. A bit... pedantic, possibly.'

'How are the goblins taking it?'

Puck dropped his eyes and wiped an imaginary spot of milk from the draining board. 'Er... okay.'

'What? Freckles is taking it okay? I don't believe you!' She walked over and made as if to knock on the wall.

'Well, possibly not okay, as such. But they'll get used to

each other, I'm sure. Eventually.'

She turned away and stamped her foot. 'Hazel!' she said.

'Madam?' a fruity voice, deep from the moist heartwood answered her.

'Ah!' she said, stepping back in surprise. 'I didn't see you there, Hazel. How are you? I haven't seen you for ages.'

The spirit bent low and took her right hand tenderly in its twiggy grasp, lifting and bending low over it, pressing its dry, bark lips to the tips of her fingers in a courtly manner. 'Nor I you, Madam. But one feels all the better now that one is here. It is, as always, a total pleasure.'

'Yes. Good.' She looked over at Puck, who still had his back to her. She extricated her hand, which the spirit still held, nestled like a baby bird among its fingers. 'I'm going upstairs, to wake Oberon and Mr Dobie. We'll be down soon. Puck, wake the goblins, will you.'

'Farewell for now, dearest Lady,' crooned Hazel. 'À bientôt.'

'Whatever,' said Titania and disappeared into the hall.

Hazel went over and stood behind Puck at the sink, and, placing its hands on his shoulders and resting its sinewy arms with all their weight against his back, put its smooth, bark cheek against his and sighed.

'Hazel,' Puck complained as he sank beneath the heavy spirit. 'Don't lean!'

'Sorry, my dear boy,' cried Hazel, leaping back. 'It's just that it is so nice to be back with one's own kind, you know. One has been lonely. Time drags when one is alone. Do mortals not know that it is unkind to plant a single tree, on its own, with just a bed of gabby pansies for company, in shouting distance of a few brainless shrubs? Ah, the tedium. It was perpetual.'

Puck gave him a kindly pat on his back, feeling the smoothness of the bark stretched over infinite power. That was the thing about these tree spirits. They might look fragile, and Hazels could talk the hind leg off a donkey, but they were so *strong*.

'Hazel, mate,' Puck said, trying to make him feel useful. 'Will you just give a gentle tap on the wall and get the goblins up? We can't let things slow down now, especially now the Unseelie know what we're up to. They're not likely to leave us alone and I don't really trust them, I have to say.'

'Nor I,' said Hazel, giving the plaster a cursory tap that made a noticeable dent and made three of Mrs Jones' kitchen cupboards fall off the wall.

The goblins popped out of the wall quicker than Puck had ever seen. Usually, they needed several calls, but today they were assembled in a sort of a line in a winking.

Hazel beamed at them benevolently, not seeming to notice that Freckles at least hated the very sap in his veins. 'No need to bang like that,' he said, crossly. 'A light tap is ample. Innit, Puck?'

Puck wasn't about to take sides. 'Several light taps, yes,' he said. 'But this morning, we need to be up and about, not skulking around playing cards and watching television programmes which even Hazel can tell are meant for children.'

'Even Hazel?' the spirit asked, on a rising tone.

'I just meant,' Puck sighed, 'that you don't have much experience of television.'

The tree spirit subsided. 'Sorry, dear boy. Excitement has made one sensitive. You are of course, completely accurate in your assumption. One indeed has very little, one might almost go so far as to say *no* experience of the televisual arts.'

'Per-lease!' said Freckles, clapping his trotter to his woefully low forehead. 'Why not just say yer've never seen the telly?'

'As the dear creature says,' agreed Hazel, 'One has never,' it coughed deprecatingly and smiled a small smile, leaning forward to share the fun, '*seen the telly*.' It straightened up, its facial bark split in a delighted grin.

The goblins cast up their eyes, except Bill, who could only do one at once. Bill was settling in quite nicely, and had become totally fixated on the Queen. There seemed to be something hidden under its coat, which it guarded with an arm curved out at a rather uncomfortable-looking angle. Its excitement was showing itself in little bobbing motions of the head and a frantic scratching at the floor. It squawked quietly to itself, a chuckling noise as of a clown convention in a very deep hole, far away.

They heard the others coming down the stairs, Oberon's steps apparent by the way he only used every fifth tread. Titania's light footfall was slower than usual, and it seemed to be keeping time with a step so soft and hesitant that it was hardly there at all. They could hear her murmuring encouragingly as Mr Dobie made his modest, unassuming way into the spotlight.

Then they were in the room, Titania and Oberon making a stunning background to the ordinariness of Mr Dobie. In fact, he was so extraordinarily ordinary in that motley crowd, that it seemed to make him stand out. Had he had two heads, hoofs or blue hair, he would have blended with far more success. He was taller than all of the goblins, but shorter than Puck, who had settled for the average height of a mortal as being the most convenient. He wore a long, brown coat of no particular distinction, which hung lower than his knees but did not sweep the floor. He wore a muffler around his neck, which was exactly the colour of his coat, as were his hair and his shapeless hat, pulled down low. His face and hands were the same sort of brown – drab and matte, pulling light in and giving off no sparkle in return – but marginally paler. They all hoped it was a muffler at his throat – it could equally easily have been folds of neck. He was, all in all, an inoffensive little being.

Titania had primed Oberon about Hazel, and so, to save time, the King nodded imperiously at the spirit and motioned the goblins to stand around the table. He and Titania sat down, Hazel leant against the wall, Mr Dobie tried to hide behind Puck, who stood, in the manner of a regimental sergeant major, behind the goblins. Bill nudged him in the knee and he bent down. The goblin squawked quietly in his ear and Puck stood up.

'Mistress,' he said, 'if I understand him rightly, Bill has a present for you.'

Bill stepped forward and, with a flourish, brought out an egg from under its coat. Titania was a little taken aback, but reached out across the table and took it. It was still warm, but she chose to assume that was from being under Bill's jacket. She inclined her regal head and went to give it to Puck. Bill looked a little crestfallen, so, to make him happy, she examined it closely. And gave a little cry of delight. Apart from minor geographical errors – she wasn't sure that Australia should be joined to America like that – the egg was marked out in jewel colours to represent the world.

'Bill!' she exclaimed, 'It's absolutely beautiful.'

Below his quiff, Bill flushed with delight. He pulled Puck down again and whispered, in a breathless squawk, his message to his Queen. After a few frowns and misunderstandings, Puck stood up and said to Titania. 'Apparently, Majesty, Bill has laid this egg for you, to show his belief that you will soon have the real world in your hand again.' Bill nodded and grinned, bobbing up and down in embarrassment and delight.

The goblins clapped their trotters together and cried variants on the theme of 'Good Old Bill.' Titania blushed prettily and gave the egg to Puck, who put it in an egg cup on a shelf, where they could all admire it.

'Bill,' said Titania, reaching forward to stroke his bouncing quiff, 'I have never had such a thoughtful gift.' She leaned back and swept her gaze over them all. 'I think Bill is right. We have Mr Dobie, and Hazel. From just one broadcast.'

'And the Untheelie have found us,' reminded Thydney, ever the pessimist. He looked around the room, at everyone in turn. He lowered his voice. 'I was really *thcared*,' he whispered.

'No need to be scared,' said Oberon, clapping his hands. 'They could never beat us before, they won't beat us now.'

'Are we fighting them, then?' asked Thydney in alarm. 'Now I'm *really* thcared!'

'No, no,' reassured Oberon. 'Of course not. I just mean...' he looked frantically at Puck who, as always, stepped into the muck his Lord was knee deep in.

'What the King means,' he said, 'Is that the Unseelie pose no threat to us. They are as weakened as we are, although in a different way. They have mastered technology, and we haven't. But they never had the love of mortals, because they're seen as cruel and vicious. And Scottish. We are the pretty sparkly ones.'

They all looked at Mr Dobie.

'...by and large.'

'And Squeaky has run off,' Bertie volunteered.

'He'll be back!' Oberon said, unconvincingly.

'We're still one up, though, aren't we?' said Tiny, showing his superior grasp of maths.

'Yes, we are,' Titania said. 'Indeed we are, Tiny. Next thing now is the next part of our plan.'

'A stratagem is what we need, my Lady,' said Hazel. 'A scheme, a design, an arrangement. A programme, a schedule, a project, a proposal. A proposition,' he looked proudly around, 'a plot, a procedure, a contrivance...'

'A smack right in the mouth,' interrupted Freckles.

It went very quiet.

'Well,' Freckles said, belligerently. 'It drives me mad, it does. What's the point of knowing all the long words that mean plan, if the stupid twiggy thing doesn't actually have a bloody plan.'

'It's a good point he has there, Hazel,' Oberon said. 'Do you actually have a plan?'

The tree spirit hung its head and its glossy bark seemed to dim a little.

'No' it said, in a tiny voice, no more than the creaking of a branch on a still summer day.

'Then shut up,' Freckles added, 'until you do have one.'

Mr Dobie coughed an unassuming cough.

Titania turned a bright, patronising smile on the brownie. 'Mr Dobie?' she said, in the voice that mortals used for children, dogs and the old. 'Do you have an idea?'

In a dry and dusty voice, Mr Dobie agreed that he did indeed have an idea. While he was sure that the television plan was sound – indeed, had it not brought him into the group – he wasn't sure that enough faeries watched television or had grasped the basic concept that things happening on the screen were real. What they needed to do was hang around in full view and behave in a faerie-like way, to attract the, as it were, passing faerie. As their little group had attracted Hazel last night. He could immediately put his hand on a few more Mr Dobies, to make a start.

'Er... can you behave in a faerie-like way?' Puck asked.

'Oh, yes,' Mr Dobie nodded. 'For example, I can remove unwanted smells. I can mash potatoes and mince up together quicker than any mortal. And...' he held up an excitedly quivering finger, 'you may find this hard to believe, but I can sort out sets of false teeth to the right owner even when they have been *put in the same drawer overnight!*' he beamed around proudly.

'A bit specialist, perhaps?' asked Hazel.

'Possibly a tad,' said Titania, burying her head in her hands.

'Well, I think,' said Oberon, against all perceived knowledge, 'I think we ought to get the Unseelie in on this.'

Titania threw up her head and stared at him in disbelief. 'Are you mad? That lot? You can't trust them an ell, Oberon.'

'Well, blood is thicker than water,' Oberon said, shrugging. 'We're nearer to them than to mankind.'

'At the moment,' Puck said, darkly.

'And he is my brother,' Oberon added.

'Half,' said Titania with a sniff.

'Well, all right, half,' he conceded, 'But even so, I think he's not so bad, deep down.'

The goblins all looked askance. They were with their mistress on this one.

Puck furrowed his brow a minute and then said, 'What if we do everything?'

'Everything being...?' Oberon asked, anxious for a recap.

'Television, loitering and trying to get back in touch with the baddies.'

'There aren't really enough of us for all that,' pointed out Titania.

'Not at the moment,' said Puck, 'no. But if Hazel gets out and about this evening, after dark, he might be able to drum up some more tree spirits. Mr Dobie can find a few more... er, Mr Dobies. My Lord, you can, perhaps, think up a few new goblins.' Bill clapped his hands and did little abortive jumps in excitement. 'Perhaps based on a few different animals,' Puck continued without a pause and Bill subsided. 'My

Lady, you and I can perhaps go out and behave a bit like fae-ries. A spot of light flying, a few manifestations, that kind of thing.'

'What about us?' Tiny asked.

'You can stay here, make sure that the goblins Lord Oberon creates are... fully functioning, as it were. I know we're all very fond of Bill, but... well, I'm sure you get my drift. One of you can watch the television,' a forest of trotters went up into the air, 'er... Bertie, you seem to have fairly so-phisticated tastes. You can do that.'

Bertie trotted off happily, determined not to waste a mo-ment.

'What about finding the Other Lot?' asked Hazel, surpris-ingly short and to the point.

Titania looked at Oberon and said quietly. 'When the King has finished goblinning, I believe he can help us there.'

'I'm sure I don't know what you mean,' Oberon said, archly.

'And I am sure you do,' said Titania. 'You found Leanne easily enough The Other Night. I'm sure you'll find her again. Particularly since I am pretty sure Benedict doesn't intend to leave us alone for too long. So,' she said, getting up sharply. 'To your places, everyone. If you can't do anything until it gets dark, get some rest, or practice. That's what Puck and I intend to do, don't we, dearest Puck?'

With a nervous glance at Oberon, Puck nodded.

'My room, I think,' said the Queen. 'More swooping space in there.' She hooked a finger through a buttonhole and hauled Puck out of the room. The others looked wistfully after them, except Bertie, who was already glued to the televi-sion. He had to wonder, though, how a rerun of 'Postman Pat' was going to help. Never mind though, Mrs Goggins was having a bit of a crisis over a stamp, and he wanted to see how it all turned out.

23

Puck had never been in the bedroom of his Queen. He looked around, breathed in the scent of woodland flowers and musk that could never be captured in a bottle but was the encapsulation of Titania and Oberon. The curtains were still drawn, and the room was filled with a faint glow from the rising sun outside, shining through.

'Come on, Puck,' said Titania. 'Let's shove this bed over to one side to give us more room.'

'Shove, Mistress?' asked Puck. 'Why not start with moving it *without* shoving?'

'What an excellent idea,' she said. She waved her arm in an imperial gesture at the bed. It didn't move. 'What an excellent idea,' she continued, 'if only it worked.'

'Shove it is, then,' he said, leaning on the bed.

He pushed it into a corner, leaving a square of fluff behind.

'I will take a broom before,' he muttered, nostalgically, 'And sweep the dust behind the door, and cleanse this hallowed house.'

'Oh, Puck,' she said, stroking his cheek. 'You are sweet. But the hoover is broken and I don't think a broom will get fluff up. Let me try moving it with magic, if I can't shift a bed.'

She took a deep breath, closed her eyes and blew gently onto the floor. The fluff coalesced into a cloud of pale blossom, which rose into the air and spiralled round, before dis-solving into lightly fragranced powder.

Puck sneezed. 'Right,' he said, wiping the powder from his face with his sleeve. 'We'll just get rid of this dust and then we can begin.'

She looked a little crestfallen.

'Sorry, Mistress,' he said, 'but you have to think mortal. The effect was lovely, the fragrance exquisite, but if you make them sneeze, they'll run for a tablet to stop it. If you cause dust, they'll rush for the latest type of anti-static polish and self-cleaning duster in the wink of a faerie eye.'

'I've never really understood them,' she sighed. 'You really have an amazing grasp, Puck.'

'Well,' he said sadly, 'Don't forget I was with a mortal, more or less, for years. Poor Cobweb, she seemed to take on all the worst aspects and not bother with the rest. Like intelligent conversation, watching sunrise, walks in the rain, like you see in the cinema. She was keenest on new brands of shampoo, latest disposable nappies and donuts. Oh, and pizza with cheese in the crust.'

Titania was clearly trying to understand. Her hair just *was* like that. Babies were what happened to other people. She wasn't keen on food. Sunrise was the best part of the day. Rain was the best time to walk – it washed her face and hair and the drumming cleared her head. Intelligent conversation, though – anyone who hung around with Oberon and goblins would always be rather short of that. She gave herself a little shake.

'This isn't getting us anywhere,' she said. 'Does your glamour work properly, yet?'

Puck shook his head. 'The flying's fine. I get a bit tired – I think putting a girdle round the earth will have to wait a while, but mainly it's coming along okay. I can't really do the size thing too well if I'm doing anything else, like, when I'm flying, I have to stay the same size.'

'That could be a problem,' Titania mused. 'How did you manage last night?'

'Well, I was a bit stuck, anyway. I had two goblins up my jumper and I was carrying Hazel's stick, which weighs the same as the whole tree. It's a perception thing, apparently. I find that I lose the thread when he really gets going.'

'Yes,' said Titania, sitting on the edge of the bed. 'It's a shame it was a Hazel spirit.'

'It wasn't likely to be anything else, was it?' Puck pointed out. 'The other trees aren't bright enough to work out what's going on.'

'Very true. And I suppose it could be worse. It could have been an Elder – I haven't met one yet that I like.'

Puck took a spin round the room. He landed, teetering on the bed-head, arms outstretched. With a pop, he disappeared and for a millisecond his clothes hung in the air, before collapsing in a heap on the pillow. A small, muffled voice came out of the pile. 'Look away, Mistress. I need to get dressed again.'

She turned her back.

'Mistress?'

'Yes?'

'Can you shake my shirt out – gently? I can't get out.'

She turned and picked up his shirt, and shook it gently out onto the bed. A tiny Puck dropped out of the sleeve and bounced onto the duvet. He tried to hide behind a button, but she carefully picked him up and stood him on her palm. He stood there in the classic man-caught-in-shower pose, hiding what he considered his best assets behind both hands.

'Please, Puck,' she breathed gently, ruffling his hair. 'Don't come that with me. I've seen all you have to offer many a time. Why so modest?'

'Habit, Mistress,' he said. 'Mortal women get the wrong idea if a milkman turns up on their doorstep with no clothes on.'

'Well,' she said with a smile, 'Even at this size, I can see you've kept yourself in trim.' She tickled his midriff with her forefinger. 'What do mortals call this?'

'Mistress!' Puck was appalled.

'No, not *that*! I know what they call *that*! I mean, this. This muscly bit, just here.' She tickled him again.

He looked down proudly, smoothing his hard stomach muscles with the palm of his hand. 'A six-pack, Lady,' he said proudly.

'Well,' she put him down again and turned her back as requested. 'You're very handsome, Puck. You haven't changed a bit.'

'Thank you, Mistress,' said Puck, reaching his favourite height and wriggling to get comfy in his skin again. He picked up his clothes and clambered into his boxers and trousers, shrugged into his shirt. 'All right, you can turn round now.'

Titania spun round, a broad grin on her face. How could Puck have forgotten that she didn't have to be facing him to see whatever she chose. And he *had* kept himself nice!

'Mistress?'

'Yes?'

'When I was small just then, did you think I was a bit... well, greener than usual?'

'I didn't like to mention it.'

'Does it show now I'm bigger?'

She took his chin in one hand and turned his head from side. 'Hard to tell in this light, but perhaps just a bit. On the edges.'

He went over to the dressing table and peered into the mirror, pulling down his lower lids and sticking out his tongue. She came up behind him and put her hands on his shoulders.

'It doesn't show,' she said, trying to reassure him. 'Anyway, I like green.'

'It makes it a bit hard to blend in, though, being green.'

'You won't have to blend much longer, though, will you?' she said. 'Not when we're Back?'

Puck didn't answer.

'Well, will you?'

He stood up and smiled at her in the mirror. He sighed and turned round. 'No, Mistress. That's right. I can be as green as I want.'

He moved into the middle of the room and started doing little jumps, while getting a bit smaller, along with his clothes this time, then a bit bigger, then smaller again. It was the faerie equivalent of aerobic warm-ups.

'Puck?' she said.

He stopped jumping. 'Yes, what?' he said, a little more curtly than he had meant to.

'If we don't manage it, manage to get back, I mean, what will you do?'

'I think the milk round's been reassigned,' he said, with what he hoped was a light laugh. 'They don't like milkmen who abandon their float in a hedge and disappear.'

'No, I mean, really *do*,' she said.

He sucked in a huge breath and stretched, with his arms over his head. He relaxed back and said, simply, 'I think that I will join Cobweb.'

Titania said, quietly, 'I thought so.' They were both still for a moment, listening to faint sounds from below as Oberon's goblins did or did not pass muster. Bertie had moved on from Postman Pat, but not far – Pingu was still a far cry from being helpful, but Puck knew when not to push it.

Puck was the first to move. Turning a back flip, he said, 'Come on, my Lady. Let's get on. Otherwise, we'll have no one to blame but ourselves. Let's see what you can do.'

Titania sank to a picturesque heap on the floor at his feet, decked out suddenly in gossamer and gauze.

'Well, I can dress myself in all this faerie stuff.' She took up handfuls of the fabric and let them fall around her. 'Can you do that?'

Puck waved an arm and was clothed, briefly, in a tight fitting outfit of shimmering leaf green. Ivy twined in his hair and his legs became goat-footed and hairy. Pan-pipes filled the air.

Titania clapped her hands. 'I've always liked the faun look,' she cried. 'Can't you make it last longer than that?'

Puck wiped his hand over his forehead. 'I'm sweating as it is, but I'll practice. I think we'll chalk that one up as a win to you. Your turn.'

'A competition! What fun.' Titania was nothing if not competitive. She furrowed her lovely brow in thought. Then she cupped her hands together and blew gently between her fingers. When she opened them, palms up, a Red Admiral butterfly sat there, wafting its wings softly in the warmth of her skin.

'Very nice,' Puck said. 'But it's Autumn out there. Don't let it out, it will die.'

'So thoughtful,' muttered Titania. She blew again on the butterfly, as gentle as a thought. It briefly became a chrysalis, a caterpillar and finally a minute egg, which disappeared with a faint implosion.

Puck applauded. 'Good,' he said. 'Very good, Mistress.' He was thinking hard. Manifestations had never really been his thing. 'May I think for a moment?'

'Of course,' said Titania, looking up at him.

He went to the window and looked out. Three women were walking up the road, chatting and laughing as they went. Puck reached out and felt that they would be an easy target. Without turning round, he said quietly, 'Over here, Mistress. I'm going to give something a try.'

She joined him, tweaking aside the other curtain.

'Do you see those women?'

'Yes.'

'Watch.' He bent his mind and sent out waves of sleep to them. One of them curled up in one movement straight away, and lay on the early morning pavement. The one whose arm she had been linked with staggered with her weight and looked down as her companion fell, but was also asleep before she hit the ground. The third one looked around anxiously, scanning the sky and surrounding houses. She looked across the road and then, to his amazement, straight into Puck's eyes. She bent down briefly to check whether her friends were only sleeping and, on finding that they were, looked carefully both ways and crossed the road with a purposeful stride.

Puck and Titania pulled back into the room and looked at each other with wide eyes.

'She saw me,' he said.

'Who is it?' said Titania.

'What?'

'Well, she must be one of our Folk. Otherwise, how is it that she isn't asleep and how could she see you?'

'I'm perfectly visible, Mistress,' Puck pointed out.

'Yes, but she knew where to look.'

A hammering came at the front door.

'Titania,' Oberon called plaintively up the stairs. 'Door. I'm a bit busy.' His voice was backed by a disquieting mixture of bleating and a strange hissing. The kitchen door slammed shut.

The hammering came again, and this time the letterbox rattled as well.

'Go down,' whispered Puck. 'But be careful.'

'Why me?' she whispered back. 'It's you she saw.'

Puck heaved a sigh. 'All right, Mistress. Don't come out unless I call you. It might be another Unseelie.'

Titania nodded and gestured him out of the door. As he went down the stairs, the letterbox rattled again and a voice said, 'Come on, Puck. I know you're in there. It's Mab.'

Titania's head appeared in the bedroom doorway.

'Mab?' she called. 'Is it really you?'

The voice through the letterbox called back, 'Mistress? Titania? Puck, you imbecile, let me in. And you'd better wake those two up as well. They'll get a crowd around them any minute. But let me in, first.'

Puck opened the door and Mab rushed in. The only faerie Titania had never fallen out with, she was her best friend, favourite and lady-in-waiting all rolled into one. She was mischievous, funny and altogether, as far as Puck was concerned, a pain in the neck. In his experience, a whoopee cushion is only funny once. And not all that funny then. To gain a bit of time, he stepped outside and concentrated hard on the two comatose women across the road. Slowly, they woke and scrambled to their feet, dusting themselves down.

One of them, looking around her, said, 'Hey, where's Mab?'

'Who?' said the other, dusting herself down and pulling at her skirt, which had rucked up as she slept.

The first looked puzzled. 'I don't know,' she said, slowly. 'I just thought... wasn't there someone else with us?'

'Don't think so,' said her friend.

'What happened there?' said the first sleeper.

'Where?'

'Just then. Didn't we... I dunno, go to sleep or something?'

The other laughed, uneasily. 'Don't be silly. In the street?

No, of course not.'

'Why have you got that leaf in your hair, then?'

The woman reached up and picked it out. 'Autumn, innit? Fell off of a tree, I expect.'

The first woman was not convinced, but, still looking vaguely about her for Mab, she allowed herself to be led on up the road.

Puck did a little caper in the hall. 'Not bad, not bad,' he said to himself, rubbing his hands together. 'You're coming on, Puck.'

The girlie noises coming from upstairs didn't tempt him to go back up. Instead, he turned on his way into the kitchen. The farmyard sounds had been creeping into his subconscious for a while, and he thought it was time to investigate. A quick check had confirmed that it wasn't coming from Bertie's television marathon. The set was showing a news update and Bertie was snoring in front of it, a beatific look on his little piggy face. Never mind, Puck thought, I'll get on to that problem later.

He opened the kitchen door and was met immediately with shouts of 'Shut the door, shut the door. The goat'll get out.'

'Goat?' he said, slamming the door to. 'I don't remember saying anything about a goat!'

24

The kitchen was worse than Puck's worst nightmare. Oberon had wandered through the animal kingdom, it seemed almost at random. Some forays had been fairly successful. The cache of goblins happily playing hop-scotch near the sink seemed a pleasant little crew. They had soft, grey, short cropped hair, even on their ears. Their eyes were soft and gentle, their teeth a little rabbity – and with good reason.

The goat was standing at bay next to the back door. Its head was lowered and its front feet splayed out defiantly as it held off all-comers.

'How did that happen?' Puck asked, tersely.

Oberon spread his hands innocently. He looked up at Puck imploringly from the floor behind the table, where he had taken cover from the infuriated goat. 'I don't know,' he said. 'I had done quite well. Take the rabbits, for example,' they all waved their small, soft hands at him and smiled. 'Nothing wrong with them, would you say?'

Puck shook his head.

'Charming little chaps and,' Oberon dropped his voice, 'absolutely *hopeless* at cards. I shan't be playing with that other cheating lot any more, I can tell you.'

Freckles, from his vantage point up near the picture rail, gave a snort.

'I tried a few other things. Cats don't work. Look like

something in a carnival. They had to go.'

'To go?' Puck asked. 'You didn't just let them out, did you?'

'No, no. Of course not. What do you take me for? I just unthought them. They were only kittens, anyway. But, the goat...'

'Yes?' Puck drummed his fingers.

'Well, I was getting a bit tired of cute. You know, rabbits, cats, sheep...'

'You've got goblins based on sheep?'

Oberon was annoyed. 'They're rather attractive, actually. Curly hair, fair mostly, but the occasional brunette. Good knitters.'

'Female?'

'Yes. Sheep are, aren't they?'

'Mostly, I suppose. May I ask where they are now?'

Oberon waved a dismissive hand. 'The lads said they would look after them. They took them into... the... wall.' He stopped and looked up rather, Puck thought, sheepishly. Through the plaster came the sounds of roistering grunts and faint, slightly querulous, female laughter.

'Females probably weren't my best idea, were they?'

Puck pressed his lips together and shook his head. Freckles snorted again. 'Now he realises!' he said. 'What that poor hen is thinking about it all, I really dread to fink.'

'Sorry,' said Oberon, in a small voice.

'And the goat?'

'Sorry, yes, the goat. I thought a goat would make quite a good model. Handsome, in a rugged sort of way, as a kind of a change from...' he looked up at Freckles without moving his head.

'Careful,' the goblin warned. It was not having a good day.

'As a kind of change. And I think I was a bit influenced by the Three Billy Goats Gruff thing. But, it must have been when whoever it was banged on the door, I lost my concentration, and when I turned back, there it stood. A goat.'

The goat was fixing Puck now with its baleful cat's eye. It pawed the ground in a thoughtful kind of way and chewed a little. From the remnant hanging out of its mouth, Puck could see that it had once been Freckles' coat.

'Who was it, by the way?' Oberon asked.

'Who was what?'

'It. At the door.'

'Oh, that.' Puck had the feeling that if he looked away, the goat would have him. He considered flying, but the room wasn't high enough to get far enough away. He considered shrinking, but wasn't sure yet about getting the clothes to join in. He thought that probably, it would be worse being butted by an enraged billy goat whilst nude than when fully clothed. 'It was Mab.'

'What, *our* Mab?'

'I think if we think of her more as the Queen's Mab, Sire, we'll have fewer arguments. She hasn't forgotten the Leanne thing yet.'

'True. But old Mab, eh? How is she looking?'

'Very well.'

'Still the same old Mab?'

'She hasn't used a trick flower on me yet, or hit me over the head with a wet haddock, but I think time should put that right,' Puck said, with a sigh.

Oberon laughed and slapped his thigh. 'Good old Mab. What a laugh, eh?'

'A scream, Sire,' agreed Puck.

The goat, sensing that it was no longer the centre of attention snorted loudly and struck its hoof on the ground with a dull ringing sound. Puck wasn't sure, but he thought he saw steam coming from its nostrils.

'What are we going to do about this, Sire?' he said, risking a wave of the arm.

The goat followed the movement and looked menacing.

'I thought that perhaps... you would be able to do something?' said Oberon, with an ingratiating rise to his voice at the end of the sentence.

'I'm glad you put that as a question, Sire,' said Puck. 'Because, as you might have guessed, the answer is, I can't. You have always been stronger than me, remember. I can't undo what you've done. You'll have to do it yourself.'

Oberon sighed and rose in one movement, like the formation of mountains in miniature. He came round from behind the table and faced the goat, which immediately looked puzzled. This wasn't right. Deep inside its head it knew that everyone hid when it blew down its nostrils and did the hoof thing. What was going on? In the pause afforded by its puzzlement, Oberon grabbed its horns and laid his head against its Roman nose. Puck noticed how his hair curled and meshed with the goat's topknot and how somehow *alike* they were. Light dawned – now he knew why his Lord had chosen a goat!

Oberon was obviously thinking very hard. His eyes were screwed up and his lips pressed tightly together. After a few seconds, he opened his eyes to find his view was still full of goat. 'Oh, that's enough,' he said crossly and, drawing his head back, nutted the goat firmly between its eyes. With a wave of one hand, he turned away, massaging his forehead with the other. The goat disappeared, with an incredulous bleat.

Freckles slid down the wall and stood looking at the spot where the goat had been, marked, inevitably, with evidence of its existence.

'Cor,' he said. 'I never seen you do that before, Sire.'

'No, well,' said Oberon, sitting at the table and holding his head in both hands. 'It doesn't take a genius to work out why, Freckles, I'm sure. That really hurts!'

Puck allowed him a moment in his private world of pain. When he lifted his head and got his eyes back into focus, Puck said, 'So, where are we then, Lord, goblin-wise?'

'Er... rabbits. Sheep. I did a few more hens, you know, so Bill feels a bit more at home. I did a few more pigs, because they are my favourites,' he smiled regally at Freckles who was delighted.

'Well done, Sire,' said Puck, genuinely pleased and secretly rather surprised. 'Have a rest, now. Why not go and join Bertie in his television watch? You might be able to guide him a bit.'

Oberon stood up majestically. 'Do you know, I think I will,' he said. 'Tell Titania and Mab to pop in when they're ready. I expect they have a lot to catch up on.'

He strode out of the kitchen and they heard him say, 'Budge up, old chap. I can't see the screen.'

Puck looked around the kitchen and asked Freckles, 'Where's Mr Dobie and Hazel?'

Freckles tutted. 'Mr Dobie's gone for a rest, poor old soul. That stuck up stick is hiding in his twig, over there on the windersill.'

'I suppose that's all right. Neither of them can really get much done yet. Leave them where they are.'

Freckles looked up at Puck and said, 'Is Mab really here?'

Puck nodded.

'She's a bit of a larf, in' she, ole Mab?'

Puck nodded again. He didn't trust himself to speak.

'How did she find us, vo?'

'Now, that I don't know. She seemed to be just walking along. With a couple of mortals. She had really blended in – I didn't even recognise her. But she's always had a face a bit like a currant bun, don't you think? Very mortal.'

Freckles snickered.

'And yet, she knew me straight away, from right across the road and through a net curtain.'

'Vat's good, vo, innit?' Freckles looked up into Puck's face.

He forced himself to see the bright side. With the goat gone, it was possible to hear gales of laughter coming from Titania's room and his heart sank with every guffaw. 'Yes, yes it is, mate,' he said, forcing a smile. 'It proves our Folk are out there. All we have to do is find them.' He suddenly had a thought. 'Why aren't you in the wall, having a good time with the sheep?'

Freckles looked at him frankly, goblin to elf. 'I don't really find them vat attractive, to tell yer ve trufe.'

'To each his own,' agreed Puck, and, hiding a smile, went off into the hall. From upstairs he heard more laughter; from in the sitting room a celebrity cook was asking what was he like. He decided a walk was in order.

He put on his coat and opened the door. It was another bright and sunny day, unseasonably warm, and he chose to take it as an omen. He strolled down Ellesmere Crescent and out onto the main road. The mid-morning rush was well under way. Women pushing buggies were in the majority and some of the babies looked at him, with that old person's look which so many small children have in their eyes. He came face to face with one so outstandingly ugly that for a minute he thought he had found another of the Faerie Folk. His eyes travelled up to the mother, proudly standing behind the pushchair, waiting to cross the road. He took a startled breath. No, not a changeling. Just what mortals called genetics.

He tuned his ears to hear more distant sounds. The drum of the traffic died away first, the chatter of the women next. After the babies' cries became fainter, he could hear the twittering of birds in the trees and flying overhead. Then the whine of insects, high above, borne on the warm air coming in from the West. But beneath it all, there was another noise, and he knew that it represented their greatest enemy. It was the ringing of tills, the whirr of electronic banking, the soft sound of an ATM disgorging money.

He let his ears pop back to the here and now. Sticking his hands in his pockets and pursing his lips into a soundless whistle, Puck swung off down the High Street, a being millennia old, caught for ever in the body of a lithe and handsome nineteen year old. He caught some admiring glances and wondered how bad could being young and gorgeous be? Also, he thought he could smell a distant All-Day Breakfast. He was feeling better already.

25

I n Titania's bedroom, the Queen and her reinstated handmaiden were having a high old time. Mab was a good natured faerie, much given to the practical jokes which Puck saw as his own domain. It was always she who made the milk go sour, who hid the keys, who stopped the bread from rising. The cottagers at the sharp end didn't usually see the joke, but Mab could laugh for hours at the sight of a puzzled farmer trying to work out how the cow got on the roof.

Back in the woods, she would put nettles in the faerie beds, harness bumble bees and ride them until they were too tired to raise a buzz and generally be a laugh from morn till night. Everyone loved old Mab – what a joker.

So, she had been rather surprised when, as the Faerie Rades broke up into smaller units, and finally became twos and threes, how none of the other faerie actually wanted to wander off with her. She had eventually been left alone to fend for herself and so she had been doing, moving on when her relentless japes had worn her welcome out.

From time to time, she had considered trying to find some of her old faerie friends. Sometimes, she was sure she had spotted one on the street, but by the time she had negotiated the traffic, and got to the spot, they would be gone. Sometimes, she would even see a lissom foot disappearing around a corner. But she got used to the company of mortals in the end, and, in many ways, preferred them to faerie.

But, now she was back with Titania, she felt better than she had for ages. They had talked about the Old Days; there was so much to say. Both of them had drawn a veil over recent times. They would look to the future; that was the only way forward. Mab had loads of ideas, and some of them were quite sound.

Titania had always felt that the children were the best way to increase their profile. The children had always taken them more seriously. Look at those two little girls that time, taking pictures of them. That the adults didn't believe them was not Titania's fault – she and her remaining court, at the nadir of their powers, had dressed up to the nines and posed until their wings hurt. But, in the end, even the children had denied that they were real. Even that Doctor, what was his name? Conan Doyle? Even he had gone off on a silly tangent about spiritualism and clever detectives. But then, like the Unseelie, he was Scottish. She had lost several of her faerie that day and her fall dated from then. And Mab liked children. Their humour was about at her level, and she always got a laugh out of them. So she was in agreement with Titania – get the kids and you'd eventually get the grownups. In fact, if you had the time, they became the grownups. Titania put the bad memories of the faerie photos behind her. She gave Mab a sudden hug.

'I am so glad you're back,' she said.

Mab smiled at her. 'Glad to be back,' she said. 'Ever hear of any of the old crowd? Mustardseed? Cobweb?'

Titania looked down. 'Both gone, I'm afraid,' she said quietly.

Even Mab's famous good humour couldn't find a joke from that piece of news. 'I'm sorry,' she said.

'Nothing else to say, is there?' said Titania. 'Mustardseed went many years ago, Cobweb only the other day. She nearly made it, but, in the end...'

'I expect it was Puck's fault,' said Mab, acidly. There was no love lost in the other direction, either.

'No, no,' the Queen was quick to say. 'No one's fault. Except, perhaps, her own. But we shouldn't think badly of her.

She couldn't help it.'

'Food and men, that'll be at the bottom of it. And babies. That was Cobweb all over.'

Titania smiled. 'Yes. I think you've more or less captured that in a nutshell. Talking of which, you'll never guess what we've got downstairs?'

'The King?'

'Yes. But why should nuts make you think of Oberon? No, what I mean is we've actually got a tree spirit, living in a twig in its glass of water on the windowsill in the kitchen!'

'Excellent. It can get a bit of a network going... wait a minute. Nutshell. Don't tell me it's a Hazel?'

Titania grimaced, her lovely face a mask of rueful apology. ''Fraid so.'

Mab drew a huge sigh. 'Oh, no. I don't suppose,' she said hopefully, 'that it has learned not to be a knowall, over the years?'

'How sweet of you!' laughed Titania. 'No, if anything, it's worse. It was growing on the grass outside the Parliament place, you know, where they make laws and stuff. It thinks it knows it all. Apparently, it was once a background to a television interview with someone it calls Pax Man. It considers this to be the highest fame a tree spirit can reach.'

Mab had once briefly lived in a monastery – lots of scope there for blowing up habits, spiking the wine and generally causing consternation. So she had picked up a bit of Latin – 'Pax means peace.'

'Does that help at all?'

'No. I just thought you might like to know.'

'Perhaps,' Titania said archly, 'you would be happier downstairs with Hazel.'

Mab broke into giggles. 'No, no,' she cried, holding up her hands as defence. 'Anything but that.' Her tone became more thoughtful. 'I'd like to see the King, though.'

I'll bet you would, thought Titania. Aloud, she said, 'I think he's busy. Puck gave us all jobs to do.'

'Puck did?' Mab was incredulous. 'Does he give the orders around here, then?'

'Of course not!' Titania's response was perhaps a little too vociferous. 'No, no! *We* still give the orders. It's just that... well, he's spent a lot of time with mortals, more than we have, and he has a lot of good ideas. Plus, the goblins like him. Oberon likes him. Mr Dobie is sleeping in his bed, so obviously he is very grateful. Hazel thinks he is impressed, so he likes him. And,' she lowered her lashes, 'I like him.'

Mab tutted. 'Well, I know *that*,' she said. 'We all used to know *that*. Have you ever... done anything about it?'

The Queen drew herself up and her voice was very regal. 'I don't know what you mean!' she snapped.

Mab nudged her, instantly regretted it and moved away slightly.

'Well?' the Queen said. 'What do you mean?'

'Sorry,' said Mab, flustered. 'I didn't know you wanted an answer. What I mean is... the King is still very lovely, I imagine?' she put in a question.

'As the day. What do you mean?'

'Puck is still very handsome, nineteen, lithe, sinewy, in good condition. Works out, I expect. Got his flying muscle back in working order already, I wouldn't be at all surprised.'

'Hmm,' said the Queen, wondering where all this was leading.

'The King still not quite there, flying wise? Bit out of condition?'

'Mab, I'll have you know, the King still attracts a crowd wherever he goes. That's why we don't go out much. Women get confused. If he lets his glamour go, trees blossom, eggs hatch, women walk into lampposts.'

'Different look, though, isn't it? Oberon is lush, Puck is... perky. Looks as if he could...'

'Titania?' came a voice from the hall. 'Are you bringing Mab down to see us, or are you going to keep her to yourself all day?' The King was bored with programmes on straying husbands. It made him edgy.

The Queen pointed a royal finger at Mab. 'I'm watching you, Mab. You haven't changed an ell. If you try and make trouble...'

'Me, Mistress?' She turned a face as innocent as the morning to Titania, who turned onto the landing. The face she turned to her interlaced fingers was different – full of mischief and as sly as a forest of apes. She would have to be careful, but... this could be fun.

She followed the Queen downstairs and into the kitchen. It wasn't the perfect room for a meeting with your King after so many years, but the glamour which had been taking root over the last few days never really left it and, despite the fact that the goblin tree hadn't lasted very long, there was still a vaguely woody air about it.

Oberon was sitting at the table, apparently engaged in arm wrestling with a pig. Mab blinked, and her faerie eyes looked out. The King was sitting at the table, arm wrestling with a goblin. She thought she recognised it – it was the one called Freckles, she was pretty sure. The King was winning, but only because the goblin was letting him. All this she took in in a few seconds. She gave a small cough. The King looked up and, letting go of the goblin's trotter, leapt to his feet.

A mist, swirling grey around him, pricked with silver lights, haloed around his head. His curls mingled with the smoke, which carried with it a smell of autumn bonfires, dry leaves twirling down through sun-moted air and the animal smell that was Oberon. Hazel's twig, leaning in its glass on the windowsill, sprouted one tiny, fresh green leaf.

He moved forward to where Mab had fallen to the ground in an awestruck curtsey. He had pulled out all the stops and the effect had bowed her to her knees.

'Oberon!' snapped Titania. 'Stop that this minute.'

He looked at her under louche lids and stuck out his bottom lip a fraction. 'Just practising,' he purred.

Mab, released from his spell, got unsteadily to her feet and was sitting on a chair. Titania patted her shoulder. 'Don't worry about it, Mab,' she said, kindly. 'He's always doing it lately. The goblins tell me Mrs Jones next door is now on tablets for her nerves.'

'I... I just wasn't ready for it,' husked Mab.

'Of course not,' said Titania, shooting an accusing glance at Oberon. 'Freckles, fetch Mab a drop of dew or something.'

'Have you got anything stronger?' Mab asked, hopefully.

'Bit early, innit?' Freckles asked. He had thought as soon

as he laid eyes on her that she had the look of a drinker. That life and soul of the party type often was, in his experience. They took the party with them, wherever they went and the price for that was that they were usually carrying a six pack of extra strong lager.

Titania looked prim. 'We are trying to go back to faerie habits when it comes to food and drink,' she said. 'A lot of Cobweb's trouble was down to too much mortal food.'

Mab sighed. Titania had always been a bit like that. Rules for one but never for her. Mab would bet anything she liked the odd tipple, but doubted she would ever admit it.

'All right then,' she turned to the goblin. 'Dew it is.'

Freckles went to the fridge and opened the door. Mab peeped in. Yes, as she suspected – a jug of dew, a bottle of tonic and a lemon. What a hypocrite. Freckles poured her a tiny glassful of the colourless fluid and, sipping it, she had to admit, she did feel a bit better.

'Feeling better?' asked Oberon anxiously.

'Yes, thank you, Lord,' she said, casting her eyes down.

'We're really pleased you're here,' he continued. 'Where have you been? Have you been by yourself? How did you find us? Got any good ideas?'

Mab held up a hand. 'Please, Lord,' she said. 'One at a time. I've been all over, as a matter of fact. I've even...' she lowered her voice, 'been *Up There*, you know, North of the Border.'

Titania tried to conceal her interest. She wanted to know what Mab had discovered without letting out the news about the Unseelie. 'Er... anyone around?' she asked.

'The odd Fachan, by all accounts. There's so much room up there, loads of mountains and stuff. It's all a bit wild, for my taste. But the Court seems to have either died out or moved on. At least, I didn't meet any of them. I think I may have heard a Bean-sidhe, but I was staying in Glasgow, so it was difficult to know what some of the noises were.'

Oberon made the sort of noise that faerie make when they are about to speak, but a goblin hacks them very painfully on the shin with a trotter.

'At first, there were a few of us, we kept together, looked

after each other. But as time went by, we drifted apart, and for years now I've been on my own, moving on when people got suspicious. Sometimes, I even tried makeup to look older, if I was happy somewhere, but it didn't really work.'

'You've been with... mortals, then?' Titania asked.

'Mostly. I was quite famous for a bit, on the stage, you know, Music Hall.'

'Really?' Titania and Oberon were impressed. He'd been a bit of a stage door Johnny in his time.

'Yes. My speciality was "Nobody Loves a Fairy When She's Forty". It used to bring the house down.' She sighed reminiscently.

'I sin yer!' cried Freckles, excitedly. 'Dahn at the old Bull and Bush!'

'Ah, happy days,' mused Oberon.

'Where was I all this time?' Titania asked.

'Oh, probably doing something highbrow with a painter or composer or something,' said Oberon.

'I know how to enjoy myself,' said Titania. 'I have a sense of humour.'

There was a pause.

'And then, of course,' Mab continued, 'I didn't so much find you as you find me. I was walking along with a couple of friends from where I live, when Puck suddenly decided to put them to sleep.' She turned to Titania. 'Why did he do that, by the way?'

'Practising,' said Titania.

'Oh. Right. Well, as soon as they dropped like that, I knew it was likely to be one of our Folk. I looked across the road, and there was Puck, clear as day, peeping round the curtain. I came across the road and,' she spread her arms happily, 'here I am!'

'Things are beginning to move at last,' added Titania. 'If Mab was out there, there must be others.' She turned to her handmaiden. 'Can you fly, by the way?'

'There hasn't been the call, but I expect I could, with a bit of practice.'

'Make that a priority, then,' Titania told her. 'I've worked out that, if we get a few more of us airborne – can Mr Dobies fly, by the way?'

Oberon snorted. 'Don't be silly. He can hardly *walk*!'

'Yes, silly of me. If we get a few more of us airborne, we can cover a lot more ground. Trevor was right...'

'Trevor?' asked Mab, eyebrow raised.

'Don't ask,' said Titania, flapping a hand at her. 'He was right, about needing to get a meeting arranged. Where he was no help was in his method. No good putting posters up and such – how would you word it, what could you say? But if a few of us get up there, skim over crowds, hide under glamour so that mortals can't see...'

'But so that Faerie Folk can see,' Mab continued for her.

'Yes, right, and when they spot us, we tell them about the meeting...'

'.. .and they all come...'

'.. .and then they all tell at least one other faerie...'

'We'll be back on top before they know what's hit them!' finished the King in triumph.

Titania looked puzzled. 'Hit them?' she said.

'Mortals,' he explained. 'They've got what's coming to them, surely. For ignoring us all this while.'

'I don't want to hurt them,' said Titania.

'A bit of a rough house, though, surely?' said Mab. 'A few pinchings, hundred year sleeps, that kind of thing'

'I like to think,' said Titania, her voice tight with annoy-ance, 'That we have evolved beyond that. No, what I had in mind was a compromise. They believe in us, making us strong again. We retire to woodland glades, where we live unmolested, as we used to do.'

'We're not the only ones who have evolved,' said Oberon, television-watcher extraordinary. 'They'll want to what they call franchise us. They'll want our story for the newspapers. They'll make dolls that look like us...'

'Poppets,' breathed Mab.

'...they'll write a pop song about us. There'll be a film, a television series. They'll copy our clothes, our hair.'

Titania was crestfallen. 'No, no,' she said. 'I just want things to be like they were before.'

'No chance,' said Oberon, turning his back. He had secretly been looking forward to the publicity, even while he knew she wouldn't go for it. 'Once they've discovered us, they'll never let us go.'

'We'll have to cross that bridge when we come to it,' said Titania firmly. 'We're in a bit of a cleft stick, here, aren't we?'

Hazel suddenly materialised from his twig. 'Something one can help you with, Mistress?' he asked in plummy tones.

'Er, no, thank you, Hazel,' she said. 'It was just a figure of speech. But we are, aren't we?' she continued. 'If we appear to them, they'll want to sell us. If we don't, we'll just waste away.'

'Well,' said Oberon, standing up sharply. 'I'm off for some flying practice. Selling's bad, but diminishing's worse. Bags I the big bedroom – I need the space.' And he swept out, giving little hops and swoops as he did so.

Freckles looked at the two faeries sitting there. 'Come on, you two,' he chivvied them along. 'Get those wings a-beating. We've got work to do.'

26

When Puck got back half an hour later, the house seemed empty at first. The kitchen was deserted, except for Hazel's twig, which, though very small, seemed to fill the windowsill with its presence. The goblins were quiet, sleeping off whatever it is goblins do when nobody can see. Bertie was watching a business programme with apparent attention, when viewed from the back. From the front, his closed eyes rather gave the game away.

Puck tuned his hearing a little finer. Oberon was right; his ears were getting more pointed and, with their change in shape, more sensitive. Out of the corner of his ear, he could just catch faint sounds, wing beats and happy laughter. It was the sound which had lulled him to sleep and the sound which had woken him for millennia. He hadn't expected ever to hear it again.

Turning his head this way and that, homing in on the sound, he made his way through the kitchen and out into the tiny garden at the back of Thirteen, Ellesmere Crescent. The sound was louder here, but still no more than a moth's wing-beat in the silence of the night. He could see nothing at first, but then he spotted Hazel, standing at the bottom of the garden, lounging against the fence and nearly invisible. The autumn sun shone on his shiny coat, and the edges of his slender body blurred into the golden colour of the larch panels. He was holding out one finger and was smiling at it.

Every now and then, he raised his head, and followed something, invisible to Puck, with his eyes. He saw Puck standing in the doorway, and beckoned him down with his other hand.

'Come down here,' he said, just above a whisper. 'Look at this.'

Puck walked down the crazy-paved path and joined Hazel against the fence. 'What?' he said, barely keeping the excitement from showing in his voice.

'Look there,' said Hazel, pointing. Then, to the space in front of him, said, 'Play fair, Mab. He's got to get his eyes adjusted.'

A tiny noise sounded in Puck's atuned ear.

'They will stay still for a minute,' Hazel said. 'Look there. Just at the end of my finger.'

And, sure enough, just beyond the twig, outstretched into the air, was Titania, no bigger than a mosquito, and making the same humming sound with her wings. Around her flew Mab, circling and spinning with the joy of being alive, being a faerie, being airborne, after so long.

Puck's face split into a huge grin. 'My Lady,' he cried, and sent the Queen tumbling backwards, on the force of his breath.

'No, no,' said Hazel, hurriedly. 'Quietly. And try and hold your breath when you speak. In fact, best of all, don't use your mouth at all.'

In his head, Puck said again, 'My Lady. Mab. You're flying!'

'Wheee!' said Mab, circling his head. The Queen, more sedate, perched on one toe on the end of his finger and did a stately pirouette, then curtseyed.

'Indeed, Puck,' came her voice, somewhere in the back of his brain. 'I had forgotten how wonderful the cool air felt on an Autumn day. We are so small, we feel the beat of a bird's wing disturb the air a mile away. So be gentle.'

'Don't make yourself so small, then,' advised Puck.

'We will be seen otherwise,' said Mab, in his head. 'We wanted to practice and the King pinched the big bedroom. Mr D. is asleep in your room, so we thought we'd come out here. We stayed in the shelter of the fence and made ourselves smaller and smaller, until Hazel could only just see us. Then,' she spun off in a spiral round the garden again, 'we flew!'

Puck almost clapped his hands, but remembered just in time and smiled again instead. 'Let's go in now, though, shall we? It makes me nervous, you being so small. And we need to get tonight sorted. There's lots to do.'

The faeries clasped hands and flew in a looping curve up the garden, landing on the back step and popping back to their mortal-size in one fluid movement. They skipped and hopped as they landed and disappeared from the bright sun into the dark inside with one step.

Puck turned to Hazel, to see the tight bark of his face stretched in a grin.

'We're one step nearer,' the spirit said. 'I feel it in every fibre.'

'One step,' agreed Puck. 'One step at a time. Anything else happened while I've been gone?'

'Not really," said Hazel, who wasn't going to admit that, for most of the time, he had been out in the garden, lounging on the fence and soaking up the sun. 'Did you do anything exciting?'

'No,' said Puck, licking his lips to remove the last remnants of bacon grease. 'Nothing much. Just a bit of a walk.'

'Let's go in, then,' said Hazel, ushering Puck ahead of him up the path. 'I'm getting quite excited. Did you know my twig has a leaf on it?'

There seemed no answer to that, so Puck said nothing as they walked back up to the house.

Benedict and Leanne were busy too. Nothing as energetic as flying, naturally. Benedict was more of a thought faerie, especially in daylight, when his powers were weakest. James was by his side, as he lay on his beautiful pale leather sofa, peeling him the occasional grape and trying to sound intelligent. Of the two actions, peeling the grape, even without an opposable thumb, was by far the easiest option.

Benedict was tapping an unnaturally long finger nail on the arm of the sofa. Leanne was leaning her chin on one hand, and looking out at the panoramic view of the river, snaking below. The television was on, with the sound off, as was Benedict's custom. A slight shimmer in front of the screen gave away the presence of the Unseelie goblins, doing their best to remain aware and functioning without a mobile phone to cling to. Benedict had called a few home and they had reluctantly left their posts. The owners of the phones were staggered to find that, suddenly, there was no background mutter and hiss on the line, that they could talk without getting cut off or cross-connected to a chatline costing £10 a minute. But experience had taught them not to get excited. Normal service would, unfortunately, be resumed as soon as possible.

The goblins were there to watch out for any more unscheduled appearances. It was a hard job for them – they weren't very good at focussing on mortal faces. Gadgets were their forte – machines, gizmos, call them what you like, they were easier to recognize than people. But their Dark Lord had given an order. They were clinging too near the edge of existence to wind him up. He had a shocking temper – it was his best feature.

Leanne looked round. Did Benedict look happy? She couldn't be sure. He specialized in Saturnine and it suited him down to the ground. He looked so like Oberon sometimes, she could hardly believe it. Except that Oberon was more... well, just *more* really. She sighed loudly. He took no notice.

'Benedict?'

'Yes?'

'I've been thinking.'

'Good. That's what I told you to do, I think. The question is, have you thought of anything yet? Or are you still at the random stage?'

'I just need to get something straight.'

'Which is?'

'Are we going to get in touch with... the Others, at all? If we do, are we working together?'

'It depends what they want?'

'Well, they want to be powerful again, don't they? Isn't that what we all want?'

'My dear woman,' Benedict leaned forward, with his smile that wasn't a smile. 'I already *am* powerful.'

'Yes, yes of course you are, Benedict.'

'Before you go any further. O... O...'

'Oberon,' James said, helpfully.

'I know, I know. His people call him Lord. Or Sire. I like that. So in future, that's what you can call me.'

He missed the dangerous twitch of her nostril. James saw it and hurriedly put down the remaining grapes and beat a hasty retreat.

'Which would you prefer?' she asked, coldly.

He smiled again. 'You choose.'

'If you are so powerful,' she said, through gritted teeth, 'why do you need labels like "Sire" and "Lord"?'

'I don't need them. *You* do. Everything's become far too familiar around here. We need a bit of dignity around the place. However, we were talking about power.' He reached out with his left hand and gestured round the room. 'I control phones, computers, television, both cable and satellite – I couldn't have any more power. But I have a feeling, just a hunch, that Titania doesn't want power at all.'

'Oh, come on,' said Leanne. 'You must be joking.'

'Pardon?'

'You must be joking, Lord. She needs power like the mortals need air.'

'Hmm, yes. But not power over them, you see. To her, the mortal world is something that happens to others. She'll just want to retire to the quintessential woodland glade and be adored.'

'But Oberon, he won't be happy with that.'

'Right. He won't. And that is where my dilemma lies. If we help them, against the mortals, and we win, which we will, of course, it won't be over, will it? The battle that always was going on in the background will be on again, and we've all moved on. The stakes are higher. It will be to the death, this time.'

James had crept nearer again, his eyes wide, his jaws slavering.

'Oh, Master,' he cringed. 'Will it, will it? I'd love that, wouldn't you?'

Benedict looked at him and then patted him on the head.

'I rather think that it depends on whose death we're talking about, James, don't you?'

'What if we don't help them, Sire?' said Leanne, heavy on the irony.

'Well, in that case, I don't think either of us will win as such. I am quite content as things are, or should I say, were, but if that mad lot are going to be upsetting the apple cart all the while... things might become difficult.'

'How so, Master?' asked James. He had scented a fight and didn't want to bother with all this talking.

'Well, we can't have been the only ones who saw that goblin last night. Some other faerie, theirs and ours, will have seen it too. Plus, some mortals who look at things properly will have seen it. These media types, they don't miss a trick. I control several TV stations, as you know, but there are some mavericks who I have no say over. They might well investigate and find out more than they can handle. Then it will be "shock, horror, journalist goes mad" all over the tabloids. Then a faerie – probably one of ours, I'm afraid – will sell its story to the *Sun*... and that's it. Gaffe blown. Back to draughty castles and howling around cottage eves at full moon for you, Madam.'

Leanne shuddered. She'd had enough of that. Cruising the A3 was the only acceptable equivalent. 'So, we are finding the others, are we?'

'Yes, I think that would be wise. We have an address for them, don't we, James?'

James looked stricken. 'Do we, Master?'

'Yes. I specifically remember an address changing hands last night. What is it?'

'I have no idea, Master.'

'Leanne?'

'I don't know, Lord. It was you Puck told it to, wasn't it? Lord.'

'I have better things to do than remember addresses,' snapped Benedict. 'I have people for that. And you two are the people. So, what's the address?'

The bogle and the vampire shrugged their shoulders and shook their heads.

'Something, Something Crescent,' offered James.

'Oh, yes, very helpful,' sneered Benedict. 'And what town, may I ask?'

'I know that,' said Leanne. 'You remember, I... met him. It's in Guildford.'

'Oh, yes,' Benedict said heavily. 'You met him. Of course, I'd forgotten that. Well, Madam, I think you'd better nip out when it gets dark and try and meet him again.'

'But, Lord, it could take weeks,' she protested.

'No, I don't think it will,' the Dark Lord said reflectively. 'If I know Titania, she'll waste no time in finding us. And having O...O...'

'Oberon.'

'Whatever. Him, waiting on a roadside with his thumb in the air is the best way to do it. The way she'll figure it out, it worked once, it'll work again.' He sighed. 'No subtlety, you see.' He suddenly yelled at the shimmering cloud that was his goblins. 'Haven't you lot got anything better to do than hang around in here watching tv? Clear off out where you belong. There are computers need hanging, phones need blocking. Where my profits would be without prime time help lines, I dread to think.'

With a muted cry in a register that reduced James to tears, they swarmed into a cloud, and dispersed out of the window, over the City to do their fell work.

He looked at Leanne. 'Still here?'

She stood up. 'It isn't night time yet, Lord,' she pointed out.

'Well, get back to your office, then. Blight a few careers or something, whatever it is you do.'

She slammed out of the apartment. She'd show him. She'd find Oberon that very night and then... she paused on the stair. The last time she'd found Oberon was all a bit hazy still. She'd concentrate harder the next time. Now she knew how much she had to lose. Howling round cottage eaves indeed. Not if she had anything to do with it, she wouldn't. She clattered down to the floor below, and let herself into her office. Her secretary looked up and said, 'Ah, just in time for the casting auditions. The hopefuls are in your office.'

Leanne smiled mirthlessly. Benedict knew her so well. She went into her office, to blight a few careers.

21

The kitchen was wonderfully peaceful, empty of goblins, livestock and any evidence of their presence. Puck felt a little guilty. He felt, as a prime mover in the restoration of Faerie, he ought to enjoy their company more, and yet, somehow, the more was not always the merrier.

Titania sat sprawled on a chair at the table, her cheeks a faint and beautiful pink, covered with the damp down found on a baby mushroom just pushed out of the earth. Her eyes were closed, her mouth still smiling, with the pleasure of her flight. Mab was altogether a more homely faerie, but still the exertion had brought colour to her cheeks and her hair lay in damp tendrils on her forehead. Puck risked a comment.

'Flying suits you, ladies, if I may say so.'

Titania inclined her lovely head. 'Thank you, Puck. You must join us next time. You always knew how to set the pace.'

Mab thwacked him on the arm. 'Ta, Puck. Glad you liked it.'

Puck rubbed his arm reflectively. In a way, he welcomed the punch. Now he didn't have to wait any longer for the first one. He could unclench his teeth.

'I wonder how Oberon is getting on?' Titania asked, pushing herself up from her chair.

Puck darted forward. 'Don't get up, Mistress. I'll go and see.' He hadn't heard Oberon flying around when he'd come in and he didn't want to spoil the moment. Because he knew full well what the Queen's reaction would be, when she found the King stretched out on the bed, spark out.

Puck flew up the stairs, for no other reason than because he could. He landed briefly in the doorway of his bedroom, co-opted by Mr Dobie. The old brownie lay on his back, snoring gently, a thin snake of drool making its way from the corner of his mouth into his thin hair. He was a harmless old thing, though, and Puck drew the door closed quietly as he left.

He threw open the door to Oberon's room. It was total déjà vu. The King also lay on his back, snoring quietly, although, thankfully there was no drool. In fact, the King slept as picturesquely as his consort cried. There were no dried scaly bits at the corner of his mouth, no print of the pillow outlined in livid white against a red sweaty cheek. Just a beautiful man, lying half curled to one side, one hand on his chest, the other, with fingers slight bent into a light fist, laid against his cheek. He had a smile playing over his lips and his eyelids quivered as he dreamed his faerie dreams. The glamour lay over him like a blanket, and butterflies rested in his hair, beating their wings in time to his soft breathing. It was a lovely sight.

'Lord!' said Puck, loudly.

Oberon sat up, the butterflies disappeared. 'What? What?' he cried, knuckling his eyes to wake himself up.

'Flying tired you, I expect, Sire,' said Puck, with heavy irony.

The King looked hurt. 'It certainly did!' he exclaimed. The short sleep had made him sulky. And his dream had just been getting to the good part.

'Did you manage to do much?' asked Puck. He wasn't going to let his Lord off the hook that easily. Especially when the rest of them were doing so well.

Oberon nodded elaborately. 'Oh, yes,' he said, continuing to nod. 'Oh, yes. Loads and loads.'

'Show me.'

'What?'

'Show me a bit of flying.'

'You're being a bit forward, aren't you, Puck?' said the King, trying to change the subject.

'Possibly, Lord. Show me.'

The King got down off the bed and shook his clothes to make himself more comfortable. He shot his cuffs, bounced twice on the balls of his feet and coughed. And then, to Puck's amazement, he soared up to the ceiling, where he circled lazily around the central light fitting. He hovered in the air, turned a languid circle and floated down to the bed again, already in a position for sleep. As he closed his eyes, he said, 'Close the door on your way out. I need my rest if I'm to be out searching for Leanne tonight.'

Puck was speechless with surprise. He backed out of the room, pulling the door closed as instructed.

Oberon opened one eye to check he had gone and allowed himself a little chuckle as he turned over and made himself comfy. The chuckle was slightly hysterical – he had surprised himself with the flying, which he hadn't been practicing at all. It was amazing what a faerie could come up with, when a telling-off from Titania was on the cards.

By now it was mid-afternoon and the atmosphere at Number Thirteen was getting tense. The goblins were coming out, in dribs and drabs, rubbing their eyes and yawning. The sheep were terribly shy, and tended to keep together, looking from under their lashes at the other goblins, and giggling. Tiny and Thydney were displaying a tendency to strut, matched only by Bill and his new cohort, to whom it came naturally. The rabbits started playing as soon as they had room. Puck was startled to see they had found a ball from somewhere and were pretty good at what looked like baseball. He would never cease to be surprised by goblins. Freckles was very cynical about the whole thing and sat with his chin on a trotter, pretending to have nothing to do with them. Bertie was still watching television. An afternoon soap had caught his attention, and he sat on the edge of the sofa, trotters clasped in front of him, desperate to know the fate of the deceived wife and her husband. A small tear trickled over his bristly cheek. Puck didn't have the heart to tear him away.

Puck told his Queen, with truth, that the King seemed to have flying licked. She and Mab, who both had harboured suspicions about his application to the task, were suitably impressed. But even so, Titania wanted him down at the planning meeting, and so Freckles was despatched to wake him and Mr Dobie.

Titania flicked her fingers and the furniture of the kitchen disappeared and a grassy bank took the place of the units along one wall. Hazel gave a little cry of delight and planted his feet in the soil at one end. The goblins sat down in semi-ordered rows at the faeries' feet. Mr Dobie was given a red spotted mushroom to sit on, because his knees were none too supple and eventually they were ready to begin.

Before they could start, a short scream was heard through the party wall. Titania's transformation had not stopped at the boundary and Mrs Jones's kitchen had become rather too glade-like for her fragile psyche. Mr Jones rushed off to fetch her tablets. On the way down the stairs, he took a couple himself. It must be catching, what she had. They sat down on the grass and muttered incoherently, plucking at random stalks. But soon, they didn't mind too much.

Titania gave a rueful little grimace. 'We'll have to make it up to them, when we're back,' she said. 'We've been quite difficult neighbours, one way and another.'

The goblins coughed and shuffled. She didn't know the half of it, and, with luck, she never would.

Puck clapped his hands together and brought the meeting to order. Faerie had never been this organised, and he knew he had to make the most of their attention span, which he estimated would be extremely short. Bill was already scratching away and clucking happily to himself, and one of the sheep was absentmindedly chewing a hank of grass. But every face turned to him, green freckled, mild and ovine, sharp and beaky, currant-bunny, smooth, wrinkled, handsome, beautiful.

'The queen would like to say a few words,' Puck began.

'Would I?' said Titania. 'Well, everyone, you all know

why we're here. I'd just like to say hello to the new goblins among us,' the sheep lowered their heads, nudged each other and giggled. The rabbits bounced up and down and waved extravagantly to everyone. The chickens didn't seem to notice. 'We're here to make a few last minute adjustments to plans already laid and to plan what happens next. So far, we have planned that Hazel should go out at dusk to find other tree spirits and if possible, bring them back here. He'll need someone to help carry their twigs, if they are willing to come.' She lifted her head and looked over the company. 'Anyone?' A sheep tentatively lifted her hand, followed by all of the others. Titania looked at them, her head tilted sideways. 'Yes,' she said, 'that should work. You look nice and strong and,' she smiled at Oberon, 'if I may say so, dear, you've done a very good job on the girls. In a dim light, they'll pass for mortals, without too much trouble.' The sheep didn't know whether to be pleased or not by that remark, but Oberon was smiling, so it must be all right. They smiled happily and one of the bolder ones waved at Hazel, who smiled politely.

He leaned over to Puck and muttered, 'One dreads this evening. They have absolutely no intelligent conversation.'

Puck patted his twiggy hand in sympathy. The Queen was continuing. 'Mr Dobie, now I believe you are going to find some more... er... Mr Dobies. Is that right?'

The little brownie nodded, his beige cheeks showing the slightest sign of a blush.

'Are you all right to get to where you need to be?'

He muttered something.

'Pardon?'

Puck leaned nearer. He stood up and looked at the brownie in amazement. 'Apparently, Mistress, he has a bus pass,' he said, in an incredulous tone.

Titania blinked. 'How incredibly...'

'...far sighted,' Puck put in quickly. The brownie had begun to look rather crestfallen.

Oberon joined in on cue. 'Yes, indeed. Very far sighted. Now, Mr Dobie,' he leaned forward and spoke slowly and clearly in a voice which obviously annoyed Mr Dobie very much, 'if I were you, I'd set off now. Then you won't have to do too much of the journey in the dark. Is that all right?' In his normal voice, he said to Puck, 'Make sure he's got some money for tea and toast, or whatever it is they eat.'

Mr Dobie slid down off his mushroom and bowed to Titania, before gathering up his voluminous coat and making for the door.

'Don't forget to bring them all back here, Mr Dobie,' called Titania as he stumped out. They heard the front door slam. 'You've hurt his feelings, Oberon,' she snapped.

'What happened to dear?' asked Oberon.

'What do you think?' she said curtly, turning her back ever so slightly.

Puck groaned. Not already, surely?

'Mab,' Titania continued, 'you have been with mortals more than the rest of us, except possibly Puck. We'll need somewhere to meet.'

'What's wrong with here?' Puck asked.

'Too small, surely,' said Oberon.

'What's size got to do with it?' Puck asked, earning him a raised eyebrow from Mab. 'Yes,' he said to her. 'Har, har. But seriously, we can get into any space we like, can't we? We can just get smaller and budge up a bit.'

'In theory, yes,' said Mab. 'But not everyone has got the shrinking thing sorted yet. Not with their clothes anyway.'

Puck looked at Titania who had the grace to blush.

'We don't want a load of naked faerie caught in piles of clothes all over the place, do we? We need a hall of some kind,' said Mab.

'Ah,' Oberon enthused. 'A Hall. Decked with every faerie device, a Hall of infinite size, but that can yet be encompassed in a nutshell.' He clapped his hands and smiled around. 'Always my favourite venue for a party.'

'Indeed, Lord,' said Mab, sketching a small bow. 'I was thinking more in terms of a church hall, though. Scout hut. Community Centre. That kind of thing.'

'How do we find one of these things?' asked Puck.

'We just look for one. There's often a caretaker or something who can make the booking. We just have to decide when we want it. Oh, and pay, of course.'

'When do we want it, then?' Titania asked.

'Tomorrow night?' suggested Puck.

'Vat's a bit soon,' said Freckles. 'Will we 'av got enough to make it worf our while?'

'Two nights from now, then,' said Titania. 'We can't hang about. With Squeaky out there on the loose and the Unseelie knowing about us, we can't afford to linger.'

'True,' said Mab. Talk of the Unseelie unsettled her. They had absolutely no sense of humour. 'I'll pop out now, then, and see if I can find some. Can I have some money, please? I may have to pay a deposit.'

Oberon reached for his back pocket, but Puck stopped him. 'No, Sire. I think the deposit should be real money. We can pay the rest with yours. It won't matter by then.'

'Don't be late back,' Titania reminded her. 'We'll need to be flying before too long.'

Mab waved a casual hand and went out, glad to be back in the fresh air, away from the massed goblin odour. She didn't know how her Lady stood it. Just used to it, she supposed. She looked both ways at the gate. The main road was her best bet, she thought, and set off. This morning, she'd been a sad and lonely faerie and now she was an important cog in their way back to the top. How she loved the smell of the greasepaint, the roar of the crowd. As the Queen's hand-maiden, she'd be an important person. Woodland glade? No way.

Back in the kitchen, the last few jobs were being handed out. Puck would fly with the Queen and Mab. Oberon would go looking for Leanne.

'And *only* Leanne,' said Titania, acidly. 'No random wom-en, if you don't mind. We haven't got the time.'

Oberon looked the picture of injured innocence. 'As if...'

'Just remember. I *will* know.'

Oberon dropped his voice to a mutter. 'No you won't,' he said.

'You seem to forget,' said Titania, her voice like some-thing breaking off from a glacier, 'that I will be flying around, invisible when I choose to be. So, watch your back, Oberon!'

The goblins craned forward. They loved a good fight. But

they were to be disappointed. Oberon gave up and leaned back on his bank, chewing a blade of grass.

'Whatever,' he muttered, mulishly.

Titania smiled round the goblins. 'I think that the rest of you ought to stay here,' she said, in her best Queenly voice. 'We may be sending some of our Folk straight back here, if it's best for them. So you must be here to make them welcome. Except Freckles and Thydney, of course.'

'What have you got for uth to do, Mithtreth?' Thydney asked, excitedly.

'You'll be going with the King,' she said. 'Just to keep a few more eyes on him. And if he shows any sign, any sign at all, of not sticking to the plot, I give you my permission here and now to do whatever you see as necessary to control him.'

The two goblins looked at each other and hugged themselves in anticipation. Whatever they saw as necessary! What bliss! They scurried over and popped into the wall, to make their plans. Oberon gave a groan and sucked more furiously on his blade of grass.

'Don't sulk, Oberon,' said Titania, as she swept out. 'It makes your eyes look piggy.'

Tiny was outraged. 'And what's wrong with that?' he asked huffily, as he went over to chat up a rather attractive sheep.

28

Mab swung off down the High Street and soon came to a Methodist Church. She couldn't read the board outside very well, but could glean enough to tell that the caretaker was the Minister and that he lived in the Manse round the back. She edged down the side of the building, which had become hemmed in by a DIY store on one side and a newsagent on the other.

She went through a wicket gate at the back of the alleyway and found herself in a totally unexpected oasis of calm green, fronting the Manse, an elegant Victorian building of two wings, held out to the garden like arms. Late chrysanthemums glowed against a wall over to her left and a shower of Michaelmas daisies lolled in the opposite flowerbed. She stood still for a moment, clearing her lungs of traffic fumes and gathering her thoughts together. The Priests she had come across had tended to be rather unworldly men, with the possible exception of the ones who used to visit her backstage in her Music Hall days. But you couldn't be sure, these days, so she had decided to say that their meeting was an open meeting to discuss a possible Christmas Panto. She thought he might like the Christmas connection.

She stepped onto the gravel path and her feet crunched loudly. A woman, who had been bending down, weeding, among the chrysanthemums, straightened up, hands in the small of her back and called, 'Hello? Can I help you?'

Mab waved and went over to her.

'Oh, do be careful,' said the woman. 'This grass is sodden. Don't get your shoes wet.' She herself was wearing Wellingtons, a headscarf and a gardener's apron. She had to be the Minister's wife.

'I'm looking for the Minister,' said Mab.

'I'm afraid he's out,' she replied. 'Can I help you? I'm his wife.'

'It's about hiring the hall,' Mab explained.

The woman wiped her hands down her apron and hopped lightly out of the flowerbed. 'I know where the diary is,' she said. 'Come with me and we'll see if the day you want is free.'

'It's an evening I'm after, initially,' said Mab.

'Hmm, that may be difficult,' said the woman. 'Evenings are very busy, as a rule, with badminton, tai chi, line dancing. We even have,' she lowered her voice, 'alcoholics anonymous.'

Mab bridled. She could give it up whenever she wanted. What was this woman getting at? 'Is the night after tomorrow night free?'

'Hmm. Wednesday?'

'Possibly.'

The woman gave her a funny look. 'Yes, as a matter of fact, it is. The psychics had it booked, but they had to cancel.'

Mab had heard this one. 'Unforeseen circumstances?'

'No, the hall wasn't big enough, so they've gone to the school down the road,' replied the woman, giving Mab a searching look. 'My name is Mrs Harrington, by the way. Phoebe.'

They were in the hall of the Manse now, Mrs Harrington kicking off her Wellingtons and leading the way into the study. She picked up the diary from the desk and flicked through it.

'Here we are,' she said. 'I'll just write in your details. Name?'

'Mab,' said Mab. 'Er... Mabberley. Miss Mabberley. Well, more of a Ms, really.'

'And are you representing a group of any sort, Ms

Mabberley?' asked the Minister's wife.

'Yes. We're a dramatic group,' and that wasn't much of a fib, thought Mab, when you took everything into account. 'It's our first meeting.'

'How thrilling,' said Mrs Harrington. 'I like a nice bit of amateur dramatics, myself. Of course, Thomas isn't so keen...' she gave herself a little shake and smiled at Mab. 'Do you have any deposit with you that you could give me?'

'Oh, yes,' Mab said. 'How much would you like?'

'Er... five pounds would be adequate, I should think.'

Mab hadn't thought this through. She was useless with money and usually just offered it to the person concerned and they helped themselves. She had tended to rely on the home grown stuff, and was ill at ease with real currency. She held out a couple of notes. Mrs Harrington just looked at it.

'Five pounds, then,' she said, making no attempt to take anything.

Mab pushed the notes a bit nearer.

'Haven't you anything smaller,' Mrs Harrington said, in a tight voice.

'No. Sorry.'

'In that case,' said the woman, turning away. 'We'll just forget the deposit, shall we? I'm sure you can sort it out with Thomas later on.'

Mab put the notes back in her pocket. 'As long as you're sure,' she said. She was puzzled. She'd never had that reaction before. Anyway, she couldn't stay there all evening; she had places to be. She held out her hand to the woman; she had learned that they expected it.

Mrs Harrington put out her hand and tentatively took Mab's. Her hand was incredibly soft and, Mab was surprised to feel, clean, the nails shaped smoothly, no dirt, calluses, nicks or scratches. In other words, rather like her own, whatever the job in hand. Mab momentarily tightened her grip, then let go. She peered into Mrs Harrington's face and met a blank gaze.

'It must be quite hard, being a Minister's wife,' she said, 'in your position.'

'I don't know what you mean,' the woman said, backing

away.

'Well, how will you manage it?' Mab asked. 'I am merely curious. When he starts to look his age, and you don't.'

Mrs Harrington now had her back to the desk and was staring at Mab. 'Please go away,' she whispered. 'I really don't know what you mean. You're frightening me.'

'Yes,' Mab nodded. 'Yes, I expect I am.' She turned to go, then spun round on her heels, deliberately letting herself leave the ground as she did so. 'I have an idea,' she said, brightly. 'Why don't you come to our meeting on the night after to-morrow?'

'Wednesday.'

'Yes. Come along. You'll enjoy it.'

'I couldn't possibly. My husband...'

'If you don't come, I'll fetch you,' warned Mab.

'No. No, don't do that. I... I'll come. I'll be there to open the door at seven. But I may not stay.'

'We'll see,' said Mab. 'I think, once you're there, you'll want to stay.' She paused again. 'Tell me, do you have any children, Mrs Harrington?'

'Yes,' said the woman, sadly. 'I do. These are their pictures.' She held up a photograph of two children, a boy and a girl, with beautiful, identical faces and mops of curls, one blonde, one dark.

'I take it they don't take after their father,' Mab said, drily.

'No,' the woman's voice was almost a whisper now. 'No. They're more like my ... side of the family.'

'It's funny, isn't it,' said Mab reflectively, 'how once they've grown past that hideous phase, our children are very lovely.'

'*Our* children?' screeched Mrs Harrington, her voice high and dusty in the airless room. 'Whatever do you mean?'

Mab patted her arm as she turned to go. 'Just come to the meeting,' she said. 'If it's any comfort, I know what you're going through.'

Suddenly, Mrs Harrington was the Minister's wife again. 'I am having serious second thoughts about letting you have the hall,' she said frostily. 'But I suppose I can't go back on it now. I'll see you on Wednesday. At seven.' She ushered Mab out of the door, and closed it firmly behind her. Mab stood there for a second before walking away down the path. If she'd had any doubts that Mrs Harrington was faerie, they were wiped away by the sound of soft weeping coming through the door.

29

Puck was thoughtful when Mab burst in with her news. Titania was ecstatic, swooping round the room with delight. She landed next to Puck, and planted a kiss on his nose.

'Why the long face?'

'You've lived practically next door to this woman for quite a while, and yet you've never met her or if you have, you haven't noticed what she is.'

'Why should I have met her?'

'Because you worked in a supermarket,' Oberon put his oar in. 'Everybody passes through there in the end.'

Mab said, 'I got the definite impression that she keeps herself to herself. She probably married this Minister bloke because she could hide behind that wall. I hope she comes to the meeting, though.'

'Why?'

'Well, because the children were about ten or twelve – they'll be turning soon, one way or another. Also, she must have been with him for a while now, and he'll start to comment on how she doesn't show her age. Then his hair will start to fall out, his hips will go and he'll be a candidate for Mr Dobie's help. And she'll still look twenty. She'll have to be off, soon. Does she take the children? What does she tell him? Does she still love him?' Mab wiped away a tear. 'I hope she doesn't.'

Puck, though not Mab's greatest fan, was perceptive enough to see what was happening and put an arm round her shoulders.

'How did *you* manage?' he said quietly.

She sniffed. 'I was lucky. The children very definitely took after their father.' Oberon offered her a hankie and she blew her nose furiously. 'It's still hard, though.' She brushed away the last tears. 'I'm not good at numbers, but I would imagine that the boy would be about sixty now.' Her brave smile nearly broke Puck's heart. He suddenly saw the soft centre under the wisecracking exterior, but knew she wouldn't appreciate his sympathy. He gave her a little squeeze and she moved away.

'It's very quiet,' Mab observed.

'Hazel's gone out with the sheep. I've told him not to bring any elders home with him, nasty, vicious things. Also, nothing that's gone too feral. The rabbits I've had to send back into the wall. Their ball games were getting on my nerves.' Titania flexed her wings. 'I'm getting a bit nervous all round, to tell you the truth.'

Oberon gave a little experimental jump. After his fluke of earlier, he was constantly afraid that he'd forgotten how to fly.

'Please, Sire,' said Puck, 'remember that you mustn't do that while you're waiting for Leanne. The goblins told me about that accident last time.'

'Accident?' Titania raised an eyebrow.

Oberon shrugged. 'Just a couple of women not watching the road.'

'Perhaps you could wear a hood, Sire, or something like that.'

'Or perhaps not!' said Oberon. 'I'd look like that stupid dog of Benedict's.'

'It doesn't have to be an anorak, Sire. What about a hat, then?'

'No. No hats. No hoods. I won't stand under a light, this time. I'm not waiting for a lift in general, am I? I'm waiting for Leanne. She'll see me even if I'm in shadow.'

'Especially then, probably,' said Mab, sharply.

'She's not so bad,' said Oberon, reminiscently, then coughed, remembering the Queen and her promise to be watching him.

'Let's not squabble,' said Titania. She certainly looked nervous, pacing about and wringing her hands, giving little hops and skips.

'What's the matter, old thing?' Oberon put his arm round her. 'I thought you were looking forward to this.'

Titania broke away from him. 'Well,' she said, stamping her foot. 'It's him.' She pointed at Puck.

'Me? What have I done?'

'Talking about why didn't I recognise her and everything. I can't do everything, you know.'

'It wasn't meant as a criticism, Mistress,' Puck said. 'I was just thinking aloud.'

'Well, don't,' snapped Mab, rounding on him. 'You've made our Lady nervous now.' She turned her back on him and bent down, wiping up Titania's silver tears.

Puck looked at Oberon, who shrugged. 'Don't look at me. I don't understand them,' he said. He glanced out of the window. 'Ah, well,' he said. 'Duskish. I'll be off. Meet you back here, that the plan?'

Mab nodded and mouthed over Titania's head, 'Behave yourself.'

'He'd better,' said Titania, through Mab's hankie.

Oberon whistled up his goblins and adjusted his coat. 'Are you up for a bit of a fly later, lads?' he asked them. Two trotters held out straight were their answer, but without the thumbs the message lacked a certain something. 'I'll take that as a yes,' Oberon said, swooping down the hall like the most beautiful bat in the world. 'See'ya,' and he was gone.

'Someone's in a good mood,' said Mab, thinking to take advantage.

'He's working,' snapped Titania. Mab had forgotten that, whilst Titania could say what she liked about Oberon, everyone else had to remember that he was the King and, as such, infallible. As far as Puck could calculate, everyone was equal now, in the snapper and snappee stakes.

'What size are we going to be?' he asked, to change the

subject.

'I've been thinking about that,' said Titania, sniffing prettily and dabbing with the hankie. 'I think quite small to begin with, but big enough to cope with wind and similar. Then, if we see a likely candidate, we'll land and approach on foot. Then, if we're wrong, it won't matter.'

'Good idea, Mistress,' gushed Mab.

'A touch time consuming, though?' added Puck.

'Possibly, at first. But what I think is that probably singletons like Mab and this Minister woman are not the normal thing. Most of our Folk will be in twos, like the King and me, you and Cobweb, Puck, possibly even bigger groups still. So, when we find one, we actually find two or more. Then, if they can still fly, they can help and soon we'll have hordes.'

'Hordes, Mistress?' asked Mab nervously. Hordes made her immediately think Unseelie.

'No, not *Hordes*! Just hordes, as in a large number. Lots, then.'

Mab was happier with lots.

'How many will we need, Mistress?' asked Puck.

'However many we find,' she said. 'However many we can find before the morning. And don't forget, there's tomorrow night as well. And by then, there should be faerie flights all over, gathering our Folk.' She stood on tiptoe, clasped her hands and closed her eyes. 'It will be marvellous,' she breathed. 'My Folk, gathered about me again.'

'And the Lord Oberon, Mistress,' suggested Puck.

'Hmm? Oh, yes, probably,' she said dismissively. 'But I was always everyone's favourite, Puck. Don't forget that. Then, when we've all gathered, we can... do something... to make mortals believe in us properly, give us our strength back. We'll be Back. Just like the Old Days.' She subsided onto her bank, smiling happily.

'Any idea of what we'll do?' asked Puck.

She looked vague. 'I don't know. I suppose I thought... something to do with television, perhaps. This Web thing Benedict was talking about. Personal appearances.' She flapped a hand at him. 'We'll think of something, never fret. Anyway,' she jumped up, 'We should be off, shouldn't we?

How are you at changing size now, Puck?'

He wiggled an uncertain hand at her. 'Most of the time, okay.'

'Fairly noticeable when it's not okay, though, isn't it?' giggled Mab.

'Let's just hope, shall we,' he said, sarcastically. 'And if I don't manage it, well, at least I will have given you a cheap laugh.'

Titania wagged a finger. 'No squabbling, I said. The other thing, what about clothes?' She swept her arm across her body and stood there in the most wonderful dress, stars caught in gossamer, underlaid with butterfly iridescence. She caught their expressions. 'Less?' she said quietly.

They nodded.

She swept her arm again and took out the stars.

As one faerie, they pressed their hands, palms down, on the empty air.

She turned down her mouth, but got rid of the butterfly element. 'It's getting very dull,' she sulked. She toned it down a bit more until they nodded and gave her the thumbs up. It was still very beautiful, but not what she considered quite the thing for a Queen about to come back into her rightful Kingdom. As they turned their backs, she put a few stars back in. But they knew their Titania – they had allowed for that in the first place.

Puck was neat but not gaudy in a close fitting, dark green. Mab nodded approvingly. 'I like that,' she said.

He smiled. 'A little something from my days as Robin Hood,' he said. 'I've always liked it. Lincoln is the new green.'

Mab wore a dress modelled on Titania's, but, for she valued her position, not as fancy. No stars, no glitter, but an impeccable cut and sweep to the fabric. There was a flower on her left breast, which Puck knew was a trick one – he could see the hole. Mab was back.

They had decided to leave from the back garden. It was dark there, no street lights on the service road behind the houses and not many people about at this time of the evening. They stood together, slightly self-consciously, and, hand in hand, took off in a spiral to the sky, getting smaller and smaller as they rose. At about bumble bee size, they stopped. It was comfortable, invisible and it was Puck's favourite size anyway.

Mrs Jones had been feeling better. The tablets had worked and she had decided that the kitchen was just an optical illusion. She didn't seem able to actually put her hand on the cooker, though, so Mr Jones had gone off for some chips. He had been gone rather a long time. This was because he had spent twenty minutes sitting on the corner, smiling at a carrier bag caught in some railings. But he was back on track now, and would soon be arriving with cod and chips twice, the Monday pensioners' special.

Mrs Jones had decided that a breath of air might help, and anyway, it would get her out of the kitchen. The sitting room had been a no go area since the morning, when she had found some rabbit droppings in the hearth. She was standing, feeling better, looking up as the stars came out one by one, when she saw something move out of the corner of her eye.

She refocused and, sure enough, three faeries, two female with big, shiny wings, and one unmistakeably male in tight green rigout, passed overhead. One of the female ones waved at her, and she heard a distinct 'Cooee!' She went back indoors, and made for the stairs. Nothing odd happened up there, unless you counted the other night, when she had woken up in Mr Jones's bedroom. She shuddered, but carried on up the stairs anyway. Now, where were those tablets?

'Mab, really!' scolded Titania. 'I believe you scared the poor old soul.'

'I was only being friendly,' said Mab. 'I think if a mortal thinks they're seeing things, they'd rather think they were seeing *friendly* things. Don't you think so, Puck? Puck? Don't you think so?'

But Puck had flown on ahead. There was something in the woman's expression that had alerted him to the brevity of his costume. He was making some last minute adjustments.

30

Oberon was standing casually by the side of the road, whistling aimlessly through his teeth. He liked wide open spaces, even if he did get buffeted from time to time by the wake of giant lorries. It was a dry night, with no wind. He could hardly keep his feet on the ground, he was so excited. It wasn't that Titania wasn't perfect. It wasn't that she wasn't beautiful. It was just that... she was *so* perfect and *so* beautiful. She knew all his tricks. But Leanne – he could still impress her, despite her Unseelie ways. He swayed lightly from side to side, with the joy of being King of the Faerie Rades.

The car pulled up, almost silently. He bent down and looked in.

'Hello, Oberon,' she said.

'Leanne!' he tried to sound at least a little surprised. He got in.

'Benedict said I'd find you here.'

'Oh.'

'Don't sound so disappointed. You were waiting for me, weren't you?'

'Well, yes.'

'Then don't be ungrateful. If he hadn't made me come here, you could have waited all night.'

He shrugged.

'I'll take you back to Benedict's penthouse.'

'What, straight away?' He turned on the glamour, thick and strong. The pheromones were so heavy in the air she could almost feel them condensing on her skin. 'Ow.'

'Ow? Oh, I see, you're carrying goblins, are you?' she leaned sideways slightly and called, soft and low, 'Come out, lads. I know you're in there.'

Freckles and Thydney popped out onto Oberon's lap and clambered over onto the back sill, where they lay on their stomachs, trying to look endearing. Drivers behind, briefly eating Leanne's dust, wondered where she had bought the nodding goblins – very funky.

'Thorry I kicked you, Thire,' said Thydney.

'Just doin' our job,' added Freckles, bestowing a ghastly grin on Leanne.

'Don't mention it, boys,' Oberon said. 'But I know what I'm doing.'

'I think that's what they're afraid of,' Leanne laughed, and reached behind her to ruffle Freckles's bristles. 'But they needn't worry. My Lord has you sussed as has your Lady. So, straight to his flat, I'm afraid, Oberon. Things are on the move. No time for fun.'

Oberon sighed. 'That's what I'm afraid of,' he said.

Benedict was pacing back and forth across his perfect cream carpet. He was soundlessly trying out the King's name in his head. In his head, it all worked just fine – Oberon. Just like that. Try it out loud, though, and what did he get? 'O...O...O...'

'Oberon, Sire,' said James, appearing silently at his elbow.

Benedict spun round angrily. 'I know, I know. And James?'

'Yes, Sire?'

'I do wish you wouldn't creep up like that.'

James looked crestfallen. 'I can't help it,' he said apologetically. 'It's my feet. They just don't make a noise.'

'We'll have to get you shod, or something,' Benedict said.

'Ooh, really, Sire, that would be wonderful!'

'Weirdo!' muttered Benedict and resumed his pacing. He would have to settle on something else to call his half-brother, but he couldn't think of anything. Obviously, 'mate' was out of the question. Initials might work, he used them all the time in meetings, but that would just leave him saying 'O' again – as far as he was aware, he and Oberon didn't have another name, which was why he had adopted McAdam – son of Adam had tickled his irony bone. Never mind, it would just have to resolve itself. Such things usually did, he found.

The buzzer on the intercom went and he called to James. 'Let Lady Leanne in, would you?'

'We're in,' Oberon's voice buzzed in his ear.

Benedict controlled his muscles quickly and managed not to jump. Ignoring Oberon for the moment, he turned to Leanne. 'Well done,' he said, patronisingly. 'That was quick.'

'I was waiting,' said Oberon. 'We need to get a few things sorted out. Titania, Mab and Puck are flying tonight and tomorrow. We have a meeting planned for the next night. What have you got in mind for your next move?'

Benedict sat down languidly and crossed his legs, playing for time. He looked at Leanne and waved a hand. 'I believe you have the floor, dear,' he said.

She glared at him, but began anyway. 'Benedict has had goblins watching TV in case any more of your Folk or our Horde shows up. They are also keeping what I suppose we must call ears to the ground and reporting back if they notice anything.'

'And have they?'

'Have they what?'

'Noticed anything. Seen any more of our Folk on the TV?'

'Not as yet,' she smarmed. She poked his midriff. 'Why don't you unload these two? They could go into the other room and start watching. The more eyes, the better. I assume you've made them with just the two? I wasn't looking.' The goblins jumped down, and sank up to their ankles in the deep cream carpet. She pointed out the door and they scampered off. There were sounds of bouncing on the kingsize bed. Leanne raised her voice to cover it. They didn't need Benedict being pernickety now. 'I expect that our goblins will save up sightings and report nil at once.' She smiled again. 'Time management. I don't expect you've had much use for it. Would you like me to explain?'

'Don't push it,' growled Oberon, shoving his face into hers. 'I'm very even tempered, as you both know, but you also know you don't like me when I'm angry.' He calmed down instantly, and the others breathed again. 'I have also had one of my goblins watching the television, but so far he hasn't seen anything that would be of interest.'

In fact, at the very moment he was speaking, Bertie was jumping up and down on the sofa, pointing with a frantic trotter. On the screen was a still picture, rather blurred, but unmistakeably Squeaky. He was caught in a classic guilty pose, turning round from foraging in a bin, head turned to the camera, arm deep in the rubbish. The camera switched back to the studio, where the newsreader had been joined by a serious looking man with a whole lot of writing across the bottom of the screen. Bertie correctly assumed that meant he was important.

'Professor Gwyddion,' the newsreader was saying, 'this photograph was delivered to our offices this morning by a member of the public, who had captured the creature on film in the early hours while he was walking his dog. Do you have any idea what it can be?'

The professor steepled his fingers and tapped his chin thoughtfully. 'In my work as Visiting Chair of Zoological Anomaly at the University of Saratoga, I see many creatures, as you call them, which currently defy classification.' He stopped speaking and smiled enigmatically at the newsreader, who seemed startled that he had finished so soon.

'Erm, yes.' He pressed his earpiece in more tightly, as his editor screamed from the control box. 'Could you, though, tentatively provide a genus into which this animal might be placed?'

The professor continued smiling and nodded his head in

an enigmatic way.

Sweating slightly, the newsreader asked, 'In a few words, Professor Gwyddion, before we close, what is this animal?'

'I have no idea.'

'Thank you, Professor,' said the newsreader, as the music signalling the weather started to swell.

The Professor leaned back in his chair as the lights dimmed. 'I think that went pretty well, didn't you?' he asked.

All the newsreader could do was look at him with open mouth. He recovered enough to say, 'Come on, now. Off the record? What is the bloody ugly thing?'

The Professor gathered up his long coat and stood up. He leaned over and shook the man's hand. 'Well, a goblin, obviously. I thought you knew that. A bit startling for before the watershed, though, I thought. If you want to make a feature programme or anything, when you have more convincing footage, contact my agent. Leanne Shee. She's in the book,' and he turned to go.

The newsreader grabbed his sleeve and stopped him. 'We'll do a piece to camera now,' he said, hurriedly. 'This is huge news.' The way he saw it was, it was either huge news, that a goblin was loose in Hyde Park, or it was huge news, see a Professor go stark staring bonkers on prime time television.

Without apparent effort, the Professor freed his arm. 'Can't stay,' he said. 'I have some people to see. Urgently. Some other time, perhaps.'

Bertie didn't know quite what to do. Poor old Squeaky, out there, foraging in other people's left offs. Not too bad in itself, possibly, but he was all by himself, and no goblin liked to be alone. He ran round in aimless little circles for a while, shaking his front trotters in distress. Everybody was out somewhere, or useless. He would just have to sit down and wait for the others to get back. He settled back on the sofa, and within minutes was doing what he did best. His gentle snores were soon mingling with the muted television and peace descended again on Thirteen Ellesmere Crescent, except for the occasional short scream echoing through from next door.

Leanne's mobile shrilled. Her ringtone was based on the shriek of a bean-sidhe she had once known up in the Highlands. She flipped open the phone.

'Yes?'

The others craned nearer to hear the other side of the conversation, but she half turned away. With a sly glance at each other, the brothers just tuned themselves in anyway.

'Leanne? It's Gwyddion here. Were you watching just now, the news? I was on.'

'Any fee?'

'No.'

'Well, why are you telling me, then? I'm a bit busy, Gwyddion, to tell you the truth. Can I catch you later?'

'Not if I can help it,' he said. 'No, I wasn't ringing so you could have your pound of flesh,' his laugh was hollow. 'I was ringing to tell you why I was on.'

She sighed. 'Go on, then. Why were you on?'

'Someone has taken a photograph of a goblin in Hyde Park. It was an item on the news.'

' *What!*' they chorused.

'Is somebody with you?' Gwyddion asked, nervously.

Leanne made a rapid decision. 'Yes. Benedict and Oberon.'

'*The* Oberon?'

'I wonder why you think there might be another,' she said, curtly.

'No reason. Is this anything to do with the goblin?'

'Not directly, but I think he knows something about it. It's one of his, I think.'

'Ugly enough, certainly. Look, can I come over? Where are you?'

'I think you should. I'm at Benedict's. Do you know it?'

'Yes. Could you open a window. I'll be with you in a twinkling.'

'Okay. See you in a minute, then.' She crossed the room and opened a window.

'Who was that?' Oberon asked. 'Why did you tell them I was here?'

'A client,' said Leanne. She turned to Benedict. 'You remember Gwyddion, don't you?'

'The wizard?'

'Yes.'

'I don't think we've ever met,' said Oberon.

'No, I don't expect you would have done. He's a bit Celtic fringe, Arthur, Merlin, Taliesin, that kind of thing. He's dropped the Welsh accent now, I'm glad to say. Dresses a bit more normally as well – he was difficult to find jobs for, dressed like something out of Tolkein.'

The two faerie kings turned as one and spat silently over a shoulder.

'He's been the brains behind most of the famous magicians over the years, Maskelyne, Houdini, Blaine. But now, he fancies himself as an academic.'

A voice in her ear said, 'That's because I *am* an academic, dear lady.'

'Hello, Gwyddion,' she said, without turning. 'Introduce yourself. I'll get James to bring in some refreshments, shall I? We need to get plotting.'

'Planning,' corrected Oberon. 'I think Titania prefers plans to plots.'

'She's changed a bit then, since the Old Days,' muttered Leanne, leaving the room.

The tall man in the long sweeping coat extended a hand, but both faeries chose to ignore it. He looked at them searchingly for a moment and then bowed his head, hardly more than a nod, but it satisfied them and the atmosphere lightened.

'Gwyddion,' the wizard said. 'Professor at the moment, but in general, I try to be what the times demand.' He looked scarchingly at Oberon, then at Benedict. 'I am beginning to wonder, though, whether the times might be changing very fast right now.'

'We hope so,' Leanne said, coming back into the room

with a tray of nibbles and a jug of water. 'Oberon, could you explain about the goblin? And you could also fill Gwyddion in on what's been going on so far? Benedict and I need to summon up some of his goblins. I think time management has to take second place to finding out what the bloody hell is going on.'

Making a mental note to put her in her place when he had time, Oberon sat on the leather sofa with Gwyddion and started from the beginning. 'The other day, the wife – Titania, you know – came home from work...'

Making a mental note to put her in her place when he had time, Benedict went with Leanne into his bedroom. They cleared a space, not because they needed physical area to do their fell duty, but because it reminded them of the castle Up There.

'Creatures of air, come to me,' intoned Benedict.

'Creatures of water, come to me,' hissed Leanne, raising her arms.

Benedict stopped. 'Water?' he said. 'Do we have to? You know what a mess that makes. The weed, the drips...'

'...the blood...'

'...the horse shit...'

'Oh, come on. The nuckalevee hasn't turned up in centuries. I think the poor thing has gone a bit senile.'

'Oh, no! I'd forgotten about the nuckalevee! I was thinking about the kelpie.'

'Fair comment. Look, probably we won't get many. But we'll have to try. We can't have the Other Lot outnumbering us at their meeting, can we?'

'All right, all right. But if they turn up, you'll have to tell them not to make a mess.'

She sighed. It was all the computers – he'd lost touch with reality. 'Creatures of air, come to me.'

'Creatures of water, come to me.'

James stuck his head round the door. 'Did you call, Lord?' he said, brightly.

Benedict sat down heavily on the bed and put his head in his hands. He looked up at Leanne. 'What do you say we go for a bit of a fly? If it's working for them, who knows, it might work for us.'

Leanne brightened and spread her arms experimentally. 'I could fancy a bit of exercise,' she said. 'And I know just where to start.'

'Oh, where?'

'With Black Annis. She lives in Hainault.'

'Really. I didn't know. Have you the address?'

Leanne avoided his eyes. 'Let's say, I know where to find her. Excuse me for saying this, Sire, but should we practice, first?'

Benedict was already crouched on the window ledge, looking down at the sparkling river below. He made as if to leap, but then climbed back down into the room. Crouching over his virtual kingdom all day may have made him rich, but it hadn't kept him fit.

'Just a little swoop round the room, perhaps,' he said. 'Just to get the old wings back in trim.' His back had sprouted two leathery excrescences, tattered and black, which, as he flapped them, gave off a smell of graves and dank, wet places. James inhaled deeply.

'Oh, Sire,' he said, ecstatically. 'My favourite smell. Just like the Old Days.'

31

Titania, Mab and Puck found it hard to keep their mind on the job. Mab in particular had always had the attention span of a firefly and the others had to constantly pull her back to the here and now, as she spun this way and that.

It was the time of evening when the streets were empty of casual wanderers. Everyone was scurrying, to and from home and work. Titania saw some of her erstwhile colleagues, walking down the High Street, cigarettes on the go, gossip in the air. She was pretty sure that she may have been the subject, but she could soar above it these days and she wished them the joy of it. What they were looking for, none of them could encapsulate in one sentence. It would be someone who was standing, not rushing. Someone who would be looking at what stars could be seen above the orange glow of the city. Someone who might be lolling against a tree, head back to lean against its bark. Someone who might be looking at something that the rushing humanity couldn't see.

Suddenly, Puck grabbed Titania's arm and pointed downwards.

'There!'' he said urgently. 'Look, over there.' Sure enough, they could see a faint figure, talking animatedly to a willow tree on the edge of the silted up stream on the edge of the recreation ground. It looked out of place among the abandoned trolleys and burger wrappers caught in the tree's roots. They swooped down to it, landing cautiously behind the trunk and then stepping out, full size.

The spirit raised its head from its earnest conversation. A grin split its bark. 'Mistress!'

Titania sighed and faced Puck crossly. 'Keep up, will you, Puck?' she said. 'It's Hazel'.'

'Sorry, Mistress,' said Puck, sheepishly.

'Never mind, Puck,' said Hazel, kindly. 'You spotted one from the air, and that's the main thing.' He gestured to a grey spirit, slowly detaching itself from the tree under which they stood. 'This is Willow,' he said, by way of introduction. 'Willow, this is...' but the Willow spirit had sunk to her knees in a low curtsey to the Queen. Behind his twiggy hand, Hazel whispered, 'She's quite slow-moving, but quick enough mentally, one thinks. Just not quite,' he gave a small, discreet and self-deprecating cough, 'in one's league, one thinks you'll find.'

'Well, there's a mercy,' muttered Mab, stepping smartly behind the tree and shrinking to bumble bee size again. 'Come on,' came her tiny voice. 'We're wasting time.'

Hazel and Willow raised their arms to the trio as they spiralled off into the orange glow. 'Don't forget your twig, my dear,' said Hazel, in an avuncular tone. 'Don't want you fading away, do we?

As the Queen disappeared from view, quicker than a flying spark, Puck tried hard to keep up. 'Don't be cross with me, Mistress,' he begged. 'Hazel is right. I recognised him. So now we know it's possible.'

She turned her head and stopped, treading air as he caught her up. She smiled at him and said, 'You're right. I'm sorry. Let's get on, and, while we fly, tell us what to look for.' She linked an arm in his, and held out the other to Mab. They did a bit of formation flying, just for the fun of it, as they swept over the city, heading for the country where they knew their Folk were happiest.

With the orange glow at their backs, they could see more clearly. Mab stopped suddenly, dragging the others back and for a moment, there was an ungainly tangle of gossamer, wings and legs. When they were separated, with Mab's hair finally loosened from Titania's coronet, she couldn't get her bearings and spun round disconsolately on the spot. But then Puck saw what she had noticed. Below them, tucked into a hedge bottom, the tiniest spark of light, winking slowly, but irregularly, on and off, off and on. Sometimes, it would go out for several heartbeats, but then would twinkle madly for seconds together. They looked at each other and, as one faerie, dived to the road on the other side of the hedge and grew to mortal size.

'This is no good,' said Mab. 'I can't see anything now.'

'That's the trouble,' said Puck. 'I don't know how big that light was. There's nothing to judge it by. It might have been a firefly or it might have been a bonfire.'

'More a firefly, I reckon,' said Titania.

'Or a torch,' offered Mab.

'Definitely not a bonfire, though,' said the Queen, definitely.

'Sshh!' Puck put his finger to his lips and touched the Queen lightly on the arm. 'I can hear something.'

They listened, but the sound had stopped.

'I can't...' began Mab.

'No, hush,' said Puck. 'There it goes again.'

This time they all heard it, faint but distinct. Sobbing, as if some small creature was breaking its heart on the other side of the hedge. Among the sobs, there was sometimes a tiny wail, followed by a sniff. It appeared to sometimes pull itself together, but then would be off again.

'I don't care who or what that is,' said Titania, suddenly. 'We've got to help it.' She was down to flying size and over the hedge before either of the others could stop her. The sobbing was briefly replaced by a small shriek, then silence. Before they could move, they heard the welcome sound of a laugh. Looking at each other with grins broad across their faces, they jumped in the air and shrank.

Mab didn't know quite what to say. Puck had left his clothes behind again. 'Ermm, you've... you're...' she pointed vaguely.

'Oh!' Puck dived back behind the hedge. 'Be with you in a moment.' There was rustling as he wrestled with the now enormous clothes. 'It's the excitement.'

'That's what they all say,' muttered Mab, flying over the hedge to join her Mistress.

A sight to gladden any faerie breast met her eyes. The Queen was crouched in front of a velvety mushroom, dusted with earth where it had only just come through. And on it, sat the sweetest little elf Mab had ever seen. About half Titania's flying height, he sat cross-legged on his mushroom, wiping away his tears with the back of his hand. He was dressed in palest green, like just-popped blackthorn buds and on his head was a tiny acorn cup, still soft and new.

'Hello,' she said, crouching beside her Queen. 'Who are you?'

His brow creased a little. His bottom lip trembled slightly and he gulped before he could answer. 'That's the trouble,' he said, with another sniff. 'I don't know.' His little light flickered and went on and off as he trailed off into sobs, quieter now, but not easily dispelled.

Mab was enchanted by the creature, but had never had a very long fuse. 'Of course you do!' she snapped. 'Everyone knows who they are.'

'Well, I don't,' he said, reaching for Titania's hand for comfort. 'The only thing I know is that I was sitting on this mushroom in the dark. And then you were here,' he pointed at Titania. 'And then you.' He pointed at Mab.

It was not good timing, but Puck suddenly came barrelling out of the sky over the hedge and landed in front of the mushroom.

'Who are you?' he asked, a little testy and breathless after the problem with his clothes.

The poor little thing burst into tears again, and this time couldn't be comforted.

'Puck, you dolt!' the Queen snapped. 'Can't you see he's nervous?'

'And frightened,' said the elf through his fingers. 'I don't know what's going on.'

Puck looked down at it. 'Bit of a wimp, isn't he?' he said, dismissively. 'What's its name?'

By now thoroughly fed up, the elf leapt to its feet. Putting its hands on its hips, it said, 'Just listen, you great lump. I don't know who I am, because until you three turned up, I didn't know if there were any more living things about. I just suddenly was on this mushroom,' he kicked it peevishly. 'In the dark. By myself. Don't keep asking me who I am, or what's my name and nil that nonsense, because I don't know, all right? So just don't!' He sat down suddenly, arms folded, lips compressed and eyes dosed.

The faerie flight were staggered. Finally, Mab ventured, 'It's got a bit of a paddy on it, hasn't it?' she said.

The elf opened its eyes and looked at her steadily.

Puck had been thinking. 'So, you just were suddenly here?'

'Did I not say that?' it said crossly.

'Just checking.' He turned to Titania and pulled her slightly to one side. 'I think it's new,' he whispered.

She turned her head to look more closely and agreed. 'Everything looks very new born,' she said. 'But how can it be?'

'I think,' he said, 'that what with Bill on the television, some of your magic leaking next door...'

'I do not have leaky magic!'

'...well, whatever, us flying about, that kind of thing, I think the time is getting ripe for more belief. I think this little bloke,' he looked over his shoulder at the elf, and waggled his fingers at him in what he hoped was a friendly way, 'I think someone just thought him. Or hoped him, perhaps.'

'Hmm,' Titania tapped her front teeth with a forefinger. 'I thought that several children noticed us when we were in London. Could it have been one of them?'

Puck was thinking hard, thinking how slack they had been in the last few days. Oberon, floating drunk out of the pub, the leaking glamour at Number Thirteen, whatever may have happened to Trevor... he blushed to remember what he had done with his serviette in the cafe he'd been in that very morning. But in his defence, he'd thought one more mouse, albeit purple, would blend quite well. It was no wonder that there was the odd new elf. With his arm round Titania's shoulder, he turned back to the mushroom.

'We're sorry for all the questions,' he said to the elf. 'We think you're new.'

'Didn't I try to say that?' it said.

'Yes, yes, we're sorry. We also think that it might be our fault.'

'Don't apologise,' the elf said, stretching. 'Now that you're here, I feel much better. And I'd rather be than not be, if you see what I mean.' He vaulted off the mushroom and stood on the ground at their feet. 'What're we doing now?'

'Can you fly?' asked Mab.

'Don't be ridiculous,' said the elf. 'I didn't even know I could stand up until just now.'

'Fair comment,' said Puck, twisting Mab's arm up behind her back before she could reach over and throttle the cheeky thing. 'If you're a typical elf, you won't be able to.'

The elf gave him an appraising look. 'You look like an elf to me,' he said.

Puck looked at his feet. 'Perhaps,' he said. 'But I'm a bit special. And I've been around a long time. I think the best thing you can do is see if there are any more elves, new or not, in this area. If there are, get them together and make your way into town for a meeting not the next night from now but the next. We'll pop by later to see how you're going. Keep your light on, if you can.'

The elf gave an experimental twinkle. 'It seems all right when I'm feeling happy,' it said.

'We won't bother looking for it, then,' said Mab, sarcastically.

'Now, now,' said Titania. She was feeling more regal by the minute. A whole new elf made her feel as if her kingdom might be on its way back after all. She bent down and spoke to the elf in what she hoped was a queenly tone, but which only succeeded in getting right up its nose. 'Just trot along now, my little man, and find some more like you. We'll be along again later and we'll tell you where to meet.' She patted him on the head, and off they flew.

The elf stood there, alongside his mushroom, staring after them. For a moment, he considered not doing anything the snooty thing had told him to do. Who did she think she was, taking advantage of an elf just because he was new? But then, the darkness, and the quiet snufflings of carnivores much bigger than him unnerved him, and he scampered off over the grass, eyes peeled for twinkling lights that weren't reflections in the eyes of wandering foxes and badgers. Better to have condescension than crunching, he decided.

'What a dear little thing,' said Titania, still in Queen mode.

'Are you joking?' Mab said. 'It's pretty, I grant you, and it may help to bring in the punters, but it's got a shocking temper. Still, as long as it keeps its mouth shut, we should be all right.'

Titania didn't like it when Mab resorted to her Music Hall idiom. 'It's not all about punters, Mab,' she admonished.

'Yes, it is,' Puck said, flying round them in lazy loops. 'We do need the more picturesque faeries to bring the mortals round to our way of thinking.'

'Which is?' asked Mab.

'That we exist, of course,' said Titania, who was practising trailing clouds of sparkling smoke as they flew. She trailed a hand lazily through it.

Puck coughed. 'You look a bit like a firework, my Lady,' he protested.

'Rather common,' said Mab, who knew a clinching argument when she thought of it.

The smoke disappeared. They flew on in silence for a while.

'There's one,' said Mab, diving. Seconds later, she was back, rather red in the face.

'Well,' said Puck, in the absence of an explanation.

'Courting couple,' she muttered.

Titania and Puck giggled behind their hands and they flew on. A small knot of trees appeared on the horizon. A faint glow was issuing from among the trunks at the edge. This wasn't a twinkling light like the elf's, more of an absence of darkness than a presence of light.

Puck pointed silently and they skirted round the wood, so

they could approach from the other direction. Not all lights were from their Folk. The Unseelie had lights too, corpse lights, phosphorescence of decaying things and they had to be careful.

As they got nearer, though, they could hear singing. They looked at each other, hopefully. The Unseelie weren't known for their singing, that was certain. Howling, screaming, baying – yes. Siren songs, possibly, but they were far from the sea. This singing was quite tuneful and very jolly.

Puck nudged Titania. She bridled a little, but realised it was just to attract her attention. Even so, she must remind him later not to nudge Queens. It was rude. She turned to face him and, in the gloom, could just see as he mouthed 'Dwarves?'

It was years since she'd seen a dwarf. She had usually come across them when Oberon was trying to get round her after some misdemeanour. Then, he would visit the dwarves and get them to make her something, usually metal. Gold, or silver. The dwarves would parade in front of her, holding their caps nervously in front of them, and present her with the jewels or whatever Oberon had splashed out on this time. There were always seven of them, for some reason. Yes, she quite liked dwarves. And, from what she could remember, usually fairly even tempered. If there was one thing that recent events had taught her, it was that her Folk were generally a rather grumpy lot.

They got nearer still, and peeped out from behind a tree. Sure enough, gathered around an open casket, the contents of which spread the light that wasn't light over their faces, sat the obligatory seven dwarves.

Puck stepped out from behind the tree.

'Hello,' he said. 'Mind if we join you?'

'Watch it, boys,' said one of the dwarves. 'He looks a bit fly. Probably selling something.'

Titania and Mab had the sense to stay behind the tree. Dwarves were notoriously immune to feminine charms, as a general rule.

'No, I'm not selling,' Puck said. 'I'm here on behalf of Titania and Oberon, your Queen and King, to call you to arms.

To bring Faerie to its rightful place again.'

The dwarves looked at each other in the nacreous light. They sucked their teeth and shook their heads. Finally, one spoke.

'I dunno,' he said. 'From what I remember, Oberon never did nothing for us. What we've got, we got for ourselves. Why should we help him now? It'll only be so he can have all the aggrandisement and grind our faces under his boot.'

'And he's a bad payer,' added another.

'Bad payer?' a dwarf from the other side of the ring laughed, like a door grating closed at the mouth of a mine. 'I wouldn't say he was a bad payer, would you?' he nudged the dwarf to his left.

'No, I wouldn't. I'd say he wasn't a payer *at all!*' he said in reply.

Titania, hidden behind her tree, was outraged. Mab held her arm to keep her hidden.

The subject of payment had really started them off. Puck could have kicked himself for mentioning Oberon at all. He had spent many a night down dwarf mines, with more excuses for not coming up with the agreed fee. But it hadn't all been his fault. Some things, like the king's first born daughter, a mountain made of crystal, straw spun into gold just didn't fall into even the King of the Faerie Rade's lap. He edged away from the circle.

'Well,' he said, quietly, 'if you happen to be in Guildford not the next night from this, but the next, we're having a meeting, Church Hall, High Street, you can't miss it,' and with that, he dashed round behind the tree and with one bound, the three were flying.

The dwarves sat there, very thoughtful.

'A meeting,' one said.

'A meeting, brother,' said another. 'Perhaps we can encourage the downtrodden faerie to arise and cast off their shackles.'

'Yes,' one dwarf got up, leaning heavily on his pick, 'Let us gather more of our brothers, and march to this meeting, where we will open the eyes of the rank and file of faerie.'

The circle shuffled awkwardly.

'No, don't let's get any others,' the first speaker eventually said. 'If we're going to divide the spoils of faerie between the deserving, we don't want to have to spread it too thin, do we? There might not be enough to go round.'

Muttering agreement, the seven dwarves hurriedly buried their treasure, and turned their little legs in the direction of the city.

32

Eventually, Oberon stopped speaking. Gwyddion blew out his cheeks and leaned back on the sofa. 'I had no idea,' he said, eventually.

'None of us did,' Oberon reassured him. 'I suspect that, if Titania hadn't lost her temper with everything, we would have just faded away. It may well have taken a while, but we would eventually have disappeared, with no one to notice we had gone.'

Gwyddion sprang up, clapping his hands. 'But now we're on our way!' he cried. A spritzer of lightning flashed from ceiling to floor, leaving a dark, smouldering burn in the centre of the top-of-the-milk carpet. Oberon and Gwyddion looked at it in dismay.

'Perhaps if we move a piece of furniture?' asked Oberon, veteran of domestic disasters without number.

Gwyddion flapped an impatient hand. 'There are more important things afoot than floor coverings,' he boomed. 'Benedict won't mind a little scorch mark.'

James came into the room to remove the tray and, seeing the burn, gave vent to a little scream. He pointed at the mark with a trembling paw.

'Who did that?' he asked, frantically. 'Did you do that?'

Oberon looked affronted. 'Do I look as though I do cheap conjuring tricks?' he said, haughtily. 'It was him.' He pointed to Gwyddion.

James scrubbed at it ineffectually with one foot. 'You'll really be for it when the Master gets back,' he warned. 'He turned the last cleaning lady into a frog for breaking a mug.' He looked reflective. 'There was a bit of a stink about that, as I remember. It cost him a lot of money, in the end.'

'The family, I suppose?' Gwyddion said, sympathetically.

'Yes,' said James. 'Not so much the frog thing. It was more the stepping on the frog thing...' His voice trailed away. 'Well, how was I to know she was behind the door.'

The wizard and the faerie were lost for words. Fortunately, James' attention span was short.

'So,' he said, pulling himself together, 'finished with the tray, are we?'

They nodded.

'Are my Master and the lady in the bedroom?'

'Yes. At least, I imagine they're still there.'

James knocked and, receiving no answer, looked in. He knew his Master was mostly hot air when it came to women. It was more years than James could count – which needn't be a long time, but was in this case – since he'd caught him in any kind of compromising position.

'They're not here,' he said.

'They didn't come this way,' Oberon said.

Gwyddion pushed his way past them both. He considered himself a bit of an expert in sleight of hand, after so much practice. He glanced round the room and then went back into the sitting room, closing the door behind him.

'In my considered opinion,' he said, gravely, looking from King to Butler, 'the birds have flown.'

'Typical,' Oberon spat. 'Typical of him to do a runner, just when things are starting to get a bit hectic.'

Gwyddion looked puzzled, then, 'Oh, I see. No, I mean, quite literally, they have gone for a fly. The window is open, you see.'

'Ah,' Oberon looked relieved. Leanne was a bit of an itch he couldn't scratch. It would be a terrible waste if she had disappeared back to some draughty castle or other.

Freckles' head suddenly popped out of the plaster, up high, near the mirrored ceiling, ''e's right, Master,' he said.

'We nipped in 'ere when they come in. They did a few scary fings and ven flew off.'

Oberon waved regally and Freckles disappeared. It was fun in these walls. Miles and miles of them and some weird stuff to explore round every corner.

Gwyddion turned to the bogle, standing to attention in the doorway. 'James,' he said, 'does your Master have any other... contacts, with whom we might get in touch?'

James scratched his head thoughtfully. Then, he bent round and started a rhythmic biting at the base of his tail. He dropped down on his haunches, and scratched along the carpet, a look of total bliss on his face. The two immortals looked away, embarrassed. In the ensuing silence, James got back to his feet and gave a discreet cough.

'I must apologise, my Lord, Sir. Occasionally, the... er... dog gets the upper hand. It won't happen again.'

Gwyddion gave a nervous smile and reminded him. 'Contacts?'

'I'm afraid I don't know how Sir is with gadgets, Sir.' He looked at Oberon and smiled. 'I know that my Lord Oberon is not...'

'I know, I know,' said Oberon. 'Common knowledge, no need to dwell on it.'

Gwyddion said, 'I'm not the whiz your Master is, James, but I can use a telephone, things like that.'

'In that case, Sir, my Master's telephone has one hundred pre-entered numbers. The first ten are his main contacts, day to day, one might say.' He waved an expansive paw towards the console, where Benedict's working day was spent.

'Thank you, James. Do you think your Master would mind if I were to...' he mimed button pushing, holding his hand with thumb and little finger extended up to his face.

'Personally, Sir,' said James, heavily, 'I would be so worried about the carpet that a little telephoning would hardly count.' He bowed and withdrew.

Gwyddion settled himself down in Benedict's chair. He picked up the phone and tentatively dialled a number. He looked up at Oberon. 'Answerphone,' he mouthed. He put the receiver down quickly. 'I really hate those, don't you?' he said.

Oberon twitched one corner of his mouth infinitesimally. How would he know?

He wandered over to the window and looked out at the view, the river dark and glossy, lights dancing and twinkling on its slightly oily surface. He squeezed his eyes shut and opened them again. Were the lights all reflections, or did some of them really have a life of their own? Even he couldn't tell, not from this height. Until proved otherwise, it cheered him to think they might be some of his Folk, massing down below. He leaned his head against the glass. It was so cool, to his hot and fevered brow. He really wasn't used to all this thinking. He let his mind drift off, trying to find Titania...

Suddenly, someone was banging on his head! No, not his head, but the glass on which he leaned. His eyes flew open and focussed. Leanne hung there, just outside, gesturing for him to open the window. It crossed his mind that, for many a Highland crofter, this would have been the last thing they ever saw on earth. He struggled briefly with the catch, then the window swung wide and Leanne flew in on a breath of fresh night air. Oberon didn't close the window, but looked out, right and left.

'Isn't Benedict with you?'

She was in the centre of the room, looking at the scorch mark. 'Who did that?' she asked.

'Never mind,' Oberon said impatiently. 'Where's Benedict?'

Leanne gave a little smirking laugh. 'He's coming up in the lift,' she said. 'He's had to walk from the bridge. He'd got a bit tired and didn't have the energy to re-cross the running water.'

She looked round at Gwyddion. 'What's he doing?' she asked Oberon.

'Getting in touch with some of Benedict's contacts,' said Oberon.

She reached across and snatched the phone out of Gwyddion's hand. 'You haven't spoken to any of them, have you?' she asked.

'No. I think they're mostly office numbers. There's no reply.'

She blew out a relieved breath. 'They're all mortals, you fool. Benedict doesn't trade with faerie, good or bad. He says you can't trust them.'

'Well,' Oberon said, 'he should know.'

'If they had any funny phone calls from this number, they would sell their shares in Benedict's companies immediately. The markets all over the world would go into a nosedive. The world would plunge into recession. There would be wars. And, worst of all, Benedict wouldn't be worth a bean.'

The door burst open. 'Why wouldn't I be worth a bean? Who did that?' he said, spinning round and pointing with trembling finger to the scorch mark.

Gwyddion slowly stood up and raised a tentative hand.

'I can't leave you alone for a minute, can I?' he said. 'And why were you sitting in my chair?'

Gwyddion was about to answer when he wrinkled his nose, fastidiously. 'Whatever is that smell?' he asked.

The odour coming through the front door and down the hall was almost visible. It slunk along the floor and wisped up the walls, tainting everything it touched. Polished metal tarnished at its passing and wood, patinated with the ages, dulled and became grey. Only James, looking out from the kitchen door, seemed to enjoy its pervading presence. It was followed swiftly by a banging and scratching at the door.

No one moved and the banging became louder.

'Open the door, James,' said Benedict quietly.

'Who is it?' whispered the bogle.

'Just open the door.'

'It's her, isn't it?' James whimpered, his pleasure in the smell gone. 'It's Black Annis.'

The banging at the door redoubled in volume and a strange, creaking voice was added to the general cacophony. There were words in there, but nothing any of the faerie inside could make out. The only thing that was clear was that they were full of spite.

'Yes, it is,' said Leanne, sharply. 'Now let her in, do, before she breaks the door down.'

James flung back the catch and leapt aside as the most revolting creature lurched in. Oberon looked at her with detached interest, Gwyddion, whose experience of such horror was less, recoiled in repulsion. She was bent almost double, so that she had to squint up at them from one red-rimmed and bloodshot eye. Her hair was matted solid around her face and down her back, and occasionally it moved slightly, apparently of its own volition. Her skin was cracked and filled with grime of a sort Gwyddion did not want to consider. Drool had hardened around her mouth and formed an armour plate down her front. Her hands were claws, one clutching a carrier bag, from which small, furtive eyes peered, accompanied by rustling, as of many feet and legs trying to get comfortable. The other claw held a stick. The nails on this hand were long and black. Had Gwyddion been able to get close, he would have seen small pieces of hair and fur sticking out from under those ragged talons. As it was, he backed away, pressing his hand to his mouth.

The creature's mouth opened, showing one black tooth, hanging precariously in the front. A scaly tongue flickered briefly in the cavernous opening and, in a dry voice Black Annis said to Benedict, 'Aren't you going to introduce me, Lord?'

Benedict coughed and indicated Gwyddion politely with one hand. 'I'm so sorry,' he said. 'Gwyddion, I'd like to introduce Black Annis, our most senior Hag. Annis, meet Gwyddion. He's a wizard, who has most recently been in show business,' he said it as if the words hurt his mouth, 'but you may know him best from King Arthur's court.'

She cackled phlegmily. 'Oh, yes,' she said, winking her rheumy eye. 'Those knights, eh? They were the boys!' She gave a reminiscent sigh.

Gwyddion's lips moved aimlessly. What he wanted to say was: the lads I knew wouldn't have given you the time of day, Hag, but he couldn't think of how to word it without giving offence. Before he could speak, however, a strange shimmering began in the hall, and finally centred on Black Annis. As he watched, the shimmering thickened into a gelatinous fog, with lights flickering within it. After a few seconds, a beautiful woman walked out and undulated up to Gwyddion. She clasped him round the waist and whispered, 'Just one kiss, Lord?'

Before any of the others could stop him, Gwyddion bent his head and kissed her — but only for the microsecond that existed for him before he found he clutched the foul Annis to his chest. She cackled madly as he threw her away from him and rushed from the room, clawing at his mouth. The next sound, apart from his retching, was running water and gargling, scrubbing and towelling.

Benedict smiled wryly. 'Not lost your touch, then?' he observed.

She sighed. 'Dun't last, laddie,' she said. 'That's the longest I've managed in... ooh, I dunno. Years.' She nudged Leanne in the ribs with a spiky elbow. 'They was good days, though, weren't they, lassie? Round those cottage eaves we'd go, share whatever we caught, eh? Still, nothing lasts forever, not even us. Although,' she gave Oberon the once over, 'You're in pretty good shape, Oberon. How's the good lady?'

'Well, thank you,' Oberon said. He knew not to mix it with Annis. She was truly evil, more than Benedict and Leanne; they were just greedy. Annis was *hungry*.

A final flush signalled Gwyddion's return. Annis looked round the company as best she could, from her hunched position. She admired the room. 'Better than a doorway, laddie,' she said, thumping Benedict on the arm. She made her way across to the sofa, stopping on the way near the burn mark. 'Somebody's made a bit of a hash o' your fancy carpet, though, I see,' she remarked. 'Get that dog o' yours to gi' it a bit of a wash.' Her eye flashed bright. 'Or ha' ye found the bean-sidhe yet? She's a bonny one wi' the washing, if ya dinna mind the blood.'

She bounced experimentally on the sofa and then stretched out on it.

'I'm fair worn out,' she murmured, as she closed her eyes. 'Switch off the light and close the door as ye go out.'

Stunned into silence, they all tiptoed from the room, leaving the cream leather sofa to Annis and her smell.

33

Wednesday morning dawned on Ellesmere Crescent in its usual way. Bit of mist, bit of sun, bit of screaming from next door as Mrs Jones awoke to face another day.

Titania was lounging on her grassy bank, looking languid and lovely. The goblins were out of sight, mainly because there was no room for them in the kitchen, but partly because Titania had felt that the general atmosphere was improved without very excited pigs, sheep and rabbits present. Mab was outside, leaning on the gate, scanning the pavement from left to right, trying to pick out any Folk making their way to the Queen.

Puck was upstairs with Oberon. The King was in a funny mood and Puck was worried about their meeting due for that night. He had the gist of what had happened at Benedict's, and Oberon's main complaint had been that nothing had happened. Leanne was playing hard to get.

'Sire,' Puck said. 'I don't like to see you like this. Leanne is a one faerie vampire, you know that. She's nailed her colours to Benedict's mast – which I must tell you is only a figure of speech,' for Oberon had turned a lover's tortured gaze on him, 'and so she's his come what may. She's always been the same. Famous for it.'

Oberon sighed. 'I know,' he said. 'But she's too good for him.'

'Very possibly, Sire. But she isn't too good for you. She's a vampire, Master. Please try to remember that.'

'Yes, I know. But she wouldn't bite me!' He looked rather wistful.

'Sire, she'll be at the meeting tonight. You'll see her then. But, really...'

'Just because she doesn't fancy you, Puck,' Oberon whined.

'For which I will be eternally grateful, Sire. Things are difficult enough, without that added complication. My bedroom is chock full of Mr Dobies. Who would have thought there were so many? They were up till all hours, playing dominoes and cribbage. The clicking nearly drove the goblins mad. There was quite a deputation waiting when my Lady, Mab and I got home.'

'How did it go?' asked Oberon, without enthusiasm. He was trying to think of a link to Benedict and Leanne, just to be able to say her name.

"Very well. Over the two night's flying, we found some elves – they'll be going straight to the meeting, by the way – some dwarves, although I'm not sure about them. They've gone a bit funny over the years. It seems they've caught a bad dose of politics. Mab spotted a few faerie strolling round town; she's got them coming over tonight. I'm not sure about them, I must say – they might be Horde, but never mind. Benedict will be at the meeting to keep order amongst his horrible lot.'

Oberon smiled at the memory of Gwyddion and Annis. 'You should have seen Annis and that wizard!' he said. 'How Leanne and I laughed.'

Puck sighed and rolled his eyes and carried on as if the King hadn't spoken. All the world is bored by a lover. 'Hazel has found a whole load of tree spirits, although the pig-headed creature ignored what the Queen said and brought home an Elder. She is busy trying to cause trouble with all the others, by gossiping and lying about them.'

'Gossiping? Lying? Just sounds like Faerie to me.'

'Possibly. But she's a nasty piece of work and I may be using her twig to light a bonfire shortly. Then there's that

Minister's wife. The Queen spotted another brownie doing that lollipop thing on the crossing outside the school. And,' he looked across the landing at the firmly closed door, 'we have a seemingly inexhaustible supply of Mr Dobies.'

Oberon took up the recital. 'Benedict is calling his goblins today and will be bringing a random sample with him tonight. Apparently, they can't all be spared from whatever it is they do. James is coming of course. Gwyddion, Annis and Leanne,' he lingered over her name, lovingly. 'As well as that, the bean-nighe has been sighted working in a launderette somewhere in Brighton. Leanne was going last night to see if she could find her. She gets the sack quite often, as far as I could gather from Annis, for ripping the shirts quite badly and keening rather a lot. But she should be there.'

'Oh, nice,' said Puck, with little enthusiasm. The one time he'd seen a bean-nighe he'd nearly swallowed his tongue. She was homely, even by Horde standards, with an enormous nose and no visible mouth. Her lank hair was plastered with the blood of those shortly to die. It was hard to imagine her being related to Leanne, but they were sisters all the same.

'Benedict has decided to leave the nastier ones alone,' Oberon continued.

'They come nastier than Black Annis?' Puck asked.

'Well, yes. No. Not nastier, just... messier. You know the sort of thing that passes for beauty in the Horde. No skin, one foot, that kind of thing. He thought perhaps we'd start with the more attractive ones.'

'Well, they say beauty is in the eye of the beholder, but... Black Annis? Attractive?'

'She's practicing her other form. By tonight she ought to be able to hold it for quite a while.'

Puck shuddered. 'Let's hope so.'

'Leanne also suggested we leave the kelpies and nuckalevee and those watery ones alone. They don't really travel and Benedict has a rather nice carpet in his flat.' He remembered Gwyddion's little accident. 'Or had, perhaps I should say.'

'Oh, yes,' Puck said, 'don't let's spoil Benedict's carpet!'

'Don't be petty, Puck. We won't have to see any of them after tonight, if we don't want to...' his voice trailed away.

Puck just slapped his shoulder, hobgoblin to King and went downstairs to see how the Queen was faring.

She was still lounging, practicing Queenly looks on one of the chicken goblins which was scratching around in the doorway. She was waving one hand in what Puck privately thought was a rather condescending way.

'Ah, Puck. What do you think of the wave?' She did a few more for good measure.

'Very regal, Mistress,' said Puck. 'Do you think we ought to have some kind of plan in mind for tonight?'

Her eyes glazed slightly, as she looked into the future that would be her world. Her voice dropped to the timbre of the lightest breeze through ancient woodland trees. 'This.' She flung out her arm in an encompassing gesture, sketching in the air the canopy of green, the soaring larks, the nodding wildflowers. Cruelly, he considered what would happen if he flung out an arm and sketched in the six lane motorway, the choking fumes, the roadkill. But his Queen was beautiful, fragrant, near and needy.

He smiled at her vision and said, 'Yes, Mistress. But we have a lot of work from here to there. What direction is the meeting going to take, do you think?'

She looked at him in frank amazement. 'Well, mine, of course,' she said. She went back to practicing her wave.

He watched her for a moment more, just for the pleasure of it. Then he went out and joined Mab.

She turned briefly to look at him. 'Oh, hello, Puck.'

He nodded.

'Excited about tonight?'

He shrugged, without speaking.

'Well, I'll tell you how I feel, shall I?' she said. 'I don't care if you don't like me. It's not how I was expecting it to be. The Queen is as snooty as ever, Oberon doesn't give me a second glance, the Mr Dobies give me the ab-dabs and the goblins smell. The elves are snotty little blighters and the dwarves are plotting their own thing, and I don't think it involves a king or queen.' She stopped speaking.

'And?'

'And what?'

'There's an "and" in there somewhere. I can feel it trying to get out.'

'And I'm scared out of my wits at the thought of the Horde in the same room.'

'And?'

Her voice was very quiet. 'And I could really do with a drink. The queen is driving me mad with her drop of dew thing.' She looked at him. 'Let's forget our differences, shall we? I know you sneak bacon sandwiches when you're out for a walk. Tell me where the vodka is hidden and I won't tell the Queen about your meat abuse.'

Puck considered his options. No one had insisted he give up bacon, but obviously the goblins took it a bit personally. He could refuse to tell her and no harm done. But he felt a bit sorry for her, so he told her. 'It's not hidden. It's in the cupboard, next to the television.'

'I've had that. I want to know where the rest is hidden.'

'There is no rest. That's it.'

She bowed her head down on her arms, folded on top of the gate. 'But there's always more,' she whispered. 'There's always more.'

'Not here,' Puck said, stroking her back. 'You'll either have to tell the Queen and take a lecture, or buy some of your own.'

'Got no money.'

Puck reached into his back pocket. He handed her a ten pound note. 'This won't buy you much, but it's all I have left. Don't drink it all at once.'

She looked up at him, tears in her eyes. 'You're not so bad, you know,' she said, reaching up and giving him a faerie kiss.

He put his arm round her waist and held her close for a moment. She leaned on him and hid her teary eyes in his shoulder. The strength flowed, one to the other as they stood there. Passers-by, on their way to work, were cheered by their glow.

Puck broke their embrace. 'I must get on,' he said. 'Lots to do, lots to do.'

She looked at him curiously. 'Surely, everything's ready,

isn't it? It's not as though we need a disco or bowls of crisps or anything,' she gave a little laugh.

He nodded. 'Yes, it's almost done. Hazel and the others are already there. The goblins will take their twigs round later. They're going in small groups. That way, if any of them gets spotted, they won't be quite such a shock to the mortals who see them. One goblin, you can pass off as a trick of the light. A whole gobble of them; well, it might cause a bit of a riot.'

Mab pictured the scene and couldn't help a guffaw. 'It would be wonderful,' she spluttered, her tear-stained cheeks glowing with the excitement.

'Don't even consider it,' he warned. 'The Mr Dobies are going to amble round in ones and twos. They are also best not seen in a group, but they're so bland, I doubt whether any mortal would remember them from one minute to the next.'

'What about the elves and dwarves and faeries?'

'They're going straight there. That is the main problem, as far as I can see. We'll just have to trust our judgement about letting them in, if they're just there by word of mouth.' He looked a little concerned, but then shrugged it off. 'But, hey! Who's going to come, if they're not one of Ours.'

'Anyone who's one of Theirs,' said Mab, suppressing a shudder.

Puck looked solemnly at her. 'You're going to have to stop this,' he said. 'We've got to have them, at least at first. Personally, I'd rather know what they were doing. That way, I'm not looking for them behind every bush.'

'Or thinking they *are* the bush,' said a voice at his elbow.

Mab and Puck looked down. They could see nothing to account for the voice.

'Who said that?' Mab demanded.

'Me,' came the voice.

'And you are?'

'The Thyme Faerie.'

'I didn't know there was one,' said Puck, without thinking.

'Oh, very nice,' the voice said. 'All right to lollop all over, oh yes. When it comes to being invited to meetings, that's a different matter, I suppose.'

Mab edged away, back into the house. These flower faeries could get quite nasty when pushed and lots of them could sting, or were poisonous. She wasn't very up on plants.

Puck got down on his hands and knees. 'I'm terribly sorry,' he said to the plant. 'Of course we'd like you to come. And, bring your friends, if you like. Do you need a lift of any kind?'

The voice was rather less huffy now, and it said, 'Thank you, no. We can fly.'

'You kept that very quiet,' Puck observed.

'We didn't like to butt in.'

'How very... punctilious of you.'

'Don't use long words on me,' another voice chimed in.

'Who was that?'

'Me. Over here. Dead nettle. *Common* dead nettle, to be exact.'

Puck knelt up straight and spread his arms. He spoke to the little front garden at large. 'Please forgive me for not inviting you,' he said, in a voice that would carry. 'You're all very welcome, of course.'

Mr Jones, opening the front door to take the wife for a bit of an airing in the Morris Minor parked at the kerb, jumped back into the hall as if he'd been shot. 'Don't go out there, Doris,' he cried. 'That young bloke she's moved in next door is asking the garden to a party. Best you don't see.'

There was a wail from the kitchen. 'Oh, where's those tablets?'

But Mr Jones was already climbing the stairs.

34

Titania's bedroom was a hive of activity. Like a young faerie setting out on her first Midsummer Eve, she had tried on dress after dress. Mab fluttered around, having settled for a classic pale gown and gossamer wings, which folded, when not in use, into a translucent cape at her back. Oberon had escaped hours before, his usual black enlivened by a discreet gold circlet, nestling in his tumbling curls. The whole house was abuzz with suppressed excitement, as Puck put everyone through their paces, checking and double checking that they knew what they had to do. The goblins he was sending out in strict rotation, with instructions to be quick, to be discreet and, most importantly, if seen, to disappear into the nearest wall. Several sheep had come back twice, unable to find their way.

Freckles and Tiny had automatically taken on the roles of marshals, lining the goblins up and generally behaving as though they were wearing uniforms. In fact, a close examination would have shown a pair of clumsy epaulettes, sewn by inexpert trotters, clinging precariously to Tiny's sloping shoulders. But they were happy, and no trouble, so Puck let them do their own thing.

The Mr Dobies were causing their first problem. None of them wanted to go until they had watched their afternoon quiz shows. They were all gathered round the television, shouting out random and invariably wrong, answers to all the questions. With each answer, there came a chorus of 'wasn't the answer in my day.' Again, Puck had enough to do and left them alone. He just hoped that they could shuffle fast enough, when the time came, to get round to the Hall in time.

Otherwise, everything was going frighteningly well. He had a few minutes in which to dress. He had decided on the tight green number, with the leaf-like edging. It set off his boyish build a treat and with his hair lightly gelled and a spot of borrowed glamour from Oberon, he was a sight for sore eyes. He remembered that Annis would be there, shuddered and toned it down a bit. But he was still a knockout – he could be nothing else.

Oberon was sprawled on the bank, where the cooker had once stood. His magnetism was leaking everywhere and exotic blooms were growing, visibly growing, inch by inch, up the sapling in the corner. Their heady scent filled the air and the room was heavy with the sound of drowsy bees. Puck would have given anything to just lie down at his Master's feet, to soak up the atmosphere, to dream the afternoon away until some frolic should present itself. He folded at the knees and his lids grew heavy.

'Oy,' said Freckles, still in RSM mode. 'No sleepin' on the job. Goblins all in place, tree spirits' twigs on the Hall windersill. Tiny's out in the front garden now, it's alive wiv midges. He's sortin' it art.'

Puck sprang up. 'What's he doing?'

'Sprayin'. Swattin'. I dunno.'

Puck dashed out into the hall and met Tiny as he hurtled in through the door.

'Ow!' he squeaked, 'They bite!'

'They're flower faeries!' Puck said. 'Not midges, you stupid creature.'

'There're clouds of them out there,' Tiny gasped. 'Look.'

Puck peeped through the letterbox and sure enough, the air was thick with a seething cloud, which was centred on the front gate of Number Thirteen.

He went out and stood on the path. 'Clear off,' he hissed. 'People will see.'

A cacophony of tiny voices came out of the cloud. He couldn't make head or tail of it, but he assumed they were complaining. In his experience, that's what flower faeries did, most of the time. It's too hot. It's too cold. Haven't got enough water. Too wet... it went on and on.

'I don't mean clear off,' he said. 'I just mean, don't make a cloud like that. Disperse. Go round to the Hall, if you like. There's a nice garden there, according to Mab. Why don't you wait there? We'll be along ourselves soon.'

Grudgingly, the cloud broke up and, like smoke, disappeared on the air. Puck went back inside. Tiny was in the kitchen, having a nasty little bite on his ear tended to by a concerned sheep. He was leaning his head against her soft chest. He looked very content, in the way that only pigs can.

Puck called up the stairs for Mab, who appeared on the landing looking harassed.

'What time do we have the Hall from?' he asked. 'You look very nice, by the way.'

'I don't know,' she said. 'Evening. Any time now. So do you.'

They smiled at each other.

'Can you bring the Queen down, then?' asked Puck, all confusion. 'We ought to be getting ready for the off.'

Mab glanced over her shoulder. 'She's not dressed yet,' she said.

Puck tutted. 'Tell her to wear Tam Lin's favourite.'

Mab wrinkled her nose. 'Are you sure? What about...?' she gestured to behind Puck, where Oberon stirred on his bank.

'Just tell her that.'

Mab went into the room to relay the message, but it had already reached the Queen. She stood there, in a robe of deepest burgundy, trimmed in gold. Although its folds hung heavy and luxurious from the high waist, it swung in an invisible breeze as she stood there, waiting for Mab's approval. The sleeves were tight to the wrist and over her hand, laced over with gold and gossamer. In her hair, piled on top of her head, a tiny crown was visible, made of fireflies and spiders' web, dotted with fresh beads of dew, trembling forever on the edge of a leaf.

Mab sank to her knees and bowed her head. Titania reached down and drew her up. She planted a faerie kiss on her cheek. 'C'mon, Mab,' she whispered, 'Let's do it!'

She swept out of the room, and it was drab at her going. Mab gave herself one last glance in the mirror. Upstaged, outdone, but it would do. Downstairs in the hall, Puck was looking pleased with himself – that dress wasn't only Tam Lin's favourite. Oberon was simmering with rage, but it only added to his almost overpowering presence. Titania was looking up at her King through lowered lashes. A glance at the two of them explained to Mab why Puck had chosen that dress. Leanne wouldn't stand a chance.

Titania raised an arm to tone down her appearance for the walk round to the Hall, but Oberon grabbed her wrist. 'Allow me,' he said, and swirled his black cloak into the air, around them both. With a snap of his fingers, they disappeared. A small wisp of smoke was all that remained to mark their position. Puck tried the finger thing, with its usual result. Mab slipped her arm through his.

'Freckles, Tiny,' she called over her shoulder. 'Make sure everyone is out of the house in the next little while. We'll see you there.'

The two goblins stood in the kitchen doorway, saluting so hard their trotters trembled at their low brows.

'Let's go, then,' she said to Puck.

In the doorway, he turned to face her. 'What if this doesn't work?' he asked.

'We won't know about it, will we?' she said. 'So it doesn't matter. Let's look at it as just another gig. They can't eat us.'

'That's the trouble,' said Puck, as they let the door close behind them. 'Most of them can,'

❀❀❀❀

Benedict was hunched over his laptop when Leanne arrived.

'I thought you'd be ready,' she said, curtly. She sniffed. 'No Annis?'

'No, she's gone on ahead. With Gwyddion.' He didn't

look up.

'That's a bit hard,' she said. 'He's terrified of her.'

'He scorched my carpet.'

'Yes, but even so.'

James came in, dressed for the road. 'Hello, Lady. You're looking lovely as always.'

She looked down at her sober City suit and smoothed it carefully. 'Yes, thank you,' she said. 'I know I am.' She was thoughtful. 'I wonder what Titania will be wearing? Something over the top, as usual, I expect.'

James looked pensive. He always wanted to roll over and have Titania tickle his tummy. He couldn't help it – instinct was instinct after all.

She tapped her foot. 'Benedict, will you come on, please? We don't want to be late. Have you got those goblins rounded up, by the way?'

Benedict looked up, exasperation in his eyes. He pointed to his laptop. 'I'm putting them in here. They're so labile without a phone or something, so I've downloaded them as attachments. They'll all be in here in a few more minutes, if you'll just be patient.'

She mouthed, 'Sorry,' and sat down on the edge of the sofa. The scorch mark now looked rather worse, being bald in the middle and rather discoloured at the edges.

She pointed at it to James and raised an eyebrow.

He mimed an old fashioned washing board and grimaced. She nodded. So her message had reached the bean-nighe after all.

Finally, Benedict closed his laptop and said, 'What are you waiting for? We should be off.' He strode to the door, whipping his overcoat from the peg as he went.

James courteously held open the door for Leanne and closed it softly behind him. His loping walk hid his excitement. From tomorrow, or at worst the next day, he and his master would be back at home, sweeping over the heather of the Highlands, as they flew, sickle moon at their backs, the smell of their terrified quarry in their nostrils.

'Come along, James,' he heard Benedict snap. 'I'm holding the lift.'

'Sorry, Master,' said James and he ran round the corner, allowing just a little lolling tongue to show. Soon, soon he could get rid of this awful anorak, or perhaps use it as a bed before the roaring log fire. Oh yes, James was looking forward to the meeting. It was the first day of the rest of his endless life.

35

Phoebe was waiting in the lobby of the Hall when Puck and Mab arrived. She was dressed more or less how she had been when Mab had seen her last, but minus the gardening apron.

'Hello, Phoebe,' said Puck.

'Puck,' she nodded.

Mab did a double take. 'You know each other?'

'Yes,' said Puck, taking Phoebe's hand and smiling encouragingly at her. 'When we were in Greece that time. She was quite famous locally then.'

Phoebe looked down modestly. 'Some of the women even worshipped me,' she blushed. 'It all got a bit too much. I just like gardening, that kind of thing.'

'She's too modest,' Puck said. 'Radiant and bright her name means. She shone brighter than all the rest in those days.'

'Not *all* the rest, Puck, surely,' the Queen cut in, sweeping through the lobby.

'Naturally not, Mistress,' Puck said. 'You remem...'

'We've met,' said Titania, sweeping out again.

Phoebe turned to Mab. 'You see why I wasn't sure I should come. It's not just the children, although, obviously, that's a part of the problem. I just never got on with...'

'...the Queen,' Mab finished for her. 'Don't let it bother you. Not many people did. Are there many here?'

Phoebe sprang back into being a Minister's wife, letting out the Church Hall. 'Loads. It's nearly full. And my garden is still awash with flower faeries. I didn't know there were still so many around. I see a few, of course, from time to time, but there are clouds of them out there. Plus some elves and some faeries who seem to have gone a bit native.' She sighed. 'A bit like me, I suppose. And there are some dwarves in the kitchen. They seem to have another agenda altogether, and called me sister all the time. I suppose they are part of this, are they?'

Puck nodded.

'Well, I suppose you know what you're doing. Also, Black Annis is here. I've put her in the annexe for the moment. The goblins have been complaining about the smell. She's with a wizard and a rather unpleasant old woman who I can't place. There are other odds and ends, the odd bogle, and there's something in the footballers' shower. It looks rather like a frog with pointed teeth, so that's probably one of Theirs. And the Queen and King of course.'

'Thanks, Phoebe,' said Puck. 'Are you coming in?' He held the door open for her, on the Babel of voices coming from the large room beyond it.

She shook her head. 'No,' she said.

'But you must,' Mab told her. 'You can't just... not come,' she finished lamely.

Phoebe took one of Puck's hands and one of Mab's in hers and squeezed tightly. 'I have been thinking about this since I saw you, Mab. I have lain awake, thinking, crying, going over things in my mind. Thomas has assumed I'm praying and has left me to it. He believes you shouldn't interrupt when a person's talking to God.' She smiled weakly. 'He's a good man, generally speaking. He does his best. But what man is equipped to deal with a faerie in a dilemma? Then, last night, when it was dark and quiet, and I had already decided to come to you tonight, I heard someone call my name.'

'Phoebe?'

'No. Mummy. And that decided me. You've got hosts and hordes of faerie and other things with no name. My children have only got one Mummy. And I'm it. So,' she raised both their hands to her lips and bestowed her last ever faerie kisses, 'this is goodbye. I'm just so sorry it comes so near to hello.' And without another word, she turned and was gone.

Mab and Puck stood there in the gloomy lobby, tears in their eyes. Puck raised a hand and brushed them away. 'We're going to have to get used to a few more of those, I expect,' he said, his voice rough with tears.

Mab could only nod, her lip trembling.

The moment was shattered by the growl of a powerful car drawing up outside.

Mab grabbed Puck's arm painfully tight.

'Ow,' he shook her off.

'It's them,' she whispered. 'It's them, Puck.'

The door crashed back. Benedict strode in and shrugged his coat from his shoulders and threw it to Puck, who sidestepped smartly so it fell to the floor, slick with the passage of so many feet, trotters, hooves and similar.

'Ah, Puck,' said Benedict unpleasantly. 'What a joker, eh? And Mab. Long time no see.' He swept through, into the room, where the noise was temporarily stilled.

Leanne leaned over and chucked him under the chin. 'Hello, Puck,' she purred. 'Master inside, is he?'

Puck would have nodded, but her talons were pressing in just under his jaw. He blinked with the pain.

'I'll take that as a yes,' she said. She glanced disparagingly at Mab. 'Hello Mab,' she threw over her shoulder. 'Nice frock.'

Mab clenched her fists and started to follow her. 'Bitch!' she said, through gritted teeth.

'No such luck,' said James, as he loped into the Hall, letting the door slam behind him. No more of this butler stuff for him.

Mab and Puck watched them go in silence.

'Of all the ignorant...' Mab fumed.

'Don't let's sink to their level,' begged Puck. 'Once this evening's over, we can do what we want. But for now, behave.'

'Just a little trick,' she said. 'Just a puddle on her chair. Just a rat in her handbag.'

'She'd love all that,' he said, ushering her through the door. 'And think how much worse her tricks would be than yours.'

Mab thought; she shuddered... and found herself a seat.

❁ ❁ ❁ ❁

Titania, Oberon and Benedict sat on the dais, with Puck, Mab, Leanne and James in the front row. Some of the audience was visible, some not. Annis had joined the crowd, and had a fairly large margin around her. Faeries have a very delicate sense of smell. Gwyddion found he could stand near her now – he feared that every scent organ he had once possessed had curled up and died, but it meant he wasn't being jostled.

Oberon leaned forward and asked Puck what to do next. The thought of having him up there with him was total anathema, but he was a bit stuck when it came to initiative. Puck looked behind him. Most elements seemed in place. The dwarves were standing down one edge of the room, arms folded across their chests, staring straight ahead. Down the other aisle, the tree spirits stood, silver, brown, green and palest moon white. They were completely still, except for the aspen, trembling in its own private breeze. The row of apparently empty seats had to be where the elves were gathered. Goblins were dotted about, with Freckles and Tiny standing importantly at the back, eyes swivelling around the crowd. Shimmering lights filled some areas of the audience, a cloud of flower faeries had settled above a pot plant in a corner. A whole row of Mr Dobies waited patiently for the bingo to begin. One or two shifted awkwardly, wishing they had brought their inflatable cushions.

Puck whispered back, 'Give them another little while, Lord. There might be a few stragglers.' In particular, he thought, Phoebe, although in his heart he knew she wouldn't be back.

Oberon leaned over and relayed his thoughts to Titania.

'I'm going out for a while, then,' she said. 'I can't stand the smell in here.' She looked pointedly to the back of the room, where Annis was amusing herself by poking a goblin in the back with a blackened talon. 'Come and get me when you're ready to start.'

She floated gracefully to the door, and hovered, waiting, until Oberon took the hint and opened it with a flick of his fingers. A small sigh of pleasure rose from the crowd, with an undercurrent of dissent from the general area of the dwarves and a cry of 'poser'. The voice sounded uncommonly like James'.

In the cool gloom of the lobby, she let herself touch the floor and leaned against the wall, heart pounding. She knew she looked beautiful. She knew that the vast majority of the crowd were her Folk. But how could she convince them that they must rise, must fight the deadening effect of mortals on their world? Some of them were happy as they were. Not all of them minded being less than they had been. She had realised, looking into the flinty eyes of the nearest dwarf, that she was the one with the most to gain, and so the most to lose.

She squeezed her eyes shut to stop the tears.

'Hello, darlin',' said a voice in her ear. 'Am I too late?'

She opened her eyes and stared. A few inches from her, was a being nearly as lovely as her Oberon. He was tall, and broad and had straight hair flopping over a smooth and un-lined brow. He was smiling, showing even, white teeth, with one missing just at the edge of the smile. He was wearing jeans, worn pale in places to show the outlines of the muscles in his thighs and a heavy, navy blue jacket, with a leather yoke. He exuded a smell, which, while not up to Oberon strength, did strange things to her.

'Er...' she straightened up. 'Not at all. Go right in.'

He leaned on the wall, pinning her in with his arm. 'Un-less you've got any objections,' he said, almost in her ear, 'I'd rather stay out here with you.'

She flicked a glance to the door. It seemed firmly closed. Oberon need never know. She remembered Leanne and made up her mind.

'Why not?' she purred, looking into his eyes. She put a gossamer hand on his chest and stroked the edge of his coat, worming in so that she was lightly scratching his chest, scat-tered lightly with springing hairs.

'What's your name?' she asked.

'Nick. What's yours?'

She pulled a hair lightly. 'Oh, you,' she said. 'As if you don't know that.'

His lovely brow crumpled with the effort of thought. 'Well, I don't,' he said simply.

'Well, who do I look like?'

He took in the dress, the crown. 'A queen?' he guessed.

'There,' she said, 'I knew you knew.'

'Er, right.' These am-dram types always took things too seriously. He only came to meet women, but he didn't usually pull as quickly as this. He was glad the Minister had told him about this audition night, while he was retiling the bathroom in the Manse. It was going to be fun.

She reached up, her lips fluttering on his. He reached down to kiss her harder, but she pulled away. She nuzzled in his neck, her hands reaching under his coat and round his waist under his shirt. He pushed her gently against the wall, reaching round to unfasten her dress. It didn't seem to have zip or anything, so he started to gather up its folds, yards of fabric draping over his groping hand. She had meanwhile pulled his shirt out of his trousers and was stroking his back with fingers that felt like fire and ice on his skin.

With his free hand, he turned her head out of his neck and searched across her velvet cheek for her mouth. As he reached her lips, he also reached the top of her leg with his hand. Under the velvet heaviness, he felt thighs like marble, smooth and cold, but warming under his touch. He pressed his mouth on hers, probing with his tongue, probing with his fingers.

She stiffened, then pulled away.

'What do you think you're doing?' she hissed.

'I... I'm doing what I thought you wanted me to do,' he said, puzzled.

She looked deep into his eyes. She saw within them – nothing. He was a mortal! Whatever had she done?

She pushed him away with a strength that Trevor of Home and Wear would have recognised immediately. She shoved him out of the door, and leaned on it, breathing heavily.

'What did I do?' came plaintively through the wood.

'My mistake,' she replied briskly. 'I thought you were someone else.' She brushed off her dress, straightened her crown, and went back into the Hall.

36

Oberon had seen things on the television. He knew how meetings should be conducted. Someone banged on a little box thing with a little hammer. He just leaned forward and waited. In seconds, the room came to order. He spoke.

'Thank you all for coming,' his voice hummed straight into the hindbrain. Even Annis stood up a little straighter and listened. 'I know a lot of you have taken risks to get here, and we are very grateful. Most of you know why we're having this meeting. It's good to see so many of you – I don't think the Queen and I had any idea that our Folk were still so many. And I'm sure that there are many more.'

The dwarves were already mutinous. Oberon decided to honour them with his attention.

'Do you have a problem over there?' he asked, smoothly. 'Something I can help you with?'

One dwarf stepped forward. 'We don't see what all this King and Queen thing is all about,' he said. 'We haven't got no kings and queens, did away with all that years ago. We share everything equal, that's what we do, don't we, lads?'

There were general noises of consent, and then another dwarf stepped forward. 'We don't...'

The first dwarf turned. 'Excuse me, brother,' he said. 'I believe that I was addressing the chair.'

The second one was outraged. 'I can speak if I like. You're

no better than me.'

'Well, I'm the spokes-dwarf.'

'Not.'

'Are.'

'Not.'

'Are.'

'Perhaps you'd like to continue this outside, brothers,' Benedict stepped in. His meetings had often ended like this.

James stood up and opened the door. The dwarves flowed out in a scuffling throng and soon the lobby was filled with the sound of steel toecaps striking sparks off hard little shins.

Oberon clapped his hands softly and all attention was again on him. The reason most of us are here, perhaps I should say, is to think of a way, or ways, to...' he leaned across to Benedict, who whispered in his ear. '...raise our profile. In other words, bring the Realm of Faerie back into kilter with the realm of Mortal Men.'

There was a smattering of applause.

Benedict spoke. 'What we must remember though, is that times have changed. Technology is a big thing these days and with it, a lot of the imagination of mortals has died. I'm sure you all remember in the Old Days, how easy it was to scare a traveller to death.'

There was a shocked hush over the Hall, broken only by a spine chilling cackle from Annis and a splashy chuckle from the bean-nighe.

'Well,' Benedict corrected himself, 'Perhaps that wasn't too mainstream, but I'm sure you can all think of your own examples. The point I'm trying to make is that now, mortals have seen it all. On film, on television. They don't have to imagine it, it's spelt out for them in gory detail. So, we have a difficult job in hand, but I'm sure you're up to it.'

There was more applause, this time with a scaly, dry over-tone to it, as Benedict's particular followers joined in with gusto. Black Annis spat enthusiastically to show her approval.

'My plan,' Benedict continued, 'is to make our presence felt on several levels. I happen to own a couple of television channels, and have either complete ownership or a very important share of all of the most commonly used Internet Service Providers.'

Blank stares met his eyes as he looked out over the audience.

'Trust me on this one,' he said. 'I know what I'm talking about, even if you don't. I can put things out on the World Wide Web,' mutters of approval met this, webs were something faeries understood, 'to prepare mortals for the ultimate revelation.

Explain, Leanne.'

Leanne got to her feet and faced the crowd. 'I am a theatrical agent,' she said. Silence greeted this, which she took to be hostile. 'Well, someone has to be,' she said. 'There has already been a television appearance of one of Oberon and Titania's house goblins,' there was a chuckle of excitement in Bill's corner of the room, with muted cries of 'Go, Bill.' Leanne waited for quiet. 'Thank you. This attracted a degree of attention, and was followed up very quickly with a photograph of yet another of the Royal goblins, who I believe has become feral.' She turned to Puck. 'That's right, isn't it?'

He nodded.

'The mortal who took this picture sent it in to a television news studio, in which Benedict happens to have a controlling interest. They made it into a small news item, using Professor Gwyddion, at the back here,' she gestured and he bowed gravely, 'as an expert. On air, he didn't name the creature as a goblin, but he did tell the journalist in private. I know they are anxious to do a programme on it. I think we should let them. With, I need hardly say, an invited audience,' she swept her arm again, 'and panel.' She gestured to the dais. 'Well,' she asked the room at large, 'what do you think?'

A cacophony of talking, whistling, grunting and spitting met this question. A singing in her ears indicated to Leanne that the Flower Faeries were all for it as well. The door crashed open and a dwarf tumbled in, with bloody nose and black eye.

'Did you say we're going to be on the telly?' he asked, excitedly.

Leanne looked at him coldly. 'I hardly think so,' she said.

'You don't seem to know how to behave.'

'No, no,' said the dwarf, coming further into the room. 'You see, there's been a coup, sort of thing, and Grumpy has been deposed. Not that he was ever in charge, understand, but if he thought he was, which he did, now he knows he's not. In charge,' he finished lamely.

'Come back in, then,' said Benedict. He had been tossing a few ideas around lately with his development boys. It never hurt to have a cheap source of gems at your disposal. Think of silicon! 'But behave, or you're out for good.'

The dwarves trooped back in and stood quietly, bloody and bowed, in a line down the side of the room.

'Before we go any further,' Oberon said, feeling his grasp on the meeting getting very tenuous, 'I think we should vote on this. Our idea was to try and spread the rebirth of faerie by word of mouth. All those in favour, raise your hand. Or whatever,' he added, catching Thydney's eye. Oberon raised his hand. Titania raised hers. Eventually, a few trotters and hooves went up around the room. The sheep goblins were otherwise engaged, having crowded round James, for the feeling of security he gave them. The other goblins were therefore sulking and not really listening. Puck and Mab raised a tiny finger to about chest height. Oberon smiled brightly. 'Right, then. All those in favour of the t...'

He got no further. A forest of hands, wings, twigs and other limbs he didn't want to consider shot up into the air. They waved frantically, to emphasise the point. Benedict sat back, examining his nails minutely and trying not to smile too broadly. Leanne grinned and sat down.

When the noise had died down, Benedict got to his feet. 'Now, a television programme takes a day or so to set up, even when its news. Until then, I want you all to stay in touch with Oberon.'

Titania, silent until now, mulling over her near miss with the mortal, spoke up. 'Wait just a minute. Why can't they stay in touch with you? You're the Communications King after all.'

Benedict shuddered. 'My dear Titania,' he said. 'I live in a beautiful and very exclusive penthouse apartment. I don't have the room. Anyway, most of this lot are Yours. Mine are accommodated adequately, thank you.' He thought of his carpet. 'Although if any of mine wish to stay in touch with you, rather than me, they are more than welcome.' He glared at Gwyddion. He spoke to the room again. 'So, as I say, don't wander too far, stay in touch with the King and Queen here, and we'll let you know the next move. I shall be leaving a few of my goblins here, so that lines of communication remain open.' He lifted his laptop in the air. 'So, that's all settled, then.' He sat back, beaming happily. 'Except one thing. Leanne. The camera.'

'Camera?' Puck said. 'Who said anything about a camera?'

'Well, some of this lot won't show up, will they?' Benedict said. 'We'll have to check that first, otherwise the mortal television watching public will see a table, a few chairs and an empty auditorium. Not *very* useful, would you say? Also, my plan is to put pictures of the more obviously faerie in amongst websites. Frequently visited ones.' He thought for a moment. On some of the favourite ones he knew about, the goblins would hardly look odd at all.

Puck subsided. He knew he looked horrible in pictures. He had seen some. He looked... like he was. A goat-footed hobgoblin, slant-eyed and wild-haired. If he was going to be on television, he wanted to look like he did now, young and handsome. Not as old as time and ugly. Benedict shot him a cruel smile.

'Not to worry Mr Puck,' he said, smacking his lips with relish. 'They can do wonders with makeup, these days.' He bared his teeth in a wolfish smile.

Leanne was lining the audience up in orderly rows and snapping with a digital camera. Some of them she didn't bother with at all. The Flower faeries, for example, though beautiful under a microscope, were invisible to a camera and therefore not any use in a studio. They buzzed and whined round her head and then shot off in a swarm to sulk back near their plant. The camera loved the tree spirits. Their slender bodies and perfect skin just came alive in its eye. The dwarves had a tendency to look rather alike, but, spread them out and they'd be all right. The goblins, they knew about, so, apart from some of the sheep who were too vain to be ignored, they were allowed to go. Just one Mr Dobie was snapped. Seen one, seen them all.

Soon the Hall was all but empty. Titania was sitting at the table on the dais, still wrapped in her own thoughts. Oberon was glowering at Leanne, willing her to take his picture. He'd give her something to remember him by. He gathered his glamour around him and waited.

When the last dwarf had stumped out, the Council turned to and on each other.

'Thanks for sharing your plan in advance,' spat Puck.

'It works, doesn't it?' asked Leanne.

'Yes, but that's not the point.'

'Now then,' said Oberon, smoothing his curls and presenting his best side to Leanne, who still held the camera, 'Leanne is right. It does and will work. When the mortals see us, either on this Spider thing...'

'Web.'

'Yes. This thing, or on the television, they will all believe in us again. Their belief will make us strong, stronger than before, when they didn't communicate beyond the next village. It will spread round the world in...'

'Forty minutes,' said Puck, nostalgically.

'Or less,' added Benedict.

'And we will come back into our Kingdom.'

'Kingdoms.'

'Yes, sorry, Kingdoms.'

Titania stirred. 'Everything will be like it was again. We'll rule the woods and the water and air. Mortals will fear and love us. They'll leave food out for us, we will visit their homes in disguise, we'll play tricks, we'll watch the spiders build their webs, we'll sleep in the down-filled nests of robins.' She sighed. 'Won't it be wonderful?'

The rest were silent.

'Won't it be wonderful?' She looked round anxiously.

Benedict laughed, too loud. 'Let's talk about that, after the broadcast, shall we?' he said. 'Personally, I should miss my little pent house, but to each his own, of course. For example,

I know Leanne can't wait to get back to those cottage eaves, can you, dear?'

James rolled his eyes and laid his head on his paws. He had sidled nearer to Titania, having finally shaken off the sheep, and was lying at her feet. Without thinking, she reached down and scratched his back with her slender fingers.

With a happy sigh, James rolled over to have his tummy tickled.

37

From the next morning, for a week that seemed to stretch into eternity, each member of the Faerie Rade and Unseelie Horde did what they had to do. For some, this was a lot. Leanne cancelled all appointments and spent hours in her office, on the phone, cajoling, bullying and threatening producers and journalists. Her secretary, forbidden to get involved, spent her time filing her nails and reading magazines on how to be beautiful and desirable. That she would never be either bore testament to Leanne's skills when it came to choosing staff. Her policy was that you didn't need competition sitting at the front desk.

Benedict was truly happy. He spent his days hunched even more tightly over his console. He had dropped the pretence of eating and James just tidied up around him, for the look of the thing. Benedict tracked the hits on the websites where he had inserted pictures of his court and the Other Lot. They were increasing. Chat rooms were full of the gossip about the goblin faces. He was wryly amused to find that Freckles now had his own fanzine. Despite promises to the contrary, he hadn't put Oberon, Titania or Puck on any sites at all. He and Leanne had agreed that what was needed was the sudden impact of them, all on screen at once, when the lights came up on the fact programme of the year. He could feel the trophy in his hand already. He had also fought shy of putting Black Annis out. Even on the World Wide Web, there were some things that people didn't want to see. She was it.

In fact, that was the only down side, as far as he could see. She had been more difficult to dislodge than to find. She had taken up residence in the hall, having decided that, after all the years on a park bench, she couldn't sleep on beds. It was his belief that she just did it so that, on the rare occasions that he passed by, she could grab his ankle and mutter some lewd remark. Gwyddion had stopped coming round altogether. He was planned as the resident expert on the forthcoming show and had decided that it was Leanne he really needed to see. But really, it was Black Annis that he *didn't* need to see.

Titania and Oberon were in a bit of a cleft stick. They had accepted as natural the fact that they would be the stars of the show. After a small rebellion, they had also accepted that Puck, Benedict and Gwyddion would also be on the podium with them. They had given instruction to all their Rade that they were to stay in touch. A representative of each therefore appeared each morning, and Titania gave them an audience, lolling on her bank. She let the rabbits crop the grass, as long as they cleaned up after themselves. Otherwise, there wasn't much to do. She just lounged, and practiced ruling. The sheep were good for this. They liked a bit of discipline and could stand still for years if required.

Oberon was less content. He was bored already, and that was with the programme to look forward to. Whatever would he do, in a woodland glade for eternity, with nothing to do but smoulder at passing faeries? He quite liked this mortal world. It was interesting. Now he was getting out and about a bit, there were places to do, people to see. And, whatever Titania might say, some of the mortal women were really quite attractive. And willing. Titania had been a bit odd since the meeting. He didn't know why.

Puck was busy. Puck was always busy. He had taken on the task of letting out an Unseelie goblin every morning, to report back to Benedict. Titania had just about allowed the laptop in the house, although she said having it switched on gave her a headache. Nothing new there, Oberon had said. Hobgoblins like Puck were quick to learn, the brightest of the elves, and he had eventually managed to grasp which keys to press. Or, to be strictly honest, he pressed what keys Tiny told him to press. Tiny was disappointed that he couldn't do the job himself, but trotters were made before keys, and he just couldn't do it. A Tiny keyboard would have needed keys six inches square.

The Unseelie goblin was a strange thing, insubstantial, a mere shimmer in the air. As it emerged to make its way back to its Master, a thin shriek would escape with it, and a sulphurous stench would briefly fill the room. Puck had blamed Tiny twice, before he realised the poor little goblin's innocent expression had been because it was, indeed, innocent.

Mab was very quiet, for Mab. She was often seen in a corner with a few of the Mr Dobies. Her back was always to the room and she didn't say much. She had decided that the brownies were nice old things. She had misjudged them. They were kind and gentle, quiet and non-judgmental. But, best of all, they carried all manner of intoxicating liquids, in bottles swathed in brown paper, hidden in the folds of their long, dull coats. And they were generous. She liked that in a brownie.

So, everything was very peaceful at Thirteen, Ellesmere Crescent. Mr and Mrs Jones were enjoying the quiet. They had got used to the rustlings in the walls, so they didn't even hear that any more. Mrs Jones had even got quite fond of the rather large chicken that seemed to have taken up residence on the landing. She thought she had seen it before, but didn't know where. On the telly, perhaps. She had taken to leaving out some bread and milk as she went up to bed. The chicken showed its appreciation by roosting on the bed head at night. She was glad of the company.

And then, one morning about a week later, a sleek black car had drawn up to the kerb outside Number Thirteen. Out stepped Benedict, James and Leanne. With them, looking around dubiously, was the news anchor man who Gwyddion had told about the goblin. He was beginning to outgrow his role in the studio. He wanted his own programme, even a quiz in the afternoon would do, and he saw this as a perfect way to raise his profile. But he was growing a little concerned. He didn't want to be known as the newsreader who went mad on air, introducing a load of loonies who thought they were faeries. He hung back. This didn't strike him as the gate of Faerieland.

Benedict clicked his fingers and the door swung open. Hmm, good trick, thought the anchor man, whose name was Christopher. Not bad at all. In the hall, he noticed an odd smell. A bit animally, but overlaid with something not un-pleasant. Puck appeared in the doorway and, smiling, ushered him through. Christopher made a note on a pad. Handsome, but too young. No gravitas.

Where he had been expecting a kitchen, was a woodland glade, complete with slanting sunlight, butterflies, gambolling rabbits, a little too large and wearing clothes and – and here he just stood gaping – the most beautiful woman he had ever seen, lying on a grassy bank, which seemed to be growing out of the wall. If this was a trick, he was all for trickery. He held out his hand, unable to speak. She took it and pulled herself up, and up, and up, until she floated in front of him, her face inches from his.

'Hello,' she whispered.

'She's off!' said Leanne, folding her arms. 'Puck, is your Master around anywhere?'

'Upstairs,' said Titania out of the corner of her mouth. 'But that isn't an invitation, so stay right where you are.' To Christopher, she said, 'Would you care to sit here, with me?' and drew him back to her bank.

The others turned to go. When Titania was doing what she did best, they might just as well not be there.

Benedict said, in the hall, 'Well, that's that bit sorted, then. We've got him on board. Puck, can you...' but he was interrupted by a plaintive whine from the sitting room. 'Was that James? Go and see what he wants, Leanne, could you?'

She pushed open the door, and there stood James, sur-rounded by the sheep goblins. 'They won't leave me alone,' he complained. She shooed them off, and pulled him into the hall, closing the door behind her.

'Don't keep wandering away, then,' she said, sharply. 'And pull your hood up. What if Christopher should see?'

Grumbling, the bogle did so.

'Where was I?' asked Benedict crossly.

'You were asking me to do something,' Puck said. 'Why am I not surprised?'

Leanne gave his right bicep a little squeeze and said, 'You look so capable, Puck, that's why.' Her pointed tongue flickered and he moved away as far as the narrow hallway would allow.

'Yes,' said Benedict. 'I remember. We have a broadcast time set for not tomorrow, the next day. The audience will be entirely Your Lot and mine. Titania, you and O... O...'

'Oberon,' came a voice from the stairs. They glanced up. Oberon was coming down, slinking down, from the landing. He had been building up his glamour for days and now he was so gorgeous he was hard to look at. Leanne gasped and made for the first step.

Benedict flared his nostrils and looked at Puck. 'So over the top always,' he muttered. 'Well, you three, will be on stage, as will I. The expert on anomalous zoology, in other words, Gwyddion, and Christopher will also be there. To start the programme, more photographs of... er, Squeaky, is it...? Will fill the screen and then the lights will come up on you. We've chosen you because you look...' he stole a glance at Oberon, who was enfolding Leanne like a cloud of sex hormones. She was making little involuntary sounds which Benedict found faintly disturbing. He poked her in the back and pulled her away from the King. There was a faint noise, like a Wellington coming free of mud, as she stepped back down from the step. Benedict sighed.

'Oberon!' he said, and they all looked at him in amazement. He blinked and looked around. Obviously, he could say it when he wanted to.

'Well done, Master,' fawned James. 'I knew you could do it.'

He didn't risk it again. 'I was about to say because you look normal. Very handsome and all that, but normal. Then, when the discussion has been going a while, we'll get the cameras to pan the audience a bit. That should make the viewers sit up and take notice.'

'What about the cameramen?' asked Puck. 'That sound

man was quite upset when he saw Bill on the outside thing.'

Benedict was dismissive. 'Huh, cameramen! Nothing surprises them. Cynical to a man.'

'I hope so,' said Puck. 'Because the last thing we need is for them to lose it and the programme to not go out.'

'True,' said Benedict thoughtfully. 'Perhaps I'll put a goblin or two in each camera. A bit of insurance. Anyway, as I was saying. I shall need you to be there in the morning for a bit of a run through.'

'I don't run,' rumbled Oberon. 'These days, I fly,' and to prove it, he swooped down the remaining stairs, through the hall and into the kitchen. 'What are you doing with my wife?' they heard him thunder.

Christopher suddenly appeared, looking dishevelled and startled. Benedict looked at him kindly. 'Problems?' he asked.

'No, not at all,' said Christopher, making a note and trying to tidy his hair, all at the same time. He gave them a wobbly smile. 'Fine. Yes, fine.' He edged nearer to the front door. 'I think I'll just go and sit in the car for a bit, if that's all right. Fresh air,' and he rushed out.

Puck bit his lip and Leanne looked at her nails, as if they were the most interesting thing in the world.

Benedict knew when it was time to wind things up. He ushered James and Leanne out of the door. He turned to Puck and said, 'Right. Have you got that? You three there in the morning. The audience by early afternoon. Broadcast live at seven, after the local news, when the viewers are still wondering what to do next. Got that?'

'Yes,' said Puck. 'Yes, Benedict, we'll do that.'

The Unseelie turned to go.

'But, then what?'

'Then what, what?'

'After the broadcast, then what?'

Benedict shrugged. 'Everyone just does their own thing, old chap. I'm kicking Annis out, as a matter of priority. I would imagine that Oberon will get a show of his own of some sort. You too, you're a handsome lad.'

'Lad?'

'Speak as I find,' said Benedict, 'or rather, as the punters will find. Titania will be offered modelling contracts in piles yards high. Which she will refuse, if I know my Titania. Mab will go into rehab, I hope and trust. And everything will be as it was, only better.'

'How, better?'

'Because we'll be in charge, Puck. We'll be in charge.' He swept out.

Puck leaned against the door. 'Yes,' he muttered under his breath. 'But who is this "we"? That's what I want to know.'

38

Before Puck could really take it in, not tomorrow but the next day arrived. So did the cab, laid on by Benedict, ordered over the Internet, paid for by his Platinum credit card. Oberon didn't understand it. He just got in and sat down, every inch a King. Titania was not dressed in her regal outfit; although she had been wearing it for most of the time since the meeting, sweeping in and out, checking its folds, adjusting its gold trimming, adding and subtracting glitter until she was happy with it, Puck had finally persuaded her that something a little more everyday might be best until the cameras rolled.

Puck was last to get in. 'No politics, please,' he said to the driver, through the window.

'Right you are,' he said. 'How do you stand on sport?'

'Thank you, no.'

'Films?'

'No.'

'Newspapers?'

'A bit near politics, possibly?'

'Royalty?'

Oberon's ears pricked up, but Puck cut in. 'No. Just a nice quiet ride to the television studio, please.'

The cabbie was delighted with this fare. It was a nice long way, and they looked like important people. The sort of people who he would be able to boast about to his fares for weeks to come, he reckoned. If only he knew how right he was.

Oberon drifted off to sleep. Titania stared out of the window, surreptitiously practicing her wave. Puck bit his nails. He was between a rock and a hard place. He hated taxi rides. But he didn't really want to arrive, either.

But, of course, they did. Tipped off by Benedict, the gate keeper allowed them through. The driver was convinced now.

As they got out of his cab, he turned in his seat, and said, 'Any chance of an autograph, mate?'

Puck laughed. 'I would say no chance at all,' he said, slamming the door and making for the building ahead of him. He could see Leanne, pacing to and fro, just inside the automatic doors. Oberon paused for a micro-second when the doors hissed open, but he was on a roll, and nothing would stop him now. Puck watched in horror as he gathered Leanne up then breathed again as the King gave her a kiss on one cheek, then the other. Then the first one again. Then nuzzled her neck, arms wrapped round her inside her jacket. Then the horror came back, as Titania pointed a finger and dragged him away, by the power of her will.

'Not yet, Mistress, please not yet,' he begged. 'Sire, please control yourself.'

'She's under my skin,' complained Oberon.

'You won't have a skin if this goes on,' threatened Titania.

Leanne smiled her cat's smile and smoothed her hair with the side of one hand. 'Your Master and Mistress are out of control already, Puck,' she purred.

'And where is your *Master*?' Puck asked, nastily.

'In the studio. Waiting for you.' She spun on one needle sharp heel and led the way to the lift.

Oberon and Titania stood still as stone as the little mirrored room shot up to the topmost floor. Puck didn't like lifts, either, but he had the *sang froid* to cope. His face in the polished bronze wall showed hardly any stress. Except the little tic developing under one eye. And he could control that, he was pretty certain.

The doors slid open and Titania and Oberon couldn't get out fast enough. Leanne pushed past them to lead the way again. Puck brought up the rear. It was like herding very bad-ly behaved sheep, he thought.

The studio was enormous. Wider and higher than any room the faeries had been in before, leads and lights hung down from the ceiling, which was dark and far away. Raked rows of seats rose up on either side of them, as they walked down towards the stage, a slightly raised platform, with a row of chairs and a back drop of photographs of Squeaky.

Titania was shocked. 'Poor Squeaky!' she cried. 'He's got so thin! We must find him and help him.'

Oberon glanced dispassionately. 'It's his own fault,' he said. 'He ran away from us. We didn't make him go.'

Titania couldn't take her eyes off the pictures. 'Even so...' she said, and sat down in the nearest chair. 'Will he be all right?'

Puck said, 'Yes, My Lady, I'll go and get him as soon as this is all over. But, you know, he may like it like that.' The photographs gave no indication that Squeaky was having a very good time, but Puck rather went along with Oberon's sentiments about the stupid creature.

Titania looked unconvinced, but she turned in her seat, and waited patiently for the next stage in this, the long await-ed Day.

Benedict suddenly entered, talking to a harassed-looking mortal, wearing earphones slung round his neck and the ex-pression of a man with a headache. A headache which, he knew, could only get worse.

'Oh, you're here. Good. Titania, darling, could you move from that chair to that one?' Benedict indicated the chair next to her.

She looked at it. She was comfortable. 'No.'

The producer smiled bravely. He had felt this coming. His nightmares last night had all featured this sort of thing. Along with that dragon with the... well, never mind. He just hadn't had a very good night's sleep.

'Never mind, never mind,' he said. 'We'll sort out seating later. If everyone could just take their seats, any seats, then we can sort out the lighting on your faces.'

The four of them dutifully arranged themselves, spread

out around the circle.

The producer looked around and spoke into his mouth-piece. 'Any sign of our so-called expert? Or that idiot anchorman?'

Two shapes unwound themselves from seats at the back. 'We're here,' said Christopher, voice dripping with irony. 'Sorry to have kept you.' They walked down to the front. 'Where do you want us?'

The producer was brusque to hide his embarrassment. 'Anywhere,' he said, waving an arm. Since only two chairs were still vacant, it was an easy manoeuvre. Assistants came out to measure light on little hand-held machines that made Titania's head ache. Lights rose and were dimmed, the heat increased and finally, the camera crew declared itself satisfied.

Puck was worried about how he would look through the camera. He approached one of the mortals manning the machine.

'Did I look... all right?' he asked.

The cameraman was used to this question. It never failed to irritate him. He was homely, if you liked him, ugly if you didn't, and he was fed up with these flawless faces with no brain behind asking him 'Do I look all right?' 'Yeah, mate. You look all right. Try and keep a bit more head on though, know what I mean? Those ears don't do you no favours, do they?' He wound up some trailing cable and left for a quick fag and a coffee in the canteen.

Puck fingered the top of his ears reflectively. Leanne appeared at his shoulder. 'Yes,' she whispered, 'they are a bit more pointed.' She flicked one with a pointed nail, 'I rather like them.' She whirled away to follow Benedict.

The producer clapped his hands. 'Can we just gather again for a moment, please? Thank you. I won't rehearse as such. This is to be a discussion, after all, and it always tends to sound a wee bit stilted if it's too rehearsed. Benedict? You agree?'

He inclined his head.

'So, here's what will happen. The programme will open with a piece to camera, which you will be able to watch on those monitor screens down there.' He pointed to a row of televisions along the edge of the stage. 'That has already been filmed and it includes an item that was in the news a while ago, some kind of weird chicken thing, on a political piece. We have an interview with the sound man on that day. He hasn't worked since and is suing the BBC for stress. Then we'll come back to the studio, lights will go up and you,' he pointed at Gwyddion after consulting his clipboard, 'will be asked a question by Christopher. Then hopefully, things will just take off.' He flung his arms wide and looked hopefully at them all. 'Won't they?'

'Oh, yes,' Puck said. 'Things will definitely take off.'

'Great, great. As far as time goes, I'll let Christopher know through his ear piece when to start winding up. Is that all clear?'

They nodded.

'I understand the whole audience is an invited one?'

Leanne stepped forward. 'Yes, that's right. They are what you might call... experts on the subject in hand.'

Oberon snorted quietly. Wasn't she just so witty?

'Great. Well, I must be off. Lunch is on us, of course. Benedict, if you'd like to do the honours. If anyone would like to look around, please do, but just remember to watch for the red lights. They mean filming is taking place and absolute quiet will be required. Otherwise, make yourselves at home.' He scurried off.

Into his mouthpiece, very quietly, he said to his PA, up in the control box, 'Kirsty? Have you seen my CV lying around lately?'

'I've got a copy in my PC,' she squawked in his ear.

'Print one out, there's a dear,' he said. 'I have a feeling I might need it by tomorrow.'

At first, the little group from Ellesmere Crescent stayed together. Leanne had disappeared with Benedict somewhere, and Oberon saw no point in wandering, if she wasn't around. Soon, he found a programme being recorded that he recognized. A celebrity chef was ritually humiliating a member of the public. Oberon knew nothing about cooking, but a bit of light humiliation was his stock in trade, so he signalled to the others that he would stay and watch.

Titania and Puck wandered off, up and down stairs, in and out of studios. They finally found one which was like the one they would be using, about the same size, but the audience was in, and beginning to rustle with impatience. It was a quiz show, the one that had made Cobweb upset. The contestants were in place, but the question mistress was not. The floor manager was looking at his watch and frowning.

'Watch this,' Titania said. With a shake, she had transformed herself into the absolute double of the formidable Quiz Mistress. She walked onto the stage and the applause grew, helped by flashing lights which said, although Titania didn't know it, 'Applause!' She bowed, as she had seen the real star do, and turned to the contestants. An obvious snag hit her immediately. She couldn't read anything on the screen in front of her. All she could recognise was the reflection of a face that was not her face, but which had her eyes in it, looking back at her. She decided to go for it. She smiled at the contestants, a smile that melted the knees of the men and even made the women fell unaccountably happier. They all thought the same thing. She's not so bad, after all.

The audience were shifting. What had gone wrong? She'd been up there for a minute now, and hadn't shouted at anyone. She turned to the first contestant. 'Hello,' she said, pleasantly. 'You're looking very smart. I particularly like the colour of that shirt.' This was more like it. The sting would whip round and slay him any minute. But no. 'It's exactly the colour of your eyes, isn't it? Now, would you like to tell us a bit about yourself? Take your time. You look such a nice man. I'm sure you've got lots to say.' She smiled encouragingly. From behind her, the audience started to bay. Above, or was it below, the noise, she heard Puck calling.

'Mistress! My Lady! Come away now. It's too soon.'

She turned her head and saw, to her horror, the real Quiz Mistress striding towards her. And she looked mad! Titania clicked her fingers and disappeared in a small puff of smoke. She reappeared in Puck's top pocket.

He hurried from the studio, where the audience were un-impressed. You could do anything with cameras, these days. Even when the cameras were their own eyes, they didn't believe them.

Round a corner, hiding behind a fire hose sticking out from the wall, Titania regained her proper size. She stood there, pressed against Puck, shivering. 'They sounded so... angry.'

'They were, Mistress,' said Puck. 'And so, I have to say, am I. You shouldn't have done that. It might have ruined everything. Can't you wait another few hours?'

She stamped her foot. 'What's an hour? It can be a mortal day, week or year to me. Tonight will never come.'

'Be patient, Mistress,' said Puck, risking a hug. She had become so Queenly lately.

She risked a kiss. He had become so busy and distant, lately.

They smiled at each other. A relationship that had lasted as long as theirs would never break under a few tantrums and stupid decisions.

'You won't leave me again? You'll always be with me, won't you, Puck?' she asked, holding his hand.

He squeezed her fingers gently. 'Forever, Mistress,' he whispered. 'Forever.'

Forever is a long time to an immortal. But, standing there in the grubby, draughty corridor, Puck knew he meant it.

39

The audience were in. The lights were low. The figures were dim on the platform, but it didn't matter. The whole studio knew who it was sitting there, ready to change their world. The producer came on and shaded his eyes with one hand, looking out on the rows of seats, fuller than he'd ever seen them. He caught a few details of what was out there, dropped his hand and unfocussed his eyes. He'd be better not knowing, he was sure.

'Ladies and... erm, peop...' He ground to a halt. Then, inspiration. 'Audience! Thank you so much for coming here tonight. It promises to be a stimulating conversation and I'm sure our guests need no introduction. You will see a piece of film on the large screen above the stage,' he gestured with his free arm. He didn't seem able to unclench his hand from the clipboard he held in the other hand. 'Then, if you would be so good as to applaud or... make whatever noise you feel appropriate, the guests will begin.' He bobbed a strange little bow. 'Thank you again.' He ran off, half crouching. Instead of going to the control box, he carried on running, until he reached his car. He leaped in it and drove away. He didn't stop screaming until he reached the M25. He was going home to his Mum in Brighton. It would all be all right then. It was a shame. He was missing one hell of a show.

The applause, whistling, howling and keening died away. The music faded out and the lights came up. Christopher turned to Gwyddion and asked, 'Professor Gwyddion, to what genus does the creature we have seen pictured and described in the piece just shown belong?'

The sentence was a tortuous one, but Gwyddion was ready. Oberon was still moving his lips, trying to work it out.

Gwyddion steepled his fingers in his usual way.

Christopher held his breath. Surely, he wasn't going to chicken out again. 'It is a goblin,' he said. 'Genus faerie, I suppose, although I don't believe such a genus appears in the fauna.'

The audience erupted. There were cries of 'Go, Squeaky!' and 'Good old Bill!' The cameramen kept their eyes firmly on their apertures. They didn't want to see what was going on behind them. The smell was enough to give them more clues than they needed or wanted.

Christopher nodded slowly and Gwyddion continued. 'We believe that this particular specimen,' — down in the front row, Leanne noticed a slight resurgence of his Welsh accent. She hoped he wouldn't suddenly start waving bits of mistletoe about — 'has become feral.'

Christopher nodded again, and turned to Oberon. 'Oberon,' he began.

Oberon leaned forward, smiling at the camera, and not at Christopher, as he had been told to do. 'That would be "Sire" or "Lord" if you don't mind, Christopher,' he smoothed.

Christopher swallowed. 'Sire,' he said. 'I believe that this goblin belonged to you?'

There was uproar from the back row, which the goblins had made their own.

'Perhaps I should point out here,' Puck put in hurriedly, 'that, like mortals — people, I should say — goblins belong to themselves. My Lord Oberon created them, thought them up, but from that moment, they have been their own goblins, not his.'

Cheers from the back row. Puck raised a hand in acknowledgement.

'Yes,' said Oberon, straight into the camera. 'What he said.'

Christopher continued, 'We also have with us tonight Benedict McAdam, possibly better known as head of many IT and media companies. Mr McAdam, if I may, what is your interest in this matter?'

Benedict looked out at the audience, where his Horde were more numerous than he had thought. They were punching the air in his support. He looked at Leanne, sitting on the edge of her seat, willing him to disown the whole shooting match. He looked at Oberon, so smug, lounging back in his chair. He looked at

Titania and Puck and envied them. They had already made their minds up. He missed his computer. It didn't ask awkward questions, or make him feel guilty. He opened his mouth to speak. Then he saw James.

His faithful retainer, who had been at his elbow through fair times and foul, was crouched at Leanne's feet, his head on one side. His tongue was lolling and one eyebrow was in the air. Above the hubbub, he could just hear him whine.

'Mr McAdam?'

Benedict swallowed hard. 'Well, Christopher,' he said, in his well-modulated, businessman's tones, 'I suppose I don't have an interest in this goblin at all.'

James whined and put his paws over his eyes.

'But I am very interested in my own goblins, in my own Horde, in fact. I am Lord of the Unseelie Court and so, I suppose one could say, Oberon's other half. The dark half.'

In the ensuing noise, which nearly broke the mikes, no one but Benedict heard Oberon say, 'Hardly half, though, is it, little brother?' But he was smiling as he said it.

Titania, sitting there, so quiet and so beautiful, decided that the men had had it their own way for long enough. Standing, she held up one hand. The whole studio was silent, but for the muttered conversations of the Mr Dobies, most of whom were uncertain as to why they were there. And, someone had brought toffees instead of soft centres – they weren't too pleased. Even they were quiet though, as her glamour spread across the huge studio space. The cameramen would remember little detail the next day, but, as one, they all focussed on her.

She spread her arms to the lens. From every angle, she was as beautiful as morning, as enigmatic as night. She didn't have a bad side. Her hair flew out from her head, twisting in tendrils as it did so. Flowers grew in the concrete floor around her feet. Birds sang among the wires high above their heads.

As the watching mortals gaped, some with forkfuls of television dinners dripping on forks just short of their mouths, some outside electrical shops, watching twenty identical images, in hospitals, in hotels, in pubs, they all saw the same thing. They saw the most beautiful woman in the whole world, a woman with a face that reminded every man of his first love, of his mother, his daughter, his wife. A woman who reminded every woman of her favourite sister, her very bestest friend from kindergarten, herself in the bloom of sixteen. They saw that woman smile at them. Only them. She held out her hand to them. They held their hands out to her. They believed in her.

In every front room, in every bus station waiting room, in every student squat, the air was sweetened with the most delicate fragrance a mortal ever smelled. Everyone's ears were full of sweet birdsong. Every piece of earth bloomed, while they looked at that beautiful face.

The camera closed in, her flawless skin glowing in the studio lights. Softly, so softly that each person watching knew she was speaking only to them, she said, 'Thank you.'

Her hand came up. She blew each one a faerie kiss and the screen went blank.

🕸 🕸 🕸 🕸

The security guys had never seen an audience leave so quickly. Or leave so much mess. It was weird, though. Everything felt a bit different this evening. Better. More... twinkly, Fred had said. But he'd always been a strange one.

The leave-taking on the platform had been short, but very sweet. The goblins had all rushed down to clamour round Titania. They had a surprise. If she could just give them a few minutes start, they would have it ready by the time she got there. They wouldn't say where there was, just that Puck knew.

Benedict and Leanne were talking seriously, just off stage. James was bouncing around, tongue lolling. Benedict was taking early retirement. The money would still roll in. He'd keep his fingers on the pulse. Who needed to work in an office, these days? Fincastle Mill would soon be all electric and he'd stay in touch. He kissed her gently and was gone.

Leanne sidled over to where Oberon was standing, a little bereft. She slid her arm around his waist.

'It worked, then,' he said, dolefully.

'Like a charm, I'd say,' she said, a little acidly.

'Back to the woods, then,' he said, trying a laugh.

'Not necessarily,' she said, scratching lightly on his neck with one talon. 'I could get you *loads* of work. The camera loves you.'

He looked down at her. 'Really?'

'Absolutely.' She looked across to Gwyddion. As she thought, she'd lost a client there. He was dressed in that stupid robe again, and had the staff and mistletoe clutched in one hand. Never mind. Oberon was worth a hundred Gwyddions.

Titania and Puck stood together, not speaking. She was pale with the effort, but happier than he had ever seen her.

Then, she said, 'We did it, Puck. They believe in us again.'

'I'm not sure they know it yet, Mistress,' he said. 'But I feel,' he chuckled, 'I feel as well as look nineteen again.' He turned a back flip, just to be sure.

'I feel a bit flat though, Puck.'

He stroked her back. She leaned into him.

'I've lost the King, I think.'

'Not possible, my Lady. He only loves you.'

'And fame. And Leanne. He hasn't even bothered to speak to me. He's angry about my... you know, little weakness.'

'You mean Tam Lin, Nick Bottom, that guy the other night at the meeting?'

'How on earth...?'

'Sorry, Mistress.' He shuffled his feet. 'We were a bit

bored with waiting...'

She blushed. 'Did *everyone* see?'

'No, of course not. Not everyone had the power.'

'Well, I should at least be grateful for that.'

'But I think once Mab had told the Mr Dobies, everyone knew after that.'

She covered her face with her hands.

'Don't worry though, Mistress. We love you because of your little weaknesses, not despite them. You wouldn't be you, otherwise.'

She left one silver tear dangling and sniffed prettily.

'Sure?'

'Positive. Shall we go?'

She slid her arm in his and they flew, up, up and away into the dusty dark, her faerie train growing and circling in a spiralling chatter of excitement. Mab elbowed her way to the front, and held her Mistress' skirts as they went. Out in the open air, they flew on through the dark, lighting their path with tiny torches, held aloft so not to scorch their wings. Their numbers grew with every mile, until at last, Puck tugged her arm and they dived for a glade, deep in a wood overlooking a sparkling bay, whose white sand made a marker for them.

They landed on soft moss, deep and dry. The goblins were gathered round, faces split from ear to ear with their happy grins. The edge of the clearing was ringed with Hazel and the other spirits. Only one faerie wasn't there, and his absence hung in the air like a note from a cracked bell.

Titania smiled, because they were so excited and after all, this was a New Day. No more thinking of the Old Days. She squared her shoulders and looked around at her Court, gathered about her again.

'Thank you,' she whispered, not trusting her voice. She turned away.

Puck waved them all to bed. They wandered off, in twos and threes, talking together in hushed voices. The goblins immediately started a card school on a felled tree stump. The flower faeries wove beds in grasses and trees. Mab took Titania's hand and pulled her arm.

'This way, Mistress,' she said. 'They've built a bower for you, over here. Away from the rest.'

'Nice,' said Titania, not really concentrating. If she missed Oberon this much already, how was she going to manage for all eternity?

'Please, Mistress,' said Puck. 'You need a bit of time to yourself at least. Even if you don't sleep.'

She allowed them to steer her over the mossy carpet to a perfect little bower, raised off the ground and woven of living willow. The doorway was low and covered round with honeysuckle.

Titania said, 'That's out of season, isn't it?'

'Nothing is out of season now, Mistress,' said Mab, with a ghost of a wink at Puck. 'It can be summer all the time, if you want.'

'Winter, I think,' muttered Titania, and, bending, went inside.

As with every faerie dwelling, it was much bigger inside than out. A soft glow came from beyond the moth grey curtain hanging just inside the door. A familiar smell, musky, mossy, dark and warm was creeping towards her from the next room. A faint sound was in her ears. It was the buzzing of bees, the pumping of blood in her head. She pulled the curtain aside.

'Oberon?' she said.

www.blkdogpublishing.com

9 781913 762513